T0007962

BEASTTHREE SIX

JASON KASPER

SEVERN RIVER
PUBLISHING

Severn River Publishing
SevernRiverBooks.com

ISBN: 978-1-64875-402-9 (Paperback)

ALSO BY JASON KASPER

American Mercenary Series

Greatest Enemy

Offer of Revenge

Dark Redemption

Vengeance Calling

The Suicide Cartel

Terminal Objective

Shadow Strike Series

The Enemies of My Country

Last Target Standing

Covert Kill

Narco Assassins

Beast Three Six

The Belgrade Conspiracy

Spider Heist Thrillers

The Spider Heist

The Sky Thieves

The Manhattan Job

The Fifth Bandit

Standalone Thriller

Her Dark Silence

To find out more about Jason Kasper and his books, visit severnriverbooks.com/authors/jason-kasper

To Shawn R., a.k.a. "Jag 17"

All of the great prophets of modern times have come from the desert: Mohammed, Jesus and myself.

-Muammar Gaddafi

Cleared hot–smoke 'em if you got 'em.

-Cancer

1

Ulcinj, Montenegro

Reilly and I strolled down the Korzo, a long promenade paralleling the water in the ancient seaside town.

To our left, the dark blue Adriatic coast was punctuated by weathered olive trees jutting out along the shore, some of them hundreds of years old. Korzo's opposite side held a charming array of modern influence amid historic structures—cafés and galleries interspersed amid mosques and Ottoman architecture, citadels, and castle walls in a network of streets that dated back 25 centuries.

Our destination, however, was considerably less historic.

We were approaching the Mediterraneo Liman, a four-star hotel, and beyond it, the stairs leading down to a secluded cove. But our progress was halted when Reilly abruptly stopped at a street vendor to purchase a meat-filled pastry—we'd been in this country for two days, and I hadn't seen the big medic go more than ten waking minutes without one of the damn things in his hands.

Adjusting the beach bag over my shoulder, I surveyed the sparse, early-morning foot traffic around us.

Located on the southern coast of Montenegro, Ulcinj was far from the tourist hotspots that drew international visitors—most of the chatter around us consisted of Bosnian and Algerian as much as native Montenegrin. The town was an out-of-the-way gem known mostly to locals, and in a few hours the promenade would swell with beachgoers carrying gelato and beer and flocking to the deck chairs, parasols, and bars lining the water.

Reilly completed his transaction, then turned to see my judgmental glare. His massive shoulders sagged, the pastry in his hand held at a tentative half-mast.

"Well go ahead and eat it," I said. "Stop now and you'll go into withdrawal."

Smiling, Reilly took a bite, and as we continued our walk, I felt the phone in my pocket buzz to life.

I heard Worthy's Southern accent as soon as the call connected.

"All set here. Are you still good for the meeting?"

"Yeah," I answered. "Doc had to stop for another sandwich."

"*Burek*," Reilly corrected me, mumbling as he ate.

Worthy, for his part, was less enthusiastic. "Do you want to organize the intervention, or should I?"

"He says he can quit whenever he wants."

"Classic addict behavior."

"I agree. See you in two minutes."

Rounding the hotel, we found the stairs and descended toward the sea, a U-shaped cove with a shale beach in the center and elevated sundecks on either side. I selected the right side, where a thatch-roof restaurant bar overlooked the few occupants who'd already arrived to sunbathe or swim. Two men occupied a table near the stairs, their gaze on the deck. Temperatures were in the eighties and rising fast, yet they wore very un-beachlike attire and had backpacks slung across their chairs.

Ignoring them, I turned my attention to the available chairs and approached an open set located next to a dark-skinned, shirtless man lying in a reclined position. A gold chain was draped around his neck, his mirrored sunglasses faced skyward, and one hand held a partially consumed cocktail stuffed with lime slices.

"*Dobro jutro*," I greeted him. "Are you saving these seats?"

A pause before he gave a half-shake of his head.

I withdrew a beach towel from my bag and unfurled it, laying it across the chair and taking a seat as Reilly did the same beside me.

Leaning back, I took a deep breath of salty air and glanced at the sea beyond the cove, its surface glinting with the sunrise. Reilly sat upright, focused on his pastry, savoring each bite.

Releasing a satisfied sigh, I glanced at the man beside me and asked, "Vacation?"

He gave another half-shake of his head, now seeming inconvenienced by my presence as he took a sip of his drink.

"Of course," I replied cheerfully. "So you retired here, then—I can see why. Summers are fantastic, low cost of living without EU taxes. Plenty of investment opportunities for all the pesos you saved. Let me guess, you bought a house overlooking the Adriatic to get your residence permit?"

He said nothing.

"That's what I thought. Then there's the fact that Montenegro doesn't have an extradition treaty with the US, which is a fantastic perk."

This comment served to command his attention somewhat, though I could discern that only because he issued a verbal reply—he was otherwise completely motionless, totally at ease despite my presence.

"I will make you an offer," he said, speaking with a pronounced Latin accent.

"Oh?" I asked. "I love offers. So does my friend here. Isn't that right, Doc?"

Reilly took another bite of his pastry, chewing slowly.

The man continued, "If you leave now, I will let you live."

I gave a short laugh.

"That's very generous of you, but I have to decline. You've got two options. The first is that you come with us peacefully, and we take a ride together. Easy day. Option two is that my friend here puts down his sandwich—"

"*Burek*," the man interrupted.

"What?"

"That is not a sandwich, it is *burek*. Baked pastry with filling." Sunglasses cutting to the street food, he asked Reilly, "Ground beef?"

The medic nodded solemnly. "With onions."

"A wise choice. They are excellent."

Reilly gave me a helpless shrug. "He's not wrong."

Sighing angrily, I resumed, "Fine, so my friend will drop his *burek*, punch you in the head as hard as he can—which, believe me, is pretty fucking hard—and then carry you out of here. That's option two."

"No," he said calmly, "to both."

Raising his glass toward me, he swirled it to jingle the ice. "I think I will stay right here and enjoy my beverage."

I gave him a tight smile. "I'm afraid you're not in a position to negotiate. It's going to be the easy way or the hard way. Choose now."

"At the risk of disappointing you, I did not come here alone."

"Option two, then. So be it." The man lifted his drink straight overhead, some distress signal met with a crash from the bar and a great hissing noise as I continued, "Doc?"

Reilly rose to his considerable standing height and took a mournful final bite of his pastry. Then he tossed it over his shoulder, rounded my chair, and drilled the man in the side of his head.

2

Worthy strolled beneath the thatch roof of the restaurant bar, heading straight for the counter to order a large decaf.

He turned his gaze toward the sea as he waited for his drink, surveying the sight anew like a good tourist would. The action certainly matched his attire of shorts, running shoes, ballcap, a suitably baggy T-shirt chosen to conceal his athletic build, and thick-framed, prescription-free glasses.

There weren't many other patrons at this early hour. A young couple he took to be on their honeymoon occupied the best table closest to the water while a single man in a polo shirt typed feverishly on a laptop, some poor bastard getting work done before his family awoke in the adjacent hotel.

Of most interest to Worthy, however, were the two men who'd taken up a spot near the stairs leading not to the beach but the waterside lounge below.

And that spot was where their focus was more or less directed, save the one facing him who made periodic visual sweeps of the bar. Both were fairly large, though the one who'd scrutinized him when he entered was particularly so; they wore oversized linen shirts with the sleeves rolled halfway, cuffs pulled tight against muscular forearms. He didn't need to see beneath their untucked shirts to know that both wore gun belts with a pistol on one side and an extra mag or two on the other. The backpacks slung across their chairs served a similarly easy purpose for a man of Worthy's credentials to discern—they contained first aid kits, submachine guns, and magazines.

The bartender set his decaf atop the counter and Worthy paid the woman, conducting a brief exchange in English that ended with a generous tip. It was the least he could do, he thought, because everyone in this bar was going to remember this day for the rest of their lives, particularly the honeymooners.

He moved to an open spot facing the bodyguards, and then proceeded to ignore them completely.

Unslinging his laptop bag, he set it atop the table along with the coffee before procuring a ledger and pen. His hasty scrawling would probably be perceived as work-related by anyone who saw him, though in truth he was doing something that served as a far more authentic cover—penning the continuation of a poem collection he'd been working on for some time. This was both consistent with the actions of a tourist on vacation and, regrettably, a consuming hobby that he'd done everything in his power to conceal from his teammates.

Worthy punctuated his musings by sipping decaf and responding to phantom texts on his phone, the latter intended to periodically check how long remained before the turn of the hour. And when that time came and went without any sighting of David and Reilly, he waited another fifteen seconds before dialing his team leader.

"All set here," he said when the line connected. "Are you still good for the meeting?"

David replied, "Yeah. Doc had to stop for another sandwich."

"Do you want to organize the intervention, or should I?"

"He says he can quit whenever he wants."

Worthy frowned. "Classic addict behavior."

"I agree. See you in two minutes."

Ending the call, Worthy kept the phone in his hand and dialed another number before bringing it to his ear.

"Meeting is still on," he began. "Two minutes."

Cancer sounded pissed. "What's the holdup?"

"What do you think? Doc had to stop for food."

"Christ. Don't even know why I asked. That motherfucker needs an intervention."

Worthy debated whether he should point out the contradiction of that comment, coming as it was from a fellow addict. He decided to do it anyway.

"Says the smoker."

Cancer replied unapologetically, "I can quit whenever I want."

"That's what Doc says—think about that, brother. All right, gotta go."

He saw David and Reilly shortly thereafter, both men casually walking down the stairs. It wouldn't be long now, he thought, though he didn't alter his actions in the slightest until the bodyguards assumed a laser focus on the sundeck. By now they'd deemed him a low-risk occupant, and were far more concerned with the pair of new arrivals with beach bags who'd just taken up a seat beside their principal.

Only then did Worthy replace the ledger and pen in his laptop bag and make a slight adjustment to its orientation before slipping his left hand inside and placing the opposite palm flat on the table.

Worthy had no idea how their target signaled his guardians, only that he had.

Both men leapt up in unison, one of them so rapidly that his chair toppled backward. It had barely crashed to the ground when Worthy drew his first countermeasure for their response—his left index finger clutched the ring mount atop a ten-ounce can that he withdrew from his bag and aimed at the bodyguards before mashing a thumb switch.

His last glimpse of them revealed that their eyes and mouths were open before both vanished in a white cloud of bear spray containing the highest concentration of chemical irritant available by law anywhere in the world. A two- or three-second burst was typically sufficient to dissuade a charging grizzly, but Worthy took no chances and continued spraying until the can had nothing left to give; then he dropped it in place, marrying his left hand to the front pistol grip of the MP5K submachine gun that he'd pulled from the laptop bag. Deftly sidestepping his table, he took a kneeling firing position with a point of aim on the cloud of vapor.

The bear spray dispersed to reveal one bodyguard hunched over and facing away from him; the other, impossibly, was shielding his face with one arm while drawing a pistol with the other.

Worthy shouted, "*Në tokë ose vdes,*"—on the ground or die—repeating the command when the man with pistol in hand didn't immediately comply. If anyone was going to get shot during this snatch, now was the time; at least with human pepper spray, a determined attacker could continue to function at least somewhat for a period of time before their vision was impeded almost entirely. Worthy had thirty rounds of 9mm ammunition ready for delivery and maintained his grip on the tiny weapon —at a foot in length, the MP5K was a fine choice for concealment in an ultra-close-quarters environment but not much else—but the offending bodyguard soon joined his comrade in lying down on the bar floor.

"*Duart në kokën tuaj,*" Worthy commanded, watching as both men put their hands on the backs of their heads, emitting pained wet coughs.

Rising and glancing to his left, he caught sight of Reilly taking the stairs two at a time toward the promenade, the body of their target slung over his shoulders like a rag doll. David moved behind him, sweeping his MP5K across the alarmed group of sunbathers a final time before committing his aim forward and darting ahead of Reilly.

When David cleared the first landing, Worthy shouldered his laptop bag, turned, and darted out of the bar.

3

It was still dark out when Cancer made his way down the stairs beside the hotel.

He carried a long case in one hand, his coveralls bearing a patch that identified him as a member of the hotel's maintenance team. Both were intended to deflect attention in the event that anyone saw him moving into position, but he was almost to his destination before realizing that he could have just as easily worn a tutu or a gorilla suit—no one was awake yet, his progress uncontested as he descended the final stairs amid the quiet lapping of waves.

Then, after a final glance over his shoulder, he committed.

Kneeling beneath the hotel's lower balcony that stretched out over the water, Cancer slipped into the narrow gap, crawling on all fours atop a slab of moist stone and pulling the case alongside him.

He heard an eerie succession of quiet clattering noises spreading away from him as he moved, though it wasn't until he was well concealed that he found the night vision monocle in his pocket and used it to scan ahead.

The dim green hues of his newly-illuminated optic showed the source of the noises clearly enough: crabs, some of them nine inches across, skit-tering sideways to give him a wide berth. That much was a relief, though he continued his visual sweep until confirming there were no snakes under here before pocketing the device and continuing his crawl forward.

He didn't require night vision to determine his stopping point—both the restaurant bar and the sundecks had security lights that remained on overnight, giving him ample opportunity to orient himself to the morning's objective. Then he opened his case and removed a tightly rolled mat with a valve that he blew into until it was fully inflated.

With that accomplished, he lay on his side atop the mat to retrieve his suppressed HK417 A2, an accurized assault rifle with a 20-inch barrel. Given the relatively short distance he'd be shooting, it was overkill; but given the imminent presence of innocent civilians in his target area, there was no overstating the need for precision in the operation ahead.

After lowering the bipod legs and orienting the weapon, he let the buttstock rest against his mat, placed two nicotine lozenges into his cheek, and sent David a text to confirm he was in position.

Then he waited in the tight confines, doing little more than responding to routine updates, all part and parcel of being a sniper, although the view of the Adriatic reflecting the first rays of sunrise was far better than the usual tactical fare. Shortly thereafter, he watched the bartenders and restaurant staff arrive to set up. The early patrons trickled in half an hour later, first a man with a laptop and then a young couple fawning over each other as they ordered coffee.

When a bodyguard arrived and surveyed the sundeck before heading to the bar to assess its occupants, he didn't so much as glance in Cancer's direction. His concern was with the local threats, as if he hadn't conceived of the notion of a sniper lying in wait beneath the overhang. Even if he had, it wouldn't have done him much good—Cancer was so far back in the shadows it would have taken someone low-crawling atop the rocks to find him.

The man placed an order at the bar, then made a phone call.

By the time the bartender placed a cocktail on the bar, a second bodyguard came into view, trailed by a dark-skinned man who took the drink before leisurely making his way to the sundeck. Both bodyguards took a seat at a table to watch over him, and Cancer relayed the proceedings via text before waiting for the appointed showtime.

Worthy showed up like clockwork, getting a coffee and taking a seat.

And then…nothing happened.

He checked his watch, growing increasingly irritated. David and Reilly should have been here by now, and by the time he noticed Worthy bringing a phone to his ear, Cancer's was already buzzing with the incoming call.

Worthy drawled, "Meeting is still on, two minutes."

"What's the holdup?"

"What do you think?" Worthy shot back. "Doc had to stop for food."

The sniper felt his jaw clench. "Christ. Don't even know why I asked. That motherfucker needs an intervention."

A pause on the other end of the line.

"Says the smoker."

"I can quit whenever I want."

"That's what Doc says—think about that, brother. All right, gotta go."

Cancer stuffed the phone into his pocket and resumed his hold on the HK417 well before David and Reilly sauntered down the stairs toward the sundeck. Then he aligned his scope on the pair of bodyguards, taking measured breaths until both men leapt up in alarm. They vanished shortly thereafter in a blast of white mist, and when it cleared, he centered his sights on one of them drawing his pistol.

Cancer was taking the slack out of his trigger by the time the bodyguard finally relented, lying on the ground beside his counterpart. Their total compliance was the only reason both men were still alive right now, and while he'd half-expected one of the bartenders to duck down and reappear with a shotgun to defend their patrons, they'd all remained out of sight while everyone else in the bar wisely kept their heads down.

But one of the bodyguards decided to push his luck, Cancer now saw. The second one to lie on the ground must have heard Worthy retreating, because he pushed himself upright to give chase.

The sight alone was painful to watch—the man's face crimson and eyes narrowed to slits as he fought the spray's effects while recovering his pistol. He was about to start blasting indiscriminately, maybe hitting Worthy in the back or perhaps killing a civilian in the process, but Cancer fired a subsonic 7.62 round through his sternum before he'd taken his first step.

It was an instant kill.

The bodyguard fell forward as seamlessly as if he'd slipped on ice, his corpse hitting the ground before the sniper cut his aim to confirm the other remained in place.

By then Worthy was gone from view, along with David, Reilly, and their new captive. Cancer flicked his selector lever to safe, then collapsed his bipod and laid the HK417 in the foam-lined case beside him. He flipped the top shut and clicked the clasps into position, grabbing the handle and leaving his inflatable mat for the crabs as he slid sideways the way he'd come. Once he reached the end of his overhead cover at the edge of a staff walkway, Cancer gave a hasty scan for any passersby.

Then he unwedged himself from the space, rising and brushing the dirt off his maintenance coveralls. Lifting his rifle case, he strode up the walkway toward the front of the building. Now he was down to a Glock 26 in a pocket holster, hopefully to remain unused in the coming moments.

He intercepted his teammates as they emerged on the promenade, looking for all the world like a group of drunks stumbling out of the beach-side bar.

David and Reilly forcefully held the detainee's arms over their shoulders, their weapons once more concealed in beach bags as they marched him forward ahead of Worthy, who was using a handheld stun gun to deliver periodic electric shocks to the man's lower spine.

What a shitshow, Cancer thought, though the operation had gone about as smoothly as possible so far. No small feat, given that capturing a target alive was the literal and figurative opposite of what their team had been assembled to do.

Their destination was a Škoda Kodiaq parked on the road, the flat gray mid-size crossover idling with Ian at the wheel. Cancer placed his rifle case into the cargo area, then slid into a rear seat.

He'd barely gotten the door closed before the detainee was shoved toward him from the opposite side. Cancer intercepted him with relish, grabbing the shirtless man by his hair and jerking his head back with one hand while using the other to administer an open-palm blow to his throat.

That maneuver succeeded in causing him to convulse and gasp, which in turn left him vulnerable for the reverse headlock that followed. Cancer held his neck tightly as Worthy wrenched the man's arms behind his back, flex-cuffing them together as David boarded the passenger seat and Reilly climbed in through the liftgate.

Ian accelerated forward the moment all five passengers had crammed inside—cramped accommodations to be sure, but they wouldn't be in this vehicle for long.

Cancer released his grip on the captive's throat, wrestling him upright and assisting Worthy in applying a gag and hood as David transmitted, "Raptor Nine One, Suicide Actual. Package secure, one bodyguard EKIA. Moving to exfil."

The whine of a police siren from their front caused Cancer to whip his head toward the windshield. A blue-and-white SUV was screaming toward them, speeding past Cancer's window with its light bar glaring.

He turned to watch it, seeing the brake lights activate as the vehicle screeched to a near-halt, then whipped a U-turn that took its front wheels thumping over the promenade as civilians scattered out of the way.

"On our six," Cancer called. "Doc, it's go-time."

~

Reilly pulled on his leather gloves, hastily flipping the liftgate window open as he appraised the vehicle speeding after them.

His team had been in these situations before—evading local law enforcement or enemy fighters—but never had they been so *prepared* for it, having outfitted the cargo space for the sole purpose of losing any meaningful pursuit.

Reilly snatched up a smoke grenade from a row of identical cylinders arrayed in pouches on the liftgate interior. They looked more like fireworks or party favors than the ones he was used to operating—a recessed top with pull pin, as if they'd spray confetti upon activation—but the Czech-manufactured devices were so ubiquitous in this region that it would be difficult for police to speculate who'd just snatched a resident, much less confirm it.

Holding the grenade out the liftgate window, Reilly yanked the pin and heard the dull *pop* before a plume of white smoke hissed forth, the vortex of wind sending it churning toward the police SUV. Short of hearing the siren, Reilly couldn't tell if the vehicle was still following them or not; both lanes of the promenade road were erased from view, and when the grenade became too hot to hold, he released it and procured another, repeating the process.

The transition time gave him a brief intermission of visibility that underscored the sheer absurdity of the situation: they were racing beside the Korzo promenade, and with it the various street vendors—he'd probably purchased *bureks* from half of them—along with stunned pedestrians who were staring at the Kodiaq as if they expected it to burst into flames at any moment.

He caught a glimpse of the police truck a moment before the second smoke grenade fired to life. Ian whipped the vehicle along a left curve, exposing the liftgate window to what could possibly be the last view of the Adriatic Sea that Reilly would ever get, tranquil waters soon blotted out by white smoke as they sped north into Old Town.

As the grenade began to sear his palm through the glove, Reilly dropped it and reached for another. He heard Worthy issuing directions to Ian at the wheel, interspersed with David transmitting checkpoints over the command frequency and muffled groans from their gagged captive.

Reilly pulled the pin on his next grenade and saw that the smoke seemed to be working—the siren behind him was growing fainter with each passing second.

David announced, "Doc, stop the smoke."

Reilly dropped his grenade and pulled the liftgate window shut as Ian veered down a side street, taking a circuitous route east across the northern fringes of Ulcinj. Now that they'd broken the police's visual contact with their vehicle, laying down further smoke would only broadcast their position; since the license plate number was already well known along with the vehicle make and model, their best bet now was to stay off the main roads as long as they could.

Or, he thought as a Montenegrin police sedan peeled through an intersection behind them and activated its light bar, until they were spotted.

"Aaaand they're back," Reilly said, reaching for his next grenade.

David replied, "We're almost to E851—Angel, flip to alternate route for the exchange point. Doc, keep them back, and on my mark, hit them with everything you've got."

Reilly pushed the window back open and resumed his smoke efforts, churning through two more grenades as Ian weaved between the houses of a residential neighborhood.

Then David said, "Here's the straightaway—Doc, let it rip."

Reilly dropped his smoke grenade and then went down the row of his remaining munitions, this time pulling pins and dropping them out the window as fast as he could, the Kodiaq's speed determining the interval at which they rolled and landed. No one behind them would be able to see the road for the next two and a half minutes, much less speed through that mess, but Reilly had one more trick up his sleeve. He went for it now, hoisting a canvas bag from the floor and shouting to Ian.

"Give me both lanes."

The vehicle began a zigzagging pattern across the straightway as Reilly opened the flap outside the window and upended the sack, whose metallic contents bounced and scattered off the pavement. Hundreds of caltrops were coming to rest now, each consisting of iron strips with barbed ends wrapped around each other to form a four-pointed tire deflation device.

By the time Reilly shouted, "Spikes out," he saw they were leaving the town of Ulcinj altogether, the final residential and commercial structures giving way to pasture and farmland. With the route behind them sufficiently obscured for the time being and the caltrops serving as a multiple-car pileup waiting to happen, their precautionary measures were nearly complete—but with twenty-plus minutes remaining until they were truly safe, one critical step remained.

Ian braked and pulled a hard right turn into a gravel driveway leading toward an abandoned farmhouse, the structure decades beyond having fallen into mere disrepair. More importantly to the team at present was the large shed beside it, intended to store a tractor that had long since vanished from the property.

It now held a vehicle of a different sort, revealed as David leapt out to pull open a decrepit door composed of rotting wood panels: a Renault Trafic panel van bearing the red circular icon and logo of Vodafone, one of the world's largest telecommunications companies and the chief mobile cellular service providers throughout the region. Ian pulled the Kodiaq in behind the van, killing the engine and taking the keys as the team wordlessly bailed out for the vehicle transfer.

What ensued was a Chinese fire drill of sorts: David and Worthy yanking their captive out of the Kodiaq, Cancer moving for the van's driver slot, and Ian retrieving the rifle case and emergency medical supplies to strip the crossover of anything and everything of value to them.

That left Reilly to stage his parting gift, an explosive charge that he positioned over the fuel tank to eradicate the vehicle and, with it, the mildewy remains of the shed they'd hidden it in.

He waited until his team was loaded in the van with the engine running before arming the charge and scrambling to join them in the passenger seat, a position usually reserved for his team leader—between a medic riding shotgun and a sniper driving, the roles for this phase of the operation were ass-backward from any semblance of how the team usually did business. But David and Ian had other things to worry about in the back, and as Cancer pulled forward into the sunshine and roared down the driveway, Reilly caught sight of the fading blanket of white smoke on the highway to their right.

By the time they turned onto the main road, Reilly was holding the radio detonator and craning his neck to watch the shed until the last possible second.

Ordinarily getting some distance from the Kodiaq before turning it into a smoking beacon that could be seen for a mile in any given direction would be far more preferable, but they simply couldn't risk civilians, much less police, stumbling upon the site as the final seconds ticked down. The best compromise, therefore, was to wait until their last moments of visibility before he clacked off the charge.

Finally Reilly pressed the transmit switch three times in rapid succession, and after a moment's delay, he saw a flash of light within the shed, followed by a cloud of black smoke blasting outward from the open doors. Then Cancer followed a curve in the road and a row of trees blocked the view; the sound of the blast, however, hit them then, a dull thumping *boom* as Reilly faced forward, watching the straight stretch of the E851 extending northeast and listening to David transmit from the cargo area.

"Raptor Nine One, Suicide Actual. Phase three, phase three, passing checkpoint seven. Twenty minutes from RV."

~

Ian leaned toward the man seated on the bench opposite him and ripped off the hood, getting his first in-person view of their gagged captive.

The man had put on some weight since posing for the fake passport picture that Ian had analyzed—his cheeks were more filled out, an extra layer of fat present in his chin and neck. The close-cropped hair was brown, having been dyed from gray. Or maybe, Ian thought, the reverse was true. Pictures of the man after his military service had proved exceedingly hard to find, with most dating back over ten years.

But the scar on his right eyebrow remained the same, as did his eyes, with a slight exception—they glowered at him with hatred as Ian spoke.

"Thiago Nelson de Zurara," he began, "here's what I know: you were the captain of the first *Tupi*-class S-30 in the Brazilian Navy before transferring those skills to a far more lucrative career running drugs. Last month you piloted a 36-meter submarine on a transatlantic voyage to deliver a very specific cargo. Here's what I don't know, and what you're going to tell me now: exactly how much cargo there was, who took possession, and where it's currently located."

He pulled down de Zurara's gag, and the captive used the opportunity to snicker and glance around the cargo area. Worthy and David flanked him, both men watching him closely, but it was Ian who'd spoken, and Ian who received the response.

"You *arrombados* have just grabbed the wrong man."

"No," Ian said, "we haven't. Felix Pinzon spoke very highly of you—he sends his regards."

De Zurara cracked the slightest hint of a grin at the mention of his protégé but still wouldn't address the line of inquiry.

Instead he said bluntly, "I want a lawyer."

Cancer called over his shoulder from the driver's seat, "This ain't that kind of party, asshole."

Ian quickly resumed control of the conversation, trying to focus de

Zurara's attention. They had precious little time to conduct tactical questioning, and while everything they needed to know would soon be spilling forth from this man one way or another, the truth remained that it may well be too late.

"We're not INTERPOL," Ian said. "We're much, much worse than that, and you haven't seen the tip of the iceberg yet."

Then he leaned forward and explained, "Once we reach the border, we're going to transfer custody of you to US and Albanian intelligence officers. You'll be transported via armored convoy to a fully-fueled Gulfstream sitting on the tarmac at Tirana, and they'll fly you to God knows where. But your final destination is a black site, and once you reach it—"

Cancer interjected, "Some devious motherfuckers are going to find out everything they want to know, and have a party doing it. You think we're bad, you've never met anyone who tortures intel out of people for a living."

Irritated, Ian added, "He's right," in a sufficiently sharp tone to dissuade the sniper from adding any more commentary to the verbal transaction at hand.

Ian swallowed hard and, with every ounce of candor he could muster, continued his sermon.

"Your best bet is to answer me now, and at least let us hand over a cooperative suspect. I don't really give a shit what happens to you, so take this as a statement of fact: if you tell us the truth and keep repeating it once you get where you're going, it'll save you *dozens* of hours on the waterboard table. Because if you tell a lie, then as soon as you contradict yourself—and believe me, when you're drowning, you will—things get a lot dicier."

That last line seemed to pull some strings in the captive, his gaze becoming fearful before Ian concluded, "*Capitán* de Zurara, I'm not going to ask you again. There are three things I want to know and will know, whether you say it now or later. One, the quantity of cargo on your sub. Two, who took it. Three, where it is now."

De Zurara was quiet after that, long seconds ticking by without a response.

Finally, his eyes narrowed.

"The transfer was twenty nautical miles south of Tenerife."

"Spanish Canary Islands?" Ian asked. "Off the coast of Morocco?"

The man nodded. "There were two boats at the transfer site. One was unmanned, for my crew to take to shore as instructed."

"And the other?"

"The other did not advance on the submarine until my crew was underway once more. I never saw another person, and can only presume they transferred the cargo before scuttling the sub."

Ian swallowed. "Did the cargo head east into Africa, or north into Europe?"

"I do not know. A man in my position cannot afford to know, or to ask."

"What about the cargo's contents," Ian asked. "Could you afford to know that?"

De Zurara flinched. "I made some logical assumptions."

"Then let me remove all doubt: you moved pure liquid VX. It's an odorless, tasteless nerve agent, a WMD-grade chemical weapon that's a hell of a lot more deadly than sarin. A fraction of a milligram is fatal whether it's breathed in or absorbed through the skin."

He didn't add that the VX had been obtained at great cost by a man known to him as Erik Weisz, a figurehead they'd been tracking across five countries on three continents. Weisz's overarching intentions were a mystery, but his influence was not: they'd uncovered evidence that he'd connected everyone from terrorist groups to government officials in mutually beneficial arrangements that facilitated the funding and execution of catastrophic attacks.

Focusing on de Zurara, Ian continued, "So tell me—how much VX was there?"

He hesitated, then responded shakily, "The cargo...the cargo was packaged in 25-liter jerricans."

"How many jerricans?"

But de Zurara didn't answer, seeming consumed by his own thoughts.

So Ian belted him across the face with a backhand, summoning his attention as he roared, "How many?"

"Three hundred and seven," de Zurara said in a near-whisper, appearing haunted by the prospect. "There were 307 cans."

Ian fell back into his seat, momentarily pressing his face into his hands as he calculated the total amount. That was over 7,500 liters, somewhere in the neighborhood of 2,000 gallons, every drop of it headed for an unknown target, or many of them. With that amount of VX, there were practically no limits to how much devastation a terrorist network could inflict on the civilian populace of any number of nations. Any major city in Europe could be in danger, or any major city in Africa, or both...or maybe, he thought, the substance would be diluted to expand its reach even further.

He looked up to see David watching him closely, the team leader's expression solemn as he keyed his radio and said, "Raptor Nine One, this is Suicide Actual."

The Renault van swerved through a sharp bend in the highway as Cancer negotiated the route eastward, accelerating through a great pine forest on their way to the Albanian border.

4

Charlottesville, Virginia, USA

I was halfway through unloading the dishwasher when I heard the sound of running footsteps over the cartoons playing in the next room.

Langley stopped at my side and asked, "Daddy, can I please have a cookie?"

At seven years old my daughter was, quite simply put, the cutest thing alive. Her brown eyes were watching me inquisitively, her dark hair all curls and barely restrained by the flower clips she'd applied herself. She'd also been springing up like a weed, seeming taller every morning than she had been at bedtime the night before.

I raised an eyebrow and asked skeptically, "Another one? Already?"

She took one of my hands in both of hers, batting her eyelashes for emphasis.

My gaze ticked to the staircase, currently empty.

"Hurry," I said, "before your mom comes downstairs."

Langley knew the drill well enough by this point. She moved with uncanny speed to the stove, crinkling the aluminum foil covering a plate of chocolate chip cookies my wife had baked last night and retrieving one before hastily retreating to the living room.

A creak on the staircase assured me I was too late, the final confirmation coming from Langley's receding voice calling out, "Good morning, Mommy."

My wife answered cordially, though with an undercurrent of sternness to assure both myself and Langley that she hadn't missed a thing.

"Hey, babe," I said cheerfully, "how'd you sleep?"

Laila approached without making eye contact: not a good sign.

"Fine. You?"

"Great." I handed over a thermos with the words, "Medium roast, light cream."

She accepted the coffee and hesitated.

Laila was beautiful even in scrubs and a white coat, with her strawberry-blonde hair pulled back in a loose ponytail. Her green eyes cut from the thermos to me.

"Thanks," she said flatly, then asked with concern, "Everything okay?"

"Yeah. Why?"

A pause.

"You drank a lot last night."

She wasn't wrong—I'd always enjoyed bourbon, though my consumption had been steadily increasing in direct proportion to how long I remained employed by the Agency. Laila was generally tolerant, though if I ever pushed it too far, I'd hear about it first thing in the morning.

"I'm fine," I said. "Some guys watch ESPN to unwind. I like booze."

"And am I correct in assuming that the cookie Langley was trying to hide from me wasn't her first this morning?"

"Yeah." I shrugged. "But, I mean, have you *seen* her? She's so fucking cute."

"She is cute," Laila allowed, "and she's also a kid."

"Exactly. Plus, we've got a special bond."

This caused her to scoff. "Oh, is that what you have."

Not a question but a statement, and not a particularly flattering one judging by her tone.

"What's that supposed to mean?" I asked.

Laila advanced a half step, keeping her voice low.

"It means she's not reveling in having you as a father—she's exploiting her absentee dad, David. Can't you see that? Every time you come home it's more of this bullshit, you overcompensating for being gone all the time and undermining what I have to do as the only parent who is consistently present."

"I'm just trying to be a good dad—"

"And what good does that do for Langley if she's getting mixed signals about what she can get away with? Christ, David, I'm the one who has to be the bad guy, always enforcing bath times and bedtimes and discipline while you get to drink and swoop in as the fun parent, then leave again as soon as you get a phone call summoning you back to work."

My eyes narrowed.

"If you've got this all figured out on your own," I asked, "then what do you need me for?"

Laila balked at the question, presumably taking it to be far more rhetorical than I'd intended.

"I need to get to work," she said, turning to leave before I could respond.

Which was just as well, I supposed, because what in the hell was I supposed to say to her? Very few things in life were as scary as an angry woman, and although my team had stopped a major terrorist attack a few years prior—which Laila was all too well aware of—if there was one thing my journey into marriage had assured me of, it was that any credibility-imbuing accomplishments were exceedingly short-lived in the wake of otherwise minor indiscretions. Save the world one day, I thought, and get in trouble for leaving your laundry in the dryer the next.

Which was an interesting contradiction, because while I'd be hard-pressed to remember the full content of this exchange in six months' time, I was damned certain that Laila had just seared every word into her permanent memory, adding it to the growing mental database of every argument we'd ever had. From this she could recall precise snippets at will, sometimes dating all the way back to our college days, with such bizarre specificity that I knew she wasn't making any of them up.

I heard her kiss Langley goodbye before leaving the house.

Once she was gone, I placed both hands on the granite countertop and thought, *Solid work, David*. Despite being gone a significant portion of each calendar year on training or deployment, my attempts at normalcy while home had resulted in my wife and daughter viewing me as a disposable asset at best or an alcoholic at worst.

And that was before I considered the misgivings that had been plaguing me since returning from Montenegro two weeks earlier.

The moment de Zurara informed us of a successful VX transfer off the coast of west Africa, my first thought wasn't *holy fuck, thousands of people are going to die* or even anything so justified as guilt and shame that my team had failed to prevent that payload from departing South America in the first place.

Instead I'd released a deliriously grateful sigh, overcome with a profound sense of relief that nerve agent wasn't somewhere in the US, near my family. They'd be safe, at least, and it wasn't until we'd actually crossed the Albanian border that I mentally chastised myself for the reaction.

Since then I'd felt mixed emotions about my response and what it said about me as both a professional Agency contractor and as a father. Had I always been this goddamned cold-blooded, or had my work at the front-lines of my nation's counterterrorism efforts—and seeing how perilously thin they could be at times—reduced me to such a state of selfishness that I was happy with the consolation prize of my family's survival?

It didn't help that I couldn't talk about that with anyone. My teammates would certainly understand, though as their leader I felt a certain obligation to maintain a facade of control over my emotions. And while Laila knew I was a CIA contractor, what was I supposed to tell her? "Sorry I'm drinking so much, but countless civilians are about to be slaughtered and when they do, it'll be my fault?"

The cartoons in the living room went silent before the approach of running footsteps.

This time Langley darted to my side, wrapping both arms around my waist in a bear hug.

"Daddy, can I go next door to play with Mila?"

I patted her on the back and said, "Her mom is taking you guys to camp today, but it's still early, baby girl. I'm not even sure Mila's up yet—"

"She is. I saw her playing in the backyard."

Drawing a breath, I replied, "Sure. Have fun."

Langley released the hug at once. "Thanks, Daddy. I love you."

"I love you too..."

My words trailed off as I realized I was talking to myself. Langley was already gone, racing around the corner on her way to the front door.

Now I was alone in the kitchen with a half-unloaded dishwasher, facing a reckoning with the wife that I severely dreaded. Under such circumstances, the prospect of violent ground combat seemed a pleasant alternative.

At that moment, my work phone buzzed in my pocket.

I checked the caller ID to see *JSC 6*, the initials shorthand for Jenio Solutions Consultancy, LLC, the private military contracting service that served as my cover job.

And the number 6 was a callsign suffix for a commander, the sight of it causing my jaw to settle.

Answering the call, I spoke through gritted teeth.

"Your timing could be better, Duchess."

Her voice was remarkably unapologetic. "It's time to come in to work."

"News to me," I said.

"It's news to both of us, and not an update that I'm particularly thrilled to deliver."

"Am I headed to the team room," I asked tentatively, "or the mothership?"

If my destination was the former, I could live with that—my team wasn't designed as a rapid deployment force, and was, in fact, very far from it, but we had very unique operational authorities, and the possibility always existed that our services might be needed on late notice. Even if we stood down at the last minute, it would get me out of the house if nothing else.

The mothership, however, a not-so-subtle reference to CIA headquarters, would spell trouble of a different sort.

But Duchess evaded the question altogether. "A driver will arrive within the hour. If I knew the duration of your absence, I'd tell you. Pack for an extended trip and say your goodbyes."

My stomach sank. There was only one explanation for this unprecedented turn of events, and it was one that my team had been fearing for some time.

"I don't know if that will work for my social schedule."

"Too bad," Duchess said without remorse. "Be grateful that I'm calling you personally as a courtesy. The rest of your team, David, are receiving their summons as we speak."

5

Cancer winced at the next statement from the man, spoken on the other end of an unidentified call to his work phone.

"Your presence is not optional," the clinical voice said. "A driver will arrive at your listed residence in 45 minutes, and you will meet him upon arrival."

Snorting his disapproval, Cancer replied, "Buddy, I'm in my tighty-whities with a cigarette in hand, and if I want to take an extra ten minutes to jerk off, I'm going to take it. This shit's not in my contract."

He ended the call then, leaning back in his seat before any dread could creep into his voice. He suddenly felt vulnerable, filled with an almost crippling concern not just for himself but his teammates.

This kind of notification could only mean one thing. He reached for a separate phone that was switched on and connected to a charger 24/7—a prepaid burner just like those possessed by the rest of his team, maintained for their hasty communication outside CIA surveillance.

The display showed a clear signal, though no incoming calls, and Cancer allowed himself a brief sigh of relief despite the obvious.

It wasn't that he'd told any lies to the Agency caller moments before—he was on his couch, clad in white cotton briefs and nothing else, an ember at the edge of his Marlboro Red twinkling gradually toward the filter.

The rest remained unsaid: that the call had interrupted his progress in *Battle Cry of Freedom*, a hardcover now closed on the side table beside his ashtray, and that his immediate reaction was that there were a couple possible reasons for the sudden recall. The odds were trending toward the least enviable of the two.

He grabbed the remote and turned on his television, a flat screen surrounded by built-in shelves filled to capacity with military history books. Placing the TV on mute, he flipped through channels in search of breaking news of some terrorist attack or another, but all he saw was the usual media and advertising bullshit. Not good.

Cancer pressed the filter between his lips, drawing a final inhale of his cowboy killer and stubbing it out before the burner phone gave a shrill ring.

He snatched it up, unplugging the charger cable as he answered, "Yeah."

Ian spoke over the line. "Stand by, I'm patching you into the conference call."

Shit, Cancer thought, this was every bit as bad as he thought.

A moment later the call re-connected, this time with David speaking.

"You get the call?"

"I did," he replied.

"And?"

"'And' what?" Cancer asked. "'And' nothing. 'And' we're fucked."

"All right," David said without a trace of surprise in his voice. He knew the score as well as any of them, probably more so since he was the ground force commander. "Let's get everyone else on the line and shoot them straight."

Ian spoke again. "Worthy's here, still working on getting through to Reilly."

"I just got the call," Worthy huffed a moment later, his Georgian drawl sounding especially pronounced, "and the guy sounded pissed. Pickup within the hour. This isn't looking good, fellas. I don't see anything on the news, do you?"

The little redneck wasn't wrong, Cancer thought as he conducted another sweep through the news stations to find more of the standard

American media fare: reactions to a celebrity breakup, partisan debate over a proposed tax increase on the wealthy, and a network-proclaimed 'harrowing video' of firefighters rescuing a dog from a flood. Shit.

"No," he said bluntly.

"So they've caught us coloring outside the lines. But for what? That last snatch was the closest we've ever come to a flawless and by-the-books operation in the two-plus years we've been running together."

David acknowledged, "Yeah, but what about all the missions before that? We've been off the grid more than a few times in more than a few places."

Reilly's voice came over the line.

"What'd I miss?"

"Apparently," Worthy mused, "we're all headed for a long trip to the federal pen."

Ian chimed in, "No way. Wherever we're headed, it's not a prison you can look up on Wikipedia."

"Unless we take off now. And if that's the play, then we better get moving."

Reilly added, "What if there's another explanation—what if we know too much, and they're erasing us as witnesses?"

It wasn't an inconceivable conclusion, Cancer knew, at least when coming from anyone on this call.

Previously, they'd all worked together as mercenaries for a transnational criminal syndicate, one whose ruthlessness had made itself evident in the periodic deaths of its own paramilitary teams. Himself, David, and Reilly had withstood one such attempt by improvisation and force of will alone.

Worthy said, "I hate to tell you guys this, but if that were the case, none of us would get a courtesy call giving advance notice. Cancer would have taken two in the back of the head while he was on his way to get cigarettes, David would probably get schwaked at a liquor store, Reilly shot dead at some fast food shithole, and Ian—I don't know, maybe have his throat slit at a Virgins Anonymous meeting."

"And you," Cancer shot back, "you'd get shanked at the Mossy Oak Emporium, or wherever the fuck you degenerate white trash spend your time when you're not balls-deep in your cousins. Bottom line, fellas, is we're headed for the cross, not the gallows. We answer to ourselves only, because if we answer to any court, we're all going away for a while. That's the score. And there's no running from the Agency."

Everyone fell quiet at that, seconds ticking by before David finally broke the silence.

"Shit, guys, this is it. I'm not going to tell you what to say or not say; God knows I've been the figurehead behind the majority of our indiscretions and I stand by every one of my decisions. They're going to split us up and probably tell you all that I was the first to crack and confess to whatever they found out about, but that'll be a lie. You know the military expression 'it's you and me until it's you *or* me?' Well my version is 'it's you and me until it's you and me in jail.' But I get that everyone's got lives to lead, so if you've got to cut a deal, I want everyone to put the blame on me."

Reilly objected, "We're not hanging you out to dry."

"You goddamn well better, if you're going to say anything at all. I'm the team leader, responsible for everything we do or fail to do, and frankly it's a miracle I haven't been prosecuted yet. There needs to be a fall guy. It's got to be me."

"Don't be an asshole," Worthy said, his tone harsher than Cancer had ever heard the mild-mannered pointman speak. "We've all incriminated ourselves just as much as the next guy. I don't know what they got us on, but we've got to present a unified front, and here it is: the official narrative we've provided for each one of our missions is the only one. It's that simple. They want to bring us down, they're going to have to find some hard evidence, and good luck with that—we're the only ones who've been on the ground. They're trying to dissect the truth from a few operational records, so what could they possibly know for sure?"

"The accounting," Ian replied solemnly. "We've always used operational funds however we've needed to, and I've cleaned up the numbers on the post-mission reports. I can't begin to list the transgressions off the top of my head."

Cancer groaned, reaching for his pack and shaking a fresh cigarette out of it as he issued his response.

"You dumbasses," he began, replacing the pack in his hand for a lighter, "are all missing the point. Since I've probably got a more robust criminal background than the rest of you, let me give you a ten-second PhD in how to talk to cops: you don't. Period. Doesn't matter what they say. All you tell them is one word—lawyer. Those are the only two syllables that leave your dirty little lips, and we let our legal teams talk to each other and handle the rest."

Reilly asked, "What if they don't let us get lawyers?"

Cancer sparked the cigarette in his lips, then took a drag and spoke as he exhaled.

"Closed court is still a court. Unless they're sending us to Guantanamo, they have to permit us legal representation. And I don't think there's any fuckin' room left at Guantanamo, do you?"

6

CIA Headquarters

I followed a suited man down the air-conditioned hallway under the glare of fluorescent lights, passing closed doors on either side labeled with nothing more than three-digit room numbers. Two similarly attired men trailed me by a few paces, no one speaking as we made our way deeper into a basement level of the Agency building.

Everything thus far had confirmed my worst fears.

I was met at my home not by one vehicle but three: a black Suburban and two patrol cars from the Virginia State Police. Which was great—now my neighbors could go from thinking I was a private military contractor to assuming that I was a soon-to-be convicted wife beater or worse. And while I hadn't been placed in cuffs, I was led into the Suburban by a suited man packing a concealed handgun. No official statement that I was under arrest, just an amiable "Right this way, sir." Fine by me, because I had no intentions of saying a word until I found out which of my team's many sins they were recalling us to account for.

The troopers, at least, had waited until we reached I-64 eastbound before activating their light bars, after which we made the two-plus-hour drive to CIA headquarters in record time. And after the State Police had peeled off before reaching the gate, my Suburban was waved through security at the flash of the driver's credentials; so this, I thought, was how the closed-trial process worked. None of the lackadaisical booking processes inherent in the criminal justice system, just a one-way ticket to the Agency, where they could hold me as long as they pleased while my family assumed I was abroad on yet another contractor job. Upon arrival, I'd been instructed to leave my luggage in the vehicle, and the armed man was joined by two more outside the building.

Now, as we proceeded down the corridor, not only were my teammates nowhere to be seen, but our route took us nowhere near the Special Activities Center that sponsored us. We were in an entirely different part of the sprawling complex, one whose purpose I was about to find out firsthand.

Finally we reached our destination: a closed door flanked by suited bodyguards with earpieces, one of whom reached for the handle and pulled the door open to allow me to pass.

Inside was a windowless conference room where two figures were seated at a long table: Duchess, the CIA officer heading Project Longwing, and an extremely stern-looking old white man I didn't recognize. Given his age, his sour expression, and the context of this still-unfolding nightmare, I concluded he was the most pipe-hitting attorney the Agency had to offer.

"Where's my team?" I blurted, immediately violating Cancer's maxim to say nothing.

Duchess replied, "David, have a seat."

I did so uneasily, waiting for the remaining introduction that she executed a moment later.

"This is Senator Tom Gossweiler, Chair of the Senate Select Committee on Intelligence."

That was a far more troubling development than if he'd been a lawyer —no legal representation here, but arguably the only thing worse: a man with direct oversight of the intelligence community writ large, not just CIA.

We eyed one another without speaking, and Duchess slid a photograph over to me.

I resolved to keep a poker face no matter what; this was the first piece of evidence against me and I wasn't about to give any confirmation one way or the other.

But when I lifted the picture to analyze it, I felt my eyebrows wrinkling in confusion. It was a professional portrait of a brunette who appeared to be in her thirties, a cute woman with a bob cut and modestly applied makeup. Pretty but not disarmingly attractive, a girl-next-door type who had nothing to prove.

Most perplexingly of all was the fact that I'd never seen her before in my life; I could forget names like it was my job, but never a face. Whoever she was, I hadn't encountered her on any of my team's previous missions, and at the moment, any photograph that wasn't a blurry snapshot of me executing a Boko Haram operative or torturing information out of a card-carrying ISIS logistician was a good thing.

I slid the photograph back to her and waited for an explanation.

Duchess didn't disappoint. "She was working with the Red Cross in Benghazi when she was kidnapped yesterday evening."

I wondered if Duchess was luring me into something, maybe trying to get my guard down before she let the other shoe drop. Shrugging, I said, "Sounds like a job for JSOC."

"There's a technical support team flying into Benghazi as we speak, and a squadron from Dam Neck is en route to Naval Air Station Sigonella."

I recognized the euphemism for SEAL Team Six, certainly qualified for hostage rescue and with a staging location in southern Italy, a stone's throw from the point of capture. Though shooting those operators out of a cannon at the first disappearance of an aid worker seemed a stretch, given they were always on standby—unlike my own team, which made the current summons all the more paradoxical.

So I asked, "Has anyone claimed responsibility yet?"

"The Abu Sayyaf Group."

I gave a half-smirk. "Filipino terrorists are operating in Libya?"

"The only one who matters is."

Duchess used a remote to turn on a display screen on the wall, which came to life with a freeze frame of a man I recognized at once—and the sight of him made my blood run cold.

Khalil Noureddin should have been unremarkable, little more than a promising commander in a backwater terrorist group in the Philippines. But the fact that he'd been born to an affluent family before turning into a radical Islamist at the University of London stood out, along with the fact that he'd relocated to Jolo Island and begun climbing the ranks of Abu Sayyaf. That combination of factors had made him the target of my Project Longwing team's very first mission, which should have been the end of him —only we'd inadvertently stumbled into his shootdown of a special operations helicopter, and our targeted killing effort swiftly turned into a rescue operation for the surviving pilot.

And while we'd gotten that pilot off the island after a particularly tense conversation between myself and Khalil over a captured radio, his notoriety was just beginning.

He'd proceeded to mutilate the dead pilot, posing with the desecrated corpse beside the helicopter wreckage in what had become an infamous photograph. And while US military forces swarmed the area to recover the body and helicopter, killing dozens of Abu Sayyaf fighters on the small island, Khalil had somehow escaped and was now a terrorist celebrity whose whereabouts remained unknown.

Until now.

"I don't get it," I said bluntly. "Libya's not a bad place for Khalil to go into hiding, but as far as conducting operations there? He'd need significant help from the militias."

Duchess nodded. "You're right about that. And I'm afraid this was no random hostage grab, but very possibly one intended to rattle the Senate Select Committee on Intelligence."

"Rattle the committee," I asked tentatively, "how, exactly?"

Gossweiler spoke for the first time, his hand steady as he reached across the table to place his fingertips on the woman's photograph.

"Her name is Olivia," he began. "She's my daughter."

The tension within me abated at once, replaced by a profound empathy for the man—he was no judgmental senator right now but a devastated father. And, judging by the eerie calmness with which he carried himself at present, one who remained in a state of extreme denial.

"Christ," I said, "I'm sorry, sir."

Blinking away the sting of tears that had formed without warning, I met his gaze and continued, "My team is standing by to help any way we can—"

Duchess cut me off, seemingly in an attempt to guide the conversation away from the senator before he could speak again.

"Your team," she began, "is en route to the isolation facility in preparation for an immediate deployment to Tunisia, where they will make a cross-border movement into Libya."

Nodding, I asked, "Has Khalil issued his demands?"

"Only one. And that's why your team will be flying without you."

"Without me? I'm the goddamn ground force commander."

"Cancer will serve as GFC, and we'll be augmenting the team with a fifth member who has significant operational experience in Libya. You'll meet them all in-country if we can manage it."

"If you can manage it?" I threw up my hands. "Did I just walk into the CIA or the Salvation Army?"

Duchess drew a sharp breath.

"David—shut up. You've got another role to serve, and there's no one on your team we can send in your place. In fact," she added, "there's no one else we can send, period."

My eyes narrowed at that—my hallmarks were many, few of them enviable. Anger issues, check. Drinking problem? Debatable. And while I had a tendency to make shit work out in combat, I was under no illusions that there were legions of far more qualified shooters and leaders who'd gladly do whatever their country asked of them.

By way of explanation, Duchess lifted the remote again and pressed a button, and the freeze frame of Khalil Noureddin on the television began to speak.

His face showed equal parts European and Filipino influence, with a thin beard and placid eyes. The Asian accent was delivered with an unnerving, eloquent grace.

"I have Olivia Gossweiler, daughter of Senator Tom Gossweiler. When I destroyed the helicopter and killed the infidel, there was a team of Americans present on Jolo Island to assassinate me. The leader of that team called himself Suicide. I will communicate my terms to him, and him alone. You will send him to Benghazi, or she—"

Duchess moved the remote to shut off the display, but it was too late—the camera view spun to reveal walls covered by sheets and Olivia slumped in the corner, her white blouse torn open to expose her bra, hands bound and mouth gagged with the Arabic text for *kafir*, nonbeliever, painted in blood below her collarbones. Her face was bruised, eyes swollen and streaming tears, before the image vanished to a black screen.

"Jesus," I gasped, and before I could rebuke myself for the reaction, Gossweiler spoke.

"Your role is to comply with Khalil's demand for a meeting. Reason being, he will likely fact-check you to make sure you were indeed the man in charge during the failed Jolo Island mission. We can't afford to send a stand-in and get called out on it."

My eyes narrowed at that, both out of his reference to the mission as a failure—we'd rescued one pilot, and at the time that seemed a far greater cause than putting down Khalil like the sick animal he was—and more importantly, because I was deeply unsettled by Gossweiler's current composure. He went on without waiting for a response.

"During that meeting, you will explain that your role is to maintain communications with the US government. You will promise nothing, nor do you have any authority to do so. The decisions will be made in Washington, and if any funds are transferred by way of ransom, it will be done through a series of non-governmental organizations and only to draw out the negotiations long enough for the SEALs to locate Khalil. I'm sending the rest of your team into Libya to facilitate the operators' arrival because doing so under covert authorities is the best way to set this into motion without tipping off the press. If you or your men walk into a trap, frankly, you're deniable. A member of SEAL Team Six isn't, and I don't want to risk them until conditions are set on the ground. That being said, you and your men will have all possible resources at your disposal."

It was then that I realized my two assumptions about Senator Gossweiler—that he was both devastated and in denial—may have been severely misplaced. Spending my adult life at war had made me question my own humanity on more than a few occasions, but I couldn't conceive of discussing my own daughter as a strategic pawn; was this what the job did to you, in time? Was I going to turn into this husk of a man after another few years of witnessing and inflicting carnage?

Inhaling, I said, "I understand the risks, Senator—"

"Furthermore," he cut me off as if I hadn't spoken at all, making it clear that he intended this to be a one-way conversation, "under no circumstances will you assure Khalil that we intend to comply with any demands. You are to serve as a neutral party facilitating our communication with this man for as long as is required until he's in US government custody, or dead."

I almost asked, *What about Olivia?* Duchess had discussed the SEALs as a hostage rescue force. Gossweiler seemed to consider their primary mission as killing or capturing Khalil. I was more or less a paid assassin, for Christ's sake, and yet seemed to have a hell of a lot more concern for Olivia Gossweiler than her own father.

So be it, I resolved. If he didn't care about her life, then I'd treat this mission as if it were my little girl in Khalil's grasp instead of his. And besides, I thought with a wry sense of anticipation, Khalil and I had old business to finish.

"Senator," I began, then waited for a beat to see if he'd interrupt me before continuing, "when do I fly to Benghazi?"

7

Longwing Isolation Facility
Rockingham County, North Carolina

Worthy emerged from the equipment storage room with a rifle case in each hand, the scarred plastic surfaces bearing the designations *RACEGUN* and *CANCER* written in paint marker.

He crossed the planning bay to the thumping beats of rap music blaring over a Bluetooth speaker—with Cancer in charge, no one could object—and deposited the cases next to the others. Then he paused to glance around the isolation facility, or as the team called it, the ISOFAC.

On the outside, this building was unremarkable, but that was the point.

It resided within a fenced-off swath of woods in the North Carolina countryside near the Virginia border, a location selected for the utter seclusion it provided. But this was ground zero for their every mission to date, the nucleus of planning and equipment preparation before an Agency vehicle shuttled them to Pope Field or Joint Base Charleston to meet their aircraft.

The interior reflected that, at least somewhat. The planning bay walls held team memorabilia, souvenirs captured at various hotspots around the world, and was lined by individual workstations. Ian was hunched over a computer at one of them wearing noise-canceling headphones, oblivious to the outside world as he downloaded anything and everything pertinent to Libya, with an emphasis on digital maps and overlays with historical ambush sites.

Cancer sat nearby, head bobbing in rhythm to the rap as he drafted an email response to the limited information Duchess had sent. The old sniper pecked away at the keyboard with two index fingers, a far cry from David, who was used to fielding the role of team leader and could have sent the email ten times over by now. Meanwhile, Reilly was seated on the floor, sifting through a massive spread of medical supplies as he tailored the contents of various aid bags to suit a long-range vehicle movement across the Sahara Desert.

Worthy was returning for his next load of gear when a surveillance monitor in the corner chimed.

Cancer paused the rap and turned to glare at the screen, a live camera feed of the compound gate opening to allow a Suburban through.

"Who the fuck is that?" he asked.

Worthy shrugged. "They had the passcode—must be an Agency fleet vehicle."

"Go see what they want."

Pushing open the heavy door, Worthy strode into the impossibly humid air. July in North Carolina was a force to be reckoned with, and he swatted away a swarm of gnats that descended on him almost immediately. He waited to hear the crunch of gravel signaling the arrival of a vehicle down the half-mile driveway, catching sight of the SUV as it rounded the final curve.

It wheeled halfway through the turnabout, stopping with its rear bumper facing him as the passenger door swung open and a man stepped out in a plaid shirt and jeans.

He looked to be in his mid-thirties, with high cheekbones and cinnamon skin. He had a trim beard, thick black hair styled and gelled to perfection, and eyes concealed by Ray-Bans.

"Who are you?" Worthy asked.

"Your attachment," he said with a trace of an accent that sounded

Middle Eastern to Worthy's ear. "Master Sergeant Jalal Hassan, I go by Hass. CCT."

Checking his watch, Worthy replied, "Right on. We weren't expecting you for another hour." He stepped forward to extend his hand. "I'm Worthy."

Hass accepted the handshake, then popped the Suburban's liftgate to reveal two Pelican hard cases, a rifle box, and a coyote brown rucksack filled to the breaking point.

"Damn," Worthy muttered. "You brought the whole kit and kaboodle."

"Wasn't sure what I'd need—how long do we have?"

They began unloading the equipment onto the gravel as Worthy explained, "Shuttle for the C-17 arrives in 90 minutes, and we'll do most of our planning enroute."

"All right," Hass grunted as he lifted one of the Pelican boxes off the truck and set it down. "Because I've been at this job for a hot minute, and this is the first time all I've been told is to pack for the desert and wait for a driver. What's the rundown?"

Worthy didn't answer him, instead tilting his head toward the waiting driver before pulling out the remaining equipment. Hass lowered the liftgate, then knocked on the rear window twice with his fist. The Suburban pulled away, and Worthy waited until the engine noise faded before explaining.

"Senator's daughter got kidnapped in Benghazi. She's being held by Khalil Noureddin, a Filipino terrorist we've got some history with. He demanded our team leader for the negotiations, so the rest of us are heading in as backside support ahead of a hostage rescue by DEVGRU."

Hass paused, momentarily startled, but then he gave an easygoing laugh.

"You almost had me—for a second, I thought you were serious. Sounds like the world's worst Nicolas Cage movie."

"I am serious," Worthy said.

The man scrutinized him for any indicators of an elaborate joke, then shrugged. "Guess it's a party, then. Let's roll."

"Hang on—you gangster or what?"

Hass's reply was immediate.

"With nonstop trips to the sandbox for a decade-plus? Worthy, if I were a Boy Scout, I would've quit or been fired a hundred times by now."

"I hope so, because this outfit plays by Vegas rules—what happens on our missions, stays on our missions. You get me?"

Worthy kept his eyes fixed on Hass. He was no fan of cracking down on a new guy for the sake of maintaining appearances, but shortly removed from the expectation that his entire team was getting arrested for ethical or operational transgressions—which there would surely be more of on the mission ahead—this was about the worst possible time to invite a newcomer into the fold.

Hass scratched his beard. "I'm here to enable you guys, not slow you down. If selective amnesia is part of that at any point on the op, then that's exactly what you're going to get from me. Wouldn't be the first time, and unless I bite the bullet in Libya, it won't be the last."

"Good. Come meet the guys." Worthy turned to swipe his ID on the card reader, then entered his code on the keypad before pulling the door open and leading the way into the ISOFAC.

The rap music was playing again, silenced only when Worthy shouted over it.

"Fellas, this is Hass, our Combat Controller."

All eyes locked on the airman now rotating his sunglasses atop his head, save Ian—with his headphones, he hadn't heard a thing and remained merrily working at his computer.

Speaking from his spread of aid supplies, Reilly asked, "Where are you based out of, Hass?"

"Pope Field, Fort Bragg."

"21st STS?"

Hass shook his head. "24th."

That number in the context of his job specialty was enough to get everyone's attention, elevating the man's credentials without him needing to say another word.

The Air Force's CCTs were elite enough—FAA-certified air traffic controllers, they were absolute masters of all things related to special operations air support. Typically one of them would be attached to an element of Green Berets, Navy SEALs, or Marine Raiders to manage aircraft and ensure all the bombs landed on time and exactly where they were supposed to. When Army Rangers conducted a low-altitude parachute drop to seize an enemy airfield, Combat Controllers would jump in alongside them, then mark the landing strip with infrared lights and call in the follow-on planes to offload reinforcements. Operating behind enemy lines was their bread and butter, and they'd happily freefall, fast rope, closed-circuit dive, or ride ATVs or snowmobiles alongside any elite US military team to get there.

But the 24th Special Tactics Squadron was another animal altogether. The Air Force's top Combat Controllers competed for attendance biannually at a nine-week assessment course where, if they were lucky enough to be selected, they'd attend further advanced training and eventual assignment to the unit. Those men accompanied Tier One elements like Delta Force and SEAL Team Six, in addition to CIA paramilitary teams, to execute their craft in the most austere and covert conditions imaginable.

Cancer slapped Ian on the shoulder, queuing the intelligence operative to remove his headphones and whirl his chair around.

Ian took one look at the man, immediately surmising who he was and asking, "How'd you draw the short straw for this?"

"Not a lot of Libyans in the service," Hass explained, "fewer still who are JTAC qualified. I was born in Tripoli, my family emigrated when I was thirteen, and I joined the Air Force after high school. Afghanistan, Iraq, Syria, then went back home with Ground Branch to run airstrikes during the revolution against Gaddafi, then two more trips to knock out ISIS from Sirte."

Ian asked, "Fluent speaker?"

"*Na'am, sadiqi,*" he replied, then added, "I can roll eastern and western dialects with no interpreter needed. If we end up in the south, I can hold my own, but no way I'm passing as a local."

Reilly nodded in approval. "What's your callsign?"

"Rain Man."

"So you're an autistic savant?"

Hass laughed. "If I could count cards, I'd be working on my handicap in Santa Rosa by now. Charlie Squadron started calling me that because I make it rain. We need some air support where we're headed. You'll see what I mean."

"All right, hotshot," Cancer said dismissively, "enough dick measuring." He pointed across the team members in rapid succession. "Reilly, medic. Worthy, point man and superstar shooter. Ian, intel nerd. I'm Cancer, sniper and in charge of this shitshow. David's our usual GFC, he's flying over separately. We're headed for Tunisia, then driving over the border to Libya. You smoke?"

"Sure, I'm a cigar man. Montecristo White Series, but I'll make do with anything in a pinch."

"Cigarettes?"

"Hell no."

"Good," Cancer declared, "more for me. Help Worthy get the gear together; we'll program radios and load mags on the way. Any questions?"

"Just one," Hass offered. "Who in the hell are you guys? I've run missions with a lot of Ground Branch teams, but this is my first rodeo where they took me to a civilian address with a base in the woods."

Worthy followed Hass's gaze to the team memorabilia on the walls, envisioning how insane it would look for a first-time visitor to the facility: an ISIS flag, a Soviet submachine gun, a pair of fatigue pants with a bullet hole through them, and a sawed-off shotgun collected on missions across multiple continents.

"Project Longwing," Cancer responded. "We're all contractors. Tier One guys go after the top terrorist leadership, and we do a little off-the-books 'pre-emptive' neutralization of any rising stars before they get enough experience to qualify for attention from the Unit or Six."

"Assassins," Hass said thoughtfully. "Didn't think America was doing business like that anymore."

"Yeah, well, until a couple years ago, she wasn't. We're the pilot team. And I planned on doing this before you arrived, but since you're early you'll just have to sit through it—we've got new gear issue, scumbags."

There was a collective groan from everyone but Cancer and Haas. Every mission, it seemed, was preceded by an updated GPS or radio they had to learn in record time, but then again, they'd never had a mission so time-sensitive as this.

"Jesus," Reilly commented, "how long is it going to take for us to figure out the newest bullshit? Can't this wait until our next—"

"Quiet, bastard," Cancer shot back. "If you need any time to learn this, then I'm revoking your man card."

He reached for a cardboard box beneath his workstation and set it on the desk. "Knives, assholes. The pointy end goes in first. You don't even need to rearrange your kit."

Reaching into the box, he procured a sheathed knife and tossed it to the medic, repeating the process with Worthy.

Intercepting the knife, Worthy slid it from its sheath and examined the blade.

"Whoa," he said, turning it over in his hand, "look at that false edge—this thing handles like a dream." It was also, he noted, slim enough to fit behind a mag pouch, much less within the waistband of his armored plate carrier.

"Balanced," Reilly allowed, trying to restrain his enthusiasm as he did the same.

Hass stepped to Worthy's side and said, "Can I see that?"

Worthy handed the knife over, and Hass brought it close to his face, scrutinizing the stamped text, *WINKLER KNIVES*, and the serial number *03*.

"I've got five Winklers," Hass said in disbelief, "not counting the CxC Dagger on my rack right now. I know every blade in their catalog, and this"—he held up the knife for emphasis—"isn't one of them."

Cancer replied, "That's because it's custom."

Hass shook his head abruptly, as if startled by the revelation.

"How'd you pull that off?"

This elicited a smile from the sniper. "I asked nicely. Explained I wanted something for stabbing fuckers. No pigsticker, no display piece that would take up a lot of space on our kit. Just a nice thin blade to slip between the ribs or split someone's kidney like a grape. I started bouncing designs back and forth with Daniel Winkler, and this is the result. It's a restricted production model, and they won't make them for anyone but me. You're holding one of five in existence."

Hass was mesmerized, his eyes darting over the weapon.

"Wish you knew I was coming," he said breathlessly. "You could've made it six."

"No," Cancer corrected him, "because I've been in the shit with everyone in this room but you. If you want one of these knives, fine. But you've got to earn it. Turn out to be a rock star by the end of this, and I'll drive down to Pope Field and deliver number six to you myself."

8

Benina International Airport, Libya

After close to two hours on an aircraft without functional air conditioning, I'd never so badly longed for the presence of a jet bridge.

My shirt was plastered to my back with sweat as I followed a row of debarking passengers down the plane stairway onto pavement radiating the afternoon sun's punishing effects back upward. The combined effect was like walking into the world's largest hairdryer, and while the backpack I carried held a few essentials, it was notably lighter after I'd downed about half my water bottles since going wheels-up on my final connection.

Squinting even with my sunglasses on, I scanned the tarmac as we approached the terminal—a few passenger jets from Afriqiyah and Libyan Airlines, along with a smaller unmarked turboprop. Beyond them was an Mi-24 helicopter and a pair of fighter jets—MiG-21s, by the looks of it—the trio a mere fraction of the inventory from Gaddafi's air force that had fallen into the hands of competing militias, most of which had recently been consolidated under a tenuous interim government. With presidential elections stalled due to various disputes, Libya was one spark away from falling back into an inferno that would see those aircraft, to say nothing of the vast stockpiles of weapons, artillery, and armored vehicles, scattering to militia control for the country's third civil war in just over a decade.

I entered the terminal and its partial reprieve from the heat, joining the line of non-residents filing toward a row of desks manned by customs officers. The "no smoking" signs were apparently for decorative purposes only, existing amid the lingering stench of cigarettes that only increased the further I got inside the building. Cancer would love this place, I thought. Unslinging my backpack, I retrieved another water bottle and began to drink as I waited for my turn at the customs checkpoint.

I'd been in the air or on layover for over 33 hours: BWI to Detroit, then Paris to Tunisia, before boarding a creaking Airbus A320 for the final leg to Benina International Airport. I was still twelve miles east of Benghazi, though whether I'd make it to a taxi remained to be seen; in the interests of total compliance, the Agency had communicated my arrival time and flight number to Khalil, along with the hotel I'd be staying at. He could intercept me at any point in the process, selecting a time and place of his choosing, and the only thing I knew for certain was that the terrorist already had me under surveillance. Half of the flight from Tunis had consisted of me wondering which of my fellow passengers were sent by Khalil to screen for CIA straphangers shadowing their diplomatic representative.

Regrettably for me, however, I was going in alone.

Finally my turn arrived at the customs desk, where I handed my passport to a man in blue uniform who accepted the document with a bored snatch of his white-gloved hand.

"Name?" he asked.

"Tom Connelly."

After comparing my appearance with the very recent passport photograph, he asked, "The purpose of your visit?"

"Business."

He raised his eyebrows.

Clearing my throat, I continued, "I'm a security consultant being retained by a multinational corporation, here for the purposes of an area assessment."

There was no way to tell if he understood everything I'd just said. The man robotically continued, "How long will you be here?"

"Seven days, unless I get extended."

"Where will you stay?"

"The Julyana Resort."

His gaze fell back to my passport and he began rifling through the stamps from ostensible entry to various European and African nations over the past six years. All I'd had to do was pose for a few photographs between shirt changes at Agency headquarters, and an hour later their documents people handed me a fully authentic-looking passport right down to the holograms, UV fluorescent ink, invisible fluorescent fibers, and RFID chip, along with a matching driver's license, checkbook, iPhone with pre-loaded numbers, and a company business card. All of it was fully backstopped to a front company complete with a functioning phone number, and I'd spent the majority of my travel time mentally rehearsing the particulars of my cover. Not that it mattered much.

Sure, I could fool an airport customs officer. Khalil, however, would know it was all bullshit: he'd disseminated his video of Olivia solely to official CIA email addresses, a peculiar level of restraint for a notorious terrorist figurehead. Whatever the cause for his subtlety, he'd be damned sure my real name wasn't Tom Connelly. And if he tortured the truth out of me, well, at least my family was safeguarded by a low-visibility protective detail of federal agents, and would remain so until my hopefully safe return.

The customs officer abruptly looked up and handed my passport back to me.

"Welcome to Libya, Mr. Connelly."

"Thank you," I said, accepting the fake document and pocketing it before resuming my march through the airport.

My next stop was the restroom, a tiled cell that reeked of urine and had, apparently, attracted every housefly on the continent. I dropped my empty water bottle in the trash before relieving myself of a small fraction of the fluid I'd been consuming while I still had the chance, then exited and turned right through a wave of cigarette smoke that was a refreshing alternative to the terminal's bathroom facilities.

I followed a trickle of people past a duty-free store, identifying a sign in Arabic with a picture of a briefcase that signified, I presumed, the way to baggage claim. The men around me were in Western attire, mostly jeans and T-shirts, although a few wore traditional vests with long white shirts and headdresses. Every woman in sight had her hair and neck concealed by a hijab, and a few had their faces covered as well, a reminder that almost every native in the country was a Sunni Muslim. No one looked under the age of twenty, and it didn't take a PhD to see why—even those who'd accepted the risk of visiting family amid the current political instability weren't about to do so with their children.

We filed past a security checkpoint manned by a young police officer with an AK-47, entering an open lobby and moving toward our respective baggage claims. I glanced around as casually as I could without looking like either a wayward tourist begging to get mugged or an intelligence officer trying to determine the extent of enemy surveillance.

The only standout in the crowd was a woman in a tight-fitting blouse, the silk scarf draped over her shoulders doing nothing to cover the long dark hair cascading down her back. She may have been Libyan by birth, or from any number of North African or Mediterranean countries, but I knew with certainty she hadn't been on my flight. Was she at the wrong baggage claim, or simply here to meet a friend?

My curiosity faded upon the arrival of airport employees pushing carts weighed down by tagged luggage, and I identified my gray checked bag amid the rows. It held nothing of importance—clothes and toiletries for an extended stay, but certainly no trackers or digital devices—as a concession to the disquieting fact that Khalil probably had people on the payroll who had searched it long before it reached baggage claim.

And to my surprise, the unveiled woman plucked my luggage from the cart, then turned to stride away. I intercepted her with a forced smile and said, "Excuse me, ma'am. I think you've got my bag."

She looked from the bag to my face with startlingly hazel eyes before returning my smile.

"I should hope so, Mr. Connelly."

Her accent sounded Libyan, though I couldn't reconcile the involvement of an attractive female with the murderous lunatic I'd come here to see.

I asked, "Can you take me to him?"

"That depends on who you seek."

"Khalil Noureddin."

"And he knows you as?"

"Suicide."

Her expression grew solemn at the confirmation, words curt as she dropped my bag and replied, "Follow me."

I hastened to recover my luggage, then caught up with her as she walked toward the exit.

As we proceeded, she asked, "Did you bring any weapons with you?"

"No."

"Any digital devices that can be tracked?"

Now she was just trying to catch me in a lie. We both knew my possessions and I were going to be scanned in short order, and while the CIA had low-key transmitters that could evade detection under most circumstances, in the end we decided it wasn't worth the risk. I was here at Khalil's mercy, and here I would remain until we could find a way to turn the tables.

"I have a phone," I admitted. "That's it."

"Computer, tablet?"

"No."

"Is anyone following you?"

I sidestepped an old man walking the opposite direction, then responded, "Besides your people? No."

"Mr. Connelly, if we find that you are not being truthful—"

"I am here to facilitate Olivia's return," I said forcefully, "and I haven't done nor will I do anything to compromise that. No one came with me."

"I am very pleased to hear that." She stopped beside a door, shooting me a suggestive glance. I pushed it open and held it for her as we stepped outside, back into the smothering afternoon heat wave, the air thick with sand and car exhaust.

My escort led the way down a row of stopped vehicles, and I could make out our destination at once—amid the taxis was an ominously unmarked van, dented and bearing patches of rust. I glided out from beneath the overhang, pausing to switch my luggage from right hand to left in an effort to expose myself to any CIA-hacked surveillance cameras or aerial coverage. The odds of being sighted by the latter were slim—rolling me up at the airport was a smart call due to flight paths forcing the Agency UAVs to maintain a wide berth—but this was my last opportunity to signal my location, and I was going to make the most of it.

The woman knocked on the van's passenger side window and I caught a glimpse of a middle-aged Libyan man behind the wheel, a scarf pulled over his nose below aviator sunglasses and a camouflage ballcap.

Then the van door slid open and she stepped aside with the words, "Goodbye, Mr. Connelly."

I rounded her to see three men in the back—chest racks with extra magazines, two Kalashnikovs and a Beretta AR70/90, all three in ski masks—and felt my stomach twist into a knot as I set my luggage aboard the van.

Crouching to enter, I'd barely made it inside before the men grabbed me by the arms and threw me down, pinning my wrists behind my back and handcuffing them. Turning my head sideways and spitting out a mouthful of dirt, the last thing I saw was the woman closing the van door before one of the men pulled a hood over my face and the outside world turned to black.

9

Ian piloted his Land Cruiser through the blinding sunlight, leading his team's convoy down a dusty, cratered highway stretching east across Libya. Personnel from the American Embassy and CIA Annex in Tripoli had traveled a reverse route when evacuating the country for Tunisia at the outset of the Second Libyan Civil War in 2014; now the team was going back in, having crossed the border along an old caravan route before reaching the highway years after the last US diplomatic presence.

To his left were the Nafusa Mountains, a desert range rising 2,500 feet as the barrier between the Tripolitanian Plateau and the coastal plains beyond. The craggy brown peaks represented a former rebel stronghold but were now a patchwork of towns and tribes with ample guerilla warfare experience that the team had no interest in negotiating by vehicle or otherwise.

Faced with the obvious issue of having only five men and three vehicles, they were running a modified task organization with only two team members—in this case, ground force commander and JTAC—relegated to passenger seats.

That left Hass riding shotgun beside Ian, and in the hours they'd been on the road, not more than two minutes of silence had lapsed between them.

"You've got to understand," Hass said, continuing their conversation while monitoring a small video display in his lap, "that Libya is totally fucked as a matter of Gaddafi's own design."

"How so?" Ian asked.

"He came to power by coup, and he had no intentions of being overthrown the same way. He'd pit tribes against each other by allocating land to one or the other along the fissure lines of contested areas, underpay his army, make sure there was just enough instability and infighting that no group ever got powerful enough to challenge his rule. Back in 2011, the only thing the entire country could agree on was that they wanted Gaddafi out, and as soon as he was gone, all those longstanding rivalries came back in force."

"Right," Ian confirmed. "Split into the Government of National Accord out of Tripoli, and the House of Representatives out of Tobruk. Second civil war."

Hass laughed, glancing over at Ian with an incredulous expression.

"Shit, if it were just a civil war there'd be a clear winner. What happened after Gaddafi was really a proxy war. The UN, Qatar, Turkey, and most of Europe backed the GNA. The HOR fought against them with help from the UAE, Saudi, Egypt, and Russia, plus Italy once they decided they couldn't handle the influx of refugees. Every one of those countries still has people on the ground right now in violation of the ceasefire. By the time we get to Benghazi, you won't have any fucking clue who you're looking at."

"Does the US still have people here?"

"If we do," Hass mused, "I have no idea where they're at."

"Meaning?"

"Depending on the administration, we backed both sides at various points. Same as the French and Brits."

Ian shook his head. "No shit."

"It's all a game, brother. Everyone either wants to stop terrorism or get their hands on the oil here, or both. And everyone's trying to be in the good graces of whichever political party comes to power. Now that the war's on hold but no one in Libya can agree to the particulars of a presidential election—delayed twice now, with no end in sight—the whole country's a powder keg."

Ian had already decided that Hass was an invaluable asset to the team; JTAC qualifications aside, his understanding of the cultural considerations here was second only to a lifelong native. Paired with his special operations experience and understanding of the team's intent in operating here, he'd been a treasure trove of information that Ian had been mining for the better part of their road trip without so much as testing the man's patience —or at least, he hoped.

Hass turned the tables then, finally placing Ian on the receiving end of an inquiry.

"Can I ask you a question?"

"God knows I've been asking you enough. Shoot."

Hesitating for a moment, Hass continued, "I get that I'm here because of my background and operational experience. But who's your usual JTAC?"

"We don't have anyone who's JTAC qualified."

"Then how in the fuck can you possibly operate? Who calls in your airstrikes?"

"Hass, this is the first time we've had air support for anything but infil and exfil." He glanced at the monitor in the man's lap displaying a live feed of the MQ-9 Reaper UAV flying ahead of them as route reconnaissance. It wasn't the only one operating over Libya—Ian had learned that the CIA had a secret drone base at Bizerte-Sidi Ahmed Air Base in Tunisia, along with a robust UAV presence at the naval base in Italy.

But only one at a time was dedicated to their ground infiltration.

Hass pointed out, "Agency's got no shortage of UAVs. How come they don't supply you?"

Ian shrugged. "Deniability, I suppose. They designed us to be cut loose if things go sideways. A few contractors can be written off as mercenaries. That's not the case if we leave a trail of bomb craters consistent with US munitions, and besides, our role is to replace drone strikes, not call for them..."

He trailed off when Hass held up a finger, indicating he was receiving an incoming radio message. Since Ian wasn't hearing it over his own earpiece, it must have been on the air frequency.

"Copy," Hass replied, watching his screen as he transmitted over the team net, "Cancer, Reaper has spotted a checkpoint-in-progress approximately twelve kilometers ahead, at that sharp bend where the highway turns northeast. Looks like five trucks with fifteen men dismounting, small arms, and an armored personnel carrier with a recoilless in the turret. Affiliation unknown."

There were a few seconds of silence—surely Cancer checking his satellite imagery from the passenger seat of the middle vehicle to determine a workaround—and then the de facto team leader replied.

"*Head north at Checkpoint 18 and take us up that side road. We'll follow it through the foothills all the way back to the highway. Gonna add a couple hours to our trip, but preferable to eating a few rounds from that recoilless if they don't like our cover story.*"

A brief pause, then, "*Stand by, have an incoming call from Raptor Nine One.*"

Hass redirected the Reaper to transition its efforts toward reconnoitering the new route, then said to Ian, "Next turn is left in five klicks, Checkpoint 18."

"Got it."

An uneasy silence followed as they waited for Cancer to deliver the update from the Project Longwing operations center. Since everything on their end had gone more or less according to plan thus far, Ian suspected the content of that message would have to do with the one team member not present in the convoy.

Finally Cancer transmitted, "*All right, fuckers, here's the update from Duchess. Suicide landed and got picked up at the airport. His cell phone went dark, but a drone spotted him getting into a van.*"

Ian keyed his mic and replied, "Where is he now?"

"*Van drove a surveillance detection route, then went to a covered parking garage. Three vehicles left that garage and began their own SDRs. Suicide could be in any one of them, and it's not going to be the last vehicle swap. We ain't gonna hear from him until Khalil lets him go, if he lets him go at all.*"

There was distinct anger in Cancer's voice, not unusual from the sniper, though in this case it was more than justified. David had just surrendered to Khalil as a willing hostage, a testament to the unfortunate reality that they had no viable alternatives at present.

Hass transmitted over the team frequency, "Three klicks to our left turn at Checkpoint 18. We've got a smuggler truck coming up, nothing suspicious."

Ian had been too lost in thought to even recognize the vehicle, and when he scanned the long stretch of empty highway ahead, he thought that Hass must have had incredible eyesight. But then he spotted it too, a cargo truck that, while distant, was so comically overloaded it presented a distinct visual beacon.

"Domestic goods and food," Hass explained to Ian, "Libya's top illegal exports. Cheap to buy here, and worth a whole lot more as soon as they make it over the border."

The already monstrous truck now approaching had its width and height nearly doubled with the strapped additions of tarp-covered bundles and mattresses, over which everything from stacks of plastic chairs and 55-gallon barrels to wheelbarrows and bicycles dangled precariously from single tie-down points. Atop it all were Africans perched at various points across the cargo.

Ian asked, "What about the people? I thought everyone leaving Libya was moving north, not west."

"Migrants who couldn't find work here. Those trucks will offload their cargo, then come back loaded with narcotics, booze, and refugees trying to make it to the coast for a shot at Italy."

"Which militias are smuggling?"

"It's not the militias so much as the Tebu. You know them?"

The truck rumbled past, its riders staring at the team convoy with curious expressions before slipping out of view.

"Nomadic camel herders," Ian said, drawing upon the precious little time he'd had to research the dizzying array of tribal, ethnic, and racial groups prior to infiltration. "Marginalized under Gaddafi, and took to making money however they could."

"Pretty much. The old government denied them education, citizenship, even healthcare. Plus forced eviction and demolition of their homes. No surprise they joined the right side of the revolution, but that didn't change the fact that they have no way to make a decent living other than smuggling, which pays the bills and then some. To the Tebu, the Sahara is their home whether it's in Libya or Niger or Chad. They know every back road, every military outpost and inspection checkpoint. Soldiers go months without pay from the government—they're feeding their families with smuggler bribes."

"A perfect ecosystem."

"More or less, yeah."

Ian considered that the cargo truck occupants' confused expressions as they stared at the team convoy was understandable. Cancer had requested armored transport, expecting to be issued a few thin-skinned Toyota Hiluxes at best, but apparently a senator's involvement counted for a lot in the equipment department. The team had arrived in Tunisia to find a trio of B6-armored Land Cruisers, which, aside from a few telltale signs if you knew what you were looking for—like the hatches for gun ports at the rear and sides—were completely civilian in appearance. Even the armored glass was mounted within ordinary tinted panels, coming as close to low-visibility transport as possible save the roof racks loaded with gas cans and spare tires, which, given this was a road trip across the Sahara, weren't optional by a long shot.

"Checkpoint 18 in sight," Hass transmitted as they approached the next intersection. "Left turn."

"*Copy*," Cancer confirmed.

Ian slowed the Land Cruiser and wheeled it left onto the dirt-and-gravel road outlet, then accelerated up a shallow grade leading into the foothills, where it carved a semicircle route northeast.

The Land Cruiser rumbled up the path, which began a series of turns winding ever higher into the rocky slopes rising to either side. Complete with rockfall and divots, it wasn't the most comfortable road to traverse; then again, Ian considered, with functional air conditioning there remained precious little to complain about, regardless of the fact that their 25-hour road trip had just increased to 27 or more. The highway checkpoint was certainly regrettable, but nothing compared to what they'd encounter if they were anywhere near the coast. With 90 percent of Libya's people living along the Mediterranean, traversing the country through the desert before moving north into populated areas was the most feasible means of reaching their Benghazi safehouse—and the local CIA asset who arranged it—with all their equipment intact, and with any chance of arriving undetected.

But that latter hope was dashed when Hass abruptly transmitted over his radio that was tuned into the air frequency, "Reaper Two Four, this is Rain Man Eight Seven, good copy. All altitudes approved, looking for you to throw Hellfires on those dismounts, stand by for 9-Line." Then, over the team net, he continued, "Be advised, we've got nine enemy moving in a file on the high ground 650 meters to our front: bunch of AKs, two PKs, couple RPGs, south side of the road and moving with a purpose. Looks like they're moving to set up an ambush."

Ian braked his Land Cruiser and transmitted before the convoy had come to a complete stop, "Road's too tight for us to turn around, and even if we reversed out there's an even bigger element waiting on the highway."

Cancer transmitted, "*Time on target?*"

Hass was scanning the monitor in his lap as he replied, "Two mikes. These guys are going to scatter soon and I've only got four Hellfires to work with. How far do you want to take this?"

"*We can't afford to get held up here, so you better turn all nine of those shitheads into crispy critters in record time. No survivors. Cleared hot—smoke 'em if you got 'em.*"

Without waiting for clarification, Hass transmitted over the air frequency, "Reaper Two Four, Type 2, bomb on target, lines one through three N/A, break. Elevation one-seven-five feet, nine enemy pax on the high ground."

Ian marveled at the speed with which Hass then rattled off the format for a close air support briefing, which continued with the target location, distance and direction of the team to the strike area, and ended with the words, "Good readbacks, request immediate push, put your first Hellfire on the two PKs at the center of the file, all headings approved, call in with direction."

Hass started the timer on his watch and relayed over the team net, "T-minus thirty seconds to drop," before switching back to his radio on the air frequency and transmitting, "Reaper, cleared hot."

With the convoy at a full stop, Ian leaned over to analyze the screen that Hass held.

There he saw the orbiting view of a nine-man enemy squad jogging along the high ground, irrefutable evidence that some spotter had called in the convoy's passage. The view zoomed in on the two central men, both carrying PK machineguns, a moment before Hass spoke on the team net.

"Be advised, round away." Then, on the air frequency, "Splash out."

Ian knew from watching countless airstrike videos what was about to occur: somewhere between two and four seconds before impact, the enemy would hear a missile screaming in and immediately transition from a determined formation to a scattering sprint in all directions. Given that there were nine men and only four Hellfires, Ian knew that Cancer's "no survivors" directive was a lost cause.

And sure enough, the file of men on the screen disintegrated into multiple groups shortly before the first Hellfire missile detonated. When it did, the thermobaric round sucked a disc of sand into the center, then up and out like a miniature nuke. Both PK gunners were off the grid, but their seven compatriots remained alive and were now running like hell in various directions.

The video feed immediately panned out as the Reaper's sensor operator struggled to keep them all in view, and Hass was sending his next transmission over the air frequency before Ian could process the sight.

"Label the first set of enemies running east as Squirter Group Alpha, break, squirters headed west are Bravo, break, single man moving south is Charlie. Approved for immediate reattack, Squirter Group Alpha, call in with direction for clearance on final."

Only then could Ian make out the eastbound runners, a group of four men, one of whom had a rocket-propelled grenade on his back. Their exertion must have caused a strain on their ability to hear the inbound missile, because all four disappeared in the wake of another blast that had barely flashed before Hass spoke again.

"Good effects, approved immediate reattack Group Bravo, same restrictions, call in with direction."

It took only seconds for the view to pan out and realign on two men sprinting west along the high ground, one with an RPG. By the time that occurred, Ian was watching the screen transition to a zoomed-in and narrow focus—the Reaper's sensor operator lasing the target while the pilot executed the terminal controls.

The third Hellfire struck with predictable results, impacting in the two meters of space between the enemy fighters with such precision that Hass didn't need to wait for the smoke to subside; instead, he repeated his previous transmission with a slight alteration.

"Good effects, approved immediate reattack Group Charlie, call in with direction."

Ian couldn't make out the last runner amid the sweeping view on the screen, and neither, it seemed, could the sensor operator. Somewhere in Las Vegas, a young man or woman in a ground control station was feverishly manipulating the optics mounted below a Reaper UAV orbiting on the other side of the world, trying to catch sight of a terrified fighter who'd outlasted the death of his entire squad by moving alone—quite wisely, as it turned out. Hass's experience and precision in calling for close air support had resulted in an overwhelmingly successful outcome; however, Ian knew that the lone survivor, combat ineffective though he was on his own, had darted into a cave or crevice, where he'd remain until nightfall before daring to move again.

But then the impossible occurred. Ian saw the Reaper feed halt quite abruptly and zoom in with incredible speed, centering on an angled slab of rock with the slightest aberration in its shadow, a hint of movement that wasn't revealed as a partial human form cowering beneath it until the lens focused in.

"Splash out," Hass said.

That statement, Ian knew, was spoken in response to the sensor operator's announcement of "splash over," transmitted when a munition was five seconds from impact.

Ian was certain that by remaining stationary, the last enemy fighter would hear the Hellfire and run; only when the explosion blossomed on the screen did he realize the initial strike had probably left any surviving enemies with their ears ringing, functionally deaf as far as anticipating further impacts was concerned.

The small mushroom cloud dispersed to reveal a dark shape beside the destroyed rock cover, and it took Ian a moment of scrutiny before identifying it as a charred human corpse.

"Good effects," Hass transmitted to the Reaper crew. "Request BDA when able, then continue route reconnaissance, break. Raptor Nine Eight, we're requesting an immediate replacement platform for close air support."

And just like that, the engagement was over.

"Reaper is Winchester," Hass transmitted to the team, confirming that it had expended all its munitions. "Nine EKIA, advise we speed through the kill zone while we still can."

Ian was already easing his foot off the brake as Cancer replied.

"Yeah, haul ass. I want our Reaper back on route reconnaissance and getting a new platform inbound."

The entire convoy was quickly gaining speed when Hass transmitted back, "Already done."

"Guess you were right," Cancer said with rare approval. *"I see why they call you Rain Man, you cocky fuck."*

But Hass didn't reply; he was pressing an earpiece with two fingertips, listening to a new transmission.

The first indication Ian had of the message's contents came a moment later, when Hass relayed it to the team in the same clinical tone he'd used to communicate with the Reaper crew seconds earlier.

"Be advised, Reaper has eyes-on three technicals inbound from our twelve o'clock, approximately two klicks out."

Ian winced at the news—the definition of a "technical" was a vehicle, typically a pickup, with a heavy weapons system mounted in the bed. Among those options were anti-tank rocket launchers, recoilless rifles, mortars, and a host of other weapons that would make short work of the armor of these Land Cruisers.

His worst fears were confirmed when Cancer replied, *"What kind of weapons are we looking at?"*

"Three-by Dushkas," Hass answered.

The mention of that word was enough to make Ian's lungs seize up.

Formally titled DShk 1938 for the year of its inception, the belt-fed heavy machinegun fired enormous 12.7x108mm cartridges and was cordially referred to as "Dushka," Russian for "sweetie," by the Soviet troops that first employed it. Ian had shot them several times in the team's foreign weapons training, and forever ingrained in his memory—apart from its nuclear-grade muzzle blast—was the extent to which the gun could eviscerate car hulks with incredible consistency. A burst from one of those wouldn't just penetrate his B6 armor, it would shred the truck to rubble in a fraction of a second, liquifying the bodies of anyone inside.

To his credit, Cancer made a command decision with no more time than it took Ian to consider the severity of their circumstances.

"*Whoever those dismounts were, their ambush position just became our ambush position. Angel, stop short of the kill zone and establish a blocking position. We dismount on my mark and get ready to smash these fuckers when they roll through looking for us. There's not enough time for me to get the Barrett operational and move to the high ground. Doc, get your rockets ready.*"

10

The first thing I heard when my vehicle rumbled to a stop was the trunk opening overhead, followed by a man's accented voice.

"Wake up, dog. Can you hear me?"

With wrists handcuffed behind my back and the hood over my face, I could discern nothing else but the presence of light—still daylight hours, I surmised, though I was sufficiently disoriented to second-guess that possibility.

I didn't respond, mostly because I wasn't in the practice of being addressed as an animal. While canines were held in high esteem in America, in the Arab world the term was just about the most slanderous insult you could fling at someone, grounds for an immediate fistfight or worse. Not wanting to give them the satisfaction of accepting their judgment, I remained silent.

Whoever the speaker, he reversed my decision in record time.

There was a long burst of automatic fire close enough to make my ears ring before a blunt metallic ring was pressed against my temple—a rifle muzzle, its heat searing through the bag over my face.

Sufficiently chastened, I answered, "Yes. I can hear you."

The pressure of the muzzle vanished and he issued a quick order in Arabic.

Then they were upon me, rough hands grabbing at my clothes and yanking me out of the trunk. I struck the bumper and they let me drop to an unforgiving surface of dirt and rocks. I grunted with the impact, unable to break my fall with my hands restrained, then heard someone chortle the words "*Ibn al kalb*." That meant "son of a bitch," more or less, possibly the only escalation of calling someone a dog by expanding the accusation to their family as well.

Then they hoisted me upright and I heard the man's voice again, this time closer to my face.

"Are you ready to die, *kafir*?"

What the hell was I supposed to say to that? This was certainly no time for bravado, and barring any sufficient inspiration to the contrary, I sided with total honesty.

"Um, no," I mumbled into the bag. "Not really."

That earned me a blow to the stomach by a hard linear object that could only be a rifle butt. I sagged to the ground with the wind knocked out of me; suddenly an angry wife didn't seem as bad of a proposition as it had on my last day in Charlottesville.

Men jerked me upright by both arms, painfully torquing an old shoulder injury as I struggled to find my footing. Breathing with this bag over my head was difficult enough; trying to catch my breath was impossible, and I took wheezing gasps for air against the sack.

The man continued, "You will show respect, animal. *Yalla*."

They marched me forward, a man at each side guiding me by the arms over loose sand and stone. I could tell from the sound of footsteps around me that I was ringed by a large party, maybe ten or twelve in total.

That nugget of information was, regrettably, about the only thing I'd learned about my captors other than the fact that they were very, very good.

I'd tried and failed to maintain my bearings during the multi-hour drive, with turns numbering in the hundreds. Judging from the extent to which my body was jostled on the floor of the initial van, to say nothing of trunks and pickup beds after a half-dozen vehicle exchanges, the terrain ranged from smooth asphalt roads to potholed expanses to dirt and gravel paths. They'd taken me across flat surfaces, uphill, downhill, then uphill again before more flat ground, making the journey as close to indecipherable as humanly possible.

Now I had no idea where I was, only that this was no routine transfer to another vehicle. This verbal exchange was the only one that had transpired since I'd left the airport; they'd emptied my pockets immediately and swept me for tracking devices. My polite and probing attempts to start a dialogue were met unanswered, as were the repeated requests for a drink of water.

So I was fairly well parched as they led me forward, and focused my attention to gleaning whatever new information I could. Inhaling deeply, I smelled the smoke of wood fires intermingled with roasting meat—they had lots of people to feed, I imagined, though the smoke's intensity led me to believe they were marching me very close to open flame. Were they about to toss me in, I wondered?

But the light at the bottom of my hood soon faded, the sun's heat on my shoulders abating as I felt smooth ground below, the footsteps around me echoing off walls. I was indoors now, turned left around one corner and right around another as I considered whether the CIA's combination of drone and surveillance camera hacking was sufficient for them to be tracking me at this very moment. If it was, then this mission would be 90 percent in the bag; they'd generate a pattern of life on Khalil, tap his communications, and be able to determine Olivia's location in short order.

But anyone as calculated as Khalil would take suitable countermeasures before attempting anything as bold as a face-to-face meeting, which meant that the odds overwhelmingly pointed to the fact that I was on my own.

My captors guided me left around a corner and then to a sudden stop before I was forced downward into a wooden chair.

A moment of total silence, and then the hood was ripped off. I squinted in the dim glow of candles, trying to gain my bearings and, blinking my eyes clear, found a table to my front with a long ceremonial sword placed lengthwise.

On the other side of the sword, seated to face me, was Khalil Noureddin.

He scanned my face with interest, and I did the same.

I knew he had equal parts Spanish and German blood on his father's side, though his mother's Filipino descent ruled his features: thick lips and eyebrows, narrow dark eyes, a smooth complexion framed by the stubble of a beard. A good-looking man. If Khalil hadn't chosen terrorism he could have easily been cast in an Asian soap opera.

He was attired not in traditional Islamic garb but in a suit and tie; I considered whether this was some kind of power play over my decidedly casual travel attire or an effort to inject a measure of professionalism into the negotiation but couldn't make a determination either way.

Neither of us spoke, the moment hanging between us until his eyes ticked upward and he gave a small nod.

Someone pushed me forward, grabbing my forearm and unlocking the cuffs. I brought my hands to my front, resisting the urge to rub my painfully chafed wrists and saying instead, "Thank you."

Khalil gave another nod, not to me but to someone positioned behind me, and I heard a quiet metallic clanking.

It was at that moment I noticed the room was thick with burning incense, the smoky waft filling my nostrils. Then I saw the source of the metal clanks—a masked man appeared at my side with his rifle slung, carefully balancing a silver tray with two cups of tea that he set down between Khalil and me, adding a bowl of sugar cubes to the table before retreating. I could hear the subtle shift of multiple people behind me but assessed that turning to look would be considered offensive to my host and quickly rebuked. Besides, I didn't need to see them to know that there were more masked shitheads with automatic weapons, all of them ready to intervene if I made the slightest move against Khalil.

In stark contrast to the thugs who'd dragged me in here, Khalil appeared inordinately composed, almost serene, as he lifted his teacup, then motioned for me to do the same as he spoke for the first time with his graceful Filipino accent.

"Please, have some cardamom tea. It is quite excellent."

I looked to the murky brown tea and then back at him, trying not to convey my obvious discomfort at the possibility of being drugged. The last thing I needed now was to black out and then wake up to an international news report with a video of me slurring and declaring myself to be an imperialist spy or some other such nonsense.

Khalil seemed to understand, taking a sip and setting his cup before me, then lifting mine and taking another sip.

Good enough, I thought, seizing the teacup and eagerly downing the scalding contents out of severe thirst. No sooner had I set it down than the man reappeared to fill it again, and by then Khalil gestured to the sword on the table and asked, "Do you know the significance of this weapon?"

"I can take a guess."

"Enlighten me."

"Your organization," I said, taking the first sip of my second cup. "'Abu Sayyaf' means "Bearers of the Sword."'

"Yes." He nodded. "That is one reason I brought it here."

Then he straightened in his seat and continued, "You may call me Mr. Noureddin. What shall I call you?"

"I thought we'd settled on Suicide."

"That depends."

"On?"

He shot me a skeptical glance. "Whether you were truly the team leader on Jolo Island."

I sat back in my seat and met his gaze.

"You asked for me, Mr. Noureddin. Here I am."

"Perhaps," he mused, "but I am afraid I must require additional credentials. Since it would be improper to make such a demand without first presenting my own, I will remove all doubt."

He reached for his shirt collar, removing a necklace made of black cord. I wondered what the hell this was about—some kind of Islamic pendant?

But the pair of rounded rectangles dangling from the cord removed all doubt, and I reached out to accept them with the reverent sense of knowledge that I was holding something far more sacred than his ridiculous sword.

Five lines of text were stamped into the thin metal, and I keenly examined the words.

MUSANTE

ANDREW C.

6749312214
A POS
CATHOLIC

Last name, first name, DoD service number, blood type, and religion—I was looking at the dog tags of the slain Night Stalker pilot, killed on impact when his MH-6 helicopter was shot down by Khalil and his men.

Goddammit, I thought, here comes the rage.

Anger issues had been a well-earned hardship of mine, particularly after adjusting to life as a suburban father. Tamping down all that buildup of combat and the aftermath beneath the veneer of a moderately well-balanced and at least semi-adjusted member of society caused my war personality, as I thought of it, to remain largely suppressed in my day-to-day functioning.

But every once in a while, the demon reared its ugly head.

I was struck by an almost insuppressible urge to lunge across the table and attack him; they'd kill me at worst or beat me to within an inch of my life at best, but the satisfaction just might be worth it.

But that wouldn't help Olivia escape her bondage.

Sliding the dog tags back across the table, I decided to get my pound of flesh with words instead.

"My credentials," I began, "come in the form of a US Army pilot who is alive and well at the moment. But since that individual isn't here to vouch for me, let's see if my recollection of the night in question is sufficient to assure you of who I am."

He donned the necklace once more, tucking the dog tags beneath his shirt with an odd little smile playing at his lips. I looked skyward and tapped my chin with a finger, as if trying to recall distant memories that, in reality, I remembered all too well.

Then I said, "My team saw the helicopter shootdown from a ridge. Looked like you had a circular formation of RPG gunners firing upward at a central point along the helicopter's flight path. One round achieved a hit to the tail rotor, I believe, and down it went. In retrospect it was an extremely well-planned and executed operation, overcoming the disadvantages of inferior equipment through the number of personnel, extensive planning, and precise coordination of the execution phase."

Khalil was grinning with the memory, but I was about to put a damper on his spirits with no small amount of grim satisfaction.

Shrugging, I continued, "That's when my team made a break for the crash site, hoping to get there before Abu Sayyaf's finest. The first of your men we encountered were at a small camp—three of them, if I recall correctly, and their discipline left something to be desired. For one thing they had a campfire, which made them pretty easy to spot, and for another they were dancing around celebrating the shootdown. That engagement was shooting fish in a barrel—"

I stopped myself abruptly, then clarified, "Sorry, that's an idiom. It means ridiculously easy, almost not worth bothering with—"

"I know," he interjected firmly, "what it means."

"Right. So we entertained ourselves by putting as much of their brain matter into the dirt as we could, then I took their radio and continued merrily along, fully planning to pile up as many bodies as we could in fighting to reach the crash site. But there was a complication—we received word from communications intercepts that your people only recovered one American body. That meant a survivor was at large, so we set about finding him. Shooting fuckers is fun, don't get me wrong, but I'm a big fan of pilots."

His smile faded, and I knew I was venturing into dangerous waters now. But now that I was on a roll, I pushed my luck a little bit further.

"So we linked up with the pilot and began our escape."

I had to stop myself from mistakenly mentioning one key detail, that the surviving pilot was a woman, deciding against it out of fear that with a small number of female aviators in the 160th Special Operations Aviation Regiment, Khalil would do his best to track her down and finish the job.

Instead I continued, "I don't know how many 'Bearers of the Sword' were present on Jolo Island—frankly, the biggest near-miss we had involved a bunch of kids tweaking on meth and marching around the jungle with assault rifles and machineguns—but we found our match at a ravine defended by four fighters."

Khalil's expression softened somewhat. He was clearly hoping for a concession to his men's efficacy that I was in no way going to provide.

"Anyway," I went on, "half of them weren't anywhere near their weapons, which made it pretty easy for us to prioritize targets after we'd split up to hit them. We put two men on the left of the ravine and two on the right, which you probably confirmed from shell casings after we strolled off the island. But the real catch was when one of your fighters surprised us; apparently he'd eaten *so* much crystal meth that he took a few dozen rounds before going down, by which time he'd fired a few bursts from his AK and managed to clack off a grenade. After that, we pretty much took it for granted that everyone on the island heard our little scrape with the blocking position."

By now his expression was deadpan, icy eyes fixed on me.

Taking an eager sip of tea, I went on, "So we were on the run then, right until we found a nice little rock cavern to hide in. Now that wasn't going to last us long, not with your sword-bearers combing the jungle, so I reviewed the available facts. Namely, that we'd just crossed a field and, judging by communications intercepts, you had the only long-range radio. I figured you'd go to the clearing to continue managing your troops, so I decided to crawl back there and try to get a shot against you, after which, judging by the enemy fighters we'd seen, any coordinated defense effort would fall apart because the labor was geared up on enough 'whoop chicken' to stay awake for a week and a half."

Seeing that he wasn't going to interrupt, I continued, "Anyway, that was around the time that you realized a few dead shitheads were missing a radio, and called me up to negotiate the handover of the surviving pilot. No dice on that, but I did pretend your radio comms were fading so that you'd start walking across the clearing, looking for a signal—and sure enough, you did. Your radio operator presented a bit of a wrench in the plan, though, and with time for only one shot, I had to choose between destroying the radio and saving the pilot, or schwaking you and probably getting killed in the aftermath. The fact that we're having this conversation makes my decision pretty clear." After a pause, I asked, "Should I go on, Mr. Noureddin, or are my credentials established?"

When he didn't speak, I downed the remainder of my cup and asked, "Could I get some more tea?"

Khalil leaned forward and folded his hands on the table.

"Your ruse on the island was...very clever."

"Thank you."

"I appreciate cleverness," he declared, "which is why I requested you by name. There is another reason, however. Would you like to hear it?"

"Sure, why not?"

"If your government does not comply, if they usurp my instructions in any way, there will be consequences. In that event, it will not be enough for me to kill Olivia Gossweiler. I should also like to slaughter the man who evaded my forces on Jolo Island."

"Wish I could say I'm happy to help, but under the circumstances—"

Khalil laughed then, a genteel chuckle as if he were at the theater. I went quiet at the sound, then got down to business.

"I need to see her," I said. "To ensure she's safe, and confirm the status of her health."

He smiled demurely.

"You may not. And the status of her health is excellent."

I shook my head slightly. "Having the word *kafir* written in blood across her chest doesn't fit my definition of 'fine,' Mr. Noureddin. Nor does the state of her face in said video, which, if you'll pardon my candor, makes it pretty clear that you beat the shit out of her."

Khalil inhaled deeply, leaning back to examine the fingernails of one hand.

"Two of my men took certain excesses during her capture. They have been punished in accordance with Islamic law."

"I'm not concerned with their treatment, I'm concerned with Olivia's. If I can see her, I can procure any medical supplies she requires—"

"I already said you may not," Khalil snapped, his eyes going wide and focusing on mine. Without breaking his gaze, he continued quietly, "I will not repeat myself again."

Undeterred, I offered, "Proof of life, then. A video of her holding the current newspaper."

"I understand what 'proof of life' means. And as a gesture of good faith,

I will provide it. But first, let us discuss terms. From the moment you report to them, your government has five days, exactly 120 hours, to pay for Olivia Gossweiler's freedom. Four hundred million USD via wire transfer."

I recoiled at the figure. Was he starting high, expecting me to bargain with him to whittle down the cash amount? There was no way to tell, but my instructions to remain an objective third party between him and my country were clear enough.

"It may take longer than five days to collect that amount of cash—"

"It will not," he assured me. "America has a defense budget of eight hundred billion each year. Less than half a billion is a quite modest request on my part, and an exceedingly small price to pay considering her father is the puppetmaster behind your country's covert operations."

I watched him neutrally, seeking any information I could salvage from the situation. Financial analysis was a CIA specialty, what with financiers bankrolling extremist groups through an ever more sophisticated web of seemingly legitimate transfers.

Finally I said, "I will communicate your terms. But they'll need the account and routing numbers."

"And you will receive them one hour prior to the deadline. Not before."

So much for that idea, I thought.

He went on, "I will provide you with a mobile phone and its charger. You will keep this device on your person and activated at all times. My men will use this phone to order you when and where to meet."

Great, I thought, knowing full well that the goddamn thing would not only be tracking my location but also broadcasting audio to some receiving station to overhear everything I relayed back to the United States government. Khalil was no idiot.

But the ability to exploit that phone cut both ways, and if I could get it into the hands of an Agency tech expert, they could quite feasibly overcome any digital safeguards and discover a location history for the device that could lead them to Khalil.

"Very well," I agreed. "May I have it?"

Khalil gave a mirthless grin, as if I took him for a fool.

"You may have it when my men release you in Benghazi, after which you will report on the specifics of your final location."

I found that last comment odd, borderline indecipherable—he knew full well I was staying at the Julyana Resort, a detail we'd made clear to ensure his people were able to link up at a time and place of their choosing. Why would I need to report that back to him after check-in?

Before I could consider the disparity, he went on.

"And now I will tell you the second reason for the sword. If there is any failure whatsoever to meet my terms, this is what I will use to decapitate Olivia Gossweiler. And this"—he procured a dagger from a sheath on his side, its blade covered in the rusty brown hues of dried blood—"is what I will use to carve out her heart."

11

Reilly charged toward the high ground, spotting a rock-strewn crest ahead. He hoped the UAV's sensor operator wasn't misinformed in the assurance that there were no dismounted enemies within earshot: in terms of noise discipline, the uphill run was about as subtle as a gay pride parade.

The problem wasn't a matter of his primary weapon system, a suppressed HK417 that Reilly had no problem wielding with ease and precision.

But the trio of rocket launchers slung over his back were another matter altogether. Their plastic outer tubes clattered against one another at a volume that would have been comical under any other circumstances, the echoes loud and clear in the otherwise silent desert. He'd been assigned the rockets as a function of his position in the convoy—driving solo in the trail vehicle—so that if the first two trucks were decisively engaged, he could flank and send some anti-tank warheads toward the enemy at 480 feet per second.

Reilly hadn't, however, anticipated the need to haul the munitions uphill at a dead sprint; the effort was exhausting, made possible for the amateur bodybuilder only by virtue of the adrenaline coursing through his system. His job was to remove as many of the incoming trucks from the battlefield as possible before they knew what was happening; any he missed would proceed unchecked to the team's ambush below, a Land Cruiser parked sidelong to block the path and protect the remaining two vehicles, which, if disabled, would leave the team stranded in the Sahara Desert.

And any failure on his part would expose his men to the withering fire of the enemy Dushkas, though that particular motivation was countered both by the steep terrain and the fact that it had to be a hundred fucking degrees out here. It was a dry heat, sure, but every rock seemed to be reflecting the scorching sunlight back up at him to effect the feeling that he was barreling headlong through hell.

Finally he reached the crest, breathlessly transmitting, "Doc up top," and hearing Hass's response, "*Trucks are forty seconds out, tight spacing,*" before he caught sight of one of the UAV strikes and nearly stopped in his tracks.

It was easy to forget that a standard Hellfire missile was a 100-pound tank destroyer; its effects on a human body were hard to comprehend, and the evidence was scattered everywhere on the ridge.

Reilly advanced through the foggy stench of explosive residue and vaporized rock mingled with the scent of burned pork, the latter radiating from incinerated corpses that had been flung hither and yon from the multiple blasts. What at first glance appeared to be a stick revealed itself as the blackened remains of a human arm that landed beside a charred body severed from the waist down.

Tens of thousands had fallen to identical fates in places like Afghanistan and Iraq, to say nothing of Pakistan, Somalia, and Yemen, all of them victims of US drone strikes and most of them, he hoped, deserving enemy combatants rather than innocent civilians. Reilly had been on the winning side of many such engagements during his time in the military, and it had all been so clean, so clinical: neatly spoken requests for immediate close air support met by explosions and the subsequent battle damage assessments confirming that the threat had been vanquished, that fire superiority had won the day once more.

But he'd never before seen the fallout up close and personal, never had to vault the singed detritus of limbs and organs ringing craters in the earth. His boot clipped the edge of a heavy object, and he looked down to see a head with the skull half-exposed skittering across the dirt. Jesus, he thought, his team hadn't even made it to their destination and they'd already laid waste to a significant enemy force, with a far more dangerous one growing nearer with each passing second.

Reilly banished the thought from his mind, focusing instead on the task at hand as he came to a stop at a rocky outcropping overlooking the dirt road. Kneeling behind a boulder, he set down his rifle and unslung the three rocket launchers, taking the first into his grasp to prepare it for operation.

The M72 LAW, or Light Anti-Tank Weapon, was a single-use rocket system and a good one at that. Not the most accurate, not the longest range, but nonetheless the lightest, most easily transportable option capable of being utilized by a lone shooter.

And while the trio of 5.5-pound rocket launchers weren't actually M72s at all, it would take a considerably detailed effort to discern that fact.

In reality they were *Hafif Antitank Roketi*, also known as HAR-66s, a Turkish clone of the US-produced weapon system that were virtually indistinguishable in function, much less appearance. But given the massive influx of foreign aid into Libya, by Turkey more than most, this slight distinction would serve to obfuscate US involvement when Reilly discarded the used launchers in place in the event he wasn't vaporized by return fire from the Dushkas.

Lifting the olive drab cylinder of the first launcher, Reilly pulled a pin and removed a protective cover from the end before repeating the process at the front. Then he assumed a double overhand grasp and pulled his hands apart to extend the telescoping aluminum cylinder backward. Twin sights flipped up with a satisfying *click*, and he disarmed the safety by yanking out a plastic cube mounted on top. He carefully set the launcher down on its side and repeated the process with the second launcher.

Reilly could hear the inbound trucks now, multiple engines growling at full acceleration. Hitting a moving target was difficult enough, much less three hauling ass through the canyon below, the thought barely occurring to him before he pulled at the safety and Hass transmitted, "*They're ten seconds out, still bumper to bumper.*"

Grabbing the third and final launcher, Reilly flew through the armament process with as much speed and fluidity as he could under the circumstances, with sweat dripping over and under his sunglasses, rivulets clouding the lenses and stinging at his eyes. With the rocket's effective range of only 200 meters, along with the inconvenient restriction that the munitions were unguided and his targets speeding, he'd have to bring his breathing under control and do the best he could to anticipate vehicle trajectories if he was going to have any degree of effectiveness.

"*Five seconds*," Hass said.

Reilly pulled the safety and shouldered the launcher, barely having time to level it downward at his target area before the first truck whipped into view.

He didn't have time to register any details beyond the fact that the Hilux was white and bore a cannon-sized machinegun mounted in the bed; the sum total of his attention was focused on the view through his rear peep sight as he aligned it with the front leaf sight and mashed the rubberized trigger with the fingertips of his right hand.

A blast slapped through the desert air, the tremendous reverberation at stark odds with the lack of recoil. Reilly tossed the launcher aside and was reaching for the next one before the rocket impacted, its progress seeming impossibly slow even amid the tight 150-odd-meter range between him and the lead vehicle. To his horror, he saw that vehicle slip out of sight unmolested; by the miracle of undisciplined convoy spacing, however, the second Hilux gracefully intercepted the munition.

The high explosive charge within a copper cone impacted the truck bed, destroying the rear axle and causing the pickup to buck like a rodeo bronc before skidding sideways through a cloud of dust and black smoke. Reilly had the second launcher shouldered by the time a third vehicle slammed into the carcass of its predecessor, the echo of the blast followed by the crush of metal on metal.

By now the occupants of the final vehicle were bailing over the side; Reilly fired anyway, seeking to eliminate the Dushka as much as any dismounted fighters. In the event he took a bullet to the head, the weapon could just as easily be re-manned and turned against his team—but that wasn't going to happen, he saw with delight as his second rocket streaked into the pickup cab and detonated in a fireball that sent a shockwave of sand and smoke radiating into the ravine walls below.

His elation vanished shortly after he snatched up his rifle and the remaining rocket launcher to dart away from his now-compromised firing position. Incoming small arms fire hissed and cracked off the rocks around him, as the fighters who'd survived his twin rockets directed the sum total of their available weapons toward the launch site. At the moment he skidded to a halt behind his next piece of cover, Reilly heard a horrifyingly deep and rhythmic succession of booming noises that dwarfed the fading echoes below.

The lead Hilux had sighted his teammates, and the massive Dushka heavy machinegun was unleashing its fully automatic payload.

~

Worthy slid backward down the slanting rock face, narrowly clearing the edge before the Dushka's opening burst sailed overhead.

The mounted machine gunner was quick to correct the miss, walking his successive fire downward toward Worthy's only protection from being vaporized. The sound of supersonic 12.7mm bullets slamming into the rock ledge was a series of shrieks and cracks that were earsplitting even over the decibel cutoff of his radio earpieces—the Dushka was designed to penetrate armor at 500 meters, and now one was being employed against him from a stone's throw away.

Worthy's HK416 was slung on his back, his primary weapon at present a SAW light machinegun he'd stripped from the truck out of a need for higher volume of fire against a vehicle target. Cancer and Hass were higher up the canyon wall, moving between rock crevices to provide precision suppressed fire that had yet to be delivered, and now that the enemy truck had survived the initial ambush attempt, Worthy was on the receiving end and, he acknowledged with a curse amid the clouds of sand whipping overhead, in truly deep shit.

On the plus side, he seemed to be the sole focus of the enemy's fire at present, which kept the heat off Ian, who would ideally be trying to get a line of sight from his position far to Worthy's right. And contrary to popular myth, a near-miss from a .50 caliber round wouldn't result in enough shockwave to kill someone; so much as a grazing hit, however, would do the job quite nicely. Hell, he thought, if he took a short burst, his team would only be able to identify his body through process of elimination in accounting for the survivors.

Cancer transmitted, "*Hang in there, trying to get in position for a shot.*"

Worthy didn't reply, instead crawling left to regain visual while remaining beneath the line of fire.

The moment the truck rounded the bend, Worthy had fired exactly one SAW burst at the gunner—apparently a miss, along with Ian's attempt to score an immediate hit—before their intended target spun the enormous barrel toward him and its muzzle lit in a swath of flame.

The problem, of course, was that the gunner wasn't supposed to be doing that at all.

Not twenty meters behind Worthy, an armored Land Cruiser that should have been a magnet for enemy gunfire was parked sideways to block the path. Since the team could get by with the remaining two trucks, they'd offered one as a sacrificial lamb to buy them a few seconds in dropping the gunner, then the driver, of any truck that made it past Reilly's rocket barrage.

Finally the gunner directed his wrath against the unoccupied Land Cruiser, whose B6 armor essentially amounted to tinfoil against a Dushka.

Worthy didn't need to look back to know what was occurring—the bullet impacts around him suddenly stopped, while the machinegun continued firing to the sound of crumpling metal to his rear. The pointman scrambled right to attain a line of sight to the enemy truck. When he angled his muzzle around a stony outcropping, he realized that wasn't going to work.

The space beyond was a thick brown haze, the swirling remnants of rock dust and sand churned by the withering fire blocking any chance of sighting the gunner. Ian's visibility must have been likewise impeded considering the gunner was still alive. Worthy set the SAW bipod down and shot anyway, using the audio from the Dushka blasts to direct his fire as he took successive short bursts between minor adjustments to his barrel alignment. The moment that Dushka went silent, he'd hold his point of aim and continue drilling rounds at a sustained rate of gunfire until Cancer and Hass could get a clear angle on the truck.

Regardless of the dust clouds, however, his unsuppressed SAW provided a two-way sound cue for the people he was trying to kill.

The Dushka gunner responded in kind, redirecting his fire on Worthy's position.

A slab of rock from the canyon wall behind him was sheared by the massive bullets, causing a rockslide of shale that crashed downward in razor fragments. Worthy slid left, narrowly avoiding being crushed by a recliner-sized chunk that hit the ground and shattered beside him. He crawled away from the avalanche, his view increasingly reduced to a layer of clear air below a pale mist of sand.

"I'm fucked," he transmitted. "Pretty soon I'm not going to have any cover left."

Cancer replied, "*Give me a sec, almost there.*"

Bitter consolation, Worthy thought, given that one second lasted a whole lot longer at his own location than it did high above the fight, where Cancer and Hass were currently moving.

He continued crawling left, moving away from the bullet impacts in the hopes that he could reach a patch of clear visibility.

And then, as if by magic, the dust cloud before him lifted and he got his second view of the battered white Hilux.

The Dushka gunner was sweeping his massive barrel to Worthy's right, continuing to blast away. To his surprise there were other men in the back, too, firing assault rifles with wild abandon. Against the noise of the Dushka, he hadn't even heard them.

Worthy was angling his sights when the gunner fell dead amid a puff of red spray—Cancer had finally found his mark.

Worthy lowered his barrel and took aim on the driver instead, unleashing a long burst from the SAW that pummeled through the windshield and turned it into a pockmarked expanse of glass painted by blood from within. Then he swung the weapon left, seeking any runners who were dismounting the passenger side opposite his other teammates.

He found two targets, both men leaping from the bed and preparing to dart away. Worthy shot them in the back, two short bursts at an absurdly short range spaced by just enough pause to let the SAW barrel settle, the whiffing clouds of sand clearing to reveal them tumbling downward. He fired again before they'd settled on the ground, knowing by this point in his career if you had a shot, you took it—there may not be another chance, and a mortally wounded enemy didn't need excellent marksmanship to land a lucky shot in the final seconds of his life.

His tracers laced into the now-motionless men, and before the end of his burst, the SAW bolt slammed forward and the weapon went dead in his hands.

Rather than reload a new drum of ammo, he pushed the light machinegun aside and transitioned to the suppressed HK416 slung across his back. It fired the same-sized round as the SAW, albeit slower subsonic bullets, but he could make up for that with precision fire through his optic.

Sweeping his aim right, he saw a pair of dead fighters on the opposite side of the truck and no other movement. He cut his view back to the cab, delivering single shots back and forth between the driver and passenger seats.

"*Check-in,*" Cancer transmitted.

Ian said, "*Angel, I'm good.*"

"*Doc here,*" Reilly replied. "*Policed up some runners, but I think the two rear trucks are done for. Racegun, you need me?*"

"Not unless you've got a change of pants," Worthy replied, summoning another breath and glancing down to see no blood on his clothes before continuing. "No idea how I made it out of that unscathed, but I did."

Cancer spoke then, concluding this phase of the engagement in three words.

"*Clear and search,*" he said, then asked, "*Anyone have eyes-on enemy wounded?*"

Reilly answered, "*I might have one...yeah, this dude is trying to crawl, looks like he'll bleed out in a few minutes.*"

"*Keep him alive until me and Rain Man get there—I want to know who these fuckers are.*"

~

Cancer scrambled down the hillside with Hass in tow as he transmitted, "Racegun and Angel, strip what you can from the downed truck and bring the other two Land Cruisers forward to pick us up."

"*Copy*," Racegun replied, and with that Cancer directed his focus back to his foot placement, doing his best to negotiate the steep descent without tripping on rockfall and breaking every bone in his body on the way down. He could tell from the sound of boot soles scraping against rock behind him that Hass was keeping pace—the Combat Controller had reacted as fluidly as the rest of the team to Cancer's hasty orders, and achieved at least one enemy kill in the short gunbattle that followed.

They'd just reached the road when Reilly breathlessly transmitted, "*Just got to the casualty. He's worse than I thought.*"

Cancer hooked right and broke into a run down the dirt path, replying, "Then start asking questions."

"*He's unconscious.*"

"He better not be by the time I get there," he shot back, irritated, then looked over to see Hass falling into step beside him, matching his own pace.

Cancer asked, "Can you get that drone away from the survivor?"

"'Metal rabbit' the casualty," Hass replied.

Before Cancer could ask what that meant, Hass was on the air frequency, communicating his order to the UAV crew.

"Reaper Two Four, new sensor tasking from the commander. Reports on the ground, looks like possible individuals three hundred meters east, need you to confirm for PID."

Then he explained, "Boss, 'metal rabbit' is some JTAC slang they don't teach in the schoolhouse. Pilots don't know about this, it's purely for the ground guys. You don't want something to be seen, that's all you need to say for me to find priorities for every bird in the stack to push them out of the area."

"Good," Cancer replied. "I want to try out this knife."

Hass gave him a half-smirk, the expression vanishing as Cancer remained stone-faced. If this Libyan-born attachment thought he was joking, he was about to find out exactly how things worked on a Project Longwing mission.

By now they caught sight of two destroyed Hiluxes, and both men slowed to a measured walk, sweeping their weapons over the visible enemy corpses, some apparently killed by the rocket blast and others by gunfire as they raced away. Ordinarily this occasion would call for preemptive fire, generally double taps to ensure all enemy were indeed dead, delivered as soon as the bodies were visible and never any later than sweeping past them, but Cancer and Hass didn't shoot. They knew that Reilly was somewhere beyond the wreckage in what was hopefully a successful effort to keep the wounded enemy alive long enough to interrogate him.

Instead they advanced into gasoline fumes, scanning for movement among the dead fighters as Cancer transmitted, "Coming up on the trucks."

"*You better hurry*," Reilly replied. "*He's going fast*."

The admonition wasn't sufficient for Cancer to increase his pace; whatever information the casualty might possess wouldn't do them much good if he got shot in the back by a survivor.

Instead he said quietly to Hass, "Swing right."

They completed a methodical semicircle around the trucks before Cancer halted and, with his line of fire safely oriented toward the far canyon wall, began directing suppressed shots at every fallen body in sight. Hass followed his lead, and they were in short order driving subsonic bullets through the truck cabs, into corpses slumped over the truck beds, toward mangled bodies of those killed in the initial blasts. Bullets were relatively cheap and the cost of complacency extremely high, and Cancer didn't continue moving until every fighter had received another two rounds from himself or Hass.

Then he resumed his push down the road, driving his barrel toward two bodies ripped apart by Reilly's 7.62mm weapon. The medic was less than ten feet past them, on his knees and working feverishly to save a third man who lay on his back.

Cancer didn't engage the remaining bodies until he was practically on top of them. Both men had sustained multiple gunshots, the neat bullet entry holes counterpointed by the gory craters of exit wounds. But they had rifles at their sides, an AK-103 and an FN FAL by the looks of it, and Cancer angled his suppressor to deliver a headshot to each before finally proceeding to Reilly, stopping just past him to achieve a modicum of far-side security. Once he was reasonably certain no enemies were entrenched alongside the road beyond, he turned to assess Reilly's efforts.

The medic's hands were covered in blood as he retrieved items from his personal kit—no time for him to grab his aid bag—and Cancer saw that the casualty was a boy of perhaps eighteen. In Libya that was well past the minimum age for militia service, though his wardrobe was a testament to youth: with fatigue pants and a knockoff Adidas T-shirt, along with cheap, dirt-covered sneakers, this guy could have been a stand-in for the average militiaman in a dozen countries across the globe.

He already had two tourniquets ratcheted over his right arm and left thigh, and Reilly was in the process of stuffing gauze into an exit wound in his abdomen. Judging by the amount of blood that had soaked his clothes and drained into the sandy road, it was a miracle he was still breathing, if he was at all—he was completely still, expression locked in a painful grimace.

"Wake him up," Cancer said.

Reilly shot him a withering glance; the medic was pissed, he knew, not because he had to temporarily save the man—that much came naturally to the jovial fat ass, no matter who the patient was—but rather, because he'd been ordered to expend medical supplies on someone who'd die no matter what. He could recover the tourniquets and maybe even the Israeli battle dressings, but every piece of blood-soaked gauze filling those bullet holes was one fewer that he'd have available to treat an American at a later time.

But Reilly complied nonetheless, procuring a syringe and driving the needle into the man's exposed forearm in a move known in medic parlance as the "junkie stick"—no use cleaning the injection site when the patient was on a fast track toward death. Then he withdrew the plunger and observed a flash of blood before reversing the action to inject a small portion of the syringe's liquid contents.

Cancer didn't need any explanation to know that Reilly was administering ketamine, probably ten milligrams or so. At that low dosage, the effect of dissociative anesthesia would sufficiently alleviate the pain enough to allow the casualty to wake up, though not enough to send him into a nonverbal trance. And sure enough, the casualty regained consciousness with a gasp, his eyelids fluttering open.

After flashing his Winkler blade, Cancer noted with satisfaction that the man's confused expression immediately turned to paralyzing fear. No ideological hardliner, this one. Whoever he was, Cancer could tell by the reaction that money had sent him here, a motivation that wouldn't be sufficient for keeping his lips sealed.

He said, "Find out who he's working for."

Hass knelt and translated the order in far more words than seemed necessary, and Cancer suspected from the use of *sadiqi*, Arabic for "my friend," that the Combat Controller was using more honey than vinegar to obtain the information.

Then he translated, "SRC, Suliman Revolutionary Council."

"Find out their task and purpose, who gave the order to hit us."

Cancer hadn't finished his sentence when Hass continued addressing the man in Arabic, but it was no use.

He emitted a blood-choked cough before his eyes rolled skyward and went blank, crossing the threshold of death that Cancer had seen before. There was a very tangible tipping point when a man's lights went out for good, the blank gaze above all else serving as confirmation that the interview was over.

Reilly began stripping his medical supplies off the man, recovering what equipment he could as Cancer swept his barrel down the road, searching for any enemy response and finding none before calling over his shoulder, "What do we know about his group?"

Hass took up a position a few meters away, likewise pulling security, as he replied, "Militias are a dime a dozen in Libya, but I can tell you for a fact that the SRC runs out of Benghazi. No idea why they'd be out here."

Worthy transmitted, "*Bringing the trucks forward.*"

Keying his radio, Cancer said, "Angel, what's a Benghazi-based militia doing in the Sahara?"

"*Best guess?*" Ian replied. "*Running interference for any American forces responding to the kidnapping. If that's the case, there's going to be more, probably spread thin along the major avenues of approach and possibly bolstered by other militias.*"

Cancer groaned. "Racegun, we're gonna have to find a route off the beaten path."

Worthy came over the net a moment later, sounding incredulous.

"*I thought we already* were *off the beaten path.*"

"Yeah, well, we'll have to go farther. We're already down one truck, and we're not gonna survive too many more of these engagements. This infiltration just got a hell of a lot longer."

12

I felt the van come to a full halt and oriented my hooded face toward the sound of its door sliding open. Someone chuckled beside me—an unsettling development, I decided—and while I could detect some faint traffic noise in the distance, long seconds passed where nothing happened.

I'd managed some fitful sleep between vehicle transfers, an achievement born of pure exhaustion more than anything else; after the transcontinental flight and long hours of transport just to meet Khalil, I couldn't even calculate how long I'd been awake. There was nothing I wanted more right now than to get my reporting out of the way and pass out in the comfort of a hotel bed.

My first suspicion that reaching the hotel was still a long way off was when multiple men pulled me out of the vehicle and I set foot on what felt like rough asphalt covered in loose gravel. Not exactly what I'd expect from the upscale tourist district along the beach, I thought, the realization reinforced when one of them unlocked my handcuffs and shouted, "*Ismaeni! Junedee Amrikee!*"

There was precious little Arabic that I could recognize off the bat, particularly when native speakers weren't bothering to slow down and enunciate clearly. But out of my instruction in the language, the military terms bore heavy emphasis—if some local was trying to tell you there was a bomb in the road or a large enemy force maneuvering, you'd goddamn better be able to understand them and quickly.

So his last two words stood out with stark clarity as "American soldier."

A distant voice yelled, "You come back for more, America?" followed by raucous laughter.

Not good.

The next thing I heard was the van door slamming and the vehicle accelerating away. With my hands recently relieved of the cuffs, I ripped the hood off my head with the knowledge that I had mere seconds to assess my surroundings and bolt in the safest possible direction.

That instinct proved justified: it was nighttime, and the run-down urban setting was illuminated by flickering streetlights, trash fires, and the lit windows of adjacent buildings. I was facing down a street occupied only by a group of six or seven men who approached in a cluster, currently thirty feet away and closing fast. Whirling around, I saw the van's tail lights receding at breakneck speed. And looking down, I saw my single checked bag along with my backpack both dumped in a heap and topped by a plastic shopping bag that I snatched up to search.

My Agency phone was there, powered off, along with a new one and its charger—Khalil's means of communicating with me—and both my wallet and passport. I shoved the items into my pockets and hastily donned the backpack, keeping my eyes on the men who advanced to reveal an array of knockoff brand shirts, shorts and jeans, sneakers and sandals. They were a street gang of some kind, with no visible weapons; no matter, I thought, because with their numbers they wouldn't need to shoot me.

Cinching down my backpack straps, I looked around to determine the best direction to run. Was I even in Benghazi? Staying on the street was a no-go since it extended perfectly straight to my front and rear. To my left was a break between the exterior walls of separate compounds that appeared to lead through a corridor overrun with vegetation. Not a bad option.

Then I looked right to find a solid wall topped with rusted concertina wire. Upon seeing it, I understood the shouted "You come back for more, America" comment, and in what was the flimsiest silver lining imaginable, I knew beyond all doubt that I was in Benghazi. The mounted placard was long since pockmarked with bullet holes and sprayed over with Arabic graffiti. But the text was partially visible—the word *CONSULATE* above America's Great Seal, an eagle with its wings outstretched and talons bearing arrows and an olive branch.

By the time I secured my backpack for the dead sprint that was about to ensue, the gang of men was closing within fifteen feet and still shouting insults in a mixture of English and Arabic. I instinctively grabbed my luggage before recalling that it held nothing that I couldn't bear to part with, and momentarily considered abandoning it.

But this was no typical combat mission where I was loaded down with all the weapons, equipment, and ammunition required to deal death, much less defend myself; I was alone and unarmed, and had better start improvising using everything at my disposal.

Gripping the luggage handle with both hands, I spun in a quick 360 turn and hurled it toward the men.

It didn't have to travel far, only ten feet or so, and achieved that feat with considerable momentum before colliding with two of the gang members who had just enough time to block their faces before impact. Both stumbled back as I twisted left and took off like a shot, running as fast as I could into the shadowy alley between compounds and hoping to God that there was an outlet on the other side.

Thin branches and vines whipped at my body as I plunged into the darkness, following the channel between compound walls as the men behind me gave chase. In my fatigued state I wouldn't be able to outrun all of them, and that truth concerned me almost as much as where Khalil had chosen to dump me.

I was now racing away from the ruins of the American diplomatic compound that had been overrun during the 2012 anniversary of 9/11. That attack had killed two Americans, including the ambassador, before security contractors rescued the survivors and brought them to their CIA annex, which was then surrounded by militants. Another two US citizens died there, both former SEALs serving as Agency contractors, and suddenly I understood why Khalil had demanded to know the specifics of my final location.

It also informed my knowledge of his intentions; by dropping me at a spot where I was just as likely to be killed as make it to my hotel, Khalil was demonstrating that he *wanted* the negotiations to fail. If I was killed out here, then he'd hold the US accountable for failing to meet his demands and carry out a plan that he apparently had every intention of executing regardless. I had to call the Agency asap and relay Khalil's terms before it was too late.

But I couldn't accomplish that task at present, trying instead to remain upright and moving forward over a bed of loose rocks, bricks, and tangled weeds with the shouts of a small but extremely angry mob trailing me. I was encouraged, however, by the appearance of a street ahead; if my pursuers didn't lose interest before I reached it, I'd have to repeat the feverish process of trying to find the best immediate withdrawal route.

Fortunately my speed seemed to exceed their motivational capacity, with their shouts fading as I continued to run.

But one set of footfalls continued to close in, and I looked over my shoulder to see the shadow of a single man pursuing. This fucker wasn't giving up, and I had no doubt that if he succeeded in tackling me, I was one shout away from the rest of his friends joining him once more. I continued over the rockfall and located a sufficiently thick tree trunk ahead. My plan was to take him out before we reached the next road, after which he'd likely catch up with me as I tried to determine where to go. After all, he knew these streets and I didn't, and I'd have to compensate for that one way or another.

I skidded to a halt by the tree, slipping behind its trunk and trying to determine if he'd seen my move or not.

My final pursuer had grown too overconfident in both his fighting abilities and my level of fear, and I heard him continue to charge forward as I panted breaths, assessing his distance based on sound. After the entire nightmarish ordeal that ensued from stepping off the plane until now, I thought, inflicting some sudden violence would be fun.

He appeared, still at a run, and caught sight of my movement the second he cleared the tree I was hiding behind. By then it was too late—I grabbed the back of his shirt with both hands and swung him sideways, redirecting his forward momentum into a semicircle arc as he emitted an involuntary shriek of surprise.

The percussion of his torso striking the tree trunk made a hollow *thud* interspersed with a few crackling noises that I presumed were ribs breaking. If one of those fractured bones punctured a lung, he'd not only be sufficiently silenced but would die out here.

No sooner had I released him to the ground, however, than he let out a bloodcurdling cry of pain before shouting for his friends. Dropping to my knees beside him, I started to raise my fist, then thought better of it and snatched a baseball-sized rock off the ground beside me before drilling it across his temple in one swift blow.

His body went limp as I considered my next move. I could've killed him then, bashed his fucking brains out with this rock and frankly had more than enough adrenaline in my system to do so in record time. But this was no hardened enemy combatant, just some kid on the streets who no longer posed a threat, so instead I dropped the rock and continued running.

The alley ended at an arid field beside a house, where I found that what I'd presumed to be a streetlight was actually an exposed bulb illuminating a back door. I turned on my Agency phone and considered whether I should attempt a break-in to steal a car, then dismissed the thought in short order. Any homeowner here was surely armed to the teeth.

Instead I cut around the house, running through a swath of arid field to the sound of a dog barking viciously from somewhere to my left. It was certainly pissed off but not getting any closer, and I identified a paved street ahead as I pulled out my Agency phone to find that it had booted up successfully but was almost out of battery.

Dialing the number for the on-call duty operator, a Seattle area code saved under the name John Mason, I brought the phone to my ear and scanned the street in both directions to find no traffic and, thankfully, no gang watching for an American scrambling to get the hell out of Dodge while he still could.

The road extended far to my right and intersected with another street to my left. Before that junction, however, an unplanted strip of dirt extended to the next block, and I moved toward it as the call connected.

"Hello," a male voice answered, waiting for me to take the lead in how the conversation would go. For all he knew I was speaking at gunpoint right now, and that wasn't far from the truth. Besides, Khalil would hear everything I said through the phone he now required me to carry, to say nothing of any other surveillance devices he'd planted in my backpack.

"Ransom for Olivia is four hundred million USD via wire transfer in 120 hours. Clock starts now. He'll provide routing info before the deadline."

"Understood," he replied, that single word bringing me an immeasurable sense of relief. Then he went on, "What can you tell me about—"

"Nothing that can't wait," I cut him off, clearing the street and plunging forward to the next road. "I just got dropped at the diplomatic compound, have no idea where I'm going, and a bunch of street thugs are trying to kill me. Need immediate instructions on where to go, or you'll have to find a new negotiator."

"All right, hold on a sec."

Easy for you to say, I thought, from an air-conditioned office. I scrambled over a waist-high mud wall separating the dirt patch from a rectangular crop extending another half block, then trampled through a field of neatly planted bushes.

The Agency man said, "You're not making it to the Julyana, brother."

"Super. Where am I?"

"Beloun neighborhood. It's a bad area."

"I gathered that."

A pause before he asked, "Are you injured?"

I tripped on a stone, stumbling to regain my balance before trying not to shout, "Who cares?"

"I need to know where I can send you, and that depends on how far you can run."

"Pretty fucking far," I hissed, "considering the alternative is getting carved up out here."

"Okay. You're headed north right now; need you to take a right at the next street."

"Got it," I replied, though the maneuver was easier said than done. I reached the road only to find two technical vehicles less than fifty meters away, both Toyota Hiluxes with machineguns mounted in the back, surrounded by a group of armed men smoking cigarettes and bullshitting with one another. Too late to stop now, I thought, darting across the street and moving left to clear a sidewalk before threading my way between trees and into a construction site.

"I said right," the man said. His phone-tracking capability was split-second or close to it, I realized as he continued, "You're going the wrong way."

"Yeah, I heard you. I'm going to need a little flexibility to execute unless your map shows militia checkpoints."

I was careful not to say what I really meant, which was *until you get a UAV overhead.* Khalil surely assumed there was US aerial coverage over Benghazi, hence the elaborate exchanges to relay me into and out of our meeting site. But I wasn't about to confirm that for him, and when the man replied, "Understood," it was with a tone that assured me we were on the same page.

By then I was trying not to trip and impale myself on a column of exposed rebar planted in the dirt, steering clear of the low warehouses to my right.

I said, "My phone's about to die. Where am I headed?"

"The Palace Hotel, about one mile straight-line distance from your current location."

I cursed in response. That distance could easily double considering I wasn't exactly running as the crow flies—my path was one extended obstacle course of trees, rubble, and fences, most of it dimly lit by distant streetlights if it was lit at all. I tripped on something and fell hard, banging my elbow on a rock and inadvertently turning the phone into a projectile that sailed into the darkness.

Full panic set in as I leapt up, feverishly scanning the ground for my device. By some miracle it landed face-up, and I descended on the glowing screen to snatch it with my good arm before having the common sense to activate the flashlight feature and use it to light my path. Why didn't I think of that earlier?

Maybe, I decided as I continued my run, because I was so sleep deprived that remaining even semi-functional would have been an achievement. Running for my life would give me the superhuman abilities of adrenaline, but that didn't mean I was *thinking* any more clearly as a result.

Now I was operating on heavy drinking rules: focus on one thing at a time, and listen closely to anyone and everyone more sober.

With that in mind, I vaulted a pile of cinder blocks and brought the phone to my ear in time to catch my handler on the tail end of a sentence.

"– come on, if you're still with me, say something."

"Yep," I said impatiently, "just ate shit and had to find the phone."

He released an audible sigh. "As long as you're okay. You scared the hell out of me."

Panting, I replied, "Yeah, well, if I make it out of this I'll buy you a beer sometime."

"I'll buy *you* a beer," he corrected me. "Just hang in there. Keep skimming those warehouses to your right. You've got Three Ring Road ahead, then six blocks of residential to clear before you're home free."

Benghazi was a semicircle against the Mediterranean, the city limits traversed by a concentric series of five major streets. The First Ring Road skirted tourist attractions like the zoo, and each successive one was like a circle of hell extending to the total chaos of the countryside. In crossing to the north side of Third Ring Road, I'd be in a safer area though by no means able to casually stroll to my destination.

I could make out the headlights of traffic ahead, and quickly reached an onramp where a single vehicle approached.

It was a taxi.

This was a split-second judgment call—try to flag down the cab, or let it pass and continue the mile on foot?

I decided to execute the former course of action; theoretically, I could make it to my destination on foot and uncontested. But with two close calls since Khalil's men dumped me at the diplomatic compound, I increasingly viewed the city as a hostile ecosystem that would soon kill me if I remained out here on my own. I needed some local expertise, the assistance of a native Libyan, and if I let this taxi pass it was entirely possible I'd never get another chance.

Leaping into the road, I frantically waved at the taxi. To my immeasurable relief, it actually screeched to a halt as the headlights blinded me.

My first thought was that the driver viewed me as easy prey, because nothing ever worked out this well.

But a second and far more likely thought occurred to me then—whoever he was, the man behind the wheel probably saw a white man in Benghazi's early morning hours as an easy payday. Foreign military service-members and private military contractors had been operating in Libya for decades, particularly in key cities, and continued to do so today. For all I knew, I wasn't the first foreigner in crisis he'd assisted, probably in exchange for a fat stack of cash.

Rounding the side of the vehicle, I leapt into the passenger seat to find the car empty save an obese, sweaty man beside me.

"Go, *yalla!*"

Once he pulled forward, I asked, "You speak English?"

He grunted.

"*Naeam*, yes. A little. Not so good."

Fantastic, I thought, bringing the phone to my ear and saying, "I'm in a cab, need driving directions."

My CIA contact replied, "Hotel is due north, but you've got to keep going to the traffic circle and take the second exit onto Jamal Abdun Nasir Street to get there."

I relayed the instructions, pointing in the correct direction and butchering the name of the street in the process, but the driver gave a curt nod that assured me he'd understood.

Only then did I notice a pair of fuzzy dice hanging from the rearview mirror, a detail that struck me as equal parts ludicrous and inconsequential, and I was in the process of divining further guidance over the phone when the vehicle began slowing.

Looking forward, I saw a string of stopped vehicles ahead and realized I was headed straight for another checkpoint.

My first glance revealed the left lane was blocked by twin pickup trucks and a sedan, with a row of militiamen lining the median to question drivers like local cops conducting a routine driver's license check. Maybe they were, not that there were any uniforms to confirm that guess or any way that would help me if they were—but with the armed men scattered and apparently bored by their duties, I felt certain that some hasty acceleration would serve to get me out of this situation before any meaningful pursuit could follow.

I yanked the wallet from my pocket and said, "Bust it," replying instinctively as if I were addressing someone who had any idea what that meant.

"What?" my driver asked.

"Speed through it," I said, "and do it quick. Fast as you can. *Yalla*, *yalla*. I'll pay you double."

I opened my wallet to find that my cash, a weighty stack of Libyan dinars and almost universally accepted US dollars, was gone. Khalil's men had robbed me, leaving only the credit cards under the name Tom Connelly that didn't do me a hell of a lot of good at present. I couldn't exactly Venmo this dude, and my intention to wave a wad of bills in his face faltered as I continued with feigned confidence, "Two thousand dinar."

It was a blatant lie, and one I had no problem telling under the circumstances. Whether he'd intuit that I was full of shit remained to be seen, though the balance of probability fell on a resounding "yes" when he didn't reply, his eyes stoically watching the road ahead.

I quickly added, "Four thousand dinar."

"No," he said simply, continuing to brake. "They will kill me."

By now we were twenty feet from a full stop beside the checkpoint, and my options were quickly dwindling to one.

What was I supposed to do? I couldn't exactly stick a gun in his neck, regardless of how badly I wanted to out of principle if nothing else. Nor could I even attempt bribing the men at the checkpoint, much less defend myself if they refused money I clearly didn't have.

Instead I did the only thing I could, shouting at him, "May Allah curse you," as I yanked the door handle and leaped out of the vehicle while it was still rolling.

Soon I was rolling too, making landfall with a fleeting stumble that ended in a fall.

I spun twice on my side, feeling the asphalt sanding my skin away before I finally halted myself and leapt upright with an iron grip on the phone.

Vaulting the median, I heard gunshots erupting behind me.

Whether they were firing skyward or at me remained unknown—I saw no tracers, and even if I did, what difference would it make? My attention was occupied with trying not to get broadsided by the headlights bearing down on me from westbound traffic.

I scrambled across a lane, certain that I'd have time to clear an incoming cargo truck, then reversed my decision at the last possible moment and stopped on the dotted line of a lane marker instead. The truck made a halfhearted effort to give me clearance, passing so close that the wind whipped over my body along with the blast of an angry horn before the vehicle disappeared, leaving a fog of exhaust fumes in its wake.

Darting forward, I repeated the process for a group of motorcycles, the drivers swerving to either side of me by the time I realized I hadn't made it to the next lane boundary, but rather stood in more or less the middle of the fucking road.

By then I was sprinting to the far sidewalk, deciding to abandon any effort at concealment as I took the first side road northward past a candy shop before vanishing from sight as I churned breaths of warm, humid air, my legs pumping with exertion.

"On foot," I gasped into the phone, seeing a T-intersection ahead. "Which way?"

No response.

"It's real simple, asshole. Left or right, which one?"

When the line remained silent, I checked the display and found that there wasn't one—my phone was dead.

Slowing at the intersection, I jammed the phone in my pocket and instinctively selected a left turn. Then I ran down the block, headed west, searching for an alley or side street that would reorient me toward the hotel. No such luck; everything was wall-to-wall buildings or tree-lined interludes with no visible outlet. Glancing over my shoulder, I saw no one behind me and decided fuck it, I'd keep going until the next right turn.

I was further worried when that turn didn't appear for far longer than the typical city block, the next street bordered by a grocery store to my left before I hooked a turn in the opposite direction. The road was empty, proceeding between trees and buildings for one short block, then two, my adrenaline fading to exhaustion by the time I reached a four-way intersection. By then I was only fifty percent certain that I was still heading north, the fatigue and disorientation making me second-guess everything.

To my right was a large building marked by the Arabic characters for *madrasa*, school, which I took as a good thing—formal education wasn't a priority in the seedier areas of Benghazi, and this structure appeared relatively well-kept. As I continued running, I realized that I was in an increasingly urban area, unmarked buildings to either side of the road with no more concealment than a few scraggly bushes haphazardly planted beside the sidewalk. Then, finally, I saw it: the next building to my right was three stories tall, rising within the confines of an immaculate stone wall. Giant pillars supported the roof, the nearest wall glowing with soft lighting that illuminated the words *THE PALACE SUITES AND APARTMENTS*. I wasn't sure what pleased me more, the fact that I'd stumbled upon my intended destination by accident or that the sign was in actual English. Slowing to a walk, I rounded the corner and turned on a cobblestone sidewalk before scanning the street both ways and slipping through an open gate in the fence.

The front door was locked, of course, though an attractive woman at the desk spotted my attempt and buzzed me in.

The hotel lobby was an exercise in extravagance, upscale even by Western standards and a veritable Eden here in Benghazi. Marble floor, fine furniture, potted plants, and chandeliers. But the only amenity I cared about was the air conditioning—compared to the stagnant heat outside, it felt like I was drifting through clouds as I marched up to the woman, who said in flawless English, "Welcome to the Palace Hotel. How may I help you?"

Her polite expression turned increasingly to alarm as she saw me under the lobby lighting, out of breath and surely looking like I'd just lost a fight to a bar bouncer.

By way of reassurance, I said, "My cab...dropped me off at the...the wrong spot." Swallowing against a dry throat and heaving a final breath, I concluded dramatically, "I was almost mugged."

"Would you like me to call the police?"

"No," I almost shouted, then composed myself before reiterating, "no, thank you. I threw my cash but..." Another breath. "Still have my...my credit cards."

As if to prove this to her, I selected a Visa from my wallet and slapped it atop the counter with my passport and the words, "I'll take the biggest suite you've got."

Eyeing the card, she asked, "Do you have a reservation, Mr. Connelly?"

Glancing at her name tag, I responded, "Arshiya, I do not, but I'll gladly pay for thirty days in advance if it helps me get to sleep a minute faster. Charge me whatever you like."

She smiled. "Long flight?"

"Exceedingly."

"I am sorry," she said apologetically. "Of course you are welcome here; we have a spare suite available and I can book you for up to a week in advance."

"Wonderful," I replied, and meant it—going from a desperate sprint to a luxury hotel complete with a hot front desk clerk felt like a dream that I risked awakening from at any second. By then I could smell her perfume, and my man-brain perked up despite the fact that I could have fallen asleep leaning against a fence of electrified barbed wire. I was a happily married and exceedingly faithful husband, but there were some evolutionary instincts that no amount of near-death circumstances could suppress.

I looked over my shoulder as she continued the check-in process, seeing through the glass door that the street beyond remained empty. There was a security camera in the corner, and when I looked back at the front desk, I saw a second one mounted in the ceiling, filming me live.

The woman glanced at my backpack, then to the door. "Do you have any luggage?"

"The airline lost it," I said grimly.

"I am so very sorry to hear that." She hesitated, then offered, "Are you all right? There is some...some blood on your shirt, Mr. Connelly."

Looking down, I saw a spatter of red droplets across my chest, the flecks still wet and belonging to a young Libyan man whose head I struck with a rock at maximum force.

Smiling pleasantly, I said with a helpless shrug, "I get nosebleeds after I fly—low humidity on the planes. Dries out my sinuses."

No way to tell if she believed me, or even if she cared. She set an envelope atop the counter and said, "Room 204. The elevator is to your right. Is there anything else I can help you with?"

Leaning over the counter, I said, "I would do unforgivable things for a bottle of water right now."

She reached beneath the desk and procured two with the hotel logo. "Compliments of the house."

Greedily taking them along with the envelope containing my keycard, I said, "I don't deserve you, Arshiya. No one does."

"Sleep well, Mr. Connelly."

I'd downed half of the first bottle before reaching the elevator; by the time it chimed to a stop on the second floor, I was halfway through the second.

By then it took my full attention just to scrutinize room numbers—my vision was bleary with fatigue, and I shuffled down the hall until locating my room and managing to unlock the door.

Flipping on the light, I staggered through a foyer and into the bedroom before turning on a lamp.

I was so tired that the act of plugging both phones into chargers took me four or five attempts. While I waited for my Agency phone to switch back on, I dialed the single number programmed into Khalil's device.

A gruff voice responded, "Yes."

"I'm in the Paradise Hotel."

"No Julyana Resort?"

Whoever he was, his voice was maliciously gleeful, and I felt my grip tighten on the phone. "What can I say? Your drivers can't navigate nearly as well as they can cut people's fucking heads off."

"Nav-i-gate?" he asked, enunciating the word in three distinct syllables that assured me he had no clue what it meant. He could figure that out later, I decided.

I ended the call and threw the phone on the nightstand, snatching up the other one and impotently trying to turn it on as a battery logo flashed red. Goddammit, I thought, how long was this thing going to take...I considered lying on the bed as I waited, but knew that if I so much as sat down, I'd pass out within seconds and likely wouldn't hear the ringer.

Finally the phone booted up. I unlocked the screen the second it was possible to do so, thumbing at the device in repeated attempts to dial. When the call connected, I spoke quickly.

"Paradise Hotel. Room 204."

The man who'd guided me through my dismounted evacuation of the general shithole surrounding the former US diplomatic mission to Libya responded with relief.

"204, got it. Nice work getting there, and hey—"

"I'm going," I cut him off, "to sleep."

"Hit the rack. I've got you covered."

After hanging up and making sure the ringer was activated, I finally —*finally*—lay down on the bed.

The last thing I remembered was looking sideways toward the window, where the first rays of sunrise were streaming in. Jesus, I thought, how long had this entire terrible journey lasted?

Then, without so much as kicking off my shoes, I passed out.

13

Cancer exited his vehicle stiffly, stepping into a rising wave of heat amid the early morning sun.

The two Land Cruisers remained parked on the dirt path as his team performed a hasty scan of the shaded areas beneath rocky outcroppings on either side, then transitioned to a ground search for IEDs around the vehicles.

When the security checks came up clean, no one was surprised—Cancer had selected the pit stop with the help of an armed Reaper overhead, one of several that had been rotating to support their effort since yesterday's engagement. The UAV's sensor operator had confirmed that the spot had no activity, no patches of disturbed earth, and enough visual cover in the form of low rock formations to keep them unseen by any distant observers with telescopic lenses. And, of course, no traffic because, well, they were in the middle of fucking nowhere.

Diverting even further off the highways for fear of additional SRC militia activity had been an obvious tactical choice, though still a difficult one for Cancer to make. No one wanted to add untold hours to an already lengthy infiltration, least of all him, but ultimately reaching their destination with the team intact, albeit without a third of the vehicles they'd entered Libya with, remained priority number one.

"Clear," he transmitted upon completion of the checks. "Racegun, take the twelve. Doc, you're on six o'clock. We move in ten."

Then, starting a timer on his watch, he stretched to a series of pops up and down his spine.

The team moved out at once, Worthy to the front of the convoy and Reilly to the rear to monitor the road despite the UAV orbiting overhead—there was only so much security that Cancer was willing to trust outsourcing to a twenty-something nerd manning computer controls back in America. Hass, Ian, and Cancer quickly walked to the side of the road and stopped.

Then, almost in unison, the team undid their pant flies and began urinating.

It was accepted policy to piss in bottles during lengthy driving stints while on mission, though with a known stop coming up, they'd all been holding it in for quite some time now. The result was a minute-plus gap of silence save the sound of liquid piddling into sand, and Cancer was able to retrieve his cigarettes, light one and draw the first satisfying inhale, and put the tobacco and lighter away long before needing to shake off. After spending most of the night awake, the combination of nicotine and bladder relief was ecstasy, and he was irritated when the reverie was interrupted by the sound of Duchess transmitting over his earpiece.

"*Cancer, this is Raptor Nine One.*"

Pinching the cigarette in his lips to have a hand free for his transmit switch, he replied, "Send it."

"*Suicide Actual checked into the Palace Hotel in Benghazi, meeting complete. I'll push you more details shortly, we're scrambling with coordinations now, but I wanted to let you know he's safe.*"

"I thought he was staying at the Julyana," Cancer replied, momentarily confused at the disparity. It had been a point of contention among the team —they had to slog it out across the Sahara while David, the lucky bastard, took in the Mediterranean views from his coastal resort. Sure, the possibility of Khalil simply whacking him at the meeting was very real, but there was no such thing as a free lunch.

"*Change of plans,*" Duchess said icily. "*I dare say it won't be the last, at this rate. Continue your infil as planned, and I'll keep you posted.*"

Consulting his watch, he concluded, "Yep, we'll be kicking out in eight mikes."

"*Good copy. Raptor Nine One, out.*"

"Cancer, out."

He buttoned his pants and transmitted to his team.

"Well, Suicide's alive and staying at the Palace Hotel. He met with Khalil. More to follow."

Only Ian seemed to pick up on the significance, approaching Cancer's side to speak.

"What happened with David? Why the new hotel?"

Cancer took a drag off his cigarette and shrugged.

"Duchess just said it was a change of plans, and she'd tell me more later. Why, what do you make of it?"

Ian gave a slight shake of his head. "Nothing good."

Before Cancer could decide whether to inquire further or let the comment go, Hass called out, "You hear that?"

"Hear what?" Cancer turned to face the Combat Controller who stood a few meters away, looking skyward.

Hass froze, cocking his head, then concluded with a look of alarm, "Fast mover."

Cancer heard it a moment later, the sound unmistakable. This wasn't the dull, distant groan of a passenger aircraft but a throaty hiss like the sky was being torn apart—a fighter jet was streaking toward them, flying at close to full throttle by the sound of it.

"Incoming!" Cancer shouted, flicking his cigarette to the side and sprinting to the scant cover of a rock overhang ahead. A series of hasty sideward glances confirmed that his teammates were doing the same, and no further guidance needed to be issued—at this point the fighter jet was audible to everyone, the sound of its engine approaching deafening levels.

As he skidded to a halt beneath the rock cover, he could hear Hass transmitting into the air frequency, ordering the Reaper's optics back to the team in an attempt to film what was about to occur.

Cancer keyed his command radio. "Fighter airstrike inbound from the west, headed right for us." Then, taking a knee and switching to his team frequency, he said, "Closing time, boys. If this guy can aim, it's last call."

He spun to face the road, angling his view skyward as he bitterly conceded the elegance of this attack.

A patchwork of militias had taken control of Gaddafi's entire air force fleet, using the aircraft to bomb one another right up until the recent cease-fire. God only knew where all those fighters had ended up, though the current circumstances assured him that Khalil possessed at least one.

If the Suliman Revolutionary Council militiamen were serving as a disruption force to support Khalil's efforts—and Cancer didn't doubt they were—then the slimy Filipino terrorist had found an elegant workaround to the fact that he couldn't monitor every road in Libya. The convoy could have been sighted by any number of long-range observation posts hosting spotters, and with ready access to Gaddafi's lost arsenal, Khalil had opted for an airstrike instead.

The outcome was as assured as it was inevitable: Cancer's team had survived an arduous cross-country vehicle infiltration, besting all ground opposition in the process, only to be wiped out by bombs while they were fully exposed in the open desert.

Sighting the approaching fighter, a metallic triangle growing rapidly in size as it followed the road, he realized it was flying far too low for a bomb drop, and far too fast for a strafing run. Cancer made out a pair of sharply angled wings, the triple array of tail fins and vertical stabilizer clouded by an enormous foglike aura that ringed it like a halo—this fucker was flying over the speed of sound, and doing so at a suicidally low altitude regardless of how flat the terrain was. But his focus was oriented on the underside of the aircraft's wings as he tried to determine the payload. He noted with pleasure that there was none, merely a pair of sleek pods that he identified as external fuel tanks, not munitions. The aircraft was painted in a splotchy camouflage pattern of olive drab and tan, and it screamed overhead as little more than a shadow in the sky.

Then he heard—and felt—the sonic boom, a tremendous thunderclap of noise and vibration like God punching the earth, a shotgun going off in each ear at the same second. It vanished to the roar of a jet engine, and only as the sound receded did he hear Duchess urgently transmitting over his earpiece.

Ignoring her, he whirled to face Hass and called out, "MiG-23?"

"Mirage F1, single seater," Hass shouted back, then rose to a crouch and darted to Cancer's side before continuing.

"No way the pilot didn't spot us. And he was following the road, so it was probably a reconnaissance flight to vector in ground forces—we're about to get hit."

14

CIA Headquarters
Special Activities Center, Operations Center F2

Duchess keyed her hand mic and said, "I repeat, what's your status? What's the aircraft ID?"

That last question was a particular point of contention; the team's Air Force attachment, Master Sergeant Hassan, had succeeded in directing the Reaper's optics just in time for her to witness the flash of an aircraft, though the speed with which it flew rendered it little more than a blur. And while her analysts were currently trying to cross-reference the plane's blurry profile against dozens of possible candidates, to say nothing of plotting an approximate length and wingspan off the freeze frame obscured by the presence of a vapor cone surrounding it, this would go a lot quicker if she got a simple response from one of the five eyewitnesses to the flyover—preferably the designated commander, who she was well aware could hear her every word.

She looked across the tiered seating of the Project Longwing operations center, neatly organized by staff sections flanked by all necessary support personnel, to the far wall with an array of flat screens.

The central screen was the largest and currently displayed the Reaper feed, which showed two Land Cruisers stationary and surrounded by dark patches where the team had urinated without bothering to seek aerial cover. The view rotated with the drone's orbiting flight path—Duchess could make out the miniscule figures of a few team members stepping out from under the rock outcroppings, which made the delay in Cancer's response all the more frustrating. Then she heard muted chatter from a speaker box on the desk of her OPCEN JTAC, and the view shifted to a peripheral scan. Hass was redirecting the drone to perimeter surveillance, which was one more indicator she didn't need to confirm that Cancer was taking his sweet time in providing an update.

The problem with Cancer, she thought, was that he had no experience as a ground force commander. David was certainly no role model for tactful communications with headquarters, but at least he had the common courtesy to keep her posted more or less in real time.

All chatter in the OPCEN had reduced to low murmurs, her staff providing their customary deference when she was communicating with her ground team—even if the transmissions were, at the moment, one-sided.

Finally Cancer transmitted, sounding rattled.

"*Raptor Nine One, be advised,*" he began, "*the aircraft was a Mirage F1 flying at five hundred feet, going at least Mach 1, headed east, directly over the road.*"

While the aircraft was certainly an unexpected development, she wasn't surprised to hear it was following a vehicle route. With avionics of questionable reliability on Gaddafi's aging fleet, the pilot was likely using roadways to navigate to his final destination, whatever that was.

Cancer continued, "*Single seater, no visible munitions. Safe to say we're burned, need all available assets for imminent ground attack.*"

"The jet wasn't looking for your team," she responded, unsure how she knew that even as she transmitted. An unsettling queasiness was taking hold in her gut as she went on, "You're sure there were no visible munitions?"

"*Positive, Rain Man confirms. Just two external fuel tanks.*"

Duchess's heart seized up as she dropped the hand mic and called out to Wes Jamieson, her operations officer.

"Send an urgent air defense notification to the GIS," she said, citing the acronym for Egypt's national intelligence service. "Notify them of the Mirage, inbound for an imminent attack. They need to alert their air defenders and scramble fighters to shoot it down."

The former Marine looked confused but complied nonetheless, taking to the phone as she directed her attention to the J2 and asked, "What targets could that Mirage be headed for in Egypt?"

Andolin Lucios appeared every bit as skeptical as Wes as he replied in a vaguely Spanish accent, "Ma'am, they said it was unarmed."

"It's not fuel in those external tanks," she said, surprised at the control in her voice. At this point she was merely stating a fact, one that was undeniable by her own intuition as much as she didn't want to admit it.

Lucios understood the import immediately, visibly paling as Duchess went on, "Think outdoor venues, amphitheaters, soccer stadiums. Any kind of large public gathering—"

"Today is Egypt's Revolution Day," Lucios cut her off. "The entire country is celebrating in the streets."

By now Wes was looking over his shoulder, still holding the phone to his ear for further guidance after communicating the alert. Duchess said, "Tell them to focus on the largest cities. Cairo, Alexandria, Giza."

Swinging her gaze to Project Longwing's own JTAC, she asked, "How good is Egypt's air defense network?"

"Along the Libyan border?" Brian Sutherland asked rhetorically with a vigorous shake of his head. "It's nonexistent. They're worried about Israel."

The implication was clear enough—Egypt's air defenses were concentrated to the northern and eastern shores. If a fighter jet came streaking in from the west as low as it could fly, nothing in the country's arsenal was going to stop it.

Her next words were strained, spoken against a constriction taking hold in her throat.

"Give me the news."

She watched the surrounding screens come to life with various news outlets, the proceedings muted but complemented by banners with Arabic script. The Agency enjoyed 24/7 coverage of every news network in the world, accessible at a click from any number of operations centers and analysis divisions. Now Duchess could scan live coverage of crowds assembled in Egypt's largest cities in addition to smaller cities with local networks such as Port Said and Suez.

Regardless of the screen, however, the situation was clear enough: the streets and town centers were packed with celebrants waving flags and holding banners, families cheering amid military parades, stages packed with bands and singers, politicians addressing them with fervent patriotism on the anniversary of a coup d'état against the king that established Egypt as a modern republic. The crowds were out in full force in the morning hours, long before the temperature peaked later in the day.

This was an utter nightmare brewing, her perception of time distorted by the knowledge that something terrible was about to occur, and that she was powerless to stop it. She scanned her thoughts for anything else she could do to prevent the calamity, considered notifying her superiors—but no, she decided, short of an urgent, direct alert to the Egyptian authorities, she'd only pollute her lines of communication with middlemen who would be quick to rebuke her if this turned out to be nothing more than a hunch gone bad on her part.

But she knew in her gut that wouldn't be the case.

She suddenly became aware that Cancer was speaking, his voice dripping with contempt.

"*Raptor Nine One, wake up,*" he continued. "*I said, if it wasn't looking for us, then what the hell was it doing out here?*"

She transmitted back, "Stand by," then added, "shut up," before flinging the mic down on her desk and returning her attention to the screens.

"There it is," someone called, and suddenly the Reaper feed of the two Land Cruisers in Libya vanished from the main screen, replaced by a live view of a sprawling traffic circle filled with an uncountable number of civilians waving the red, white, and black national flag. It wasn't just any public space, she realized upon spotting the sleek obelisk rising from the center of the traffic circle, but Tahrir Square in Cairo: site of the Arab Spring protests that ousted Mubarak from his seat as president. Mubarak had ordered his own fighter jets to fly over the protesters in an unsuccessful bid to disperse them; now a fighter of a different kind approached, the camera's view wheeling skyward to trace a rapidly approaching speck against the cloudless blue sky.

It was flying just over the surrounding buildings, the cameraman's elevated vantage point from an adjacent structure only slightly lower than the inbound aircraft. The view swung right to follow the Mirage F1 as it initiated its flyover, visibly decelerating before the external fuel tanks emitted twin streaks of white mist that extended as it soared past and, despite the cameraman's best efforts to keep it in frame, vanished from sight.

The scene that ensued was chaos; civilians trampled one another in a desperate bid to escape what was clearly some form of an airborne attack, even though they knew not what it was. They would find out soon enough, Duchess knew; death by VX could take minutes or hours, depending on the dose, but it would occur for anyone touched by the aerosol particles now drifting downward as the blanket of mist descended over the crowd.

Duchess was scarcely breathing, the sight horrific beyond the proportions of anything she'd witnessed save perhaps 9/11. The collective focus of the OPCEN was directed at the nightmarish vision unfolding on the main screen, the entire room silent save the dimly registered voice of Wes, relaying the development to the Egypt desk, and a tinny metallic sound of Cancer's voice as he transmitted to her, speaking words she couldn't make out.

By now the cloud had descended to street level, though she barely had time to confirm that before the camera's view swung right—the Mirage was lining up for another pass, leveling out and activating whatever retrofitted sprayers had been mounted to the external tanks. Again the wings projected dual plumes of white, the fighter soaring over the square to release its deadly payload before cutting off the spray and pulling up.

This time the cameraman was able to keep the aircraft in sight; it performed a climbing, wheeling turn in the sky over Cairo and was just beginning to turn its nose downward to the innocent civilians lining the streets when a new stream of smoke appeared—not the ghostly white of aerosol VX, but a gray streak racing from the left side of the screen on a collision course with the Libyan fighter jet.

Duchess released an involuntary relieved gasp as the missile impacted with a tremendous fiery explosion. The blast resulted in a starlike puff of black smoke that hovered in place, dissipating slowly as the flaming wreckage of the Mirage fell in an eerily slow descent, rotating with its nose down before impacting in a mushroom blast of jet fuel atop a multi-story building– a hotel, she wondered?—on the east bank of the Nile.

A pair of Egyptian MiG-29s crested into view, overflying the wreckage before Duchess regained the full use of her senses.

The most composed of her OPCEN staff were turning to face her, seeking guidance in the wake of this unprecedented attack. Cancer was still trying to continue their exchange, a final sentence fragment suddenly reaching her consciousness.

"*—guidance on the Mirage, over.*"

She blinked twice, then swallowed hard, trying to sift through her priorities and finding no point of reference for how to react. What could she possibly do right now, how could she conceivably respond in any way that would do justice to what had just occurred?

Service to her ground team suddenly came to the forefront, and she snatched up the radio mic and brought it to her lips.

But before she keyed the mic, her attention returned to the main screen, where the cameraman was now zooming in on the crowd at Tahrir Square. The view panned over a scene that had gone from catastrophic to unspeakable, as the effects of VX exposure took hold on whoever had survived being trampled to death.

"*Raptor Nine One,*" Cancer said, sounding annoyed now. "*We are continuing mission, still awaiting your explanation on that fucking Mirage.*"

15

I awoke with a pounding headache, the effect of a severe dehydration hangover ending my respite of sleep after what seemed like mere minutes.

But the sky outside was bright, and I checked my watch to see that it was just before three in the afternoon. Two things occurred to me then: first, that I was ravenously hungry, and second, that I may well have missed a call or several on either of my phones—a marching band probably could have run a full dress rehearsal at my bedside without waking me. Rolling sideways, I checked the phones to see that both were fully charged, with no incoming calls. While that seemed a blessing in regard to Khalil's device, I actually checked the reception on my CIA phone to make sure it was working; it seemed almost impossible that Duchess would have let me sleep so long without requiring an update.

A refreshing change of pace, I thought, stretching my creaky limbs and fighting my way from the bed as I realized my clothes were still soaked through with sweat. The comforter was now marred by a grease stain of my exact proportions, my thighs painfully chafed and legs aching with fatigue.

Then I turned and realized for the first time exactly how nice this suite actually was.

The floor was softly carpeted beneath nightstands, a bedframe, and two wardrobes finished in teak wood paneling. I ambled stiffly to the window, looking beyond the hotel compound to see traffic and pedestrians crossing the streets—an ordinary day in full swing, no sign of militiamen, terrorists, or, clothing and Arabic signs aside, any indication that this was the war-ravaged city of Benghazi.

A trip to the palatial bathroom revealed a sink top of solid quartz with a marble backsplash, and I left the bedroom to find a small foyer with a coffee table and desk. I felt like I was in a James Bond movie, where luxury suites were the norm between gunfights and car chases; then, remembering that I hadn't so much as considered my teammates since waking up, I decided to call the Agency phone and ask for their status in veiled terms.

But before returning to the bedroom, I noticed a new detail: a folded sheet of paper that someone had slid under the door.

Snatching it up, I saw handwritten block text.

FRIENDLIES ARE HERE. UNLOCK YOUR DOOR AND CALL HOME, REQUEST AN UPDATE. TURN ON THE TV, VOLUME LOUD. REMAIN SILENT UNTIL WE GIVE YOU THE O.K.
BAD GUYS HEAR EVERYTHING RIGHT NOW.

No shit, I thought dryly, cracking my door and activating the deadbolt before letting it rest against the frame. Then I went to my phone and dialed the Agency number, which was promptly answered by a new male voice.

"Go ahead."

I replied, "Still in my room, no calls. Do you have any updates for me?"

"No updates," he said, the catch-all phrase meant to indicate that my team was proceeding with their infiltration as planned. It should have come as a relief to me, though I was instead troubled by the fact that if they had run into issues, no one from the Agency would tell me and risk distracting me from my dealings with Khalil.

I hung up before the conversation could progress, finding the remote and turning on the television set to see a reporter at his news desk speaking quickly in Arabic. Cranking up the volume, I turned to the foyer—whoever the Agency was sending to my aid, I wanted to be standing by when they arrived—only to find that I was too late.

They were already here.

A distinguished-looking man with gray hair approached the bedroom with an enormous roller case. He was clean-shaven, attired in cargo pants and a loose button-down with sleeves rolled to the elbows. Upon seeing me, he pressed a finger to his lips, and I nodded and stepped out of his way as he moved for the two phones on the nightstand.

I watched a second man enter and secure the door behind him, this one a shorter, paunchy fellow in his mid-thirties with dark skin and a goatee. He was in shabby tourist attire, khaki shorts and a T-shirt, and pulling an equally large piece of luggage forward on its wheels. He also, I noted, wore a hiking pack that was nearly as big as he was.

By then the first man had set his case on the bed and opened it, wordlessly setting up shop by opening laptops on the mattress. His shorter associate followed suit, procuring a first aid kit and showing it to me. I shook my head no, and he replaced the bag for a heavy canvas parcel that he handed over before ignoring me completely, turning his attention to an array of electronic cargo from his luggage.

Unzipping the bag, I watched them with interest. The older one had removed both my phones from their chargers and plugged them into separate laptops via red cables. The one with the goatee, meanwhile, ran a scanner over me before waving the device across every surface in the room to search for surveillance devices.

Then, as I opened the canvas pack he'd given me, I forgot about the men altogether.

There were plastic bottles of Gatorade and Pedialyte, together with an assortment of protein and chocolate bars. Manna from heaven, I thought as I twisted the cap off the Pedialyte and began chugging it. The sugar- and sodium-laced drink went down smooth and fast, and I immediately chased it with a generous portion of Gatorade before going to work on a PowerBar.

I was two bites in when the gray-haired man looked up from his fleet of laptops and shot a thumbs up to his partner, who was returning from his countersurveillance scan of the foyer.

"We're good," he said over the blaring Arabic news.

With that I used the remote to mute the TV, then said with my mouth half-full, "You guys work fast. Bring any bourbon?"

The older man didn't seem to think it was funny, which was just as well since I wasn't joking.

"Maybe next time," he said. "I'm Sam, this is Corey."

"David," I replied, shaking their hands in turn. "How's my team?"

Corey said, "Continuing infil. Delayed due to a gunfight, but no injuries, and they should make it to the safehouse later today."

I nodded to Khalil's phone, still tethered to a laptop via the cable. "So what's the deal with that fucking thing?"

Sam gave a self-satisfied grin. "We've hijacked the audio and location beacon and can pipe in whatever noise we want—TV, shower, that sort of thing—and tweak the GPS coordinates."

"Why would you want to adjust the location? I assume he's watching the hotel surveillance cameras by now."

"The security staff here is doing that for him, courtesy of a phone arrangement by his people a few minutes after you reported in. But you'll need to evacuate prior to any hostage rescue, because Khalil has a hit team on call to get you if Olivia is snatched. We can selectively freeze the camera feeds and have set up an evacuation route via the first-floor service room."

I nodded, taking another bite of the PowerBar.

"Slick. Am I correct in assuming I'm supposed to call Duchess?"

"ASAP," Corey replied. "She wants your full report about the meeting with Khalil. Particularly," he went on, now looking uneasy, "after the attack."

"What attack?"

He looked at me oddly. "Cairo. Wait, you haven't—"

That was as far as he got before his partner tapped my shoulder and pointed to the television behind me.

I spun to see the muted newsfeed now showed an aerial view of Tahrir Square, which was blanketed by an odd mix of colors and discarded flags. It took me a moment to recognize that I was looking at the distant view of human bodies, far too many to comprehend at a glance.

Sam explained, "A rogue fighter jet flew over the Revolution Day celebration and sprayed aerosol VX on Tahrir Square."

That comment hit me like a sucker punch. I couldn't bring myself to face them, instead continuing to stare at the screen as I numbly asked, "Casualty count?"

"Initial estimates are in the thousands."

I was speechless, unsure what to think or how to react beyond a deep, pervading sense of disgust. We all knew it was a matter of time before Erik Weisz employed his WMD, a prize that my team and I had failed to stop before it left the shores of South America despite our best efforts; judging by the screen, he'd succeeded in topping the 9/11 death toll in a single strike. What that accomplished for his aims beyond sewing chaos, I couldn't tell and didn't want to contemplate.

Corey spared me the pained silence, however, by pulling a cell phone from his pocket and dialing.

"Stand by," he said into the receiver, then handed it to me with the words, "She's ready for you."

Accepting the phone from him, I excused myself to the foyer to hear Duchess's voice over the line.

"David, are you there?"

"Yeah," I said, stopping before the coffee table. "I just heard about Cairo."

There was a long pause before she replied, "I need you to put Weisz aside, for now. You're the only one in a position to facilitate Olivia's rescue, and that's where I need your focus. Your assessment of Khalil is critical. I want a full debrief of your meeting, but first I need to know what you thought of his intent."

Drawing a breath, I recounted my memories of yesterday's meeting that now seemed like it occurred a lifetime ago.

"His requesting me for the negotiations was all just a bit of drama," I said. "He couldn't have cared less about the fact that I was on Jolo Island, other than to rub it in my face a bit. If he really had a personal vendetta with me, he would've debated my account or tried to determine my real identity. Khalil did neither. The meeting was all business, no mustache twirling. But he showed me the dog tags from the pilot he killed—he's wearing them, and I feel like it's all part of the act. All the nonsense of him posing with the body, cutting out that pilot's heart, was nothing more to him than a sensationalist recruiting tool. Because I got the sense that beneath the facade he's a pragmatist, and an effective one at that. If articulate speeches were more effective for his target audience, that's what he'd be doing."

"What is your assessment of his intentions with Olivia?"

"He's going to kill her," I said. "If he cared about that ransom, he wouldn't have dumped his only negotiator outside the US consulate. It's going to take a hostage rescue to free her."

"Once we find her, the raid is a done deal. The squadron is standing by in Italy as we speak, and their advance element arrives in Libya tonight."

I paused, then asked, "How are my guys?"

"They're almost to the safehouse with one enemy contact to show for it. They also," she added, "witnessed the Libyan Mirage fly over their position and reported it. We did everything in our power to stop that attack, and if the Egyptians had sufficient air defenses on their western border it never would have happened."

I shook my head.

"That doesn't make me feel any better about what happened in Egypt. But why did he hit Cairo, of all places?"

"It can wait. First I need—"

"No," I interjected, "it can't. You've already got a working theory, goddammit, so tell me."

I heard Duchess huff an impatient sigh before she acquiesced.

"Fine. July 23rd is Egypt's equivalent of the Fourth of July for America. Remember what happened on Independence Day last year?"

"The attack we stopped at the last possible second? Yeah, pretty sure I recall that one."

"Both attacks indicate an entirely new altitude of conception and planning. It's way beyond striking civilian targets; it's corroding national identity and making a mockery of sovereign nations in the eyes of the world."

"Then why Egypt? Why would he hit a Muslim country?"

"I don't think it's about Egypt," she offered. "I think it's more about Libya, about the entire proxy war. Consider how many countries are trying to get in on Libya's natural resources by backing opposite sides amid an exceedingly fragile ceasefire deal, and you can see Weisz is exploiting the fault lines of this entire region. He wants instability, he wants to pit both sides against the middle. And now that he's made an example out of Cairo, can you imagine his ability to negotiate with world powers? If you were a government decision maker and could cut a backdoor deal to keep an attack like that out of your borders, what would you be willing to give?"

"I think his ability to negotiate is a lot less than it was before he used his entire supply of VX."

Not exactly a comforting thought, I considered, but the best we were going to get.

When Duchess didn't answer, and didn't immediately turn the conversation back to Khalil, I felt a queasiness growing in the pit of my stomach.

"Duchess," I said, "he expended his supply, right?"

There was a long pause before she audibly inhaled and spoke again.

"Initial samples of the aerosol residue from Tahrir Square show an approximate 1:2 concentration of VX to water. The external fuel tanks for a Mirage hold 317 gallons each, and there were two of them...I'll spare you the math, but the bottom line is that only 200 or so gallons of VX were used. Given what de Zurara has told us, the remaining ninety percent, some 1,800 gallons, is still out there."

16

Worthy's voice came over Ian's radio earpiece, a transmission that elicited equal parts concern and relief.

"*Eyes-on the rolling door, pulling in now.*"

Cancer replied from the passenger seat, "Copy, standing by." Then, releasing his radio switch, he said, "Take a right up here and get us closer."

Ian complied, wheeling his Land Cruiser through a turn between a jewelry store and a shopping mall within the flow of late-afternoon traffic.

The streets of southeastern Benghazi had thus far presented no obstacles to the team's progress—whatever militias and off-duty soldiers and dirty cops roamed the streets after dark, he'd seen no sign of them in the waning daylight. They'd made good progress through the desert, relying on the UAVs to direct them around checkpoints and reaching the city limits before sunset.

Now Ian drove past storefronts and billboards, the flat-roofed buildings to either side finished in almost uniform shades of tan or, occasionally, painted white. The sidewalks were interspersed with palm trees and scrub brush, with an occasional pedestrian strolling through the heat. Even the traffic was orderly; the chatter of car horns was as ubiquitous in most Third World cities as it was in New York, and yet Ian heard none of that now, just the blare of radio stations from vehicles cruising with their windows down.

He was glad their Land Cruisers had acquired a healthy coat of sand and dust during their drive through the Sahara—most of the civilian cars here looked like they hadn't been washed in years.

Cancer said, "Take the next left and we'll be on the safehouse road."

The staggering between vehicles was intentional—if Reilly and Worthy ran into a trap, it was up to the men in the second truck to react—but Worthy's voice came over the net with assurances that wouldn't be the case.

"*Safehouse is clear. He's the only one inside. Come on in.*"

"Thirty seconds out," Cancer replied.

Looking over his shoulder to Hass in the backseat, he said, "This cat better deliver."

"Ramzi always delivers," Hass replied with absolute confidence. "I've only worked with him twice, but both times were like having a professional logistician making preparations for us. A bored, disinterested one, but still. This guy's been run by enough Agency and JSOC types to know the score, and he's very...how should I put this...financially motivated."

Cancer looked to Ian, who elaborated.

"His profile basically says he'd stab his mother in the street to make five bucks. On the plus side, there's nothing he won't do if we can pay him, which we can. On the downside, Ramzi will double-cross us in no time flat if he finds a better payday."

Hass conceded, "I have zero doubt in my mind about that. But no one pays better than America, and he knows that as well as we do."

Cancer frowned. "So if Khalil gets his 400 million in a few days, we need to leave town."

"Without a trace," Hass agreed, and by then the conversation was over—Ian made out the open rolling gate of a warehouse ahead, and he slowed to turn into it.

Once he did, the enormous size of this safehouse truly occurred to him. Normally, such establishments were apartments or small homes in ordinary residential areas.

Never before had he established such a setup in an actual warehouse, much less one with the storage capacity to conceal fifty-plus men.

The space requirement was for good reason, he saw upon pulling into the storage area that was largely empty save a row of cargo trucks and sedans against the far wall to his right, their bumpers neatly aligned. The first Land Cruiser was off to the left, parked beside an old silver BMW 3 series that could only be Ramzi's personal vehicle.

More notable at present, however, was Ramzi himself, approaching as Ian brought the Land Cruiser to a stop. He checked his rearview to see Worthy and Reilly on either side of the rolling door, pulling it down as he killed the engine.

Cancer waited until the rolling door was down before exiting the vehicle, and both Ian and Hass followed suit; they were the decision-making delegation who would establish a formal Agency link for Olivia's rescue with the portly Libyan man standing before them.

He wasn't some newly vetted CIA asset: Ramzi al-Muntasir had been in the recurring employ of the Agency for over a decade, setting up accommodations and facilitating the transit of various US intelligence and special operations personnel during the overthrow of Gaddafi and the ousting of ISIS from Libya in the chaos that followed.

Ramzi's suitability for the task stemmed in large part from his ethnic heritage, and after scouring his background files, Ian knew much about the man standing before them, starting with the fact that his real name wasn't Ramzi at all.

Born Edji Koki, he'd changed his name to distance himself from his birth clan, the Tebu people. With their very cultural identity threatened by the assimilation attempts of the former regime that had banned their citizenship, employment, and even language, many became expert smugglers and none more so than Edji, whose success in that racket had led to a lucrative existence in Benghazi complete with a new identity. He'd turned his back on his own people, with his first Agency handler noting that the topic of his heritage was a conversational trigger to be avoided at all costs.

But decades of smuggling had not only made him a relative fortune; he was reputed to be endowed with an intimate knowledge of every local contact, trail, back road, and secret entrance to militia compounds. Considering that alcohol was illegal in Libya despite the thriving industry in illicit narcotics and human trafficking, the man who could seamlessly negotiate passage and products across countless tribes, alliances, and militia territories was worth his weight in gold and paid accordingly.

Ramzi looked the part, too. Now in his sixties, his weather-worn face appeared creased with age, cynicism, and the unshakable knowledge that every man had his price. His beard was gray and his lips were formed into a scowl that Ian guessed was near-perpetual; his dull brown eyes were flanked by crow's feet and his pot belly suggested he wasn't one to miss a meal.

"*As-salamu alaykum*," Cancer said, the standard Arabic greeting of "peace be upon you" that would have, under nearly any other circumstances, be met with the response *wa alaykumu s-salam*. But that wouldn't be the case here, Ian realized as Ramzi replied in heavily accented but flawless English.

"I thought you were bringing three trucks."

Cancer spoke flatly. "One of them lost a fight to a Dushka."

Ramzi gave a curt nod, unimpressed and unemotional, before Hass greeted him in Arabic and received a response in the same language. They embraced and kissed one another on both cheeks—a more intimate exchange than would be reserved for a total stranger, Ian noted, but far from the two or three repetitions of that act reserved for close friends and family.

Ian himself remained unacknowledged by Ramzi, as if he weren't there at all, which was fine by him, as his aptitudes were better reserved for overseeing this exchange as an impartial observer.

Ramzi asked, "Any other trouble on the journey?"

The inquiry was a conditioned response, Ian could tell; the man clearly couldn't care less about how their infil went.

Cancer responded, "Half the population of Egypt just got killed with a nerve agent, so yeah, there was trouble."

Ian struggled to keep his attention on their new safehouse manager at the mention of the Cairo attack.

Everyone on his team had been blaming themselves for the transatlantic VX transfer, but it was a much easier guilt to shoulder when none of that substance had yet been employed. Now that Erik Weisz had inflicted such unprecedented human carnage with a small portion of the payload, and was currently at large with the vast majority, it was going to be exceedingly hard to stay focused on the current mission of running backside support for the rescue of a single hostage.

Ramzi took the reference in stride, however, shrugging to indicate he'd heard the news and wasn't particularly concerned about it.

He said, "Better Egypt than Libya" and made a *tsk-tsk* sound with his tongue. Then, without further ado, Ramzi swept his arm to the row of four cargo trucks currently being inspected by Worthy and Reilly before continuing, "As promised, four Iveco medium-duty cargo trucks. Your two sedans for low-profile work, a Kia Optima and Toyota Camry. All fully fueled, with oil changes and mechanic inspections, and the tires inflated. Keys are on the dash."

Cutting his pointer finger to a side room of the warehouse, he continued, "Sleeping quarters and toilets through that door. As ordered, I did not procure cots to avoid raising suspicion, but I can do so within several hours if you change your mind. Along with sleeping bags, pillows, and blankets as you prefer."

Ian tried not to scoff—the man was in it for a payday, no question, with the fate of the Agency contractor team and their Navy guests relegated to a distant second place.

Cancer pulled a pack of cigarettes from his kit and waved it in front of the man. "Can I smoke in here?"

Ramzi laughed.

"You paid for it. Shit on the floor, for all I care. Whatever else you need, simply tell me. I know everyone, can get anywhere, and find anything. But I want my retainer before you depart tonight—if you do not return, I would like to be compensated for my troubles."

17

Reilly scanned the rolling landscape through his night vision as a warm breeze crested over him, bringing with it the scent of calm Mediterranean waters.

The largely unoccupied stretch of coastline northeast of Benghazi consisted of a series of tightly rolling hills interspersed with snaking, brackish tributaries that threaded their way in from the sea. Reilly's team learned this firsthand during his team's three-plus-mile overland movement from the vehicle staging area, a journey he was none too thrilled to negotiate on foot. Yes, there was an entirely abandoned road skirting the coast to his front. And no, neither Cancer as team leader nor the Agency writ large had been willing to allow the staging of transportation assets so close to a major avenue of transit where a civilian vehicle could appear at any time. Not that such a possibility had ever actually occurred in the three hours they'd been sitting here, patiently waiting for the arrival of an exceedingly unique Naval vessel with a payload bay that could launch and recover everything from combat rubber raiding craft to special operations-modified jet skis.

Or, in the case of tonight's insertion, deposit eight select men from a highly specialized squadron of an already elite unit.

A voice beside him said quietly, "You okay, man?"

Reilly looked over his shoulder to see Hass lying in the prone, maintaining a view in the opposite direction beneath the section of camo netting they'd erected as a temporary hide site. Beyond him, Reilly could see the dark expanse of the Mediterranean meeting the horizon and, beneath it, the beachhead where their Navy counterparts would soon be arriving.

"Yeah, I'm fine," Reilly said. "Just thinking about the worst possible names for a boat, and having a hard time picking anything shittier than the Navy did for their flagship special operations delivery vehicle."

"Combatant Craft Heavy?" Hass asked.

Resuming his view of the landscape extending to their west, Reilly replied, "No—I mean, yeah, that's bad, pure and simple. But that's no reason to string together a jumblefuck of words in an attempt to make an acronym on top of it. What's the full title again?"

Hass supplied, "Sea, Air, and Land Insertion, Observation, and Neutralization. SEALION."

"Exactly. An animal that should be a middle school mascot at best, not slapped on a stealth boat."

"It's not really stealth, though. Just semisubmersible, with enough acoustic and thermal insulation—"

"To deserve a better name," Reilly cut him off. "And you can't tell me you're not at least a little skeeved out by working with SEALs."

"Meaning...what, exactly?"

The medic hesitated, uncertain of how to phrase his next words.

Hass served the US Air Force, but Combat Controllers were most often attached to various special operations forces of other service branches. Uncertain where the man's organizational allegiances trended, Reilly certainly didn't want to offend.

But, as Hass remained silent, Reilly chose to hit him with both barrels.

"Look," he began, "my team has had to run exactly two missions involving Delta Force."

Hass ventured, "Sure."

"Know what kind of press coverage there was?"

"Let me guess: a few vague news references to unspecified special operations forces."

"Yep, pretty much."

After chuckling, Hass asked, "So what makes you think the SEALs will be any different?"

"Oh, I don't know," Reilly began, "maybe the fact that given historical precedent, by the time we get these Navy guys back to the safehouse, they'll be working on four memoirs, two movie deals, a half-dozen magazine and news interviews, and a TV miniseries about this mission. Just saying."

"By the time we get back to the safehouse?" Hass asked incredulously. "Doc, they're probably on the phone with their agents right now."

Reilly resisted the impulse to laugh—despite the fact that they were undeniably alone out here, noise discipline was an inextricable component of surveillance, particularly at night, when sound traveled farther due to atmospheric effects. He returned his focus to the rolling landscape before him, resuming his vigil for human presence whether civilian or enemy.

Ground surveillance of the area surrounding the beach landing site, at least, was undeniably necessary. American aerial coverage had been stretched to the breaking point to cover the boat's passage across the Mediterranean. Sure, the SEALION had forward looking infrared and a retractable mast with high-definition radar, but that only went so far when it had to make it through a labyrinth of legal and illegal civilian vessels crisscrossing the waters.

Myriad fishing trawlers and massive container ships were easy enough to avoid, more or less following declared routes with GPS transponders broadcasting their location at all times.

The real problem was the never-ending torrent of rickety boats setting off for Italy, all of them filled by a portion of the 100,000-plus African refugees that used Libya as their departure point each year. By the time they took to sea, most of those refugees had already endured a journey filled with forced labor and sexual abuse at the hands of human traffickers. Thousands drowned in the Mediterranean, while tens of thousands were intercepted and incarcerated in Libyan detention facilities only to be forced into slavery or prostitution.

And despite that heartbreaking reality, which continued year after year with no end in sight, the tactical implication was that human traffickers took great pains to go unnoticed. They utilized spotter boats to detect and report government efforts to interdict them, including containment attempts by the Libyan Navy—handsomely funded by the Italians—as well as the Italian Coast Guard ships.

As a result, the SEALION had spent hours on a winding and circuitous route to bypass visual detection amid a complex web of possible compromise by a tremendous number of unidentified vessels, any of which could hold observers with night vision reporting directly to Khalil. Thus far the effort had been successful; the downside was that an extremely finite amount of US aerial surveillance could guide the boats without broadcasting an infiltration-in-progress. The combination of P-8 Poseidon maritime patrol aircraft and Reaper UAVs had barely been sufficient to collectively re-route the SEAL element through an ever-shifting matrix of Mediterranean boat traffic.

That was, of course, part of the reason that Hass had little to do but banter with Reilly as they waited; air assets were being managed by the Agency and Navy operators, who apparently had their hands full as the arrival time kept getting delayed with each diversion around competing boat traffic. The downside to these delays, however, was that each aircraft's station time had elapsed until they had to continue rotating back to base, leaving a single P-8 overhead to guide the Navy vessel.

Cancer came over the net then, transmitting from his central surveillance point among the team formation.

"*Good news and bad news,*" he began. "*Bad news is the last P-8 has to wave off, so we're the only people watching the beachhead for the next 45 minutes until another Reaper arrives. Good news is the SEALION has been cleared for a straight shot to shore, and should be arriving in ten mikes.*"

Reilly checked his watch. The linkup was supposed to occur around midnight; after the delays, it was already close to two in the morning.

"*We've only got three hours until nautical twilight, four until sunrise. Linkup plan changes as follows: I'm going to flash the SEALs into my position, and by the time they get here I want Racegun moving out on point to take us back to the trucks. Doc and Angel, you guys let them pass and bring up the rear. Forget about moving to the beach, we don't have the time.*"

"*Good copy,*" Worthy responded, "*I'll set pace for a land speed record. Doc, you just let me know if anyone's falling out of the formation.*"

"Yep, copy," Reilly transmitted back. A few miles over easy terrain should be a cakewalk, and at any rate, they'd be home free once they reached the vehicles.

They'd staged both of the Land Cruisers but only one of the Iveco cargo trucks at their disposal—tonight's linkup wasn't for the main assault force.

Instead, the team would be receiving a contingent of eight operators and technical specialists from SEAL Team Six's Black Squadron, who specialized in intelligence, reconnaissance, and surveillance. Those men had the equipment and training to tap communications and electronic signals in the interests of locating the hostage, after which they would conduct close target recon and lay the groundwork for the arrival of the main assault force.

To Reilly, the Black Squadron element seemed large; at least, until he considered how many shooters were standing by to conduct the actual rescue.

That operation would be conducted by Red Squadron, one of four within the organizational charts of SEAL Team Six who were surgically focused on killing terrorists and rescuing hostages. Their only peers in the US military were the operators of Delta Force, and while either unit could perform the mission just as well, Libya's Mediterranean coast and the ensuing possibility of a maritime operation made SEALs the force of choice.

And what a force it was, Reilly thought.

Speaking quietly to Hass, he noted, "Besides, 56 SEALs seems like a lot of dudes to stage in Italy for one hostage, doesn't it?"

"Not really," Hass replied, pausing before he elaborated on the comment. "When Captain Phillips got captured off the coast of Somalia, I had a buddy with DEVGRU's alert squadron. He parachuted in with them off the Horn of Africa, and told me they inserted close to a hundred shooters."

Reilly recoiled at the figure, citing his only knowledge of the event.

"I thought that was, like, six snipers."

"Six snipers took the shots," Hass confirmed, "but the rest of the assault force was staged on another ship in case the life boat made it to shore and the pirates took their hostage to an urban objective. And Captain Phillips wasn't a senator's daughter. Besides, bro, HR is another animal," he continued, referencing the military acronym for hostage rescue. "The name of the game is flooding in as many operators as fast as possible, with the vast majority looking for a shot they'll never get. I'm guessing that with a five-man team, you guys do things a fair bit differently."

Reilly snorted. "No shit. Everyone in this messed-up outfit gets to shoot all they want and more. I've killed a lot more people as a medic for Project Longwing than I ever did as a medic for Ranger Regiment."

"Not a bad deal," Hass noted.

"Downside is that our odds of getting killed are catastrophically higher."

"Everything in life comes with a tradeoff, am I right?"

"Fuckin' A," Reilly acknowledged, his response trailing off as he caught a flash of movement in his night vision.

"I've got movement," he transmitted instinctively, "stand by."

But the hills extending westward appeared exactly as they did before, eerily quiet and without a trace of human presence.

Cancer asked impatiently, "*What is it?*"

"Not sure," Reilly responded, "it's gone now."

He struggled to recall what he'd seen in the first place—it was little more than an aberrant spot of darkness, the distance difficult to gauge with the reduced depth perception of night vision. Could have been a person at three hundred meters, or bird or bat twenty feet away. Whatever it was, it was gone now.

Not good enough for Cancer, who sounded pissed now. "*Did you see something, or not?*"

Reilly questioned whether he'd sighted anything at all, or merely had some last-minute paranoia.

But the skin along his spine was tingling, a primordial instinct assuring him that all was not well on this otherwise quiet night.

"Yeah," he transmitted back, "I saw something. Have the boat loiter offshore, I'm trying to get visual."

He heard a scrape of movement beside him as Hass reoriented his position beneath the camouflage netting, angling for a vantage point to assist in positively identifying, well, whatever it was Reilly thought he saw.

Cancer spoke a moment later. "*The SEALION is having comms issues, all I'm getting is static. Trying to relay through Duchess.*"

Reilly didn't respond—not immediately, at least.

Hass spoke instead, whispering, "There it is."

By then Reilly saw it too, and knew that his initial guesses had been wrong; he hadn't spotted a bat or a person, but something far worse that now cleared a far hill once more.

"We've got vehicles," he transmitted, "moving fast, no headlights, straight up the coast road, two minutes out. Call the abort."

~

Cancer keyed his mic and spoke quickly.

"Trident Zero Four, I say again, abort, abort, abort. Enemy inbound to landing site."

By now he could see a row of trucks speeding down the road paralleling the coast. Reilly had the advantage to identify them first from his vantage point on left-side security, and Cancer was immeasurably grateful they'd scrapped the plan to move forward to the beach and instead remained in their elevated hide sites. So much as a bootprint in the sand could give them away if the enemy did what he thought they were about to do, and even without that means of compromise, this could turn ugly in a split second.

The lone radio response came not from the SEALION crew he was trying to contact but from Duchess.

"*We still can't reach them either, will keep trying.*"

"That's not gonna make their radio magically work," he shot back. "They're expecting an armed contingent securing the beachhead, and that's exactly what they're going to see—except it's not my men. Get the P-8 back here to sparkle the boat with an IR laser before it gets to shore."

"*The Poseidon already hit 'bingo' fuel and is fifty miles away. Unless comms come back up, you'll have to signal from the ground.*"

Yeah, Cancer thought, that was all well and good to suggest, so long as you didn't have the ground experience to read between the lines of Reilly's report.

The sudden approach of vehicles at this desolate spot told Cancer this was no chance encounter, and the fact that they were moving without headlights assured him that they were dealing with an enemy force operating under night vision—no amateur-hour militia operation. It also meant, regrettably, that any means at his disposal to visually signal an abort to the Navy would be seen by the enemy as well. Even activating his infrared laser right now would be about as subtle as turning on a flashlight and waving it at the convoy.

And it might not matter either way, he considered. After all, were these fuckers coming after the Navy boat, his team, or both? If they were only chasing the boat, then his team could feasibly remain undetected considering they were hiding beneath camo netting—provided he succeeded in persuading the Navy boat and its SEAL passengers to wave off their approach. But if the bad guys definitively knew there was a reception team in place, then Cancer and his men had better shag ass back the way they'd come while they still could.

These thoughts ran through his mind in a matter of seconds, which turned out to be more or less wasted time; since their communications were down with the inbound SEALION, the decision was made for him.

"We stay put," he told his team, continuing his transmission with a hasty order. "Hold fire unless compromised. If the boat doesn't turn around, I'll visually signal the abort and we hit these assholes with everything we've got, then break contact back to the trucks."

"*Check*," Worthy replied over the radio, followed by an identical message from Reilly.

Ian's response came verbally, spoken in a whisper from Cancer's right side, where the intelligence operative had been maintaining overwatch on the beach.

"We've got a problem," he said.

"No shit," Cancer shot back.

"I'm not talking about the bad guys. What I mean is, how did they know a boat was coming? We've had aerial surveillance guiding it every step of the way—no way this was a chance spotter on some Mediterranean vessel, and if there was anyone out here but us, we'd be dead already."

There had been several times in the history of Project Longwing where

Cancer wanted little more than to punch Ian in the face, and this was certainly one of them; but he had bigger problems at present, and said only, "Let me know when you figure it out," before re-attempting radio contact with the SEALION.

"Trident Zero Four, abort, abort, abort, how copy?"

Reilly transmitted, "*Trucks passing left-side security now, four SUVs.*"

Cancer angled his night vision to observe the convoy's approach. The vehicles were spread out, staggering their intervals to respond in case the point truck was attacked.

That lead vehicle was a large Toyota that halted directly in front of him along the coastal road, coming to a stop less than a hundred meters below without so much as the flash of brake lights. Men began piling out of it and spreading along the shore as Cancer whispered an update to Duchess, relaying the details as he was able to make them out.

"First truck dropped four men," he began. "Automatic weapons, rocket launchers, night vision, good noise and light discipline—these are professional soldiers, not militiamen. Someone's supplying Khalil with a hell of a lot better than strung-out teenagers with Soviet-era weapons."

Then he saw a bright green beam appear from one of the enemy weapons, extending to spin in circles on the ground. A team leader using his infrared laser to demarcate shooting positions in the scrub brush along the base of the hill, he knew. They were in a hurry to set up, and in his follow-up transmission to Duchess, Cancer pointed out the only explanation that could explain the developments of the past sixty seconds.

"They're setting up a hasty ambush directly at the landing site. They've got no idea we're in the hills above them, but they know exactly when and where the boat is making landfall."

"*Copy,*" Duchess replied, "*still no word from Trident—*"

Cancer repeated his attempt to contact them, this time repeating only the word "abort" in rapid succession as the first truck made a quick turn and sped back the way it had come. A Jeep Grand Cherokee quickly filled the void, moving further eastward before repeating the drop-off.

"Second truck dropped another five shooters."

He had just enough time to make another unsuccessful transmission to the SEALION as the second truck departed. Another SUV immediately drove in, this one some kind of foreign Nissan he didn't recognize, and it traveled further east before depositing its load of fighters. They were stretching the ambush line incrementally, probing further and further for any defenses on the beach before committing additional men. Not a bad play, he thought as the cycle repeated with the fourth and final vehicle, a Toyota FJ Cruiser, completing its drop of the final four men almost directly in front of Worthy's position on the right flank.

Then it too sped back the way it had come, racing to join the other three SUVs and leaving the landing site to appear as unoccupied as it had minutes earlier.

"Seventeen enemy fighters on the ground," he updated Duchess, then transmitted another abort that went unacknowledged.

The silence that ensued was terrifying; those Navy personnel were headed into certain death, and a lapse in radio comms now spelled an imminent massacre that the team didn't have nearly enough men to stop.

Unless, of course, he prevented it from happening entirely.

Cancer reached into his kit for a long cylinder that he really didn't want to have to use—a rocket flare, his last resort to signal an abort to the SEALION's crew. And while it would serve that purpose as only a blazing ball of fire in the sky could, shooting it would pinpoint his team for every one of these enemy fighters. The enemy would face precision gunfire and a deadly uphill charge if they wanted to counter-assault, but sheer numbers worked overwhelmingly in their favor. His team would have a brief head start in a three-mile sprint back to their trucks, but the odds of making it that far against a determined force of this size were slim to none.

But the math was clear enough: the four crewmembers and eight SEALs aboard that boat trumped his five on the beach. He removed the cap and its embedded firing pin from the top of his flare, then slipped it over the explosive percussion cap at the base as Duchess came over the net.

"*Still no comms, they should be ninety seconds out.*"

"I'm sending up the signal in one mike," he replied, "and then we're going to be running for our lives back to the trucks. Whatever air assets you can mobilize to support us, they better be here asap."

But both of them knew the status of their aerial support—namely, there wouldn't be any for some time—and he was left to hope that Duchess would be able to redirect fighter aircraft or similar under crisis authorities. Given that his team was chosen for their expendability, however, the words remained just that: words, the only hollow attempt he could make to safeguard the men under his care within an Agency bureaucracy more concerned about deniability than anything as trivial as saving his men's lives.

Then he transmitted to the boat, "Trident Zero Four, abort, abort, abort."

Cancer held the flare away from his body as he continued the attempts. All he had to do now was slam the base of the cylinder into the ground to send a projectile roaring three hundred meters skyward, where a low *pop* would precede a blinding orb of flame descending beneath its parachute to be seen for miles in any given direction until it burned out a minute or so later.

And well before that burnout occurred, his team had damned well better have inflicted as many casualties as they could on the unsuspecting enemy force below, and be well on their way along the return trip back to their only ground transportation.

His heart sank as he could make out the SEALION coming in over the water, a jet-black bullet appearing beneath the horizon in his night vision. Only the superstructure was visible, its twin 10-cylinder engines slowed just enough to keep the wave-piercing hull below the waterline.

"Abort, abort, abort," he transmitted. "I say again, abort—"

Suddenly the boat whipped a sideways arc in the water.

A man's voice replied, "*Trident Zero Four copies abort, moving offshore to loiter for alternate linkup. Standing by for guidance.*"

Huffing a breath and shakily pulling the flare's firing pin cap away from the primer, he said, "Guidance is there's no fucking linkup. Seventeen enemy fighters with night vision just set up an ambush at your landing site."

"*Copy. Your team okay?*"

"For now," Cancer began, all too aware that status could violently reverse course at the drop of a hat. "Do us a solid, Trident, and follow the shore to the west—I say again, the *west*—like you're still going to make the drop at an alternate site. Pull these guys out of here and away from my men."

"Good copy, we'll stay within sight of shore. Let us know when you get away clean and we can RTB."

That last acronym stood for return to base, an act that Cancer's team would have to conduct in relatively short order and with the eternal gratitude that they hadn't yet been compromised.

But first, he thought, it was time to sweeten the pot.

Keying his team radio, he said, "Crew got the abort, they're taking the boat west as a diversion."

Reilly replied, "*Looks like the bad guys are taking the bait—their trucks are heading back now to recover the shooters. Hopefully they go on a wild goose chase until we get back to our vehicles.*"

"Most will," Cancer said, then grinned. "But not all of them. We're going to let the first three trucks leave, then hit their trail element. I want to snatch one of these fuckers alive."

~

For a second, Worthy thought he'd misheard the transmission; and, upon realizing he hadn't, only one thought took precedence over all others in the wake of their failed linkup with the SEALION now racing away from the beachhead.

This was utter insanity.

It wasn't that his team couldn't outwit an unsuspecting enemy force, particularly if they let the vast majority of them depart before striking. But there was a big difference between shooting people from concealed positions and trying to keep one of them alive without compromising themselves in the process, and that was before a three-fucking-mile walk out with a live captive in tow.

Adding to his concern at present was the fact that the burden of this prisoner snatch would fall largely on him.

With only five men to monitor the beach landing site, their options were to split up into a pair of surveillance positions consisting of two and three shooters each, respectively, or to maintain a trio of observation posts by leaving one man as a singleton element.

And by Worthy's lack of a job specialty such as medic or ground force commander, and the fact that he was, sniping aside, the best shooter on the team, Cancer had sent him off alone, mitigating the risk of solo operation somewhat by placing him on right-side security to the east, where the odds of enemy approach were at their slightest.

To be fair, no enemy had come from the east; instead they'd approached from the west, but that didn't stop them from dropping a team of shooters directly below him. Those men were the last to arrive, and if the professionalism of their insertion was in any way indicative of their extraction, they'd be the last to leave.

Which put Worthy squarely responsible for taking down one of those individuals alive.

As if reading his thoughts, Cancer said as much before Worthy could reply that this sudden alteration to an already failed plan was an extremely, extremely bad idea.

"*They're gonna exfil in reverse order, which means the right flank will be the last to load. Racegun, you pick your prisoner. We'll shoot the rest—I've got dibs on the driver.*"

"Cancer," Worthy transmitted at a whisper, "this is—"

But the acting team leader was on a roll, continuing as if Worthy hadn't spoken at all, "*Once they're all dead save one, I want all of us to descend to the road and use the vehicle as cover to approach the objective. Except you, Racegun, because you'll have to make your way downhill however you can without getting shot. And no one hit the engine block—I want to steal their SUV and ride that bitch through the hills as far as we can. Rain Man, you're driving. Questions?*"

"*Nope,*" Hass replied as if this were the most normal thing in the world. "*Love me some grand theft auto, and I'm ready to haul ass out of here.*"

Reilly added his contribution to the proceedings with equal levity, "*First truck is ten seconds out.*"

Cancer said, "*Racegun, you copy or what?*"

"I hear you," Worthy replied. "But this is a terrible plan, through and through."

"*Why?*"

By then Worthy could see the ambush line below rising to a knee, then to their feet, hastily assembling in files to board their trucks as quickly as possible. The Toyota Sequoia was the first to arrive from their staggered convoy, appearing to his left with its headlights off and screeching to a halt as the first group of shooters raced to load up.

Worthy was having trouble choosing his words. This felt like a slow-motion nightmare, where everyone on his team was committing to certain death and impervious to reason.

Where to begin, he thought, then replied, "First off, they're going to notice a missing truck."

"Eventually, sure. But they're driving blackout, so unless someone gets a radio call out—and they won't, if we're shooting well—we've probably got a few minutes before they realize the last truck isn't behind them. By then, we can be halfway back to our vehicles, and after that, they ain't catching up."

The Toyota wheeled a U-turn on the beach, clearing the way for the Jeep to arrive and come to a halt. As the next group boarded, the lead SUV was gone in a flash, accelerating at maximum speed back the way it had come, headed west along the coastal road in pursuit of the SEALION.

Keying his mic, Worthy said, "There's only one way this will work, and about a hundred ways it won't. Once we commit, there's no going back."

"*Same as everything else we've done on this team,*" Cancer challenged him. "*And don't overthink this—MACV-SOG used to snatch dudes all the time.*"

"This isn't the Ho Chi Minh Trail," Worthy pointed out, all too aware that the tactics of the elite unit in question—namely, clubbing the last man in an enemy formation before darting off into dense undergrowth with their newly claimed captive in tow—bore precious little similarities to the largely open terrain of the coastal hills in north Libya.

Cancer was unapologetic.

"*Well if you can't do it, you can't...just be prepared for me to give you shit about it for the rest of your natural life.*"

"That might not be too long if I try to pull this off."

Now the second truck was leaving the area, making way for the Nissan SUV to collect its load of shooters. A minute at most remained for him to either talk Cancer out of this act of lunacy or, by not challenging it further, give his consent via silence.

Before he could speak again, Ian transmitted for the first time, his opinion as the most risk-averse among them serving as the final notice that there was no backing out of this.

"*Racegun,*" he began, "*this is our first chance to get intel that leads us to Olivia. If we don't take it, we might not get another.*"

"Fuck it," Worthy transmitted back. "Let's go."

"*That's the spirit,*" Cancer said as the third truck sped off. The final vehicle was fast approaching as Worthy scanned the row of enemy fighters lined up to board it, four men in total, and selected his target.

"I'm taking the last man, that big fucker with the machinegun. You guys put down the rest and I'll take him alive—or try to, at least."

His main consideration was selecting a target with a belt-fed weapon that would be difficult if not impossible to operate when wounded. That wasn't exactly a guaranteed recipe for success, he knew, but would increase his chances of a live capture by a factor of ten.

But the fact remained that there was a better-than-passing chance that the enormous soldier lining up behind his teammates would nonetheless maintain sufficient composure to orient his weapon and put Worthy in the unenviable position of choosing between his own life and the overall mission, with Olivia's life hanging in the balance.

His last transmission occurred as the FJ Cruiser slowed along the path below.

"I want to hit them just as the truck stops."

"*Five,*" Cancer replied as Worthy took up a stable firing position. "*Four.*"

The rules of combat marksmanship were profoundly simple—you took the most lethal shot possible, then repeated the process until your opponent was, without doubt or question, dead. Whether that took two bullets or seven or twelve didn't particularly matter, even by his own high standards of accuracy. Worthy had fired all of the above against a single enemy depending on the degree of their cover and concealment. When there was any doubt, it was best to remove it to the fullest extent possible with overwhelming fire.

But nowhere, absolutely *nowhere*, was there any provision for the deliberate use of non-lethal shots in the real world. That shit played out just fine in buddy cop movies, but on an actual objective it was beyond inconceivable to give an enemy fighter any further opportunity to send bullets your way. There were no exceptions.

"*Three.*"

The truck's momentum dwindled to a near-stop as Cancer sped up his count. "*Two. One. Execute—*"

Worthy considered aiming for his target's legs, but the risk of severing a major artery was simply too great from pelvis to ankle. And none of this insane risk, he thought with gritted teeth, would do them much good if the target bled out within sixty seconds of being shot.

Instead, he activated his infrared laser and took aim at the man's boots before firing seven times.

His attention was momentarily distracted by the simultaneous appearance of four other lasers crisscrossing the impromptu objective area as he forced his focus onto the man he'd just shot, who was collapsing to the ground behind the others with hopefully nonlethal consequences.

The machinegun fell from his target's grasp as successive volleys of fire laced into the truck cab and the falling bodies of the other fighters. Worthy swept his laser to the downed machinegun and, adding another first-ever act in combat to his achievements that day, shot five rounds into it.

"*Assault, assault,*" Cancer called over the radio.

Worthy slithered out from beneath his camo netting, rising to survey the kill zone from a standing position to find that the only movement came from his original target, now rolling to his side with a pained groan that echoed all the way uphill.

Then he took off, threading his way toward the coastal road as fast as he could without tumbling downward, keeping his barrel at the low ready in preparation to take a lethal shot if necessary. His only sideward glance revealed his teammates doing the same, scrambling toward the road in preparation for a lateral approach that would keep the now-stationary truck between themselves and the hopefully dead enemy fighters. Then he resumed his focus to find that his target was now crawling toward his weapon, one foot leaving a dark trail of blood along the road.

Worthy took a momentary halt to drill another four rounds into the machinegun, seeing the sparks of metal-on-metal impact as the man continued to scramble for it—had he disabled the bolt, rendered it inoperable in any way? No way to tell, and with his view of the weapon obscured by the enemy's body, he resumed sprinting downhill.

He alighted on flat ground and raced forward, betraying every instinct to secure his flank as he ran to his sole target.

The machinegun had been knocked to its side, resting sideways with its front sight post in the sand and the bipod extended toward him. The enemy gunner was in the process of righting it, beginning his arcing sweep sideways in an attempt to engage, when Worthy closed the final distance and drove a hard kick into the weapon.

His toes stung with the impact but he'd succeeded in dislodging the heavy machinegun from the man's grasp. The barrel was flung sideways, away from him, and he instinctively drove the heel of his still-throbbing foot into his opponent's stomach as hard as he could without losing his balance.

A vacuous surge of air erupted from the man's mouth as all breath was knocked out of him in one fell swoop, and Worthy exploited the gap to roll him onto his stomach and plant a knee into the small of his back. Swinging his weapon back on its sling, he snatched a flex cuff from his kit and wrenched one arm, then the other, backward into its loop.

He'd barely finished restraining the man's wrists when a figure appeared beside him, grabbing the machinegun and chucking it sideways toward the waves.

"That wasn't so hard, was it?" Cancer rasped victoriously.

Worthy rose to a half-crouch and stumbled backward, the exertion of the past thirty seconds suddenly hitting him all at once. Cancer knelt over the captive, flex cuffing his ankles and, for seemingly no reason other than recreational purposes, belting a swift kick into his ribs.

Then Worthy registered that his teammates were beside him, not some but *all* of them, Hass included, some delivering headshots to the scattered enemy bodies and others pulling the dead driver from the FJ Cruiser before searching it.

Reilly darted to the enemy captive as Cancer said, "Get him in the back, you can treat him on the way."

Hass shouted, "These radios have geolocation."

"Get the frequencies and leave them," Cancer replied.

Worthy caught sight of Ian performing an action as surprising as it was illogical—he pulled a water bladder from his kit, unscrewed the top, and upended it to let the contents stream out as he raced to the shoreline.

Then the intelligence operative knelt, filling the bladder with seawater from the Mediterranean for reasons that Worthy couldn't begin to comprehend. But there was no time to question it now; they had an extremely swift three-mile journey to negotiate whether the enemy truck lasted the entire way or not, and if Ian wanted to ditch a significant portion of his available drinking water, then that was on him.

Worthy's heart was pounding hard, mind delirious with gratitude at the simple fact that he was alive, even as he tried to compose himself so he could assist the men around him. But he barely managed to rise to his feet and achieve some semblance of balance before Cancer announced, "Exfil, exfil, exfil."

Then Hass was scrambling into the driver's seat, and Reilly hoisted the prisoner onto his massive shoulders and raced toward the cargo area as Worthy jammed himself into the backseat.

Then they were off, Hass accelerating the FJ Cruiser in a wheeling turn onto the sand dunes and foothills of the rolling terrain leading south, toward their vehicles. Worthy had just enough time to look out his window at the enemy bodies lying on the beach before he collapsed back in his seat, heaving ragged breaths as he watched the coastal terrain passing in a blur outside.

18

"All right," Cancer said upon exiting his vehicle in the safehouse, "we got him here—now what?"

Ian needed precious little time to issue his response; he'd had ample opportunity to consider what needed to happen, though the gravity of his decision caused him to pause a split second before responding. The ground force commander held the ultimate say in the actions of his men, though in certain instances a subordinate team member made the key judgment calls—in a mass casualty situation, for example, Reilly would call the shots.

And in matters of interrogation, Ian would decide the team's fate for better or for worse.

He replied, "Get rid of his pants and tie him to a chair. Stage a gas can in the room and be ready to do everything I say during the interrogation without hesitation. Reilly needs to rip the contents of the cell phones we recovered and send them to Duchess for immediate analysis, and Hass can refit the vehicles—probably better that neither of them sees this. Everyone needs to stay kitted-up, and let's put David on standby."

"Standby for what?"

"Those guys were professionals," Ian said resolutely, "and they don't come cheap. One of the factions vying for power in Libya must have supplied that ambush force to Khalil, which means the fighter we snagged is positioned a lot higher up the food chain. If this interrogation goes how I think it's going to, we're about to have a TST."

His mention of a time-sensitive target was sufficient for Worthy to depart immediately, moving out behind Reilly as the medic moved the casualty to an isolated room to evaluate his medical dressings with ample interior lighting rather than in the back of a moving vehicle.

The need for security outweighed the possibility of questioning their detainee on the way back to the safehouse; but the overland movement in the captured enemy vehicle had passed without incident, and the team transitioned to their original vehicles before making an entirely uneventful return to Benghazi. Their captive, despite having sustained two gunshot wounds to his left foot—one passing clean through, the other shattering the first metatarsal and shearing a pair of tendons in the process—had faced the agony of Reilly packing the wounds with Kerlix and pressure wrapping his entire foot without the benefit of painkillers, all without uttering a single word.

And that silence, Ian felt certain, meant that there was no need to bother questioning him on the way; he wasn't going to talk at all, save some extraordinary measures that were best employed in the relative security of the safehouse.

Ian started to move out to their ad hoc interrogation facility—in reality, little more than a walk-in supply closet—when Cancer stopped him.

"What about Ramzi?"

Ian sighed impatiently. "Keep him out of the room. I don't want our prisoner seeing his face."

Cancer drew his Winkler knife with a speed and fluidity that told him the sniper was all too eager to put the blade to good use, then said, "I don't think he's gonna be talking once we're done with him."

Ian put a hand on his shoulder and gave him a light shake.

"We need this guy's intel, and we don't have time to conceal the source before reporting it to Duchess. She already knows we have a captive and can verify whether he's still alive by virtue of the SEAL reporting if and when they finally make it to Libya."

Cancer looked aghast at the words, eyes ticking back and forth as he sought some flaw in the logic and found none.

Then, sheathing his knife, he asked, "So what do we do?"

"Let me handle it."

Then, without waiting for a response, he set off through the doorway into the main section of the warehouse, past the rows of parked vehicles, including those that had just returned from the near-disastrous foray to the coast. Reilly stormed out of the side room with his aid bag without so much as a sideways glance toward Ian and Cancer—for all the man's compassion as a medic, or maybe because of it, he wasn't one for torture-based interrogations. Nor, for that matter, was Ian himself, though given the circumstances of Olivia's captivity, he was willing to do what was necessary without reservation.

Passing through the doorway, he saw Worthy standing beside a gas can, watching Ian's entrance with a look of grim determination. It almost seemed to Ian as if the pointman was seeking a means to prove himself after the debacle on the beach; not that he needed to, having been put in harm's way above and beyond the rest of them. But Ian would be lying to himself if he hadn't noticed the man's facade of almost robotic perfection in combat crumble somewhat after the harrowing prisoner snatch.

And then he turned his gaze to the spoil from that most recent foray, appraising the man with his arms and ankles flex cuffed to the chair.

Ian couldn't tell his nationality, and something about that bothered him to no end.

His skin was darker than purely Anglo origins would dictate, facial features more Mongolian than Middle Eastern. Beyond that his background was a mystery; he was well-muscled, probably six-foot-two, with bulging quadriceps partially wrapped by black Under Armour boxer briefs, his desert fatigue pants pulled down to his ankles, left foot wrapped in a pressure dressing that bulged atop a bundle of gauze. The sides of his head were shaved, the long dark hair on top pulled into a high ponytail.

Without speaking, Ian lowered his assault pack and retrieved the water bladder from it.

Then he nodded to the gas can and said, "Pour some on his thighs."

Worthy didn't hesitate long, just enough to scan Ian's face for any indication that this was a practical joke in progress. No one was going to set another human being on fire, least of all Ian, but Worthy quickly did as he was told.

The prisoner jolted at the wet slap of gasoline on his exposed skin; some of it splashed on his boxer briefs, which was no doubt a sobering experience. His eyes turned to Ian, now unscrewing the top off his water bladder as he spoke.

"Many of the Libyan refugees being pulled off boats require medical treatment for chemical burns. Can you guess why?"

The man glowered at him, though it wasn't yet clear to Ian if the English made any sense. That was just fine, as whatever language the man spoke, Ian was going to hear it being shouted at maximum volume in the coming seconds.

"A lot of those boats have gas cans leaking onto the floor. And when you're sitting shoulder to shoulder on the deck, that soaks into your skin. But the burns don't happen until a wave crashes over the deck."

He held up the bladder in his hand. "Seawater contains sodium chloride—that's salt—which reacts to gasoline. Refugees have leapt into the ocean and drowned rather than endure that kind of pain. It's an excruciating process, and if you don't start talking right now, you're going to find out firsthand. This is your last chance."

The man merely stared at Ian contemptuously, as if no amount of pain would get him to talk. Whatever awaited him if he was exposed as a traitor to his own people was a sufficiently dire alternative to make him willing to endure the searing horror of a chemical burn. Ian took no pleasure in inflicting human suffering, no matter the justification; but with Olivia at large and this man serving as a possible link to finding her, then torture was by far the lesser of two evils.

He dumped a stream of salt water onto the man's thighs, stopping only when the screaming began.

But that didn't take long—one, maybe two seconds—before the captive was writhing in agony, shrieking at the top of his lungs in words so incoherent that Ian couldn't determine the language. Grotesque red splotches appeared on his legs, their outlines following the splash patterns of where the two fluids intersected like a horrific piece of modern art, and Ian was shocked to see that the blistering started almost immediately.

"Now get his balls," Ian said.

The sentence had barely left Ian's mouth before Worthy dumped a stinking portion of gasoline onto the man's crotch, and this time Ian didn't bother talking. He simply held the water bladder directly over it and tilted it ever closer to the tipping point.

"*Hvatit!*" the man screamed.

Ian halted his effort abruptly, keeping the bladder poised as he responded, "*Ti gavarish pa russki. A po angliyski ti toje qavarish, druq?*"

"Yes," the man replied in a heavy Russian accent, now looking down in shame. "I speak English."

In the brief silence that followed, Cancer muttered three words so quietly that it was unclear if he even knew he was speaking aloud.

"Christ—he's Wagner."

Ian cut his gaze to Cancer to silence him, and was surprised to see that the restrained man did the same with a look of thinly veiled anger.

"Is this true?" Ian asked.

The man didn't respond at once, instead looking from Worthy, to Cancer, to Ian with a trembling breath that ended in his jaw clenching shut. A slight angling of the bladder caused him to reverse course in remarkably quick fashion.

"*Gruppa Vagnera*," he said. "*Da*. Wagner Group."

"Unit?" Ian asked.

"*Rusich*."

Ian lowered the water bladder to his side, deliberately keeping it in hand as a reminder of the pain he could inflict at the slightest provocation.

But his mind was reeling.

While ostensibly a private military company headquartered in Saint Petersburg, the Wagner Group's cover story was quite possibly the mercenary world's worst-kept secret. In reality they were primarily former Russian servicemembers who'd volunteered for far better pay as a member of Vladimir Putin's private army, a brutal and ruthless force whose primary calling card was plausible deniability.

But that was far from their only specialty: from the Crimean Peninsula to the Donbas, Syria to Venezuela, and in a long list of African countries like Sudan, Mali, the Central African Republic, to say nothing of Libya,

Wagner operatives had made a name for themselves with systematic war crimes to include rape, mutilation, and summary executions of civilians and journalists alike. Wherever the Kremlin needed a heavy hand without a concrete trail leading back to their psychopathic and Machiavellian president, it would send the Wagner Group—no politically unstable country in which Russia wanted to expand its influence was too dangerous, too war-torn for these men.

And they were fiercely loyal to their motherland; whoever provided their services to Khalil must have paid incredibly well for the privilege.

Cancer leaned in and asked, "*Rusich*?"

Ian watched his captive and said in a flat tone, "Reconnaissance, sabotage, false-flag operations, assassination. Yes or no?"

"No," the man said, "to assassination. The rest, yes. These are our missions."

"Good," Ian said, letting the man know with his eyes that he'd deliberately inserted a falsity into his statement to see if the prisoner corrected him.

What he didn't say was that he could have gone on at length about the unit in question. Task Force Rusich, as they were often known, had a hard-earned reputation for being ultranationalist neo-Nazis who were particularly fond of collecting war trophies in the form of severed ears before lighting human remains on fire. The unit's insignia was the valknut, an ancient Germanic symbol of three linked triangles that had long since been appropriated by the white supremacy movement. A full strip search of this man, Ian knew, would likely reveal one or more swastika tattoos.

Ian forced himself to suppress the emotions that sprang into being with this recognition, focusing instead on the task at hand. Now began a very delicate balance—he had to tease information out of the man in increments, assessing its validity before moving on to the pertinent topics. To rush through risked a lie that would send them on a wild goose chase at best or at worst, into a trap.

"What's your name?"

"Arseni."

"Why were you sent on the ambush tonight?"

He hesitated, then offered, "To kill the men arriving by boat."

"Who were those men?"

Arseni gave a sharp, almost delirious laugh.

"Who? *Who?* Libyans, Americans, Zionists, I do not know and I do not care. They say to kill, and we go to kill."

"How did you know where they'd be landing?"

"What is there to know? They sent us to the coast hours before. Go to this grid, then that grid, until they gave the final one and told us we must hurry."

"Who is 'they?'" Ian asked.

"I could not know. None of us could. Only our commander spoke with them."

"Were the orders from Russia?"

"No," Arseni replied adamantly. "It was a *padrabotka*, a side job. We were never to speak of it after this rotation."

"Why did your commander agree to it?"

"They knew what Wagner was paying us for the deployment. They gave us triple that to do what they said."

Ian gave a slight nod of understanding. It was a brilliant move, if true—rather than outsource this vital task of ambushing American servicemembers to an undisciplined Benghazi militia, or infiltrating a skilled force from parts unknown with all the elevated signature that could be traceable in the aftermath, Khalil's people had simply found the most ruthless men in Libya and paid them handsomely to conduct the ambush along with God only knew what else.

Ian went on, "Arseni, one of two things will happen right now. You're going to tell me where, or how, I can most quickly find the men who gave these orders. If that happens, we will give you food, water, and medical care until we leave Libya, at which time you will be released. Or you tell me nothing useful, or worse yet *lie to me*"—he raised his voice on the last three words—"and I'm going to douse you in gasoline from your head all the way to the bullet wounds in your feet, start pouring saltwater after that, and keep you alive until I get bored. Then, the real pain will begin."

Arseni watched Ian levelly, eyes narrowed, as if trying to determine how credible this threat was. Then, before Ian could get a read on his judgment one way or the other, he spoke.

"A man delivered the first payment. My commander ordered the *nablyudeniye* so that we might find him if he failed to pay us after the job. You understand?"

"*Da*. You performed surveillance once he left."

The Russian winced in professional embarrassment.

"We tried. Me and several others. He lost us in the streets after changing cars several times, but not before making one stop and delivering two suitcases. I do not know what was in them."

Cash, Ian thought, plain and simple. Arseni was clearly describing a money man if not an outright facilitator, and the Wagner Group mercenaries weren't the only effort supporting Khalil.

"Where did he make the delivery?"

"An office building on Munequir Street," Arseni said, "southwest Benghazi."

19

The chat window on the laptop screen flashed with an update, and I leaned in to read it with a profound sigh of relief.

0247L: GFC reports en route to safehouse time now, 100% MWE, 4x EKIA, 1x EPW.

My relief was, however, interspersed with a healthy dose of confusion.

MWE stood for men, weapons, and equipment, with a hundred percent status indicating no injuries or loss of gear. Simple enough. So too was the count of enemies killed in action—the team must have been compromised, I thought.

But EPW meant enemy prisoner of war, and I could envision no circumstance where hastily breaking contact from a significant enemy force resulted in capturing one of the pursuers alive. That seemed to indicate a deliberate snatch, which was suicidal given the difference in numbers. Had Cancer ordered it? Would I have had the balls to do so, in his position?

I was standing over the bedroom desk in my hotel suite, where Corey and Sam had arranged their laptops in a semicircle and remained seated almost continually since their arrival.

Sam looked over his shoulder and asked, “How’d they manage an EPW?”

“Your guess is as good as mine,” I said. “I’ll find out when they call.”

It was beyond frustrating to not have a simple satellite radio link to my team; until they called me via the encrypted cellular network, I was reduced to getting their operational updates secondhand via a secure chat interface on the laptop.

To be fair, my access was restricted to the equipment Sam and Corey had carried into my room, which was limited by what they could erase in ten seconds flat if we were compromised. On a typical mission, my team carried military radios that could be “zeroed out”—completely wiped of data—via a series of button inputs. If one of us was about to get overrun, destroying all links to any remaining team members as well as our higher headquarters was of paramount importance.

So it was no surprise to me that one of the first orders of business was for Corey and Sam to explain the procedure to systematically zero out the laptops now arrayed before us, one of which displayed the Palace Hotel’s internal and external surveillance camera feeds. It was a chilling reminder that we were essentially operating beneath Khalil’s nose in an already hostile city in an even worse country, and after getting a glimpse of the Agency’s sweeping efforts surrounding this mission, I had no doubt that the three of us were only a very small cog in a considerable national response.

By now the Agency had tapped into every possible radio frequency as well as the overall cellular network in Benghazi and the surrounding area, searching for any abnormalities that would help guide the search. In that regard, Sam and Corey served as little more than technical support to maintain my link with Khalil while allowing me to communicate directly and securely with Duchess on the back end.

Sweeping a hand over the laptops, I asked, “You guys think any of this is going to work?”

“Absolutely,” Sam said, the confidence in his voice absolute. “Remember when the Red Brigades Marxist group kidnapped Brigadier General Dozier in Italy?”

"No."

"Well," he continued, "after some serious signals intelligence work—kind of like what we've been looking at here—a handful of Intelligence Support Activity guys were able to pinpoint the hostage location by finding abnormalities in the power grid. Narrowed it down to a single apartment that started using a lot more electricity since the day of the kidnapping, indicative of nonstop guard rotations."

Without looking up from his screen, Corey added, "And that was in the early '80s. Now we've got SIGINT drones collecting around the clock, spy satellites, cyber threat intelligence...with a senator's daughter at large, everyone and their brother is on the hunt."

I frowned. "Then why haven't they found anything yet?"

Sam turned to face me. "Because Khalil is disciplined. But eventually, everyone trips up, or leaves a pattern that's vulnerable to detection from some classified technology. The only question is, will that happen in time to save Olivia?"

My Agency cell phone buzzed in my pocket, and I answered it to hear a Southern drawl greeting me from the other end of the line.

"Hey boss, got a minute?"

It was a typical Worthy understatement, and I hastily replied, "For you, I've got all the time in the world. How'd you guys get a prisoner?"

"Cancer ordered a snatch," Worthy said, "which was exactly as terrifying as it sounds. We just made it back to the warehouse, and Ian's about to question him."

After Cairo, I'd increasingly been met with the feeling that we were playing into Khalil's hands with each unexpected turn of events. But a living captive could change all that—or affect nothing whatsoever, depending on what he knew. Now that we were about to find out one way or another, all I could manage were the words, "What do you need from me?"

"Can you break away from the hotel?"

"Yes. Why, what's up?"

"Ian wants you on standby. Said he expects a TST, and if it's close enough for us to action, we could really use a sixth shooter."

The request incited a momentary crisis of confidence in my ability to serve on an assault—Khalil hadn't called me back yet, but that could change at any moment. When he ordered me to link up I had damned well better be ready; not to mention a time-sensitive target would occur at an unknown location and I'd have to factor in transit time back to the hotel.

But if my team was headed into harm's way without any support from SEAL Team Six, then my presence alongside them could be the make-or-break point for mission success.

"I'll make my way outside," I said. "Call me back when you have more."

"Will do, boss. Now if you'll excuse me, I have to strip this dude's pants and bring in a gas can."

"A—gas can?" I asked, uncertain if he was joking. Ian wasn't about to set anyone on fire, I knew from long experience in working with him, and yet he wasn't in the habit of threatening anything he wasn't willing and able to carry out.

No response from Worthy; the line was dead, and Sam and Corey watched me hang up.

I blurted, "I need to get out of here right now."

"How long will you be gone?" Sam asked.

"Don't know yet. But they're expecting a TST, and I need to stand by for linkup."

Corey pulled Khalil's phone from the charger and handed it to me.

"Keep this with you. We're spoofing the GPS signal to show it's stationary here at the hotel and playing a continuous audio 'pattern of life' for the bug he installed. If Khalil calls, let it ring a couple times so we can cut out any shower or television noise we've got running. The audio will cut to your live feed as soon as you answer the phone, so it's imperative you don't have any background noise."

"Got it," I said. "How are the camera feeds looking?"

Sam was already analyzing the surveillance screen. "You're clear to move now, we're not expecting any staff for another twenty minutes. We'll talk you out over your issue phone."

The device buzzed in my pocket, and I pulled it out to see a Tacoma, Washington, number.

Answering the call, I said, "Good volume?"

"Yeah," Corey replied, his voice audible both in the room and over the phone. "I'll stay on the line and provide any updates until you make it out."

I gave myself a quick pat-down to confirm I had my wallet, then ordered, "Start freezing camera feeds. I'm out of here."

I exited the suite into an empty hallway, taking a right turn and bypassing the elevator for the stairs.

Then I descended to the first floor, hearing Corey's voice as I went.

"Exit the stairwell, take a right toward the fire exit. Door will be to your left, and you'll be in a camera blind spot so tell me when you get there."

I did as he said, striding onto the first floor and glancing to one side to see a hallway leading past restrooms and into the lobby. Turning away from it, I followed a short service corridor ending in a fire exit, stopping at a door marked *STAFF ONLY* in English and Arabic.

"I'm here," I said quietly, reaching for the keypad as Corey recited over the phone, "Three, four, nine, two."

After I punched in the numbers, the light atop the keypad flicked from red to yellow.

Twisting the handle, I entered a service area that extended forty feet to my exit. I was now in full view of an overhead surveillance camera, a fact Corey acknowledged as he said, "I've got you. You're clear."

A fleet of housekeeping carts lined one wall, while the other was filled with shelves holding cardboard boxes stacked to the brim with toiletries for the guests. I was moving quickly now, past a laundry chute and service elevator, eager to get the hell outside before there were any unexpected arrivals from the hotel staff.

Too late, I realized when Corey spoke again.

"Shit. Hide, now—you've got an employee moving to enter from outside."

The only problem was that there was nowhere *to* hide; the only other door led into a break room with a fridge and pantry, not to mention the cabinets for employees to store their personal supplies, and the goddamned service elevators were keyed for access.

I considered crawling behind a housekeeping cart, but there were far too many and they were lined up too neatly for me to disturb them unnoticed; barring that, I searched for a pile of soiled linens that I could conveniently dive into, which was no use either—they'd all been thrust into the chute to my left.

Which was, I saw with pained recognition, the only place I could conceal myself in the coming seconds.

I wrenched open the waist-height metal door and glanced inside to see a round tube extending vertically in either direction. Devoid of options, I pocketed my phone and struggled to lift one leg through the hatch, then the other, awkwardly slipping into the shaft and bracing my boots on the side with my back against the far wall as I wedged myself into a semi-stable position. Reaching forward, I delicately closed the door by pulling at its edge, all too keenly aware that there was no interior handle—apparently the engineers behind this contraption hadn't conceived of such a situation when designing it—and tried to get it as flush as I could without causing it to fully latch.

Trying to quiet my breathing within the echoing confines of the tube, I heard the exterior door swing open on metal hinges, then slam shut before a set of footfalls approached. Only at that point did I consider the somewhat terrifying possibility that whoever had entered could just as easily notice the laundry hatch door partially ajar and slam it shut, locking me inside; or, perhaps worse, they could open it and notice the extremely uncomfortable white man wedged inside.

Looking down, I saw a twenty foot void below. If I lost my precarious foot and handholds, I'd rocket down to the basement outlet like I was shooting out of a water slide. And if I somehow managed to escape that without injury, I'd still be landing under the watchful eye of the staff who occupied it almost 24/7. Not a good look for my first attempt to leave the hotel unseen, I thought.

It took considerable effort to track the sound of the footsteps as I tried to gauge the entrant's location in the room. I was wondering how the hell I was going to pluck the cell phone from my pocket when I heard an entirely new rustling noise, not from beyond the hatch but directly overhead.

I looked up just in time to see a billowing mass of white descending toward me. I braced as hard as I could before a mangled pile of sheets and towels fell on my head, fearful they would dislodge my tenuous hold. But they engulfed my head and shoulders instead, a moist washcloth on the back of my neck and a bedsheet across my face. I smelled body odor and the vague presence of semen, and had to fight the almost overwhelming instinct to pull the entire disgusting mass away for fear that whoever was outside would detect my presence.

To make matters worse, my ears were covered by linens, so I could no longer hear the individual in the room beyond, if they were still there at all.

Frustrated and incredibly pissed off, I gingerly pulled one hand away from the chute door and painstakingly felt for my pocket, probing for my phone and trying to slide it out without losing my grip.

Gradually I managed to bring it to my ear, huffing a breath as I heard Corey speaking.

"...you there?"

"Say again," I whispered.

"You're clear. Someone showed up to work early, but they took the service elevator down to the basement. Better get out while you still can."

"You think?" I said testily, giving the hatch a shove that forced it outward. Then I dropped my phone into the room beyond and disentangled myself from the giant wad of shit that had come close to literally and figuratively flushing me down the tube.

Then I began the process of pulling myself through the square porthole, an act that I performed with all the grace and elegance of a monkey trying to fuck a football. If strolling into a luxury hotel suite the previous morning had been the one and only James Bond moment in the course of my Agency career, then clambering through a tangle of dirty sheets and out of a laundry chute surely erased any cool-guy points I'd earned in the process.

Setting foot in the service area and closing the hatch behind me, I picked up the phone and brought it to my ear to the sound of Corey's laughter. Whirling around, I flipped off the security camera and muttered, "You better not have recorded this shit."

Then I darted for the final door, reaching it as Corey suppressed his chuckle and said, "I didn't see a thing. Take a right once you get outside."

He had just enough time to say it before I reached the exit, cranking the handle and shoving open the heavy door to step out into the early morning sunlight.

I moved quickly between the hotel and the solid compound fence, walking along a threadbare trail stamped into the dirt between yellow patches of grass—no customer-facing walkway, this—and reached an iron gate whose lock disengaged when I grasped the handle.

Beyond it was an alley between the backsides of other retail buildings on the block, and I quickly threaded my way between piles of trash and a few sleeping dogs that lined the path who barely looked up as I passed.

Corey continued, "You're headed east, and by the time you reach the end of the block you'll be well clear of Khalil's people. Cross the next street and you'll be in the retail district. We're about to lose visibility on you through the security cameras, so hit us up when you're ready to make your way back."

"No worries," I said, stepping around a fallen shopping cart now overgrown with weeds. "I'll take it from here, and—"

That was as far as I got before the line chirped with an incoming call.

"Hang on."

The voice I heard next once again belonged to Worthy; this time, however, he sounded like he was running.

"We got our TST," he began, "moving on it now. Are you standing by?"

~

Cancer braced himself in the passenger seat of the Kia Optima as Reilly swerved right through an intersection, then consulted his Android device and called out, "Take the next left. Six blocks to Third Ring Road."

"Got it," Reilly confirmed, straightening the car on its new vector and threading his way between relatively sparse early morning traffic. The medic's offensive driving was on point, Cancer thought, though he wondered if it would be enough to compensate for a deliberate detour on the way to their target.

The question of whether or not to add three minutes to their route in order to retrieve David hung heavily on his mind as he navigated with the phone. After all, any delay could be the difference between recovering intelligence that would tip the scales in their favor and failing to stop the most horrific spectacle that Khalil could devise in executing Olivia.

Then again, he had no earthly idea how many bad guys were on the objective. There were no blueprints, no reconnaissance ahead of the assault, and no option but to hit it immediately. Under those circumstances, having a sixth gun in the fight could mean nothing or everything. No right answer, Cancer realized, and no wrong one. Simply two bad options, both of which could be equally damning.

"Right turn onto Third Ring Road ahead," he said, then keyed his radio and transmitted, "We're diverting to pick up Suicide. Racegun, tell him he's got exactly one second to get in your car or we're leaving him behind."

"Copy," Worthy replied from the trail vehicle. Cancer turned in his seat to look out the rear window, seeing Ian at the wheel, struggling to keep up, then his view was blocked by a tablet screen being thrust into his face by Hass in the backseat.

"Reaper's in business," the Combat Controller said victoriously. "Looks like we've got one entrance on the west side and another on the south. Long-range communication equipment on the roof."

Cancer analyzed the rotating overhead view of a nondescript building, ignoring the roof hardware. He next had to decide whether to send everyone through a single entrance or divide his forces between both. With the need to interdict as much intelligence as possible—that was, if everyone hadn't already flushed off the objective in the wake of four dead Russians and one missing—going in both doors was worth the risk.

He turned to face forward in his seat and transmitted, "Split Team One: lead vehicle with me, Doc, and Rain Man. South side door. Split Team Two: rear vehicle with Angel, Racegun, Suicide. West side door. Clockwise direction of clearance."

Then he checked his phone screen and instructed Reilly, "Take a right at the next intersection and follow the street north for three blocks. He should be standing on the corner. Blow straight past to a left turn on Second Ring Road; Ian will have to catch up."

Reilly had barely finished confirming the instructions when Hass spoke urgently.

"Three squirters leaving through the south door, carrying packages—make that four, moving to separate cars." He laid the display on the center console and asked, "You want Reaper to follow the runners or stay on the building?"

"Keep their eyes on the building."

What he didn't say was that if Khalil's men had successfully lost aerial surveillance while transporting David, then those runners surely had the wherewithal to split up. Even if they didn't, and consolidated on some other objective, what good did tracking them do when there was no one available to hit it? Cancer's team was the only show in town, and the certainty of one known target in the coming minutes easily bested the vague possibility of a future one.

As Hass relayed the guidance to the UAV sensor operator, Cancer updated his team.

"Four squirters egressing south with equipment, heading to vehicles."

Worthy replied almost immediately, "*Sounds like the Russian commander finally reported his loss.*"

Very possible, Cancer thought—if he were in the Wagner man's position, he'd certainly exhaust all options in recovering his lost soldier before admitting to such a humiliating defeat. And if he'd sent the news immediately, why were people still evacuating the objective? It could just as easily have been cleared already.

He transmitted, "We're staying focused on the building. Assume additional squirters. Priority is capturing anyone alive, but if they're going to escape, then gun them down. This is a 'hot' objective..."

Cancer's words trailed off as he stared out the passenger window at a man looking back at him from the street corner—David Rivers, unshaven and in civilian clothes, looking like he hadn't slept in a week—before Reilly sped the car past him on their way to the target building.

~

I ran to the Toyota Camry screeching to a halt before me, wrenching open the back door before leaping into the seat. Worthy had passed along Cancer's warning that I had one second to enter the vehicle or be abandoned, and I had no intentions of missing out today.

Ian floored the accelerator before I had a chance to close the door, and by the time I did, Worthy was turning to face me from the passenger seat, grinning. "Welcome back, boss. Brought you a little something as a homecoming present."

I looked to my left, seeing a tactical Christmas: my HK416 rifle angled barrel-down with its suppressor against the floorboard, upper receiver festooned in my preferred configuration of visible and infrared laser, taclight, pressure switches, and EOTECH optic. On the seat behind it was my armored plate carrier with its mag pouches, medical kit, radios, flex cuffs, even my night vision neatly stowed.

Seizing the vest, I eagerly donned it and secured the elastic straps by way of Velcro panels, then turned on my radios before calling forward to Ian, "Where's this little hunting trip headed to?"

"A command and control node," Ian replied without taking his eyes from the road. He whipped us through an intersection in pursuit of Cancer's vehicle before continuing uneasily, "At least, I think so. Some Libyan faction or another making a power play, possibly ahead of a coup to exploit the delayed elections. The men we encountered were Wagner Group being paid triple, so if I had to guess, we're looking at someone draining the national treasury to install themselves as the next president."

That much made sense, I thought. Whichever group was trying to take over control of Libya—and there was no shortage of likely candidates—must have granted Khalil safe haven and the means to raise his profile, all in exchange for a significant portion of the ransom.

But did Khalil plan on keeping Olivia alive in the first place?

Worthy added, "Target building has squirters bailing with equipment right now, so I'd say Ian's right about it being a C2 node. We're Split Team Two, going in the west side entrance. Split Team One is hitting the south door."

I inserted my radio earpieces and asked, "Clockwise?"

"Yeah."

Keying my team radio, I transmitted, "Suicide up on the net. Cancer retains tactical command and responsibility for all comms with HQ, I'll be 2IC and take over if he goes down."

"*Copy*," Cancer replied, his only acknowledgement that I'd joined the mission, and frankly, I didn't blame him. That poor bastard had enough to worry about in juggling all the particulars of being in charge, I knew from long experience, which was why I relegated myself to second-in-command without asking for input from him or anyone else. As far as this target was concerned I was a total outsider, and trying to assume control over a rapidly unfolding situation I knew nothing about would have been a shameless ego ploy to the detriment of the overall mission.

Then Worthy continued, "Since we're looking at C2, priority is getting one or more detainees. That Russian we snatched sang like a bird, and the goal is to run the same play higher up the food chain."

"Cool," I said, grabbing my rifle and confirming it had both a full magazine and a round in the chamber. Then I switched on the optic and adjusted my reticle brightness for a daytime assault before leaning back in my seat.

"God, it's good to be back."

Then I reached into a pouch on my kit to procure my tactical gloves, pulling them over my hands before quickly doing an inventory of my kit to ensure everything was where I left it—and in the process, stopped abruptly and said, "What the fuck is this?"

"I told you," Worthy said, "your homecoming present."

I drew the knife from its sheath, assessing the thin blade with a long false edge as Worthy continued, "Cancer had them made up for us. Project Longwing special."

After testing the balance and grip, I nodded with approval.

"I'm in love."

Ian replied, "Don't mention it to our new Combat Controller. He's devastated that he didn't get one."

"Yeah?" I said. "If he keeps us alive, we'll have to change that once we get back."

At that moment I was blasted by a sense of utter relief that I was with my team once more, a simple fact that imbued me with a sense of invulnerability. It wasn't that we couldn't be killed; I could simply accept any fate so long as it occurred beside my brothers. Dying alone while operating as a singleton element in the streets of Benghazi would have been meaningless, but if I fell while fighting shoulder to shoulder, it would not have been in vain.

A sense of calm descended over me then, the Zenlike sensation evaporating when the phone in my left pocket vibrated to life.

I withdrew it, staring at the screen in muted alarm.

"Everyone stay quiet," I said, pulling out an earpiece. "Khalil's people are calling."

Then, recalling Corey's admonition to let the phone ring a few times to allow them to transition the audio effects of their digital hijacking, I waited another two seconds before answering.

"Yeah?"

A new voice spoke, not Khalil or the man I'd reported to upon making it to my hotel.

This was a young man, possibly a teenager, who said in accented English, "You will be waiting outside the hotel in thirty minutes. He wants to see you."

"Got it," I said, ending the call before any road noise could betray the fact that I wasn't sitting in my suite but speeding through Benghazi.

Then I started a timer on my watch and transmitted, "Khalil's picking me up in half an hour."

Cancer responded, "*Jesus, we're still five or six minutes out. Strip your kit and we'll let you out; you can take a cab back.*"

Checking my watch, I quickly replied, "Negative, I can swing ten minutes on the objective and still make it back in time."

"*Your funeral,*" Cancer said. "*Let's do this.*"

20

Reilly sprinted toward the target building's southern entrance, both pleased and dismayed to see that an explosive breach wouldn't be necessary—the door ahead was cracked almost halfway open. Had someone left it ajar in their haste to leave the objective, or was there a boobytrap waiting to be triggered? As the first man to enter, it was up to him to find out one way or the other.

He didn't slow his pace until he was ten feet out, and even then only to allow Hass and Cancer to close the distance behind him. It was impossible to judge their proximity by sound; between the ambient traffic noise and a passenger jet roaring overhead, he'd have to trust them and hope for the best.

Kicking the door fully open, Reilly entered the building.

He cut left to begin his split team's clockwise rotation, barely having time to pivot on his heels before being struck head-on by a man running toward him at full speed. Being of superior size, Reilly remained upright as his opponent staggered backward in what would be his only momentary chance to seize the initiative one way or the other.

This was, he knew instinctively, a situation where split-second necessity dictated response.

By team protocol as well as common sense, physical contact was as good as getting shot at in determining hostile intent; after all, he was adorned in enough ammunition and explosives to stay alive for a time even if separated from his teammates, and a desperate enemy could steal a grenade or Reilly's knife and use it against him just as quickly as he could do the opposite. Any hesitation could be fatal, and while Reilly would unquestioningly give some benefit of the doubt if racing through a crowd of fleeing civilians, this was a "hot" objective with an all but confirmed enemy force. Added to that was the fact that he was the first man through the door, and if he went down, it would expose Hass and Cancer to gunfire or worse.

Reilly didn't even waste time looking at the man's hands for a weapon, only registering by the sight of his alarmed expression that he wasn't Libyan before shoving him back with his rifle far enough to bring the muzzle upward and firing three 7.62mm rounds into his chest.

The man dropped to the ground and Reilly flowed past him along the wall, registering for the first time that he was in an honest-to-God break room. He noted a plastic table ringed by foldout chairs to his right as he advanced past a refrigerator and microwave, seeking further targets but finding none on his way to the first corner before swinging right toward the second and stopping short before an open doorway.

He'd barely slowed to a full halt when a second man plunged through the door ahead; this time, however, there was no need to second-guess his intent. Both of them pointed rifles at each other, and both began firing immediately, Reilly's only tenable advantage the fact that he was stationary while his opponent was moving. He felt the punch of bullets impacting his chest before the man vanished in a blur of movement leading deeper into the room.

Reilly tried to swing his barrel right in order to down him before he could threaten Cancer or Hass, but his effort was impeded by the fact that he was falling backward from the impact of getting shot. His only conscious act consisted of withdrawing his index finger from the trigger guard of his HK417 before he involuntarily sprayed automatic fire in a ricocheting volley.

Then he landed on his ass, frantically taking aim to see that his attempt to shoot the enemy fighter had succeeded.

The forty-something bearded man in street clothes was already toppling sideways with the bloody pockmarks of bullet holes in his chest, losing control of his rifle before additional rounds ripped into his torso and face. Reilly could only assume his teammates were finishing the job as he swung his rifle left, back to the doorway to his front, in the most stable shooting position he could manage from his sudden seated position.

There was a thud against his back, the first assurance that at least one of his teammates had entered behind him, and then he felt a hand tugging him upward by the drag handle on the back of his plate carrier.

"Come up," Cancer said.

Reilly scrambled to his feet, a hasty glance assuring him that the enemy gunfire had been stopped by his armored plate. How many missions had he been in gunfights without body armor due to the long-range foot patrols required to swiftly reach an objective in the jungle or mountains? He didn't know and tried to brush the thought aside with his gaze focused on the open doorway ahead, barely gaining his footing before Cancer squeezed his shoulder in the signal to proceed with the clearance.

He did so at once, having only a split second to determine which way to move once he cleared the threshold.

A wall extended to his front on the other side; he knew he should buttonhook left, both by virtue of a clockwise clearance and in assuming the more difficult pivot as the lead man. But under the circumstances he didn't trust himself to execute the maneuver in time to engage a threat in the blind spot, and chose instead to cede the effort to Cancer, exposing his backside as he instead proceeded forward along the wall. A set of double doors was propped open before him, and he stopped there before converging his sector of fire with that of Cancer, who was already at his point of domination at the first corner. Seeing that the room was free of targets, filled only with shelves holding boxes of printer paper and office supplies, Reilly swept his barrel back to the double doors and took a half-step left to peer into the room beyond.

He was looking into a large, carpeted space, the far wall bearing another doorway. Reilly almost immediately saw movement through it, taking aim and then lowering his barrel in the same second as the man he saw was performing the same action toward him as if in a mirror—it was Worthy, the lead man for Split Team Two.

Reilly called out "friendlies" for the benefit of Cancer and Hass; the first unsuppressed gunfire had already rung out, negating any particular need for further stealth.

But his announcement was dwarfed by a raging cacophony of gunfire that erupted in the room to his right. There was a dull expectation that Worthy would be vaporized before him, but instead bullets and tracer rounds laced into the wall beside him before he ducked out of sight. With a machinegun in play and half the assault force bogged down practically before the raid had begun, Reilly glanced left to find Cancer sidestepping along the far wall, incrementally clearing the space beyond the double doors in an effort to find the source of the gunfire. He came to a stop without firing as David transmitted.

"*We're pinned in the first room*," he began, "*can't get an angle on the stairway*."

What stairway the team leader was referring to, Reilly had no idea. Apparently Cancer had seen it from his vantage point on the opposite side of the room, though, because he took off the way they'd come, moving at a jog.

"*Sit tight, we're moving counterclockwise to engage*."

By then Reilly was running just to catch up with Hass, now the center man in the stack, as they followed Cancer back into the first room of their clearance.

No sooner had Hass cleared the doorway than he called three words over his shoulder to Reilly.

"Don't sweat it."

Reilly was confused, still reeling from having been shot, but he chalked up the Combat Controller's announcement to lack of experience in urban combat. Hass was without a doubt a god among men when it came to employing air assets in support of ground units up to and including danger close range, when the slightest error in radio communications could annihilate himself and everyone around him.

But in close quarters battle, brevity in spoken communications was paramount; barring some urgent need to relay a situational change or order movement in one- or two-word statements, speaking was more or less unnecessary until the target was secured. That was never more true than in a daylight clearance with full visibility.

It wasn't until Reilly had swept past the dead fighter with his abandoned rifle, following the two men on a reverse course to provide fire for David's split team, that he saw what Hass was talking about.

Just inside the southern door was the man Reilly had collided with upon entry; he was young, twenty at best, with the scrawny arms and undeveloped physique of a professional video gamer. His eyes were locked open, mouth agape and emitting a crackling gargle that Reilly recognized as a death rattle even between the bursts of gunfire directed at the other split team. A bloody pool expanded beneath the man, spreading to eclipse his outstretched arms.

Both hands were empty; there was no weapon in sight, no duffel bag brimming with terrorist planning materials lying beside him.

What he was doing here was a mystery, but Reilly knew at a glance that he was looking at some poor kid who didn't belong here. Whoever he was, he was fleeing the building in a desperate bid to save his life, and Reilly had killed him for it.

~

Worthy crouched lower into his kneeling position, maintaining little more than a reflexive aim into a narrow slice of the room beyond as bursts of machinegun fire continued to lace into the floor and wall.

Aside from the tactical particulars, Worthy's only conscious thought was *what in the hell is this place?*

Judging by size, the massive room before him comprised a majority of the ground floor. The space was clearly intended as an office: patterned carpet was illuminated by neat rows of fluorescent lighting, and the bare walls were more or less what he expected for a workplace of corporate drones.

There was also an impressive collection of desks and rolling chairs, but these were pushed to the walls, haphazardly stacked atop one another to make room for rows of sleeping cots that dominated the floor, topped with civilian sleeping bags and pillows. Combined with the variety of backpacks and carry-on bags beneath the cots, the lack of uniformity assured him that he was looking at a civilian living space. No current or former members of any military, however undisciplined, would leave their quarters in such disarray—the most suspicious thing about it, he reasoned, was that it existed within an ostensibly ordinary office building in southwest Benghazi, his only indication that this was more than just a safehouse.

That, and the fact that men were fighting to the death to defend it.

Another volley of machinegun fire raked the wall to his left, its source coming from the long stairwell at the far corner—these fuckers had the main entrance to the room dialed in and had begun firing moments after his split team entered the building. Whether or not they knew that a second element was maneuvering toward them remained to be seen, but with Cancer leading it, Worthy felt confident that the gunner was about to meet his fate in a particularly grisly fashion.

Cancer transmitted, "*In position, shift fire left.*"

Under any other circumstances, Worthy would have laughed.

Instead he keyed his mic and replied, "We're not shooting, brother."

There was no acknowledgement of the transmission one way or the other; Worthy only knew that Cancer had received the message when the machinegun stopped shooting, the echo of its final burst quickly fading to silence.

"*Team Two,*" Cancer said, "*move, move, move. We've got the stairs covered.*"

Worthy rose and flowed through the door with his rifle at the high ready, visually clearing the rows of cots for further threats as he advanced at a swift walking pace. He was three steps inside by the time David replied, "*Moving.*"

Sweeping his aim to the staircase leading upward from a corner to his left, Worthy got his first clear glimpse of the enemy machine gunner and considered giving him a few bullets out of principle if nothing else, but he decided against it at the sight of the man sprawled out on the stairs. His head was cratered by 7.62mm exit wounds, surely Cancer's well-justified *coup de grâce* after scoring some initial hits, and a sizable portion of his brain matter was now spilling onto the barrel of an RPK machinegun.

Worthy had proceeded halfway across the room as fast as he could when more gunshots rang out: automatic weapons fire somewhere above him. Terrified screams followed as the gunfire continued, and Worthy almost halted in his tracks out of sheer confusion.

"Go," Ian called out impatiently behind him. "They're executing people."

Worthy broke into a jog at that, not second-guessing Ian per se but nonetheless skeptical of his assessment due to the obvious contradiction—who would they be executing? Olivia certainly wasn't being held here, and she was the only hostage these people had. By the time the question arose in his mind he was at the base of the stairs, pivoting left and angling his aim upward with the thought, *here we go*.

Staircases were one of the more fickle elements of close quarters combat because they were an absolutely fantastic place to get killed. In the team's extensive training across DoD and CIA shoothouses up and down the east coast, they had negotiated these scenarios with blank munitions against well-trained men playing the role of an opposition force. There were really only two ways to move upward inside a building: slowly and methodically, as would be the case on a deliberate assault without hostages, or, when there was an imminent risk to someone you desperately wanted to survive the raid, as fast as you possibly could.

And given the inexplicable fact that *someone* was being slaughtered up there, combined with the recent death of the only known staircase defender in the form of a man with multiple headshots before him, Worthy sided with the latter.

He kept close to the left wall as he ascended rapidly, leaving space for David and Ian to fan out behind him as he approached the top to the sounds of continued gunfire and screaming. There was a closed corner to the right, which put a single buttonhook maneuver between himself and whatever threat resided on the second floor. Worthy momentarily considered whether to flow onto the top floor as he normally would in room clearing, or to perform a stationary high-low maneuver without fully committing his split team to the unfolding festivities, whatever they were.

For reasons he couldn't divine at present, he felt a tug in his gut telling him not to run into the fray.

Unwilling to contradict his instinct, he halted at the top step, knelt, and whirled around the corner to take aim into the space beyond.

~

I only had a fleeting moment to react to Worthy's sudden stop.

But my team's extensive training made my response as fluid as if I'd been expecting it—when the point man knelt, I immediately closed the distance behind him, remaining standing as I took the high slot in the two-man stationary clearance maneuver. I angled my rifle around the corner in unison with Worthy, though not as far: my role was to clear right to left as the low man did the opposite.

Two enemy fighters began firing at once, ripping wild volleys of automatic rifle fire down the hallway at the first flash of our movement around the corner.

They were spaced on either side of the hall, but their premature reaction cost them their lives; neither had the training or composure to direct their shots at the edge of the wall that Worthy and I remained tucked against, little more than our right shoulders and a fraction of our heads exposed—and, of course, our rifles, which we put into play simultaneously.

Worthy's target on the left was the first to die, his gunfire ending as he fell forward. By then I was already engaging the man on the right, ripping subsonic bullets above his tremendous muzzle flashes until they extinguished to reveal a still-standing corpse in jeans and a soccer jersey flooding with blood. An AKM rifle fell from his grasp as he dropped from sight.

I sidestepped right and moved down the opposite wall, slipping past the bodies and proceeding as the number one man before Worthy had time to rise and follow. It would be either him or Ian backing me up as I approached a door at the end of the hall where the firing continued, mercifully not at us, before identifying, almost too late, a T-intersection to my right. A side corridor, I guessed, and one that I'd nearly missed in my haste to reach the door ahead.

By then, transitioning my weapon to a left-handed shooting position to maximize the use of cover around the corner would have required me to slow and add precious time to an already-stalled assault, so I decided to overexpose myself instead, considering that the two men Worthy and I had just gunned down must have been a delaying force. The question remained, were there any others?

Lowering my rifle just before the corner to prevent flagging myself before the final commitment, I spun right and took aim down a short corridor, finding my sights aligned with a trembling man who stood not three paces ahead of me.

He was light-skinned but Middle Eastern in appearance, with the tufts of a premature goatee and a flop of curly hair slicked to his forehead by sweat—that detail stood out even before I recognized the wide-eyed terror on his face, and the overladen flak jacket wrapped around his torso. In what may well have been the fastest shots I'd ever taken in my life, I fired two rounds into the bridge of his nose.

He collapsed before me, and I momentarily considered leaping atop his body to smother the blast. But it was too late for that, and the possibility of anti-tamper devices meant that would increase the odds of all three of us being vaporized. Instead I stopped short and took stationary headshots, three more subsonic rounds thwacking into his skull with sickening effect. Then I appraised his hands, finding that the right gripped a thin, palm-sized rod topped by a red button that had gone unpressed.

I transmitted, "S-vest down," to notify my teammates that there may well be additional suicide bombers ahead. Only then did I gain the composure to give a hasty glance at his dusty flak jacket, lined from waist to chest with a sloppily sewn arrangement of AK-47 magazine pouches bulging with plastic explosive and probably shrapnel consisting of ball bearings or steel bolts as well. Twin wires of red and white snaked across the pockets, leading to the detonator in his hand. He'd probably been chosen for his youth and expendability, but his cowardice had bought me the seconds required to end his life by my hand rather than his.

Spinning in place, I saw Worthy racing down the hall past me, followed in short order by a procession of Cancer, Reilly, and a man I'd never seen before who was decked in similar tactical attire and kit and wielding an HK416.

The four assaulters chased a man at the head of the pack, who was proceeding with reckless abandon to the end of the hall—Ian, already slipping through the final door.

~

Ian entered the room with his weapon raised and froze at the sight—tactical suicide, but a reaction he was unable to suppress nonetheless.

The three shooters were facing away from him, either unaware of his team's progress to the second floor or unconcerned with their own defense. They were spread in a semicircle facing a corner of the room, where a group of men had been herded and were now reduced to little more than a pile of bodies being raked with automatic gunfire from the trio of assault rifles. The floor around them was littered with empty magazines indicating multiple reloads.

It was a horrific sight, the stuff of school massacres. There was no time for a nonlethal shot in the hopes of capturing one of them alive, only a chance to kill them as quickly as possible and hope that he'd done so in time to save at least one of the helpless victims.

All of this flashed through his mind in a fraction of a second before he fired two rounds between the shoulder blades of the leftmost executioner, seamlessly transitioning his aim right and dropping the center shooter with another controlled pair. The action was fluid, automatic, and he swept his barrel to the final enemy, who had just now realized that his counterparts had stopped firing. He spun to face the door, sternum neatly aligning with Ian's sights—and just as the intelligence operative was about to depress the trigger for the first in a series of fatal shots, he was shoved sideways with such tremendous force that he nearly went sprawling onto the floor.

Ian struggled to regain his footing in time to reorient his rifle toward the imminent threat, but it was too late; the man fell in a hail of suppressed gunfire from Worthy, who'd pushed Ian aside in the first place. Cancer appeared then, shoulder-checking Ian further to the side as he engaged and making room for the remaining assaulters to spill inside the room. By the time Ian managed to align his sights again, the former enemy fighter had been shot a half dozen times, dead long before he hit the ground.

And then, with the final threat removed, Cancer slapped Ian in the back of the head as hard as he could.

"Stopping in the doorway, you fucking kidding me?" he hissed, voice seething with rage before he turned to Worthy and barked, "Get Suicide in the car and take him back now. This dumb shit"—he nodded toward Ian—"will ride back with us."

Worthy was out the door in a flash, and before David moved to follow, he looked Hass up and down and muttered, "David."

"Hass."

The battlefield introduction between the two men ended as quickly as it began as David vanished out the door. Reilly and Hass moved toward the casualties, leaving Ian to take in the details of the room for the first time as he wondered how in the hell he was supposed to exploit this site with the limited manpower available, much less in record time before fleeing the objective.

There was a central table with four chairs, though the room was dominated by the equipment along the walls: rows of workstations with chairs for two, dual seating areas surrounded by blank screens and computer equipment along with dry erase boards, notepads, and keypads flanked by joysticks. He performed a hasty count—eight workstations in total, room for sixteen men plus four in the middle.

Ian had seen rooms like this before, but only on highly secured compounds within US military installations. Libya was the last place he expected to encounter the same, but now that he was seeing it firsthand, he suddenly understood the answer to the one question plaguing him since the aborted linkup attempt earlier that morning.

Whoever was giving orders to the Wagner Group mercenaries must have had spotters conducting surveillance on the naval base in Sigonella, Italy; it was the logical choice for staging an assault force to hit a major target in Libya. He'd feared an intel leak, of course, but the moment those arriving fighters set up for an ambush without first searching for a prestaged reception team, he knew they were tracking the SEALION and nothing more.

But how could they have anticipated the exact landing site? The Mediterranean was vast, and spotter boats or no spotter boats, Khalil's people weren't covering all of it. That was to say nothing of the fact that the SEALs vectored their force around maritime traffic right up until the last interference, after which they made a straight shot for the coast.

The Russians had appeared minutes later, and now Ian knew how.

He moved toward the central workstation, knowing beyond a doubt it served as the "step desk" to oversee the combined efforts of each individual workstation and therefore would hold the most comprehensive intelligence. But the computer system units had been removed entirely, leaving a haphazard array of monitors, keyboards, microphones, and speakers scattered across the table's surface. The four squirters to make it out before the team arrived had not only been allowed but ordered to leave, indicating they were senior management and exempt from the fate that had befallen the underlings left behind for summary execution rather than the possibility of capture.

Cancer asked, "Can you fix one of 'em?"

"I'm a medic," Reilly shot back, exasperated, "not Jesus. These guys are dead three times over—we're searching them."

To Ian, Cancer asked, "What is this place?"

"Ground control station," Ian said, darting toward the nearest set of displays, "for UAVs."

He didn't add that while Khalil's drone operation certainly wasn't Reaper-grade tech, it was sufficient to calculate the landing point for the Navy boat once it was a few minutes from making landfall. And if those assets hadn't been tied up tracking the maritime infil and subsequent diversion as the SEALION sped westward, his team minus David would have been spotted and wiped out to a man long before making it back to the vehicles with a Wagner captive.

But Cancer hadn't yet considered that unpleasant reality, replying in a confounded tone, "Khalil's got *drones?*"

Ian didn't reply, instead frantically grabbing the box of a computer system unit and yanking it free from its cable attachments. He analyzed the front, then flipped it sideways and spun it to scrutinize the back before turning and using it as an on-the-job training aid as he shouted at his remaining teammates.

"Forget the men—get these boxes from all the workstations. Strip the hard drive like so—" He spun the back of the unit to face them, demonstrating how to extract a bricklike assembly from the casing, then rotated it so they could see the front. "Then get the video capture card by pushing here."

He pressed a button to eject the flat square of a high endurance SD card, pairing it with the hard drive in one hand and letting the system unit crash to the ground. "Bag those up, leave everything else. I'll check the bodies."

Hass and Reilly scrambled away from the dead men to comply, joined a moment later by Cancer as he yelled, "Thirty seconds."

Ian slipped his two pieces of intelligence into a drop pouch before taking a series of hasty photographs of the room and moving out to the heap of bodies. Noticing several had been separated from the group and searched already, he called out to Reilly, "You find any phones on them?"

"No," Reilly shot back.

Of course not, Ian thought, these were the expendable ones: the UAV pilots and sensor operators, surely kept from communicating with the outside world for the duration of their stay. That made searching them further a futile endeavor, particularly given the extreme time constraint.

He directed his efforts against the slain gunmen instead, photographing their faces before going through their pockets. He found Libyan currency and cigarettes in addition to the tactical gear, short-range radios that he stashed in his drop pouch, and finally a single piece of paper with a scrawled note. Ian didn't care what it said, only which language it was written in, and he scanned the looping and dotted rows of script long enough to confirm his suspicions of their country of origin.

The text wasn't written in Arabic, but Farsi.

He pocketed the note as Cancer spoke loudly.

"Time's up," he said. "Doc, lead us back to the car. Exfil, exfil, exfil."

21

Duchess watched the central video display in the Project Longwing OPCEN, seeing an overhead view of four shooters scrambling to enter their Kia sedan. The vehicle performed a U-turn and sped away a moment later, almost disappearing before the Reaper's sensor operator realigned the lens to keep them in sight. Feeling the initial relief that all the assaulters had made it off the objective, she lifted her hand mic in preparation to receive the first official report.

Which, given that it was Cancer in charge, could take some time.

The vehicle that the team had staged on the west side of the target building had already departed after two of the men had raced out of the building, presumably to return David to his meeting with Khalil and not a minute too soon. At this point, he'd be lucky to make the linkup on time, if at all.

She'd questioned the merits in taking him along on a time-sensitive target; after all, what if he was wounded or killed? That was before Khalil had actually called for another meeting, which had made matters even worse—particularly in the wake of the image currently displayed on her computer monitor.

Olivia Gossweiler was centered in the photograph, wearing the same clothes she was captured in, wrists bound by handcuffs as she clutched a copy of the *Al Kalima*, the closest thing Benghazi had to a reputable media outlet. The broadsheet newspaper was from the previous day, with no mention of Cairo on the front page, and despite the fact that the bruises on her face had healed to purple-and-yellow blotches, captivity had taken its toll—she'd lost considerable weight since the first video confirmed her capture, her cheeks now gaunt. Clearly dehydrated and underfed, but *alive*, and at this point that was about all they could hope for.

As with the initial proof of life, Khalil had distributed the photograph only to select Agency email addresses to ensure Olivia's capture wouldn't leak to the media. That was of limited consolation, however, given the alternative would essentially declare open season on aid workers to any terrorist or militia looking to straphang off the publicity. Meanwhile, Khalil could simply claim public credit at a time of his choosing, or at worst after the execution.

She redirected her gaze to the central screen at the front of the OPCEN, watching the final team vehicle speed away from the target. Before it turned into the next major intersection, she received her first communications since the raid began.

"*Raptor Nine One, this is Cancer.*"

Duchess felt a tinge of satisfaction at the timing—no lengthy delay in reporting as had been his trademark thus far. Maybe the man was finally getting the hang of being a ground force commander.

She keyed her mic and replied, "Go ahead."

"*Objective complete, 100 percent MWE, Suicide is on his way back for the recall with Khalil. We had nine EKIA, a whole shitload of intelligence captured, and sixteen unarmed men killed on the second floor before we got there.*"

Any relief she felt faded to the apprehension that her ground team had inadvertently slaughtered civilians and was now covering up that fact for the benefit of the mission transcript.

"Unarmed men?" she asked, adding with an unrestrained edge to her voice, "Explain."

"*Stand by for Angel.*"

A brief pause before Ian's more nasal voice took over the radio, speaking with quick and calm precision.

"*The objective was a safehouse for a UAV ground control station. Some secu-*

rity plus the pilots and sensor operators, who were all executed once the raid commenced and they knew the operation was burned. Three men did the killing; I've got pictures of their faces but found Farsi script on a note with one body. Assess they are current or former Quds Force, and if I'm right about that, it means the pilots were probably Houthi imports."

Duchess was familiar with the Quds Force; in fact, it was all but impossible for anyone remotely involved in intelligence work to be unaware of who they were and what they did. When Iran wanted to train, equip, or advise state or non-state actors, and in particular terrorist organizations without any direct link to their government, these operatives were dispatched to operate as the Supreme Leader's hidden hand. For years they'd been supporting militias and extremist groups from Lebanon to Afghanistan and everywhere in between, and done so with such effectiveness that the US Secretary of State had formally designated them as a foreign terrorist organization.

And she was well acquainted with the Houthi movement, more formally known as Ansar Allah. As the former station chief for Yemen, Duchess had seen them go from a spawn of marginalized opposition to a fully armed, highly radicalized army of true believers wresting control of the northern portion of their country from the failed government. Their official slogan told the uninformed observer everything they needed to know about the group's aims: *God is the Greatest, Death to America, Death to Israel, Cursed be the Jews, Victory to Islam.*

And while the Quds Force had long supported the Houthis—at this point, the situation in Yemen was essentially a proxy war between Iranian influence and the widespread Saudi military intervention—she hadn't been to the country in years and any drone connection was lost on her.

Rather than reveal her ignorance, she decided to go straight to Project Longwing's veritable fountainhead of information regarding any and all things air support.

"Wait one," she transmitted. Lowering the mic, she called out, "Brian?"

Sutherland was already facing her from his JTAC workstation.

"It's possible," he said, "because the Houthis have been running a UAV they call Qasef-1, which they claim to produce themselves. In reality it's identical down to the serial number prefix to Iran's Ababil-T platform, and if the Iranians are supplying the aircraft, they're also providing advisors to train pilots and run the step desks at UAV ground control stations."

Keying her mic again, she asked, "You think the platforms were Qasef-1s?"

"*Best guess?*" Ian asked rhetorically. "*Yeah, I do. But we're going to have to crack the hard drives and video capture cards to confirm or deny that, and to figure out the scope of Khalil's operation. We got all that material off the objective but it's going to be encrypted to hell and back. I don't have the hardware to analyze it, not even close. Need a direct handoff to get it into analyst hands at the earliest possible opportunity. You have any ground agents?*"

"None that can get it pushed up the food chain sooner than an air asset. Stand by." Then, releasing the transmit key, she called out, "Wes?"

She looked left to the bearded redhead serving as her operations officer.

Jamieson said, "It'll have to be 160th off that big deck amphib. The 47s can range a direct flight, but it'll have to be POD."

Between the military and the intelligence community, Duchess wasn't sure who used more acronyms and veiled references, but as a former Marine turned CIA officer, Jamieson had certainly mastered the art of relaying as much information in as little time as possible.

The "big deck amphib" he referred to was the USS *Iwo Jima*, a *Wasp*-class amphibious assault ship that had been on a joint Italian training exercise in the Mediterranean at the time of Olivia's capture. Since that time it had been loitering off the coast of Libya, reinforced by a contingent of helicopters from the 160th Special Operations Aviation Regiment—MH-47 Chinooks among them—in anticipation of providing aerial support to the SEAL hostage rescue effort.

But the last acronym of his statement was the one that concerned her: POD meant "period of darkness," and it would be a good many hours before the sun set over Libya.

She replied, "Think outside the box. How can we recover those materials before nightfall?"

Jamieson countered, "Plenty of ways, none of which are going to go unnoticed by Khalil. We already know he's got everyone from service workers to militias passing up information. That puts airports off limits, and sending a bird into the desert in broad daylight isn't going to be any more discreet than that. Good news is we can send an exploitation team and all their gear by charter jet to Sigonella and have them ferried out on the USS *Iwo Jima* tonight so they can start cracking the hard drives immediately."

With a frustrated sigh, she ordered, "Get the tech team moving, and start planning a rotary wing handoff. I want a desert landing zone remote enough for the helo to come and go unnoticed, and enough UAV support for the ground team to bypass any and all checkpoints and roadblocks. We can't afford to lose that intel."

"Yes, ma'am."

Then she keyed her hand mic and relayed the bad news.

"Quickest will be a Night Stalker bird from the USS *Iwo Jima*, but we can't risk sending them until nightfall."

Ian wasn't any more willing to accept that unfortunate reality than she was.

"*You can't tell me there's nothing closer. Air Branch, civilian charter, something.*"

Jamieson shook his head adamantly.

She said, "With Khalil fully aware that his UAV operation got hit, and the likelihood of an extensive source network in Benghazi, we can't risk sending a plane to the airport. And we don't have any local rotary wing assets that could arrive before the Night Stalkers."

"*At least they can deliver the SEAL advance element when we do the handoff.*"

"Negative. After the failed linkup and your discovery of a UAV operation, we need to withhold them until we analyze the captured materials and get a handle on exactly how wide Khalil's reach truly is."

"*Either way, that means we're dead in the water until nightfall.*"

"I wouldn't say that," she replied. "The Wagner radio frequencies have all gone dark, but analysis of the phones you captured reveals a cluster of affiliate numbers centered at a building in northern Benghazi, which indicates it's their safehouse. One of those phone lines, probably the commander, received a series of calls from a new number immediately preceding the Navy's maritime infil attempt, so we assess that whoever that line belongs to, it's a key player in Khalil's operation."

"*Great,*" Ian replied, "*so where is that caller located now?*"

"Geolocation indicates he was placing the calls from the building you just raided, but the line went dark shortly after your prisoner snatch and it appears it was a single-use burner with no other calls placed. It's possible, however, that the caller was the same man who made direct contact with the Wagner commander. If that's the case, he's got other phones we can use to trace him—if we can figure out who he is. Were you able to get an identity from your captive?"

"*We ran out the door as soon as we had a physical address, so not yet. I'll do another round of questioning and see what shakes out as soon as we make it back to the safehouse. But I think we're looking at terrorist sponsorship from some faction of the Libyan government, because Khalil's got some serious weight behind him now.*"

"Understood. Keep me posted."

"*Copy all.*"

With that coordination complete, she turned her attention to a side screen displaying the streaming feed from another Reaper altogether—and on it, she saw a Toyota Camry screeching to a halt on a side street. David Rivers leapt out of the passenger side wearing only civilian clothes, no rifle or armored plate carrier to be seen, and took off at a dead sprint into an alley before disappearing from view.

22

I raced through the alley, vaulting a pile of trash with a cell phone pinned to my ear as I strained to hear Sam, the technical specialist who remained in my suite alongside Corey.

"Camera feeds are frozen," he said, "45 seconds to Khalil's linkup. Keep heading straight down the alley to the gate, gate to service area. We'll activate the hall camera before you pass into the lobby."

"Yeah," I panted, "sure."

"There's a worker passing through the service area; they should clear out by the time you arrive."

"Doesn't matter if they do or not—I'm out of time."

As I momentarily considered the implications of a white man barreling through a staff-only space of the Palace Hotel, one of the sleeping dogs abruptly sat up and snarled at my sudden intrusion.

"Fuck off," I managed between breaths. The dog's growling stopped.

Sam sounded confused.

"Come again?"

"Not you," I said. "Almost to the gate. How am I supposed to explain this?"

Sam responded so matter-of-factly that I found myself questioning whether he'd supported a similar effort before, and if so under what circumstances.

"We've been running a lot of audio of the toilet flushing. Tell him you ate something that didn't agree with you. That's not a joke."

I hurdled the same fallen, weed-covered shopping cart I'd encountered on my way out, a notable landmark in this short and exceedingly absurd path back into the hotel. Then I passed the heaped piles of trash before skidding to a stop at the iron gate in the solid fence comprising the hotel compound's outer door and gasped, "Code?"

"Three four nine two."

Punching the numbers into the keypad and wrenching the gate open, I proceeded onto the worn footpath threading between patches of yellow grass, then repeated the code entry once I reached the hotel's service entrance.

"Going inside."

"You're clear. Ten seconds remaining."

I burst inside the building to the air conditioning of the same utility room I'd had so much trouble negotiating on my way out. Accelerating into an all-out run, I moved past the service elevator and the laundry chute I'd stuffed myself inside less than an hour earlier, then the rows of housekeeping carts.

"Door," I whispered, and had just enough time to shoulder my way through by the time Sam replied.

"Time's up, van just pulled up out front. Good luck."

I ended the call and strode into the hallway that led past restrooms, knowing that I was now entering the view of the nearest surveillance camera. Assuming a casual gait took considerable effort—my heart rate was jacked, adrenaline not yet subsided from the raid I'd just been an active participant in, the effort to transition from a gun-wielding assaulter to a negotiator presenting an almost insurmountable obstacle.

Nonetheless I entered the lobby at what I considered to be a reasonable pace, if anything a testament to the frequency with which I'd had to feign normalcy with my wife when I was almost too drunk to walk. My efforts were aided by the sight of Arshiya, the same front desk employee who'd completed my check-in after a desperate sprint to reach the extravagant lobby that I now slipped through.

As she looked up at me, I felt my composure return almost in full; my walk slowed considerably as I found my right hand lifting in a casual wave, pointer and index finger extended in a hybrid political and machismo maneuver that was a first for me, yet indescribably casual and nonchalant.

Arshiya blushed and looked down as I exited through the glass doors, then moved past the open gate onto the sidewalk.

There, idling malevolently on the curb, was a battered gray van whose side door slid open a moment before I reached it.

Inside were three men in ski masks, the same weapon loadout as my first reception outside Benina International Airport—a Beretta AR70/90 and two Kalashnikovs, because they were very likely the same crew and because fuck everything at this point. I hastily clambered aboard before they threw me to the floor of the van and pulled a hood over my head.

"You are late," a voice hissed overhead as the van pulled forward. "Why?"

"Stomach bug," I muttered through the hood.

"Bug?"

"I was sick," I said testily to the heavily accented man, "because the food here fucking sucks."

A fist slammed into my kidney with a velocity that made me second-guess every decision I'd ever made in my life; the searing pain spreading across my rib cage was a brutal throbbing pulsation as they handcuffed my wrists behind my back, then emptied my pockets.

I felt rough hands shifting my body from side to side in what was surely an effort to manipulate me into varying positions for the benefit of a surveillance tracker.

Once they finished, I was released to lie on the floor, where I rolled onto my side, panting for breath. For the first time, I considered the mission I'd just returned from, whether or not it held any implications for what lay ahead. Chief in my mind was the question, what would Khalil do as a result of my tardiness to the linkup?

Would he kill Olivia?

I weighed that possibility against the fact that without my presence on the mission my team had just executed, two of my teammates would have been killed. That wasn't due to any particular valor or precision on my part, simply the blind luck that put me as the number one man in confronting a suicide bomber with probably a hundred pounds of explosives strapped to his chest. Could Worthy have put him down in my position? Yes, and even quicker than my already split-second response. Cancer and Reilly could have managed the same or damn close to it, and I had no idea about the Air Force cat assigned as our Combat Controller but guessed he was more than capable.

But none of them would have been the first down that hall in my absence; it would have been Ian, and there was no chance he'd have reacted in time to prevent that shaking, sweating mess of a kid from clacking off his vest. That wasn't a slight against Ian, just a simple fact. His specialty was intelligence, and despite our extensive training and rehearsals at every opportunity in the States, close quarters combat more than anything else demanded that a shooter be experienced to survive—there was a level of reactiveness and fluidity that you simply couldn't attain without sufficient repetitions, and Ian was far behind the rest of us in that regard.

He had, after all, committed the absolute cardinal sin of building clearance by stopping in the doorway of that final room. It wasn't that Ian was dumb. Intelligence, however, whether as a character trait or a military specialty, wasn't the only consideration in flowing through a building during real-world combat. Gaining that experience required one to either be very good or die in the process, a catch-22 that Ian had thus far negotiated, for the most part, by operating alongside far more experienced shooters.

So if I hadn't been there, what would have happened? Ian would have turned down that side corridor, if he'd seen it at all, and been unable to achieve a fatal headshot in the time it took that cowardly little shit to press a button. Ian would have been incinerated and, judging by the fact that he was just sweeping past me after I'd killed the man and transmitted the outcome to my teammates, Worthy would have as well.

And if Olivia died as a result, would it have been worth saving two of my teammates?

I didn't know the woman and had only briefly met her father, who couldn't have made it any more clear that his own child was a distant second to national security objectives, his own political career, or both. If my daughter Langley was held hostage, there were simply no limits to the amount of human carnage I'd gladly witness if not inflict personally to get her back—that wasn't much of a testament to my objectivity or value as a human being, but it was absolutely true as far as my instincts as a father were concerned.

In the end, I couldn't make a justification one way or the other. Instead, I came to the same conclusion I always did when trying to weigh the philosophical considerations of what I'd done or failed to do on a mission: combat was pure, unadulterated chaos. Training, preparedness, and audacity usually won the day, but not always. Far better men than myself had fallen dead on the military, mercenary, or paramilitary battlefield after doing everything right, and besides, what did the consequences matter? What was done was done, and in that equation, my own reconciliation or lack thereof mattered precious little.

The van rolled forward through Benghazi, taking me ever closer to the first of what would surely be many vehicle transitions and an ever more elaborate surveillance detection route toward Khalil.

23

Reilly braked the Kia to a halt inside the safehouse, killing the engine and exiting along with the majority of his team to see Worthy pulling the rolling door closed behind them.

Reaching back in the car to recover and sling his HK417, he walked quickly to catch up to Ian as the intelligence operative proceeded deeper into the main warehouse bay. He hadn't been able to have a private discussion with Ian while driving the team's lone remaining vehicle back to the safehouse, and sought to change that at the first opportunity.

Gently grabbing Ian's shoulder, he said, "Hey man, I need to talk to you—"

"Not now," Ian snapped, turning to slap a palm on a table beside him and calling out, "Intel here."

The team consolidated and set their bags atop it before emptying the contents of the various drop pouches as Ian said, "Cancer, I need you and Reilly, that's it."

Cancer spun toward the remaining two men.

"Worthy, you and Hass get the vehicles fueled and top off magazines. Let me know when we're a hundred percent on refit. And take the soft armor and plate out of the back of David's kit and swap it with Reilly."

He waved his finger at the medic to hurry up and remove his gear, and

Reilly looked down to see three neatly bored holes in the fabric of his plate carrier, the bullets forming an oblong triangle roughly centered on his left pectoralis. Uncannily good marksmanship for such quick shots from a solo fighter barreling into certain death with a hot trigger finger and 72 virgins in mind, he thought, and reached for the Velcro flap securing the twin elastic waistbands to hold the armor in place.

"No," Ian said, "leave it on. You're coming with me to talk to Arseni, and I want him to see we're not fucking around."

"Go," Cancer ordered, and Worthy moved out alongside the team's resident Combat Controller before Ian spoke again.

"Cancer, I need you to send up the intel. All the pictures from my camera, scans of any paper material. Photograph the hard drives and video capture cards, particularly the serial numbers, and get it to Duchess asap."

Reilly asked, "What about me?"

"Get some food, water, and your aid bag. Meet me outside Arseni's room. Once we go in, I want you to let him see what you've brought, but don't give him anything until I tell you."

"All right," Reilly agreed, and did as he was told amid the flurry of post-mission tasks at hand. He downed a bottle of water in the process, then took two additional ones and a field ration before carrying his aid bag around a corner and down a hall to find Ramzi.

The safehouse manager was standing guard at the door—or rather sitting guard, slumped in a folding chair with his M4 carbine leaning against the wall. He held a magazine idly, and glanced up at Reilly before turning the page with a smirk.

"Ah, good hunting, I see."

He looked down and saw what the native Libyan asset had: tactical gloves covered in blood from searching bullet-riddled bodies, more red flecks on his plate carrier from either the dead men or those that Reilly himself had shot. Whether Ramzi had noticed the three bullet holes remained unclear.

"You can go," Reilly said, setting down his supplies along the wall.

"The boss said I must not leave until he tells me to."

Reilly lowered his aid bag to the ground, then rose to his full standing height and faced the man, replying in a dull monotone that customarily preceded the flaring of his temper to uncharacteristically high levels.

"If you want to get paid, then get the fuck out of here. Now."

Ramzi gave an indifferent shrug, dog-eared the page of his magazine, and flipped it shut to reveal the publication—an English-language printing of *Maxim*. Then he stood to recover his M4 before sauntering down the hall.

Reilly waited for him to leave, then drove his fist into the wall with just enough force to make his knuckles sting without breaking skin.

He heard movement and looked over to see Ian approach, almost scoffing in disbelief—the intelligence operative had washed his face, ditched his tactical kit, and had the audacity to swap his sweat-soaked fatigue top with a clean, dry one. The implication was clear: he'd come across as the composed man in charge during the interrogation, while Reilly was to be the blood-splattered Neanderthal bearing food and medical treatment that would only be issued upon Ian's say-so.

Reilly had to tamp down the anger that thought evoked and, not wanting Arseni to overhear anything from inside his detention room, walked swiftly down the hall to intercept Ian.

Lowering his voice despite the distance from their captive, he asked, "What just happened?"

"It can wait," Ian said impatiently. "Let's go—"

That last word hitched in his throat as Reilly grabbed the clean fatigue shirt with two balled fists that he used to push Ian back and then jerk him closer, maintaining his grip as he whispered, "It can't wait, motherfucker, because I just wasted an unarmed twenty-year-old on what was supposed to be a 'hot' objective and I want to know why."

Ian recoiled, blinking quickly.

"Honestly?" he asked, and upon receiving no response or release from Reilly's grasp, continued, "The four senior operators who flushed with the contents from the command desk were allowed to leave. Most likely, they weren't certain that they'd be compromised just because the missing Russian wasn't supposed to know about the location in the first place. They were hedging their bets. Once the shooting started, they knew they were fucked and security gunned down the pilots and sensor operators so they couldn't be captured alive. One of them was either in a separate part of the building, or managed to escape the gunmen. That's who you shot."

Reilly released him, and Ian took a step back and smoothed his shirt-front with a sigh.

"Look," he continued, "Cancer presumed everyone on that objective to be hostile, and he wasn't wrong. Even if that guy was unarmed, you think he's innocent? Whether he liked it or not, he was facilitating Khalil's operation."

"Why?"

"*Why*?" Ian asked incredulously. "For profit. Carlos the Jackal was paid 50 million after his 1975 OPEC raid in Vienna. Khalil is asking eight times that, and judging by the UAV and Wagner support, he's got serious backing. So take it easy on yourself, Reilly. We can't afford to have you out of the fight just because you want to take your conscience for a ride."

"My conscience," Reilly responded as he took a step toward him, "is pretty damn close to the only thing separating us from Khalil at this point. Tell me I'm wrong."

Ian's mouth fell open, as if he was having a hard time discerning if Reilly was serious or not.

"Every SEAL in the advance element is right back in Sigonella after our linkup was busted, and Olivia Gossweiler is still being held at gunpoint. That means if we don't make some moves to locate her—no spy satellites, no UAVs, just *us*—then there might not be a hostage left to rescue. So no, Reilly, your conscience is far from the closest thing standing between us and the man who captured her. If you want to have a breakdown about our role in all this, do it on your own time—we've got work to do."

He brushed past Reilly without waiting for a response, then flung open the door and announced, "Arseni, let's talk."

~

Ian left the door open for Reilly, striding inside to center himself before the captured Russian mercenary even as he questioned whether he'd been too harsh on the big-hearted medic.

A moment later he concluded that no, he hadn't; there was no shortage of suitable times to question one's own participation in an ongoing military and intelligence effort, but serving as the lynchpin for a hostage rescue amid the ticking clock of an imminent execution wasn't one of them.

But before he could delve further into his own line of reasoning, his attention was occupied by the sight of his captive.

Arseni was in the same location as before, both ankles were flex cuffed to the chair legs, blood now soaking through the pressure dressing on his left foot. His face was taut with the pain from his foot or chemical burns or both. Ian shot him a withering glare even as he second-guessed what was about to occur.

The last thing he needed was any event or circumstance, much less a softcore assault by a fellow teammate, that would throw him off balance before a critical interaction with a captured enemy prisoner. It would be one thing if he had a full staff of psychologists and professional interrogators to support the timing and pacing of a preordained sequence of controlled sessions that could be adapted as needed, but having returned from a time-sensitive target after a single hasty session with no one but himself to procure further information was another matter entirely. Ian compensated for that disparity with a forcefulness in his voice that he rarely utilized.

"You have withheld critical information from me. I want to know why."

Arseni shook his head quickly.

"*Bred*. I have withheld nothing."

Turning to Reilly, Ian gave a determined shake of his head. "Get the saltwater, and the gasoline. Along with my knife—"

"Wait," Arseni blurted.

Spinning back to face the restrained man, Ian said, "I thought this was going to be friendly. I haven't asked you for anything that would hurt your comrades so that when this is over I could return you to them without any accusations of collaboration on your part."

What he deliberately withheld was the fact that he didn't need any further information on Wagner's activities—the CIA's analysis of Arseni's phone had clarified not only their staging area but the regrettable fact that since the prisoner snatch, the Russians were cut off from further contact with Khalil's operation.

Ian continued, "But you know the score in Libya. Your government has sent you here, sure. And you guys accepted the *padrabotka* to attack a force arriving by way of the Mediterranean, which I understand. Money is money, and I won't fault you for that."

Arseni said nothing; his eyes were ticking back and forth between Ian's, an imploring gaze trying to anticipate where this was going.

What Ian really wanted to know was the identity of the man who'd liaised between the Wagner Group force and Khalil's efforts in Libya. Precious little was more effective in accomplishing that than accusing a captive of lying by way of a deliberately false piece of information that needed to be corrected in order to avoid further torture, so that's exactly what he did.

Ian progressively raised the volume of his voice during the next sentence, ending it just short of a shout.

"I want you to say what was at the location my men just attacked—you know, so *say it*."

The Russian was flabbergasted, quickly sputtering, "Intelligence operation, maybe. People who knew where the enemy would arrive. I did not see inside the building, only the address. We never returned."

No mention of UAVs, Ian noted, his gut instinct telling him that Arseni simply hadn't known. Which was fair enough, as Ian hadn't even arrived at that conclusion until he saw the inner workings of a ground control station.

"But you knew of that location," he continued, "by following a man. A man you saw."

"*Da, da*," Arseni readily agreed. "Exactly."

Ian regretted what he was about to do; Arseni probably had no idea what he was getting at, but the best possible way to discourage a lie under the circumstances was pain.

He took a rapid step forward and landed an open-handed blow across Arseni's left thigh. The slap of his palm against the medical dressing covering the blistered chemical burn caused the Russian to unleash an anguished cry that echoed around the room.

Ian repeated the process on the right thigh, waiting a beat for the screaming to subside before placing a boot sole atop Arseni's wounded foot.

Without taking his eyes off the Russian, whose face was now contorted with unspeakable pain, he thrust a finger backward at Reilly and went on, "One of my people was shot because of your failure to warn us. Two more were fucking killed, all because you failed to mention we were going up against Quds Force."

"What?" Arseni gasped, now in more shock than pain. "*Net*, no. How could I know this?"

Ian removed his boot from Arseni's bleeding foot and sent a vicious slap across his cheek.

"Because the man you followed was an Iranian."

Arseni's eyes flashed the briefest glimpse of relief, and he yelped an awkward laugh before replying, "No. Maybe some of the bodyguards were, I do not know. But the man called himself Zaahid Amer. Tall, as thin as a twig, and had a severe limp of the left leg. Not from Iran, though—he was a *pesok chernyy*, you understand?"

Literally translated, the term meant "sand black," though Ian could divine both from context and his prisoner's affiliation with the *Rusich* faction of Wagner Group that he meant a dark-skinned man from the desert. There were more offensive terms he could have used, yet he'd withheld his outburst to what was, for him, a relatively neutral designation. Had he finally figured out that his interrogator was Jewish and tempered his response accordingly? Ian's thoughts then pivoted to the very possibly immense disparity between what Arseni had said and how he'd interpreted it.

"A Libyan?" Ian asked.

"No," Arseni said, then corrected himself. "Maybe. He may have been from Niger, or Chad. My commander said he spoke with a Tedaga or Dezaga accent. I saw his skin, and I know this was not a lie."

This was an interesting development on two fronts, Ian thought.

First was that regardless of how many times he'd visited Libya as a member of Wagner Group, Arseni understood the cultural nuances of the country's nine living languages, the two he'd just mentioned belonging to a single ethnic group.

The second source of curiosity, of course, was that a neo-Nazi had bothered to learn that fact at all.

"*Abyasni*," Ian said, demanding an explanation in Arseni's mother tongue for emphasis.

Arseni readily responded, "Tudaga, Umbararo, the rock people. Whoever he was, the Sahara was his home. You see? You understand?"

Ian understood well enough—the man Arseni had tracked through the streets of Benghazi was of the worst possible ethnicity as far as the team's intent was concerned. The Agency's intelligence supply, and therefore his team's, decreased radically the further south into the desert that they needed information.

But that wasn't his only concern at present; there was exactly one man who could immediately confirm or deny this information, whose one and only hot-button topic as per his previous handlers' reports was the matter of his ethnicity.

Arseni had made his point, however.

He'd cited three terms: Tudaga, Umbaro, and rock people. All were synonyms for the same group who made the Sahara their home. Ian knew them as the Tebu, as did the two native-born Libyans in the safehouse.

One of those men was Hass, but the other had been raised in the Tebu culture and long since turned his back on his own people.

~

Worthy was halfway through topping off the fuel in the newly returned Kia sedan when Ian appeared at his side and spoke quietly.

"I need you to come with me."

Setting the gas can down, Worthy asked, "Everything okay?"

"Maybe. You've got your pistol?"

"Sure, but what—"

"Come on."

Only when he'd turned around to follow did Worthy realize he was the last one to be summoned. Hass and Cancer were already standing by, and both followed the intelligence operative to the old silver BMW 3 Series parked in the corner of the warehouse bay, its driver's door open.

Inside sat Ramzi, one leg dangling outside the vehicle, his face concealed by a *Maxim* magazine that he held over the steering wheel.

The four men came to a stop, following Ian's lead as he declared, "We need your help."

Ramzi didn't look up from his magazine, idly flipping a page as he responded with a bored yawn.

"*Hasanan*. What may Uncle Ramzi do for you."

"You said you know everyone."

The man chuckled softly, apparently at the sight of something on the magazine page, and Ian started to repeat himself before Ramzi replied, "I do."

Nodding with a defiant expression that seemed to say *prove it*, Ian continued, "We're looking for a Tebu man."

Worthy's first thought was that the intelligence operative was a hypocrite if ever there was one. His exceedingly short brief about how to handle Ramzi consisted mainly of an admonition not to mention the Tebu people, being that the asset was more or less a closeted member of that tribe, and now Ian was doing just that.

Ian quickly continued, "Very tall, very skinny, with a pronounced limp on his left leg, uses the alias Zaahid Amer, facilitates the operations of foreign actors in Benghazi and—"

But that was as far as he got before Ramzi flung his magazine sideways, then leapt out of the car and shouted, "*Tint rabbok!*"

That explained why Ian asked if he'd had his pistol, Worthy realized; for a moment it appeared as if Ramzi was lunging forward to attack, but instead he used his raised fist to make an angry hammering motion at the ceiling as he cried, "That bum, that Gaddafi bitch!"

"Oh," Ian said with palpable relief. "So you do know him."

Ramzi was shouting in Arabic now, a long sentence that ended in a phrase that Hass converted to English.

"A snitch, like an Uncle Tom." Then he asked Ramzi, "*Kayf?*"

Spinning to slam his car door shut at maximum force, Ramzi kicked the front quarter panel and started pacing like a caged animal along the wall behind him, gesticulating wildly as he shot off more words in Arabic.

Hass raised his voice over Ramzi's to translate.

"His real name is Ghalibun Sharif. He was an informant to the *Mukhabarat*, Gaddafi's secret police, accepting money to rat out any Tebu safe havens that hadn't yet been persecuted. Thousands lost everything they had because of this man, hundreds were tortured to death in prison. Maybe a thousand or more—*madha?*"

"And he tried," Ramzi went on, finally stopping in place and mustering enough composure to transition to English, "to have me killed."

Cancer lit a cigarette and replied, "Then you wouldn't mind returning the favor."

Ramzi shook his head solemnly. "Death is far better than that *manyoka* deserves."

"Good," Ian said, "because we don't want him dead, we want him alive, and we'll do whatever it takes to find out what he knows. Now, how can we find him?"

After a brief snorting laugh, the Libyan said, "Sharif is an addict. When he is not on the streets with his bodyguards, he is at his home with his drugs and his whores. But you will never be able to capture him."

Angrily blowing a cloud of smoke, Cancer shot back, "Why not?"

"Listen to me carefully: a *surm* such as this can only have a home in one way. It is surrounded by a three-meter wall. Inside is a courtyard house, and militia security is too great for twenty men to overcome. The five of you do not stand a chance."

"How many stories is his house?"

"Only one."

Cancer nodded. "Big courtyard?"

"With a garden and a fountain. His blood money has provided this. Why?"

"Because," Cancer explained with audible irritation, "a three-meter fence and a one-story house means we could see inside the courtyard. Are there any tall buildings around it, any vantage points for a sniper?"

Ramzi folded his arms.

"Sharif is a bitch player, but not foolish. There are tall buildings, yes. All are too far for a sniper. Otherwise he would be dead already."

"Ramzi," Worthy began, sparing Cancer the trouble of interrupting his latest drag to ask, "what's your definition of 'too far?'"

"More than a kilometer. Perhaps two."

Worthy glanced over at his current team leader, a man whose normal specialty on the team—other than serving as its second-in-command—was accurately placing precision gunfire at ludicrous distances, and doing so extremely well.

"You brought the Barrett, right?"

Cancer gave a self-satisfied nod, exhaling his next gray plume without speaking.

Cutting his eyes back to Ramzi, Worthy concluded, "Brother, I think you've found your shooter."

No sooner had he finished his sentence, though, than Ian objected to the solution.

"Killing him would be counterproductive," he said adamantly. "We'd sever Khalil's access to a major player but not gain any additional intel. That's not good enough. What we need is to roll him up alive and see what he can tell us."

Ramzi reiterated, "You will never get inside his home."

"And," Worthy pointed out, "we don't have the time or manpower to follow him long enough to chart a pattern of life and try to take him while he's on the move. Killing him will have to suffice—it's better than nothing."

Ian was unconvinced.

"No, it's far worse. The Wagner Group has been cut off, so Sharif is the only link we've got to Khalil and his people. If he drops dead, we won't even have that."

"Ian," Cancer said firmly, turning his back on Ramzi to face the intelligence operative, "you lost all credibility when you froze in the fucking doorway on our last objective. And this isn't your call to make: it's mine. I say killing Sharif will serve our purposes, so he just became a dead man walking. That's final."

Worthy saw the sniper give Ian a wink then, though what the subtle cue meant, he had no idea.

24

Someone ripped the hood off my head a moment after I'd been shoved into the chair, and upon seeing Khalil seated across from me, I knew at once that there would be no tea at today's meeting. He wouldn't even have my handcuffs removed this time, perhaps ever again.

He was in a different suit, a tailored navy jacket over a crisp white dress shirt with no tie. Glancing at his open collar, I saw the black cord holding the slain pilot's dog tags. I wondered if this son of a bitch had been wearing them as a war trophy ever since the shootdown, and concluded that he had.

We faced each other in a different room than the previous meeting, though I was reasonably certain we were in the same building—once again I'd been led past a wave of wood smoke and burning meat, and once more the room was filled with incense. Now I was certain they were trying to cover up a smell, something that could assist us in determining this location, however general. What was it—seawater? Manure from a farm or crop? The fumes of some nearby factory? It had to be significant. I filed the thought away, confident that Ian would, if I lived long enough to tell him, come up with some well-informed guesses.

Remaining alive, however, seemed like an ever-dwindling possibility.

Khalil's eyes had a measure of contempt I hadn't seen in our first meeting—or maybe contempt wasn't the right word for it, perhaps it was simply a new perspective on my intentions in Libya. Whatever the case, it was clear to me that *he knew*, not just that his UAV facility had been raided but that I was personally involved.

But when he spoke, it was in reference to something far worse.

"The latest update from Cairo," he began heatedly, "is five *thousand* Muslim dead. They are not finished counting, of course, and there will be many more. It would seem the Jews have outdone even themselves."

I reeled at the statement.

"You think Israel attacked Cairo? According to the news, that jet launched from somewhere west of Egypt—"

"Of course it did," he nearly shouted. "Because the Zionists do not claim responsibility for their crimes. Instead they use spies and assassins: Mossad and Kidon, Aman, Sayeret Matkal, Shayetet 13, Unit 504. And the Western world's response is no different than it is to the theft of the Palestinian homeland and the murder of its citizens: they do nothing. Except America, of course. She actively supports these sins with military, financial, and political aid at every opportunity. The blood of those innocent Muslims is on the hands of your country as much as the Jews."

This was no feigned anger, I could see at once—Khalil was genuinely outraged by the Cairo attack, possibly more so than myself even considering I shouldered the blame for the missing VX that was used. Worse still, I had no recourse to correct or alter his opinion. To even attempt it would be to either accuse him of being a conspiracy crackpot or expose my personal knowledge of the VX's source, which the Agency had definitively traced to Erik Weisz.

I stayed silent instead, waiting for the vein in Khalil's forehead to subside as he gradually calmed himself.

But the anger remained, as palpable as the scent of incense in this room, as he continued speaking.

"I have already vowed vengeance against anyone who trespasses against Islam, and this attack has doubled my resolve. Whatever the final number of Egyptian dead, know this: a greater number of your people and Zionists will pay with their lives. For what we cannot achieve through a single strike, we will accomplish through repeated attacks. The believers are accomplished in killing Jews, but there remains much work to be done on the fat underbelly of America—your subways, your unguarded trains, your state fairs. The hospitals and day care centers that have remained safe while your country drops hundreds or thousands of bombs in Muslim nations each and every day, decade after decade. 9/11 was your country's starting point for a War on Terror, and Cairo will be ours."

Only then, however, did he reference the target from which myself and my team recently extricated ourselves.

"Which brings me," Khalil said with a panted huff, "to a setback that my people have suffered."

"What setback?" I asked innocently.

Leaning forward to fold his hands on the table between us, Khalil said, "Tell me where you have been, Suicide."

I shrugged. "Sitting in my suite at the Palace Hotel."

"Until you left for...where, exactly?"

I answered flatly, casually, "I didn't leave. Not until your people picked me up."

My expression was placid, but my mind raced through the various intricacies of Sam and Corey's manipulations of my cell phone as well as the device Khalil gave me—continuous audio surveillance, false hotel room noises, a spoofed geolocation signal—and wondered if one or more had failed. Or maybe, I thought, Khalil had simply stationed an observer somewhere who had escaped our detection and seen me running into or out of the alley.

But there was only one way to proceed, and that was with the sociopathic confidence that he may suspect my involvement but couldn't possibly know for sure. Whether or not that was true was anyone's guess, but self-incrimination wasn't in my repertoire of survival techniques.

"Why," he asked quietly, "do I not believe you?"

"You don't have to."

"No?"

"I've kept your cell phone with me at all times, exactly as instructed. Trace the GPS history if you like, or ask the front desk staff. There are cameras in the hotel, and I'm sure you have the means to obtain all that footage. I'm here for one reason: to ensure Olivia's safe return. Anything that reduces the chances of that happening has nothing to do with me. So if you don't believe me, you don't. But until you show me some evidence that I've violated your instructions—and you can't, frankly, because I haven't—then I think our time would be better spent discussing your payment."

He seemed to have finally cooled off, at least somewhat.

"Then discuss it."

"Of course," I said hesitantly. He wasn't going to like this next bit, but I had my marching orders on what information to relay. "The only question is one of timing."

Khalil flashed a courteous smile. "My deadline is quite clear. And since a wire transfer is virtually instant, the timing represents no problem at all."

"It's a matter of assembling the funds amid national policy. They will have at least fifty million by the deadline, but getting the rest—"

"National policy," he cut me off, his smile fading to an icy glare, "being that your country does not negotiate with so-called terrorists. So your politicians seek to route that money through various non-governmental organizations and charities to obfuscate their source, and maintain their own innocence while standing by a policy that they themselves violate. How uniquely American."

"The details are above my pay grade. All I have for you at this time is that message, and one more."

"And the other?"

I drew a breath before continuing, "The remaining 350 million will take an additional four days. By 11 p.m. on the 31st, it will be ready in full."

"Very well," he said, so graciously that for a moment I thought he was going to accept unconditionally.

But a moment later he said, "And my counteroffer: your government has just lost 24 hours from my previous deadline, which was already quite generous." He checked his watch. "In 53 hours and 17 minutes, I will kill Olivia Gossweiler and post the footage on every major international media outlet. The only further question is whether you will relay those terms or not."

Swallowing, I said, "I don't see why there would be any question. My job is to maintain communications between you and my country, and that's exactly what I'm going to do."

"If I allow you to."

"Meaning?"

"Meaning," he went on, "that I know you had a hand in the setback of which I speak. I warned you when we first met, Suicide, that there would be consequences if my instructions were usurped in any way. Your government is about to learn exactly what those consequences are."

Huffing a breath, I replied, "You have yet to explain how I or anyone else has failed your demands. If you think I'm not playing ball, fine: show me your evidence."

I regretted the words as soon as I said them, seeing in his face that he was going to take that demand and contort it into some horrific spectacle that I was unlikely to survive.

Further confirmation came with his next words, spoken with a smile.

"As you wish, Suicide."

25

Duchess almost jumped at the first ring of the desk phone in her personal office, quickly snatching the receiver from its cradle.

"Yes?"

Jamieson replied, "He just entered the Special Activities Center, two minutes out from you."

"Thank you. Any updates?"

"Nothing else, ma'am."

"Call me soonest if that changes, meeting or no meeting."

She hung up the phone, giving a final glance around her office to ensure it was sufficiently tidied up. Then she focused on her computer screen, where every conceivable briefing, timeline, and operational map were ready and waiting in neatly aligned windows whose placement was staggered by relevance and currency.

Duchess was exceedingly wary about this meeting request, in her private office no less; Senator Gossweiler was well-equipped to grease the wheels for Project Longwing or smother it in the cradle, as he preferred. That was more or less his prerogative as the Chairman of the US Senate Select Committee on Intelligence, which was formed after 1975 congressional investigations revealed hard evidence of CIA-sponsored assassinations against foreign political officials among other notable indiscretions.

And while the Agency was now ending more lives than ever courtesy of a robust and well-honed UAV program, the notion of targeted killings by a ground team far outside declared areas of conflict remained a largely political tightrope that Project Longwing was testing with each mission. The fate of the program was in question well before this point, and now that Senator Gossweiler's daughter remained a hostage in the wake of a WMD attack against the largest city in the Middle East, she had no idea where she stood.

She rose at the knock on her door and said, "Come in."

An Agency escort opened the door to allow Senator Thomas Gossweiler to enter—he was attired in a suit and tie as always, silver hair immaculately combed, though his face held an air of exhaustion that she'd never seen in their previous interactions.

"Senator," she said.

"Kimberly," he acknowledged, stepping forward to allow the escort to close the door behind him.

She found it irritating that he was one of an exceedingly small group who referred to her by birth name rather than her hard-earned Agency moniker, but she smiled warmly as she extended a hand toward the visitor chair opposite her desk.

He lowered himself into the seat and asked, "Any word on Rivers yet?"

"No, sir. He's been dark for"—she checked her watch—"ten hours and counting. The remainder of his team is proceeding as per our last situation report."

Then, still standing, she asked, "Can I offer you something to drink?"

"Water," he said, "frozen into cubes and floating in three fingers of single malt."

"I'm afraid my options are limited to coffee, tea, and unfrozen water, Senator."

"Then nothing for me."

Duchess sat down across from him, trying to anticipate his intent.

Gossweiler abruptly winced and said, "Christ, Kimberly, what type of father have I been? There was a time that little girl had me wrapped around her finger. Then I put my career first and the next thing I knew, she was in her thirties and running around the world as an aid worker. Now this."

Duchess had every operational detail ready and waiting on her computer, and was prepared to answer each question to the level of granularity that Gossweiler usually demanded.

But seeing him in the chair across from her, she came to realize he hadn't come here to scrutinize intelligence—if anything, this was a form of therapy for a disgraced parent who couldn't discuss the issue with anyone else.

She nodded slowly, considering that he hadn't seemed nearly so troubled when they first received news of Olivia's capture; as Duchess was preparing to deploy David's team, the senator's main concern seemed to be getting Khalil off the proverbial battlefield by any means necessary.

Then she responded, "I don't think there's a parent alive who hasn't felt blindsided by how fast their children grow up. And as for placing your career first"—she reached forward to rotate one of the photo frames on her desk to face him, then sat back—"you're not the only one. But you must admit, Senator, that our work has stopped a lot of the evil that would otherwise prevail."

"We've stopped some of it," he agreed, looking thoughtfully at the framed picture and then back at her, "but not all. There's always another 9/11 brewing, another Cairo. And what concerns me more is the fact that every time we cut a head off the Hydra, two more grow back to replace it. I bet you can't find an analyst in this entire goddamn building who can list them all without reading a chart, and that's not counting Weisz in the equation."

"Finding Erik Weisz may be the closest anyone ever gets to killing the Hydra, sir."

Gossweiler released a weary sigh. "If and when that happens, you and I both know the next one is somewhere in its infancy, waiting to fill the power vacuum."

"Which is why our jobs—our careers, as you put it, Senator—are so important."

"With innocent civilians paying the price for our failures, and our families paying the price for successes they'll never hear about. Where does that leave us?"

She flashed a sad grin. "We pay a price of a different kind, I'm afraid. I think about that every time I walk into my empty house."

“I think about it every time I can’t sleep,” he seamlessly replied, now staring hollowly at her desk. “Every night, actually, since he took her.”

Duchess saw the pain in his eyes, his expression seeming to mirror the same doubts and fears in her own soul.

Reaching down to pull open her bottom desk drawer, she set a bottle on the desk and followed it with two glasses.

“It’s not single malt,” she offered, pouring two equal measures of amber liquid, “but it’s the best I can do.”

She set the bottle down and handed him a glass, then took her own and lifted it.

“To your daughter, Senator.”

“To Olivia,” he agreed.

And then, in unison, they took their first sips.

26

Reilly sat on the roof of the Land Cruiser, cradling his HK417 with his legs dangling off the side. This had to be the most lax security he'd ever pulled, he thought, scanning the desert with the benefit of night vision and paying particular attention to the direction of the nearest road to his front.

But that road was over two miles distant, and if anyone approached, he'd be able to see them coming over the flat stretch of desert. That was to say nothing of the advance notice provided from the MQ-9 Reaper circling somewhere overhead, which could detect any incoming traffic a hell of a lot sooner than he'd be able to locate it through his optics. The UAV's pilot and sensor operator, along with the Agency officials who had cleared it for tonight's excursion, however, were less concerned about the small team on the ground than they were the 26 million dollars' worth of hardware that would soon be arriving.

He looked up to see the dazzling array of stars, tens of thousands of pinpricks of light amplified to a brilliant glow under his night vision. It was the kind of panorama he'd never been able to envision growing up in southern California, and now that he was sitting amid what had arguably been the most peaceful moment on this mission or any other, the predominant emotion was dread.

His earpiece came to life with Cancer's voice.

"Doc, what's your SITREP?"

The request for a situation report caught him off guard; Reilly was used to being a shooter first and medic second, not the appointed leader of a split team on top of the rest. But Libya had stretched them thin, and in retrospect, he'd wished they'd brought more guys.

Reilly glanced over his shoulder to see Ian seated atop the other Land Cruiser, facing the opposite direction. Hass was dismounted, using his infrared floodlight to perform a ground sweep; between the night vision and the two ridiculously oversize long-whip radio antennas rising from his kit, he looked like a giant insect.

"All good," Reilly replied. "We're twelve minutes from showtime, no issues. How's everything going on your end?"

"*Regular fuckin' slumber party,*" Cancer replied.

Reilly hesitated then, knowing that Cancer was about to sign off and not sure that he wanted to know one way or the other. But curiosity got the better of him and he keyed his radio once more, asking, "Any word on Suicide?"

"*Yeah. Word is he's still off the grid after fourteen hours. It ain't looking good.*"

"You think he's dead?"

"*The fuck do I know?*" Cancer replied. "*But if we're betting on it, yeah. Khalil figured out he was on the op and didn't like it. Or Suicide is alive and in an orange jumpsuit while Khalil gets his camera crew together.*"

Irritated at the lack of emotion as well as the pessimistic assessment, Reilly responded, "You don't sound too distraught over the possibility."

"*I am distraught. You want to take your anger out on someone, go punch Rain Man in the face—he's probably hoping Suicide gets schwaked just so he can inherit the knife.*"

Hass came over the net then, pausing his clearance effort to reply.

"*Too soon, Cancer. But if worse comes to worst for him, that Project Longwing Winkler is going to need a good home.*"

Cancer ignored the comment but probably appreciated it—gallows humor was more or less standard fare among fighting men who had little other recourse in dealing with the blind chance and dumb luck that combat presented more often than not.

Then the sniper transmitted, "*To be honest, I don't like this bullshit any better than you do. But all we can do is continue keeping Duchess up to speed and letting the situation develop. You think I'm wrong, then I'm all ears on what we should be doing differently.*"

But Reilly had nothing to offer; if anything, he'd been hoping for some glimpse of optimism from the acting team leader, but that kind of perspective wasn't in the man's constitution.

Sensing that no response was forthcoming, Cancer concluded, "*Let me know when you guys are on your way back.*"

"Copy," Reilly answered. The main topic of conversation underscored his grim mood—despite the remoteness of their location, regardless of the orbiting Reaper to keep eyes out for any signs that they'd been compromised with negative results, he felt like enemy contact was imminent. This was going to be a repeat of their failed linkup with the SEAL advance element, he sensed, where everything was going according to plan until the last second when everything went sideways in the worst possible way. After all, who in the fuck could have anticipated that Khalil would have drones?

He heard footsteps approaching in the dirt behind him and looked over his shoulder, expecting to see Hass.

Instead it was Ian, the skinny intelligence operative clambering over the Land Cruiser's bumper and hood to mount the roof, where he took a seat beside Reilly.

When Ian didn't speak, electing instead to clear his throat and hawk a wad of spit into the dirt below, Reilly said, "Thought you were supposed to be pulling security."

"If they manage to surprise us out here, we've got bigger problems. But relax, no one's coming."

"That's what we thought about the SEALION linkup. So what is this, a social call?"

"Two things," Ian clarified. "One, I owe you an apology about what happened back at the safehouse. The interrogation with Arseni."

"The first one, or the second?"

"Either. Both. I stand by my actions, because if there was an easier or less violent way to extract information, I would've done it. We didn't have time to waste. Then again, I know it rubbed you the wrong way and it wasn't my intent to offend."

Reilly snorted.

"What are you trying to say, that I have feelings and shit?"

"Yeah," Ian mused. "Something like that, which makes you an anomaly on this team. I mean, obviously Cancer's a total sociopath, and the others are probably just tamping down whatever they feel to look tough. But I know it hurts you to see anyone suffering, Nazi or otherwise."

Reilly, unsure how to respond to that, settled with the words, "Apology accepted. What's the second thing you wanted to talk about?"

"David."

He felt Ian's gaze upon him, looked over to see the lenses of the intelligence operative's night vision. At this range they were regarding each other as a green blur, with their optics adjusted for far more distant focus, and both men quickly redirected their attention to the desert beyond.

Then Ian said, "I don't know where he is any better than you. But you know the saying, 'if you're going to be stupid, you better be tough?'"

"Story of my life," Reilly muttered.

"Well, David's not the brightest, but he's one tough son of a bitch. I've known him longer than anyone on the team, and believe me when I say that if any of us can survive impossible odds, it's him. I was certain he'd be killed so many times before Project Longwing that if Duchess tells us he got executed, I'd still need to see a body to believe her."

"Here's hoping it doesn't come to that."

"Here's hoping," Ian agreed. "What else is bothering you?"

"Oh, I don't know...maybe the fact that Khalil had fucking UAVs."

Ian released a quiet laugh.

"Yeah...not saying I was expecting it, especially an operation as big as the one we found. But as far as criminal and terrorist organizations go, Khalil's not the first and certainly won't be the last."

"Really?" Reilly asked.

"The Mexicans have been using them for years. Human traffickers run drones to probe border crossings for law enforcement before sending people across, and small-time narcos fly drug bundles over the boundary. The cartels have drones fly aerial reconnaissance before they move their armored fighting vehicles or land their planes—hell, they've even weaponized them, especially the CJNG, with C4 and ball bearings."

The thought sent a shudder up Reilly's spine.

"That's a scary thought...so they're, like, flying IEDs?"

"Exactly," Ian said. "They call them *drones artillados*. And that's nothing compared to the Middle East. ISIS was running upwards of a hundred drone attacks each day at the height of their power, the Houthis have flown them into Saudi air defense radars, and Hamas uses them to bomb the Israelis. Hezbollah uses them to surveil Israeli nuclear facilities on behalf of Iran among many other things like dropping cluster submunitions."

"Jesus."

"And here's a little poetic justice for you: this all started with the CIA. In 1986 they started the Eagle Program to build UAVs, and one of the first things they planned to do—until the proposal got nixed—was weaponize one with either a rocket or explosives for use in a kamikaze mission, and use it to kill the man responsible for the West Berlin discotheque bombing: a dictator by the name of Muammar Gaddafi."

Reilly wasn't sure how to respond to that; taken in the context of their mission in Libya so far, the irony was almost overwhelming.

And as it turned out, he didn't have to respond at all.

Hass came over the net then, speaking quickly. "*One minute out.*"

Ian and Reilly clambered down from the Land Cruiser's roof, and the medic retrieved a kit bag from the rear seat and quickly confirmed it was zipped fully shut before slinging it over his shoulder and searching the sky to the west. Hass joined them a moment later, jogging over as he transmitted on the air frequency. To Reilly, it was almost inconceivable that he couldn't hear anything yet, but after a few seconds had passed, he realized why.

The helicopter was cruising incredibly low, a nap-of-the-earth run as fast as it could fly. The sound of its double rotor assemblies was audible almost as soon as he identified the shadowy black orb coming in over the horizon without so much as a single infrared running light to show for it. Total blackout, the same as its landing zone—Hass could have erected any array of strobes or ground markers to guide the pilots, but they simply didn't need it. This was the equivalent of sending in Michael Jordan for a game of one-on-one against a middle school JV player; nothing about the flight or landing on the ground required the best helicopter pilots in the world to make the trip, but this aircraft and its crew was the closest rotary wing asset that could range the trip from the USS *Iwo Jima*, so that's how this brief exchange had to go down.

Hass raised his voice over the sound of the incoming rotors. "You want me to—"

"No," Reilly cut him off, donning a pair of clear shooting glasses beneath his night vision. "No, I got it."

Then he transmitted to Cancer, "Eyes on the bird."

And as that bird got closer, Reilly was struck—as he always was—by how absolutely *massive* it was.

The standard Army CH-47, more colloquially known as the Chinook, was a beast. It had a rotor diameter of sixty feet—and two sets of those rotors, thank you very much—over a fuselage large enough to transport a full platoon of soldiers. From its first operational deployments since the Vietnam War to the continued use of updated variants in the current day and age, it was a time-honored staple not just of the United States but militaries around the world.

But compared to the aircraft now approaching, it looked absurdly banal.

There was only a slight change to the nomenclature, from CH for Cargo Helicopter to MH for Multi-role Helicopter, but in terms of visual and operational disparity, that amounted to a world of difference.

Exactly one unit in the world flew the MH-47: the Army's 160th Special Operations Aviation Regiment, who by virtue of their role in spiriting shooters to and from some of the most austere environments on earth, at night and often at high altitude or inhospitable weather conditions, required far more than the standard military aircraft could offer.

He could make out some of those additions now, the most striking and obvious of which was the extended spike of an aerial refueling probe extending from the nose like a medieval lance. Bulbous, long-range fuel tanks flanked the sides, over which he could make out partial glimpses of a pair of six-barrel rotary miniguns and another pair of M240 machineguns sweeping over the ground, the weapons operated by crew chiefs who'd send a hailstorm of death upon anyone foolish enough to shoot at them. Less evident but there nonetheless were the various bolt-on attachments to facilitate multimode radar and forward-looking infrared technology that allowed the pilots to hug the terrain in zero-visibility conditions, to say nothing of the various rocket countermeasures like flare and chaff dispensers.

Nor did aircrews of this caliber settle for anything as unsightly as the olive drab warpaint of the standard military helicopter: every 160th aircraft was painted black.

In short, it looked like a standard Chinook both on steroids and attired as a ninja. Twenty-seven thousand pounds of dark metal and sex appeal, Reilly thought, watching the aircraft thunder alongside his position in a gradual descent to send a blasting spray of scorching rotorwash and sand in all directions before it touched down, alighting gently on its landing gear with the lowered ramp facing him.

Reilly ran forward with the kit bag, charging through a hot wave of exhaust until he'd cleared the rotorwash and could make out a crew chief in his night vision, standing inside the cavernous fuselage with a safety lanyard tethering him to the rear of the bird.

Charging up the metal ramp, Reilly unslung his kit bag, filled to the brim with the hard drives and video capture cards they'd seized from the drone command center, and handed it over as he shouted amid the sound of the blades, "This is everything."

The crew chief accepted the package and, to Reilly's surprise, set it aside to pick up a far larger duffel bag that he handed over with the response, "Resupply, and a little something from our guys to yours. Happy hunting."

Reilly took the bag, unprepared for how heavy it was—fifty pounds, easy—and called back, "Thanks, brother."

"NSDQ."

Reilly chuckled as he turned away and jogged down the ramp. NSDQ was the unit's motto, *Night Stalkers Don't Quit*. The men and women of that elite organization liked to reference it at every opportunity, and for good reason—their stated guarantee to the ground units they supported was arrival on target plus or minus thirty seconds, in any conditions, under any circumstances, anywhere in the world.

He hadn't yet arrived at the trucks when the hammering sound of the MH-47 rotors crescendoed into a roar, and he took a knee in anticipation of what amounted to a shockwave of air and sand as the helicopter broke its contact with the ground. Spinning in place to watch, he saw the gigantic aircraft ascend vertically for fifty feet or so before dipping its nose and throttling away in a wheeling turn.

Its engine noise faded as he closed the final distance with the Land Cruisers. Ian was already in the driver's seat of one in preparation to lead the way back to their safehouse, while Hass stood beside the second to ride shotgun while controlling the Reaper to navigate them around any checkpoints.

"The Golden Duffel," Hass said as Reilly dumped the bag into the rear seat. "Guess they deemed us worthy."

Reilly had no idea what that meant, and quickly adjusted the focus of his night vision and unzipped the bag to scan the contents.

Just when he thought he couldn't like Night Stalkers any more than he already did, they'd found a way.

Beneath the particulars of a combat resupply—5.56 and 7.62mm magazines loaded with subsonic ammunition, alongside a trio of HAR-66 rockets to replace those he'd shot at the militia technical vehicles—was the real prize, the very sight of which caused Reilly's spirits to lift.

Candy bars, chewing gum, cigarettes, and a case of Coca-Cola, every amenity the team would take for granted in the States appearing as a heaven-sent taste of home now that they were several gunfights deep into their Libyan mission.

Zipping the bag shut, he closed the rear door and moved to the driver seat. The night sky was quiet once more, with no indication that one of the most advanced aircraft in military history had touched down a minute earlier.

Reilly put the truck in gear and accelerated to follow Ian in the lead vehicle, transmitting as he drove.

"Cancer, this is Doc. Handoff complete, we're heading home."

27

I felt the vehicle brake to a stop, my breaths growing more rapid against the hood over my face as I tried to brace myself for whatever was about to occur.

After the usual succession of vehicle transfers away from the meeting site, I'd been placed into my current trunk and there I'd remained for hours—sometimes moving, sometimes parked for great periods of time, but not released.

What kind of game was Khalil playing now? I couldn't begin to speculate, only knew that whatever his plans for me, this went far beyond his previous surveillance detection routes. I'd been through three of those already, two for the first meeting and one on my way to the last, and this was not only different but wholly terrifying in a way I'd never experienced outside combat. My only consolation was that if he wanted to kill me, he could have done so long before now; whatever his intentions were, I assumed that my role in his eyes was to serve as a living witness.

Unless, of course, he planned to release me in an even worse part of Benghazi than he had upon my last return trip. Dumping me at the US diplomatic mission was crude poetic justice, to be sure, but I wouldn't be getting off so easily a second time.

I heard the trunk opening overhead, and at least two men wrenched me out before standing me upright. They marched me a few steps away from the vehicle—it was impossible to discern the setting with the bag over my head—and unlocked my handcuffs.

One of the men said, "Your evidence, Mr. Connelly."

Pulling the bag from my head to see it was nighttime, I feverishly tried to assess my surroundings, to distinguish threats from near to far as I prepared for another sprint through the streets with what I could only hope was a sufficient level of navigational support from the Agency.

But as the vehicle pulled away, I saw that the sidewalks around me were eerily empty. I looked down to find my wallet and two cell phones on the pavement, bending to stuff them into my pockets before looking left and identifying the side of a three-story building with soft lighting illuminating the letters *THE PALACE SUITES AND APARTMENTS*.

But unlike the first time I'd gazed upon this sight with breathless relief, I saw the presence of new lights as well—the alternating flickers of a red and blue glow.

Turning toward the hotel, I broke into a run.

Soon I saw why Khalil's men had dropped me off nearly a block away—the street outside the hotel was filled with civilians packed in around police cars. This wasn't the United States, after all, it was Libya; there was no police cordon, no yellow tape or row of perimeter officers keeping the crowd at bay. Any pedestrian gawker who wanted to stroll in to watch the crisis-in-progress could and did line up, and I forced my way through the crowd until stopping at the far edge.

Between the street and the hotel's outer compound wall was a sidewalk lined with dead men, women, and children. I saw a family of five clustered together in a heap, the youngest daughter no older than my own; beside them were three women in hotel uniform including Arshiya, the front desk clerk who'd handled my check-in. She'd been shot six or seven times in the chest, as had most of the victims, I saw at a glance; their bodies were also damaged by the fragments of grenade shrapnel that had in some cases dismembered them horribly and in others sheared limbs completely. Policemen continued to shuttle fresh cadavers out of the hotel, and I muscled my way through the crowd along the sidewalk until I found Sam and Corey, recoiling at the sight.

They'd fared far worse than most of the hotel occupants—Sam's face was a cratered mess, his clothes and what was left of his gray hair soaked in blood and gore, serving as my only positive identification. Corey had likewise been shot in the face with what must have been an automatic burst at near-point-blank range.

Unlike the rest of the fatalities, however, their bodies bore wounds in excess of the damage caused by bullets; their chests had been carved open, hearts surely removed just as the pilot's had been on Jolo Island. Khalil's twisted calling card, I thought with disgust, and a message not just to me but to the Agency representatives who would eventually claim the bodies.

Scanning the crowd for expats, I found a man with European features and approached him with the question, "What happened?"

He squinted at me as if I was insane, and I hastened to offer, "I just got here."

Nodding, he replied in a British accent.

"Massacre, mate. Gunmen stormed in and blew away everyone, room by room. I didn't see it happen, but I bloody well heard it. Sounded like World War III from my flat."

I said nothing, able to muster only a dumbfounded nod.

He asked, "Were you staying here? The police are asking for statements."

"No," I muttered, leaving the man where I found him and slipping back through the crowd. Now I knew the reason for my prolonged trip back—it had nothing to do with detecting surveillance and everything to do with the time required to summon an attack. The identity of the assailants didn't matter; any number of militias would gladly take the job if money was on the table. However many casualties there were, Khalil may as well have been pulling the trigger himself.

Drawing my Agency phone as I distanced myself from the hotel, I dialed the number for John Mason and waited for the call to connect.

Once it did, I spoke immediately.

"I'm sure you've heard by now, but the Palace Hotel got hit."

The voice that responded sounded like it belonged to the same man as before. "Can you confirm or deny that—"

"Confirm," I said without further prompting, "no survivors."

What I wanted to say was "two more stars," a reference to the Memorial Wall at the CIA's Original Headquarters Building. The marble surface was marked by a hundred thirty-plus stars etched in by chisel, one for each Agency officer who died in the line of duty. Most were members of the Special Activity Center or its predecessor departments, roughly a quarter of the stars had no name attributed due to the secrecy surrounding their deaths, and one—in a controversial move regarded as either an insult or a long-overdue recognition of the mental effects of war rather than the physical—was a female CIA officer who killed herself less than 48 hours from boarding a flight home after a year in Afghanistan.

"It was clean," the man said abruptly, then added, "your room."

"Are you asking or telling?"

"I'm telling you. It was clean."

That was all the clarification I'd get that Corey and Sam had successfully zeroed out their extensive array of computers. I envisioned their horrific final moments—they'd have seen the gunmen flooding into the hotel over their live camera feeds and immediately wiped the hard drives before they could be captured intact. That procedure was designed to take less than a minute from start to finish, which didn't leave them much time to run; not that it mattered, I thought. They'd probably transmitted the situation to the Agency and remained in place to oversee the digital clearance, knowing full well that no rescue was coming for them. The closest thing to cavalry in Benghazi was the rest of my team, currently occupied with God knew what after our raid on Khalil's UAV operation.

Then the man asked, "Can you find a taxi?"

"Why?"

"Because we booked you a room at the Julyana. Right now, that's the safest place for you."

"All right. Be advised, Khalil refused to accept a delay in payment and shaved 24 hours off his deadline as a result of me bringing it up."

I could practically hear the man's grimace as he responded, "Understood."

"I'm on my way to the Julyana, will call in once I arrive."

"Safe travels."

I put the phone away only to feel it scrape against Khalil's device in my pocket, and was struck with the unsettling realization that I was tethered to that fucking thing once more. No more location spoofing or mock audio—now they'd know exactly where I was, hear everything that occurred within the phone's recording radius. My days of leaping into a team car to find all my kit and join them on a raid were over; should they, I wondered, have existed in the first place?

The truth was that while I'd saved the lives of two teammates while on that objective, an equal number of Americans had just been slaughtered as a result along with a whole lot of civilians. That alone was a zero-sum game with no rhyme or reason. Whatever I did, however I responded to the jests and parries of Khalil's plot, this situation was totally fucked.

I didn't know if I was sick of this or wanted more, if I was rejecting it all or utterly addicted, and it may not have been my place to say. Maybe my wife could make that judgment, but I sure as hell couldn't. All I knew was that I was living life in the only way I knew how, existing amid death in all its forms whether inflicting it as an aggressor, witnessing it as a horrified observer, or, in the worst of circumstances, sacrificing those around me while I, as the least deserving to live, continued to survive against all odds.

Finding a taxi approaching down a side street, I flagged it down and began my trip to the Julyana Resort.

28

The sunrise would have been more beautiful, Cancer mused, if he hadn't been required to lie in position for most of the night that preceded it.

Still, his elevated vantage point afforded an impressive view over a slice of northeast Benghazi, a war-ravaged city that had fallen into a recent uneasy peace. The buildings in his line of sight could have been confused for those of just about any other developed area of the world; then again, he reasoned, he was looking at a particularly affluent area. He made out the distant sound of the *Adhan* over loudspeakers below, an echoing Arabic chant calling all Muslim men to the nearest mosque for the sunrise prayer.

Beside him, Worthy asked, "You need to go pray?"

Cancer lifted his head to look over his teammate, lying in the prone behind a spotter scope, just in time to observe Ramzi rolling his eyes.

"Do I look like a good Muslim to you?"

Worthy drawled with genuine innocence, "No judgment, man. Just asking."

"Relax," Cancer said, returning his gaze over his sniper rifle, "he probably drinks more booze than we do. You're not in any danger of offending him."

Eager to defend his honor, Ramzi declared, "I could drink *twice* as much as both of you put together."

Case closed, Cancer thought; Ramzi's boundaries, beyond those related to his Tebu heritage, were fairly hard to discern if not altogether nonexistent.

The fat bastard had, however, been far too optimistic when he'd declared that yes, there were elevated buildings overlooking their target's home, albeit at great distance.

Once they'd begun planning in earnest, Cancer had been horrified to learn that the man's definition of elevation was tempered by lack of travel experience—the tallest building in the entire country was only 35 floors, and it was five hundred miles away in Tripoli. Here in Benghazi, the highest point they could attain was on the roof of the Tibesti Hotel, which was nowhere near Ghalibun Sharif's home.

But hope sprang eternal in Libya, and Gaddafi had barely been sodomized with a bayonet—and then shot repeatedly, for good measure—when the new administration bankrolled a series of high-rises to reclaim Benghazi's rightful throne as the country's business capital.

Of course, little of that had come to pass.

The descent into civil war, or rather its second civil war in a three-year period, had left those promising high-rises abandoned as a series of gutted construction sites, some of them still bearing damage from artillery bombardment. And while the one they occupied at present had fared pretty well considering many of its counterparts, it was left with a top floor only eight stories high. Sufficient for sighting his target, Cancer thought, but just barely.

And despite a long night spent on surveillance with a steady rotation of nicotine tablets tucked in his cheek, hoping for the appearance of a limping stick figure to enter the courtyard, he'd had no such luck. There was no getting off this mission early, he knew now; they were in it for the long haul, and Cancer desperately hoped that Ramzi knew what he was talking about when it came to their target's daily routine.

More to annoy the only Libyan present than to make any request for confirmation, Cancer asked, "You sure this guy's going to come out?"

Ramzi remained adamant.

"If you had a garden such as this, would you?"

It was a fair point.

Due to the elevation difference, Cancer could only make out roughly half of the square courtyard at the end of his scope. But it was an impressive sight: heavily planted with flowers and shrubs, with multiple paths converging on a central fountain that spewed water from a tall, birdbath-looking fixture into the circular pool below. Even that was only visible through the enhanced magnification of his scope, mounted atop the tremendous sniper rifle he'd been manning for hours.

His Barrett M107 was supported at the front by a height-adjustable bipod and at the buttstock by a monopod that removed any meaningful shoulder fatigue from the equation. Which was a good thing, because with a total weight just under thirty pounds, the sniper rifle was enough of a pain to haul into and out of position, much less support over an extended duration at the firing point.

Cancer heaved a long sigh as Ramzi reiterated, "Sharif will appear. Probably soon. The only question is, will you be able to hit him?"

He replied, "Buddy, I've got a 1,580-meter shot and this rifle can send a round almost two kilometers."

"But," Ramzi taunted him, "can it do so with accuracy?"

Cancer gave a scoff of disdain, as if to avoid stating the obvious fact that the answer depended on who was behind the trigger.

In truth, however, it was a valid question.

The M107 boasted an impressive ten-round magazine that could be discharged with devastating speed if necessary, but the convenience of the rifle chambering its rounds automatically came at the cost of an imaginative number of moving parts. The complexity of that construction took its toll on accuracy, which was only about a third of that of its bolt action counterpart. At this range, there would be close to a six-foot margin of error between his point of aim and the bullet impact.

That didn't matter much if he were using the weapon in an anti-materiel capacity that it had been largely designed for, shooting at engine blocks and the like across the vast ranges of open Libyan desert. Cancer had packed the weapon for just such an employment, and would have put it to good use on infil if the goddamn Reaper had sighted the incoming technical vehicles when they were more than a minute or two away.

But an engine block was a far bigger target than a single man, and a rail-thin one if Ramzi's description of Sharif was accurate. That size disparity made a world of difference when pushing the weapon's maximum effective range for vehicle targets and far exceeded it for personnel; granted, however, the .50 BMG round didn't need to pierce a man's heart to kill him. So much as a shoulder hit would be more than enough to remove Sharif's arm, not just the use of it but the entire goddamn limb. He'd bleed out long before he realized what was happening, but a near-miss would be as good as a total miss, and Cancer wasn't used to operating so close to the margins of his own abilities, considerable though they were.

From his position behind the spotter scope, Worthy announced, "We've got movement in the windows. Ramzi, better make sure your earplugs are in, and be ready to give us positive identification."

Worthy had set up an identical spotter scope for the Libyan, carefully adjusting its orientation and focus atop the bipod and warning him not to touch it, just to look. With the magnification set to 40-power, the slightest bump would send it wildly off the mark—and Ramzi had done so three times thus far.

Cancer rested his cheek against the guard on his buttstock, taking in the view of the courtyard with a laser focus.

Worthy said, "Door to the courtyard is opening."

Keeping his crosshairs centered on the fountain, Cancer would be the last to sight Sharif if it was, in fact, him striding into the garden; his goal was keeping the scope, and therefore his barrel, precisely aligned for what may well be a split-second shot at or near the courtyard's central fountain.

"This is him!" Ramzi cried.

"Sharif is moving toward the fountain," Worthy confirmed. "He's alone."

Sure enough, Cancer saw an exceedingly skinny Libyan limping past the vegetation at the right edge of his scope.

He carried a teacup in his right hand, stopping to delicately set it atop the fountain's concrete rim and procuring a cell phone from his pocket. Cancer kept the man centered in his crosshairs as he placed a call and, infuriatingly, Ramzi began hissing in a whisper.

"What are you waiting for? Shoot him!"

"Shut up," Cancer said without breaking his line of sight through the scope. He wasn't about to tell Ramzi why he wanted the call to be completed, nor could he relax—Sharif was mere steps away from vanishing behind the garden leaves or worse, the nearest wall of the courtyard, if he chose to saunter so much as a few steps in any given direction.

But his target replaced the phone in his pocket in relatively short order, then reached down to recover his teacup.

Cancer adjusted his aim, evenly took the slack out of his trigger, then pulled it to the breaking point to crack off his first shot.

The blast was tremendous, like a cannon going off, but, owing both to a cylindrical muzzle brake that deflected exhaust gases and a strengthened recoil buffer, the effect on Cancer's shoulder was more of a push than a sharp jolt, akin to firing a shotgun rather than a regular sniper rifle.

Given the incredible distance, he had time to reacquire his point of aim while the bullet was still ripping through the air, and Cancer was taking the slack out of his trigger a second time when a great geyser of water shot upward from the fountain's pool. Sharif jumped back, arms flailing as he staggered to remain upright with his bum leg; Cancer fired a second round by the time the man had composed himself to begin a limping run back the way he'd come.

The concrete fountain exploded, a blast of dust and water shearing the giant birdbath mid-stalk and sending it toppling into the pool. A third shot would be too little too late, Cancer knew—Sharif was already gone from view—but he pulled the trigger anyway, then observed that in addition to the fountain damage, a single shattered teacup now lay in the walkway. The last round impacted several feet to its right, violently puncturing a slab of flagstone that would serve as a permanent reminder of how close Sharif had come to dying that morning, if he ever returned here at all.

Cancer doubted that would be the case as he flicked his selector lever to safe, then leapt up and tried to shake blood into his legs as he collapsed his bipod and muscled the giant rifle sideways and back into its open case. Worthy was likewise stowing his spotter scope, slinging his HK416 in preparation to lead them back down the stairs to their waiting vehicle—and by then, Ramzi was absolutely losing his mind.

"You missed!" Ramzi shouted, probably oblivious to how loud he was being with his ears plugged. Not that it mattered much, considering how loud the weapon itself was, but his outcry annoyed the hell out of Cancer nonetheless.

"Lose the earplugs," he replied, "you're screaming."

Then he turned to follow Worthy toward the stairs, determined to make his exfil regardless of whether Ramzi decided to follow or not.

By the time he reached the stairs and began his descent, Worthy was already turning on the first landing, clearing the way as pointman. Cancer moved as quickly as he could to pursue, but the weight of his rifle case prevented him from coming anywhere close; it also, regrettably, slowed him to the point that he could still hear Ramzi's accusations as the fat Libyan thundered down the stairs behind him.

"You faggot," he gasped, trying to keep up, "you missed."

Cancer responded while taking the stairs two at a time.

"Everyone has bad days. Wind must've picked up."

"There was no wind!"

Turning at the landing, Cancer took the next flight down without response.

To Ramzi's credit, it only took him another few seconds to realize what had just occurred. And when he did, he exclaimed, "You missed on purpose!"

Smiling, Cancer called back, "Why do you say that?"

"You never intended to kill him."

"Maybe I'm just a terrible shot."

Ramzi wouldn't accept this, and when he spoke again, the rage in his voice was mounting to unprecedented levels.

"You lied to me—*why?*"

Cancer stopped at the next landing, but only long enough to fix his gaze on Ramzi and ask, "Would you have led us here if I didn't?"

The Libyan fell silent at that, and without bothering to look back, Cancer continued, "And relax, fucker. We'll find out where he's going."

"No," Ramzi insisted, panting as he thumped down the stairs behind Cancer. "Now he will disappear."

Disappear, Cancer thought, yes—at least as far as anyone in Benghazi was concerned. But the irrefutable facts remained that to Sharif, the UAV ground control station had been raided less than 24 hours before an ostensibly botched assassination attempt against him. He was going to flee to the highest degree of safety he could, which meant deeper into the bowels of Khalil's operation. Doing so would require him to make contact, to convey his circumstances, and to feverishly request protection for his troubles in service to the terrorist mastermind.

Whether Khalil would help him remained to be seen.

After the failed maritime linkup by the SEALs, it was clear enough that the Americans were coming no matter what. The noose was tightening around the terrorist operation here, one way or the other, and no one would understand that better than Khalil. It was very possible he'd kill Sharif just to seal the source of compromise, just as the former Quds Force mercenaries had gunned down the UAV operators who, if captured alive, could have provided an encyclopedic knowledge of what they'd been tasked to do, and how they set about accomplishing that task.

But Sharif's fate didn't concern anyone. What truly mattered was what he did in the coming days—or hours, if he didn't live long enough to see his next sunset.

Unbeknownst to Ramzi, the Agency had committed the vast majority of its aerial assets to a continuous rotation that would follow Sharif wherever he went, to say nothing of monitoring his communications using an array of highly classified resources whose technology Cancer would probably find mind-boggling if he had the compartmentalized security clearances to know about them. As it stood, however, he didn't much care how the CIA tracked the man now limping his way to perceived safety, only that they did. In this more so than anything else, he felt certain that the odds were in America's favor.

Sharif represented close to the only thread the Agency had to follow toward Khalil and with him, Olivia. Now that they had it, they weren't going to let it go.

29

"*Raptor Nine One, Cancer.*"

Duchess reached for her hand mic and replied, "Send it."

"*Fired three shots toward Sharif, he's on the run.*"

"Copy."

"*Exfil in progress.*"

She didn't even bother responding to that—her attention was focused instead on a screen at the front of the OPCEN, where the transcription of Ghalibun Sharif's previous phone call was appearing as fast as the translator could type.

[call begins]

SHARIF: *Peace be upon you. Have there been any changes with the weather?*

UNKNOWN: *Close your mouth. I will send for you when the time arrives.*

SHARIF: *Do not forget about me, friend. I should like to be safe before the ghibli.*

UNKNOWN: *Stay where you are and wait for my call. Do not contact me again.*

[end call]

. . .

Analyst comments: *"Weather" likely refers to an established plan or timeline of operations. "Ghibli" are sandstorms endemic to North Africa. Possibly a codename for the hostage (OG), or a reference to US reprisals for her capture.*

Duchess wanted to dwell on that exchange, to shake out some semblance of meaning beyond the obvious, but her satellite radio crackled to life once more—there was always something, she thought.

This time, however, it wasn't Cancer who transmitted.

"*Raptor Nine One, this is Angel.*"

Managing a team through a single ground force commander while directing the efforts of her own OPCEN staff amid the constant influx of new intelligence could be maddening. Now that David's team was split into three elements, with two CIA officers dead along with 31 others in the Palace Hotel, to say nothing of the VX attack against Cairo, she felt like her composure was coming apart at the seams.

Grabbing the hand mic, she replied, "Go ahead."

Ian continued, "*We're back at the safehouse, and I wanted to see if you had any further intel on the materials we sent. Is now a good time?*"

"No," she replied without thinking, then added, "but based on how things are progressing with Sharif, I don't think we're going to have a better one anytime soon."

In truth, the exploitation team aboard the USS *Iwo Jima* had already made landmark progress in sifting through the items captured at the UAV ground control station, transmitting their findings back in four data clusters so far.

And while Duchess had only personally reviewed the highlights of those transmissions, leaving any thorough dissection to the analysts on her staff, her computer displayed a live document being updated continually by each staff section as they summarized their ongoing assessments.

She began reading from that document now, starting at the top and working her way down.

"We've confirmed the UAVs in question were Qasef-1s, clones of the Iranian Ababil-T platform. They're Group 4 drones, range of just under a hundred miles, roughly two-hour station time, with a ceiling of 12,000 feet.

And the pilots were running all eight in rotation to follow the Navy boats across the Mediterranean."

Ian asked, "*Where were they launching from? I'm assuming the airfield was abandoned by now, but if we could know—*"

"No airfield," she said. "The takeoff locations appear to be mobile desert sites in the vicinity of Al Karmah and Taykah, south of the city and near enough to the coast. Those UAVs have a ten-foot wingspan, which makes them easy enough to transport in cargo trucks, and they were launching them with mechanical catapults just like they do in Yemen. And with all of our efforts currently focused on Sharif, it's unlikely we'll drum up any further specifics that will affect your team."

"*Unless*," the intelligence operative noted, "*Khalil has another UAV operation running.*"

"He doesn't. Or if there is, they are currently grounded. If that changes, we'll let you know."

"*How can you be certain?*"

"Because I am," Duchess said impatiently, thinking that Ian should damn well know better than to press her on the point.

In reality, the P-8 Poseidon squadron out of Sigonella had since dedicated two of their maritime patrol aircraft outfitted with AN/APS-154 Advanced Airborne Sensors, or AAS, to a concerted hunt for unsanctioned drone flights over Libya and the surrounding waters. Once in flight, the highly classified AAS pods could, among other things, detect and track moving targets in three dimensions from great distances.

Those planes were backstopped by a steady rotation of Navy fighter jets equipped with SLAM-ER missiles capable of receiving the AAS data and adjusting their trajectory to a moving target in real time. If a UAV threat were even a remote consideration prior to her team uncovering the ground control station, Khalil's drones would have been shot out of the sky long before the SEALION ever departed for the coast of Libya.

But hindsight was always 20/20, and the best they could do at present was to continue to monitor for aerial surveillance that had, thus far, failed to appear.

Ian finally conceded, "*All right, I get it. If you're confident there are no more drones, then I'm confident. But there is zero chance Khalil is dumb enough to place his UAV ground operations anywhere near Olivia or himself. That means we're looking at a hostage rescue well outside Benghazi.*"

Duchess responded, "For the record, my J2 agrees with you. And we were able to identify one of the executioners from your last raid: Nasser Laghmani, former Saberin Takavar Brigade who retired from the Quds Force and flipped to the private sector. Our assessment is that his presence in Benghazi was as a mercenary, and not indicative of Iranian government involvement—which is a very good thing, as far as additional enemy capabilities are concerned."

"*I agree,*" Ian conceded, "*but we still have no idea what we're up against. Wagner Group, Houthis, former Quds Force...no intelligence agency can effectively track all those elements at once, and Khalil is compartmentalizing different facets of the operation so no one compromise can take him down.*"

She was momentarily distracted when someone announced, "Sharif just reached Abraq Road, heading northeast along the coast."

Her eyes ticked to the main screen, where a live Reaper feed was centered on a Mercedes-Benz G-Class SUV speeding around a vehicle to its front seconds before a tractor-trailer roared past in the opposite direction. Sharif was running scared, and the fear was making him sloppy. No tradecraft, no surveillance detection route, just a terrified blitz toward what could only be a safe haven of sorts.

Duchess was about to reply to Ian when she saw her intelligence officer rising with urgency and quickly climbing the tiered steps leading to her desk. Then, she lost her train of thought entirely.

"Let me call you back," she transmitted. "Looks like there's been a development on my end."

"*Standing by,*" Ian replied.

She set the mic down and spun her chair to face Andolin Lucios, who held a tablet in one hand and set the other atop the desk before addressing her in a Spanish accent.

"Ma'am, there's close to a hundred hours of footage and we've got as many analysts as possible reviewing in fast-forward. So far it appears the drone pilots were primarily conducting routine orientation flights, along with patrolling what seems to be screening routes on the outskirts of Benghazi. For the most part they were keeping their UAVs in reserve—

the first and so far only concentrated effort to leapfrog the Qasef-1s in unison occurred when they mobilized to track the SEALION vessel, which is indicative of a spotting effort outside Sigonella, as we suspected."

Duchess frowned. "Then we're having this conversation now because...?"

"Because," Lucios clarified, "there's exactly one major disparity among that pattern, on a flight taken six days ago."

He set the tablet down for her to see, then pressed play on a video.

She saw the full color display of a drone feed as it followed a road that looked oddly familiar, particularly considering she hadn't seen this footage before.

"What route is this?" she asked.

"Abraq Road."

"Same one Sharif is traveling?"

"Yes, ma'am," Lucios said. "And in the same direction, heading northeast out of Benghazi."

The camera view shifted radically—no camera manipulation by the sensor operator, she could tell, but a violent 180-degree sweep of the aircraft to return the way it came.

She asked, "Am I correct in assuming this is suspicious because the bird had plenty of station time remaining?"

"That, and the fact that it had no follow-on task whatsoever. The rest of the footage, corroborated with the GPS tracking, indicates it simply resumed a standard orientation or screening flight."

"Where was the turnaround?"

He closed the video and opened a map on his tablet.

"Right here." He pointed to a small and seemingly inconsequential town just south of the coast. "Outside Al Marj, which is a dry hole to be sure. We've already run a full sweep of historical imagery with MACE-X, and there's been no unusual activity since the kidnapping."

"Then why the sudden evasive action?"

"That's the million-dollar question. I believe the drone operators were conducting an orientation flight and strayed into a no-fly area, one that they weren't aware of at the time. The speed of the correction indicates their Quds Force oversight kept that information from them, interceding only when a pilot unknowingly violated it."

"And if that no-fly area isn't to protect the town, then it's protecting what's beyond it."

"Correct, which brings us here." He swept the map east, where a mountainous and heavily forested plateau ringed the Mediterranean. "This area is known as Jebel Akhdar, or the Green Mountains. It extends across three districts between the Levantine Basin and the Gulf of Sidra. Rich agriculture, nomadic herders, heavy rainfall, and most importantly the mountain terrain has made overhead observation as well as determining routine patterns of life extremely problematic for us."

"You think that's where Khalil is keeping Olivia?"

He hesitated before replying.

"Between Sharif's direction of movement and the footage indicating the drones were forbidden from approaching it, I assess that is quite possible. Consider also that David Rivers's transportation to and from the first meeting with Khalil was just over eight hours, which is certainly consistent with a thorough surveillance detection route and multiple vehicle transfers added to what would otherwise be a two-and-a-half-hour drive in each direction. Additionally, Jebel Akhdar is of tactical and strategic significance; the Libyan resistance ran its insurgency against the Italian occupation from that area in the '30s, and British and Axis powers fought over it in World War II."

"Brian," she called out, not bothering to look up from the map.

"Yes, ma'am?" Sutherland asked.

She swung her gaze toward him, waving toward herself impatiently.

"Come hither."

Then she turned to Lucios and said, "Let me get a handle on the air piece. Circle back in ten with a list of the most likely target locations in the vicinity of Jebel Akhdar. Can I hang onto the tablet?"

"Yes, ma'am," he replied, quickly departing for his desk. Duchess had an additional few seconds to scrutinize the map projection, panning back and forth over a tightly wrinkled plateau of knotted hills and snaking roads, before Sutherland arrived at her side.

"Ma'am?"

She shrank the map to reveal the full extent of the elevated range and said, "Andolin anticipates the hostage rescue will occur in this mountain chain. Where does that leave us as far as rotary wing support goes?"

"Depends," Sutherland said, touching the tablet screen and swiping to the Gulf of Sidra, "on where the assault force is. Will you be ferrying the SEALs to the USS *Iwo Jima* beforehand?"

"Absolutely not. That would remove the possibility of a ground assault, and I want that option in play until we've positively confirmed Olivia's location. Andolin could turn out to be wrong."

Sutherland shifted the map back to the mountains, gauging the distance.

Then he said, "Andolin's not wrong very often, ma'am, but I'll play ball. Okay, so the SEALs will be pre-staged in Libya and have mobility assets provided by our ground team to make a linkup with the whirly birds. Landing anywhere along the Mediterranean is a no-go; it's too densely populated and those helicopters won't go unnoticed. My guess is that the Night Stalkers will want to go feet-dry somewhere south of Al Maqrun just like they did last night, then fly to a desert staging area."

"To pick up the SEALs."

"Right," he said, "that, and the refuel."

She looked up from the tablet, wondering if she'd missed something. "Brian, the *Iwo Jima* is less than a hundred miles offshore."

"Straight-line distance, sure. Then it's another fifty miles or so to skirt those mountains to the south, so we're talking roughly three hundred miles round trip. Plus the transit and loiter time for an objective that's well above sea level. The Blackhawks and Chinooks might be able to make that on one tank if everything goes exactly according to plan, but their two MH-6 Little Birds are limited to 267 miles."

"They can leave the Little Birds behind. What do they carry anyway, like three shooters each?"

"Six," he corrected her, "but the SEALs are going to want them in the fight, and so are we."

"I think they can fit twelve men in the other Night Stalker birds, don't you?"

Sutherland heaved a barely audible sigh before explaining, "They can, but they shouldn't have to. First off, depending on terrain and buildings around the target, the MH-6s might be the only platform that can put shooters on the roof for a top-down assault while the main force enters at ground level. Even if that's not a consideration, noise matters. Any bad guys in those mountains will hear the Chinook coming a half-mile out, Blackhawks at about a quarter if we're lucky. But the two Little Birds? Duchess, they're practically flying lawnmowers. They can deposit a dozen SEALs wherever the assault leader wants them before the enemy knows what's happening, and by the time that occurs, the other platforms are seconds out because the Night Stalkers have calibrated to an exact science how to stagger their helicopter arrival based on audio signature. In a hostage rescue scenario more than anything else, Little Birds are a game-changer."

She scoffed.

"Not if they can't make it to the ship and back, they're not."

"I don't give you problems without solutions, ma'am. Not my style. The answer to all this is a Fat Cow FARP."

Duchess blinked. "You're going to have to explain yourself, Brian."

"FARP," Brian repeated, "is a forward arming and refueling point. And Fat Cow is simply turning a Chinook into a portable refueling point by configuring it with additional tanks that can hold somewhere around 2,400 gallons, if memory serves. They can fill up a Blackhawk in twenty minutes or so, Little Birds in a lot less. And if we don't have a target by sunrise, the birds just fly back to the ship and re-cock for the following evening."

She nodded approvingly. "So all that's left is getting the SEALs into Libya."

"Right. And that's the easy part."

"Agreed. Thank you, Brian."

Sutherland took the hint and departed, leaving Duchess to call out, "Update on Sharif?"

Lucios responded, "He pulled into an auto shop in Kuwayfiyah, switched vehicles, and is now in a VW Touareg on Abraq Road. Still heading toward the Green Mountains."

Duchess had heard enough; she rose from her seat, raising her voice to address everyone in the OPCEN.

"We stand at grave risk of Khalil accelerating his timeline further as a result of our recent activity, particularly against Sharif. Given the likelihood of an imminent raid in the Green Mountains, I'm going to advise the Pentagon of the following. If anyone has any objections or insights to anything I'm about to say, now is the time to tell me.

"As soon as possible after sunset, the 160th launches from the USS *Iwo Jima* to establish a forward arming and refueling point. They'll use that staging area to position their close-combat attack and transport aircraft for immediate employment in the not-unlikely event that we attain further intelligence during or prior to the next period of darkness in Libya. If there's no action by the time nautical dawn approaches, they fly back to the ship and stage to repeat the action the following evening. Either way, we maintain forward-deployed rotary wing capability during nighttime hours from here on out."

When there were no objections, she continued.

"Next: the assault force. The SEALs are a minimum of two and a half hours out by C-17, and now that 24 hours have been cut from the deadline, we've only got one full period of darkness remaining to stage them. Since we've confirmed Khalil's UAV capability has been severed and are trending toward a hostage rescue in or around the Green Mountains, I see no reason not to close that gap. Barring any unforeseen weather events, their primary course of action remains a high-altitude parachute drop into a desert landing zone, where our ground team will be standing by with cargo trucks to transport them to the birds."

"Ma'am," Lucios asked, "as far as the SEALs jumping in, are you referring to their advance element?"

Duchess struggled mightily not to sound condescending.

"We're running out of time, and we can't risk a major setback by stalling any longer. There *is* no more SEAL advance element, Andolin; I'm going to recommend in the strongest possible terms that all 56 shooters freefall into Libya tonight."

30

Ian sat at a long foldout table in the dimly lit room where he'd remained since returning from the intelligence handoff with the 160th Chinook.

The operations center was inauspicious but had been sufficient thus far; in addition to the various ruggedized laptops providing a lifeline to the Agency as well as their mission planning software, there was a satellite radio console along with a hand mic that Ian stared at, willing Duchess to transmit so they could resume their previous exchange.

He heard the chime of an incoming email instead, cutting his eyes to the screen to see that it had come from the Project Longwing OPCEN. Ian opened it at once, carefully reading the opening lines before scanning an itemized list of locations. Then he opened the map overlay attachment, seeing the locations flagged across a satellite image of a long, mountainous plateau east of Benghazi.

Ian was so engrossed in the contents that he only dimly registered a vehicle entering the main warehouse bay, followed by the distant echoes of Cancer and Worthy talking. The sniper team had made it back, and not a minute too soon. Based on the contents of the email before him, their day was about to get a hell of a lot more interesting.

Hass reappeared shortly thereafter, trailed by Cancer with a lit cigarette in hand.

"Any updates?" Cancer asked.

"Yeah. And we'll need Ramzi asap."

Hass left to retrieve the Libyan asset, while Cancer leaned over the open laptop and asked, "What do you got?"

Ian summed up the email as quickly as he could.

"SEALs are parachuting in tonight," he began. "We've got to pick them up in the cargo trucks and bring them back here or, if they find Olivia's location by then, to a 160th staging area for an immediate assault."

"Tonight?" Cancer asked incredulously. "Sharif provide some intel I don't know about?"

"Yes and no. He's fleeing toward the Green Mountains and it looks like Olivia is being held there—these are seven locations that the Agency has identified as the most likely targets."

He scrolled down the list for Cancer's benefit, and the sniper wasted no time in choosing the one that stood out from the rest.

"Right there, number four—classified military base from the Gaddafi era."

Ian shook his head. "It's not *that* classified. The CIA had Billy Waugh taking photos of it back in the late seventies—if I recall correctly, it was an air defense site with Soviet hardware."

"If it was built for air defense, though, it'll have a lot of defensive fortifications. That sounds like an ideal place for Khalil to stash Olivia. Why don't you favor it?"

"I don't know. Because it's obvious, I suppose."

"Then which one do you think she's at?"

"Based off this information? I can't say." He steepled his fingertips and closed his eyes to think for a moment. "The main factor isn't defensibility or even remoteness from civilian population centers. Khalil would select someplace that is not only tightly controlled by some armed faction or another but deep within defended territory. Think of the kind of places that would be an insurgent's dream to operate out of, where there's only one way for vehicles to get in and a whole lot of footpaths for them to flush out in the event of a raid. Where a wrong answer at a checkpoint will get you killed whether you're a local or not."

Ramzi said, "What is it?"

Ian opened his eyes and turned to see the portly Libyan standing behind him, flanked by Hass.

He replied, "What's your level of expertise in Jebel Akhdar?"

"Jebel *al* Akhdar, the district?"

"Not the *shabiyah*. I'm talking about the Green Mountains, running across three districts."

Ramzi crossed his arms.

"I see. In this case my expertise is the same as it is in all of Libya: I have been everywhere, and I know everyone. What do you need?"

"A hostage location. There are a number of possibilities, but I'm looking for someplace with one way in and a lot of ways out. Not just militia territory, but a stronghold within a stronghold."

"That is easy. The answer is quite simple."

Cancer asked, "It is?"

"Yes. You have just described all of Jebel Akhdar."

Ian frowned. "I'm being serious."

"So am I," Ramzi shot back. "There is a main road that runs through the mountains. It is cut into the limestone, and used by many. At Qasr Libya, another road runs north to the coast. Both are safe. There are also some areas used by hikers, campers, this sort of thing. As for much of Jebel Akhdar, it is most hostile to outsiders. This is where militias hide their armories, where people who do not want to be found go to hide. A maze of forest, caves, valleys, waterfalls. Many small roads, many trails that can only be followed on foot or by mule. Dozens of tribes and just as many militias. There are fighting positions left from the Italians, some carved out of the hillsides."

Ian's expression must have conveyed skepticism, because Ramzi asked, "You do not believe me? When the Italians came, they put us in concentration camps. One quarter of all Libyans were killed in the Fascist occupation. But Omar al-Mukhtar and his thousand fighters spent twenty years fighting back. Not in Benghazi, not in Tripoli. In the Green Mountains. Same with the LIFG insurgency against Gaddafi. He could not defeat them by fighting in the hills, so he crushed the city of Derna instead. If you intend to travel off the main roads, into the wilderness, there will be much danger."

Indicating the computer screen, Ian asked pointedly, "Do you recognize any of these sites?"

Ramzi squinted to analyze the seven locations, his eyes ticking back and forth between the words and their corresponding number on the map overlay.

Finally he gave a satisfied nod. "Some of them. I have delivered *bokha*—"

"*Bokha*?" Ian asked.

Hass clarified, "Libyan moonshine."

"Yes," Ramzi agreed, using a fingertip to tap a number of the listings in succession. "I have delivered liquor as well as cigarettes and pornography to...here, here, and here. Also this one—the old Italian fortress. I went there routinely until the SRC took it over."

Cancer said, "Suliman Revolutionary Council—same fucks that came at us with Dushkas on infil. Significant?"

"Maybe," Ian replied.

Ramzi continued, "The happy news for America is that for these sites I have delivered to, I can deliver the *albab alkhalfiu*, the back door."

Hass seemed to know what Ramzi meant, and Ian asked impatiently, "What does that mean?"

"The *bokha* is forbidden, and militia commanders do not allow it. My arrangements were with the lieutenants, typically, and delivery required me to arrive at night. Never the main entrance. These hideouts, you see, have many ways for the men to flee if necessary. Hidden doors leading to trails, secret gates. In some cases an actual back door. In others"—he paused, then jabbed a finger at a nondescript point on the map—"like here, a tunnel entrance concealed in the cliff. I would bring my mules there, and the militiamen would escort me underground by lamplight."

He traced his finger to the Italian fortress and tapped the screen. "It leads here, beneath the fort. Their men would unload the mules at the final gate and take me back down the tunnel to the cliff."

"The tunnel was big enough for a mule train?"

"The Fascists were miserable dogs, but they could dig."

Cancer grunted. "All due respect to the Italians, but once the SEALs get here, they ain't going to have to sneak in the back door."

Ian felt a sudden spike of anger.

"They will, however," he shot back, "have to isolate the objective before Khalil can waltz out. Ramzi, I want you to go through this list and write down everything, absolutely *everything*, you know about these locations. Which militias were operating out of them, and when. The back doors, secret entrances, every GPS grid you've got. We'll need to know what the gates are made of, how thick the walls are, any and every data point in as much detail as possible."

Ramzi gave a theatrical groan.

"I am tired," he said, jerking a thumb toward Cancer, "after a long night beside this liar. First I rest, and perhaps when I wake—"

Ian cut him off. "An extra five thousand dollars should help you wake up. Get it done, now."

Ramzi's expression brightened, his aim achieved.

"I will make some cardamom coffee and return in five minutes."

"Make it three," Cancer said sternly.

Once the Libyan had departed, Ian looked at Cancer and said, "We're going to have to pull David back into the fold."

"What for?" Cancer asked, taking a final drag off his cigarette before dropping it and snubbing the filter with his boot. "If we've got 56 SEALs dropping in tonight, it's gonna be hard to justify the need for a sixth man on our team."

"It's not for our safety," Ian said, "it's for David's. Now that he's tied to that phone with no safety net of Agency officers scrambling the surveillance, he's being tracked 24/7. If that raid goes down tonight like everyone seems to think it will, what do you think is going to happen?"

Hass supplied, "Same thing as the Palace Hotel. Any attempt at hostage rescue triggers a hit team to enter the Julyana and start smoking people."

"Right, except since the Palace Hotel got hit there are military and police stationed at hotels all across Benghazi. Khalil won't have to send in a hit team; he's got corrupt government officials on the payroll. They'll send the shooters straight to David's room, and when he gets killed, it will be by men in Libyan uniforms."

"Shit," Cancer said. "You're right."

Ian couldn't help himself—he leaned over and slapped his acting team leader in the back of his head, albeit far more softly than when the reverse occurred after the cardinal sin of stopping in a doorway during room clearance.

"I know I'm right. Get it cleared with Duchess."

Cancer balled one hand into a fist and held it in front of Ian's face.

"Don't push your luck, asshole."

Then Hass pointed out, "One problem: David doesn't know where this safehouse is, and there's no way Khalil's tech people haven't cracked his Agency phone after having it in their possession twice now. Anything you say to David, whether call or text, will be seen by Khalil, not to mention that hotel security is probably reporting to him."

Ian nodded, watching Hass closely. "That's why we'll have to get creative. And I think I know how we can pull it off."

31

I lay on the hotel bed, fully clothed and awake, staring at the unlit ceiling as the afternoon ticked by one excruciatingly long second at a time.

This wasn't exactly a presidential suite; the Julyana Resort was an average hotel, not the worst I'd ever stayed in but far from the best. The housekeeping staff had some room for improvement, to be sure, and there was a faint smell of stale cigarette smoke that compelled me to leave the window open.

Rising from bed, I stretched and approached that window now, pulling open the curtain to appraise the only thing I had going for me at the moment.

There was a clear view of the hotel pool, filled at present with delighted children who screeched and splashed one another while their parents sunbathed on reclining chairs. All the families appeared to be Libyan—there was precious little incentive for international tourism given the political situation—and beyond the fenced pool deck was the beach stretching north alongside the gently lapping waves of a tranquil Mediterranean Sea, its surface gleaming in the waning sun. Men and women strolled along the sand, but no one so much as waded in the surf. The reason, I'd learned during my check-in process, was that while open water swimming wasn't prohibited, it was best avoided at all costs: three days earlier, the bloated and rotting bodies of a half-dozen refugees had washed ashore at Bushileef Beach a few hundred meters north of the hotel.

Despite this grim proclamation, since arriving at the Julyana, I'd eaten —quite well, as a matter of fact—showered, slept as much as I could, and remained hydrated with bottled water, trying to bring my body and mind to as close to a state of readiness for whatever lay ahead as I could manage. What that could be, I had no idea; the Agency hadn't called with anything more than routine check-ins, knowing full well that the enemy was monitoring anything they or I said. Not only had Khalil's people failed to call me to arrange a meeting, but I'd actually tried dialing them out of sheer boredom only to receive an automated message in Arabic that, I presumed, stated the user's phone was switched off. No surprise there, as Khalil had to know the sky overhead was packed with unseen surveillance aircraft working to track every signal.

Since then my hotel room had turned into a prison cell of sorts, my mood worsening with each passing hour. This entire mission had been one sucker punch after another, from the Cairo attack to my disastrous meeting with Khalil to the massacre at the Palace Hotel. I was no stranger to tactical setbacks, nor the death of comrades, nor even the soul-sucking experience of witnessing the deaths of civilians who didn't even realize they were on a battlefield in the first place—none of those events got easier with time, but there was at least *something* I could do about them, a mission-in-progress that demanded my utmost attention and focus. And under the best of circumstances, I'd soon find myself in a position to locate the perpetrators and adjudicate a much-deserved punishment upon them.

Remaining locked in a hotel room, far from my team and devoid of any updates to the overall operation, however, was more than I could bear.

A loud knock at my door caused me to whirl around, instinctively sidestepping behind the bed in anticipation of a shooter bursting inside or simply spraying bullets through the wood panel. It took me a moment to realize the absurdity of this precaution. I was both unarmed and being tracked by Khalil, so if someone wanted me dead, they'd get their wish without much effort on their part; the best I could do would be to inflict as much damage as possible in hand-to-hand combat, not that it would change the ultimate outcome. But if this was when they decided to take care of me for good, I'd give them a hell of a show.

A man spoke on the other side of the door.

"*Iidarat almumtalakat*," he said politely. Then, in clear English with a thick Libyan accent, he added, "Housekeeping services."

Both the timing and content of this announcement struck me as borderline comical. Here I was, a sitting duck in every sense of the term, riding a sudden spike of adrenaline and wondering whether the coming seconds would be my last. No self-respecting hit team would go to the trouble of attempting such a charade—at least I hoped not.

And whether because I believed him or was sufficiently bored with my state of isolation, I answered the door.

The bearded Libyan man in the hall wore a headdress, long white shirt, and traditional black vest that was not uncommon among the more devout of Benghazi's male residents. There was a single piece of luggage at his side. He held one hand over his chest in what I initially took as the Arabic gesture for gratitude; but then I realized that I'd seen this man once before under far different circumstances, and that he was holding a notecard with block letters explaining, *SAY "NO THANK YOU."*

"*La*," I said, "*La, shukran*. I don't need housekeeping."

Hass replied while gesturing for me to step out of the way. "Thank you, sir. Enjoy your stay. *Ma'a salama*."

He entered my room then, and I closed the door behind him. Locating the remote, I turned on the television, and by the time I turned back to face Hass, he'd flipped the notecard to the other side, this one bearing information in far smaller script.

I took the card from him and read it as he set his luggage on the bed, then unzipped it.

Time to go. Leave both phones here. Khalil's people are watching the exits. Sorry in advance, but this has to happen.

After squinting at the card in confusion, I saw Hass holding out a paddle holster containing my Glock 26. I allowed myself a sigh of relief at the sight, which elicited much the same reaction as seeing an old friend for the first time in years. This was more like it, I thought, eagerly donning the holster and pulling my shirt over it. My pulse quickened with the feel of a weapon at my side, spirits lifting with the heady knowledge that I would soon be reunited with my team, back in the fight in whatever capacity the Agency asked of us. If Hass thought this meeting was worthy of an apology, he was sorely mistaken.

But he turned back to the bed, indicating the remaining contents of his luggage. At the sight of it, my relief turned to outrage.

I shot Hass a murderous glance, but he merely gave an apologetic shrug before raising his left wrist to expose his watch and tapping the dial as if to say, *I don't like this any better than you do, but you better hurry up.*

32

Reilly started the Camry's ignition as soon as he saw Hass approaching in his native garb. Then, after another glance at the approaching Libyan, he had to do his best not to laugh uncontrollably.

Trailing the undercover Combat Controller was David Rivers in all his glory, which wasn't much at present. Reilly could recognize him well enough from context, though to the outside observer there was little indication of a white man beneath the clothes that consisted of, hysterically, a long-sleeved black dress that extended all the way to the ground, combined with a niqab covering his hair and face below the eyes. He looked for all the world like a woman—a broad-shouldered, athletic one to be sure, but a woman nonetheless.

Reilly retrieved his phone from the cupholder, closing the navigation app in favor of the camera function, and surreptitiously took a picture of the two men before returning it.

Hass let himself into the passenger seat, leaving David to open his own door and slide into the backseat.

"Just drive," David said preemptively.

Reilly complied, accelerating out of the parking lot at a leisurely pace so as not to draw any undue attention to what was a truly bizarre spectacle. The tension inside the vehicle was palpable as Hass said, "Sorry, David, but you'll want to leave the niqab over your face until we get where we're headed—cops are a lot less likely to flag us down if there's a female in the back."

"Wonderful," David muttered, his voice obscured by the garment.

Reilly followed a turn in the road toward a traffic circle where a Benghazi policeman in his white summer uniform was waving vehicles past, then took the first right to head southbound on Algeria Street. Consulting the phone positioned in his cupholder, he checked the navigational display to assess his next turn.

"Shit," he said. "There's a problem with my phone."

David asked, "What's wrong?"

Pausing for effect, Reilly lowered his voice to a sultry tone and continued, "It doesn't have your number in it, girl."

David's response was immediate.

"Ten seconds before you started running your mouth. Ten fucking seconds. Go ahead and get it out of your system."

Accelerating past a shopping mall, Reilly was all too happy to comply with the directive.

"Baby," he began, "just call me Microsoft—because I'm going to crash at your place tonight."

"Mediocre," David said, unimpressed.

"You must be a parking ticket, 'cause you've got 'fine' written all over that body."

"Ever think there's a reason you don't get laid, Reilly?"

But Hass commented, "You've got to admit he's getting warmer, though."

By then Reilly had his next pickup line locked and loaded, so much so that he rushed the delivery.

"Hope you know CPR, girl, because you're taking my breath away."

"All right," David shot back, "that's enough. I seem to recall something about a hostage who needs to be rescued. Where do we stand with Olivia?"

Reilly cleared his throat.

"They've narrowed her location down to a few likely options in the Green Mountains, just east of the city. It started with a list of seven, and they've crossed two off already."

"Crossed them off…how, exactly?"

To this Hass responded, "If I had to guess, they pulled in something sufficiently exotic to detect a mouse fart from 50,000 feet. Maybe a Triton. Those are in very short supply so it's a big deal to get a few hours' coverage, but if it's got the station time to check out the remaining five spots tonight, you can bet your ass we'll have a location."

Reilly entered the next traffic circle, wheeling left around a grassy field before merging with eastbound traffic on Third Ring Road as Hass continued, "Night Stalkers are launching from the USS *Iwo Jima* after sunset. By 2300, they'll have landed in a staging area and begun refueling their birds a kilometer upwind of the drop zone as a precautionary measure so a parachutist doesn't end up in their rotor blades."

"What's the package?"

"Two Chinooks, one of them a Fat Cow, plus two Blackhawk transports, two DAP gunships, and a pair of MH-6s."

"Christ," David said, "they're coming in heavy. What about DEVGRU?"

"SEALs will be wheels-up in a C-17 by 2100, with two and a half hours of flight time between Sigonella and the landing zone in the desert south of the Green Mountains. Time on target for their HALO jump is 2330. Once they land, we scoop them up in our trucks and, depending on how the intel shakes out by then, either drive them to the 160th birds or stash them at the warehouse before sunrise."

"And when the raid goes down—" David began.

"We," Reilly cut him off, preempting the question, "sit it out at the refueling point."

"Fine. As long as they find her."

Reilly shook his head slightly. "No need to act professional, boss. This sucks, and we all know it."

"You're right. Fuck. What time do we leave for the desert?"

Reilly guided the vehicle beneath a highway overpass and answered, "Team's already gone, bro. Staggered departure from the safehouse. Worthy took the first cargo truck to a staging point at an asset-owned junkyard in Al-Abyar a couple hours ago. Ian and Cancer should be arriving there any minute now with the second truck and Ramzi, our safehouse manager. He's a subject-matter expert on the Green Mountains and has smuggled shit into a few of the suspected hostage locations. Once we get back to the safe-house, you and Hass take off in the third truck, and I'll follow you in the fourth because we don't have any time to waste. Goal is for us to be consolidated in Al-Abyar by 1900, and we'll move out to the desert as soon as it's dark enough. That gives us about half an hour to establish the parachute drop zone while the Night Stalkers start their refuel."

"All right," David replied. "What else do I need to know?"

Reilly gave an amicable shrug. "We've still got that Russian tied up, I'm the proud owner of an armored plate with three bullets in it, and you probably would've been killed in a few hours if Hass didn't grab you."

"Super."

"All things considered," Reilly added, "you've had the cherriest assignment of the mission. The rest of us have had to put up with shit accommodations while you've been chilling in hotels."

David wasn't amused by the observation.

"You're not allowed to complain until you've had to wear a burka."

"Abaya," Hass corrected him.

Reilly seized on the opportunity to go for the jugular.

"Yeah, David, it's an *abaya*. And all you had to do was wear the damn thing, not rock your hips with that strut all the way to the car. Hey Hass, know the difference between a boner and cheeseburger? David's not giving me a cheeseburger right now."

33

"We've got a problem," Wes Jamieson called out to Duchess. "The C-17 just developed a hydraulic leak while taxiing for takeoff from Sigonella. I'm waiting to hear back on the repair time."

Duchess involuntarily rose from her seat as everyone in the OPCEN fixed their eyes on her, awaiting a response.

Rather than reply to Jamieson, she asked, "Brian, what kind of delay are we looking at?"

Sutherland answered, "Depends on how quickly they locate it, and the extent of the leak. If it's just a fitting that needs to be tightened, they'll have it up and running with plenty of time to make their infil tonight with an adjustment to their time on target. If the leak is in a hydraulic line, however, there's a chance it could push us past sunrise."

"Wes, is there another Globemaster the SEALs can cross-load onto in order to make their jump time?"

Jamieson shook his head. "Not one from the 437th, there's not. And given the air defense matrix, they'll need those advanced avionics and countermeasures. No way they can risk flying in with a vanilla C-17."

He consulted his screen. "All right, it looks like a relatively quick fix—they're quoting us mission ready within 45 minutes. The pilots can shave their planned loiter time to make up for some of that. One-hour delay to our timeline."

That timeline was relatively simple, at least on paper and at least before the SEALs got delayed—the helicopters and the C-17 were supposed to launch within minutes of each other. The Night Stalkers had a lot less ground to cover, and the near-simultaneous launch would give the helicopter crews just over an hour to refuel all their birds before the assault force parachuted in. Minimum exposure for Americans on the ground, and maximum darkness remaining in which to launch a raid if the intelligence came through as she suspected it would.

She seized her hand mic to transmit.

"Cancer, the drop ship had a mechanical issue. Anticipate a one-hour delay for the assault force, new time on target approximately half past midnight."

"*Copy*," Cancer replied, "*roll to 2430.*"

She'd barely set the mic down before her intelligence officer, Andolin Lucios, called back to her.

"Ma'am, Triton has cleared NAI 5 of suspicious activity. They're moving to NAI 4 now."

Duchess gave a curt nod, frustrated that there wasn't a better outcome as the asset screened their named areas of interest. Then again, she considered, they were extremely lucky to have that asset in the first place.

The MQ-4C Triton made almost every other UAV look like a Tinkertoy by comparison; it was longer than a city bus and weighed as much as three Reapers combined, with twice the wingspan and almost ten times the operating range. The Triton that launched from southern Italy could have just as easily flown to New York City and back before landing with fuel to spare, and contained a suite of electronic support measures that used triangulation to geo-locate a jaw-dropping array of cellular, radio, FM, satellite, and radar signals. It should have been an obvious choice to locate Olivia in the first place.

But there were only twenty operational Tritons at any given time, all gainfully employed to the highest national security directives out of a handful of strategic bases worldwide. It had taken Duchess everything but an Act of

Congress to pull a Sigonella-based Triton away from monitoring Iranian nuclear facilities and commit even a few hours to supporting a hostage rescue, which was particularly ironic given that a congressman's daughter was at stake here. The DoD wouldn't so much as entertain her request until she presented a definitive list of no more than six surveillance targets, all backstopped by corroborated intelligence. She'd succeeded in fighting for approval of the top seven out of Lucios's twelve most likely candidates, and even that had been a stretch of her personal and professional reach.

Only then in her train of thought did she realize she was still standing in the wake of Jamieson's first announcement of an aircraft update—and by the time this occurred to her, he was making his second, albeit with considerably more optimism than the first.

"Helicopters just took off on schedule. Eight Night Stalker birds wheels up from the USS *Iwo Jima* en route to staging area, flight time one hour and forty-seven minutes."

Retrieving her hand mic, she transmitted, "Cancer, be advised: rotary wing assets are airborne, one hour forty-seven minutes out."

"*Good copy*," Cancer replied.

And that was all the time she had before Jamieson's next announcement.

"Ma'am, the Night Stalkers had to send an MH-6 back. Transmission chip light after takeoff."

"Meaning?" she asked.

Jamieson shrugged helplessly and looked at Sutherland, who translated the phrase to non-aviation specialist language.

"Metal particles in the transmission oil. Unless the light is faulty, it means something's grinding and potentially headed toward a catastrophic break."

Duchess nodded her understanding and Jamieson went on, "The rest of the formation is proceeding as planned, including the remaining Little Bird."

She keyed her hand mic and transmitted, "Cancer, be advised the air element just dropped one MH-6 from the formation. Mechanical issue."

"*Copy that*," Cancer replied. "*The rest of my team should arrive in the next ten mikes or so, and then we'll head out to set up the landing zone. Estimate we'll reach our destination shortly after the helos touch down.*"

"Understood."

As frustrating as the loss of a helicopter was, the Little Birds were by far and away the least critical of the helicopters assigned to the current mission. If an MH-60 or, God forbid, one of the Chinooks suffered a similar difficulty, the SEALs would be forced to leave behind a significant portion of their assault force if not roll the entire raid back to the following night, when only a few hours of darkness remained until Khalil's deadline.

Coming on the heels of a C-17 issue, she was reminded of the drawback to all these capabilities: with incredible technology came an immense number of moving parts and points of failure, any one of which could strike at the worst possible time. And aerial assets tended to be the worst offenders.

Duchess finally sat down with admirable composure, though she allowed herself a single huffed word—"Goddammit"—under her breath.

And whether because he'd sensed her general unease or was otherwise trying to steady her nerves, Wes Jamieson approached her workstation and leaned in to speak quietly.

"The night is still young, ma'am. A one-hour roll isn't a showstopper. The operators will still have time to hit any one of those targets with darkness to spare."

Duchess eyed him warily. "Provided nothing else goes wrong, which hasn't exactly been the trend thus far."

"If something goes wrong," Jamieson continued, "and it always does, I'd rather have it happen up front and not on the objective. Besides, we don't even know if we'll be able to verify the hostage location—if Triton doesn't give us confirmation, the most we'll accomplish tonight will be getting the shooters back to the safehouse."

34

"Suicide, this is Cancer. Radio check."

No response, same as the last half-dozen attempts.

Cancer checked his watch, assuring himself that the incoming two-vehicle convoy should enter FM radio range any minute now. Under any other circumstances he wouldn't have been concerned at all, but splitting up the team over the course of this mission had taken its toll on his usual confidence—and if he was feeling worried, it was damn certain that his teammates were as well.

He shifted his seated position atop the decrepit semi-trailer—the highest vantage point he could reach in the interests of not missing a single radio transmission—and conducted another visual sweep of his surroundings.

As a short-term staging area, the junkyard on the northeastern fringe of Al-Abyar left little to be desired: it existed within a walled compound to protect the two dozen or so vehicles kept for spare parts in service of the adjoining auto mechanic shop, was sufficiently far from the main road, and was flanked by a sprawl of low buildings on one side and a vast desert on the other. Most importantly, the entire facility was owned by a vetted CIA asset, one of many kept on retainer across war-torn countries around the world.

It was getting dark now, somewhere between official sunset and the end of nautical twilight, a one-hour gap that made a world of difference in moving unobserved through the desert to set up a landing zone for the SEAL parachutists. He could make out stars in the graying sky overhead, the pink glow to his west fading ever more steadily toward the horizon. The view in the opposite direction was what held his interest, however—the Green Mountains were a black, rolling plateau rising from flat desert wilderness. Olivia Gossweiler was somewhere among those dark hills, and if all went as planned, she'd soon be rescued while a dozen or more terrorist shitheads would be reduced to carcasses.

But not by his team, he lamented.

He heard boots rattling the ladder at the back of the semi-trailer and rotated to face the intruder. Ian's face appeared over the edge, and he spoke over the distant barking of dogs in the town beyond.

"Any updates?"

"Not since I last called for you. When I hear something, you'll hear something."

"All right. In that case, I'm going to keep going over the remaining targets."

No surprise there, Cancer thought—Ian had sequestered himself inside the trailer since his arrival, setting up his laptop to analyze imagery of the possible objectives. It was a waste of time, but no worse than the available alternatives as they waited for the remainder of their team to arrive.

Then Ian asked, "You need anything from me or Worthy?"

"Yeah," Cancer said, "your Magic 8 Ball. What's going to happen tonight—will we be taking these SEALs to the helicopters or back to the house?"

Ian responded without hesitation.

"Helicopters. The raid goes tonight."

"This might be the first time you've predicted the future without some long-ass preamble of disclaimers about all the reasons you could be wrong."

The intelligence operative seemed to consider that for a moment, then clarified, "Sharif ran straight to the Green Mountains before the Agency lost visual and his cell phone went dark. That means someone punched his ticket before he could compromise the location further. The intelligence community has way too many assets focused on way too few possible hostage locations now. By tomorrow morning the SEALs will have Olivia, hopefully alive, and we'll be packing our bags. At least, that's my best assessment."

"Cool," Cancer said, drawing his pack and shaking out a cigarette. "Read anything good lately?"

"*A Savage War.* Highly recommended."

"I'll add it to my list. Still working on *Battle Cry of Freedom*."

Ian chuckled. "Have you read far enough to realize that Robert E. Lee is the man?"

"History doesn't lie—Grant kicked his ass."

"But Lee was the only military mind who could have delayed defeat for so long given the vast disparity in military, economic, and diplomatic resources."

Cancer was in the process of lighting his cigarette when he realized Ian wasn't waiting for a response—he'd already begun climbing back down the ladder to continue his target analysis.

Since they'd arrived at the junkyard, the most interesting update hadn't come from Duchess at all; just over an hour ago, David himself had checked in over SATCOM, reporting that he was en route to Al-Abyar with the remaining team members aboard the final two Iveco cargo trucks.

After that point they'd been receiving the satellite updates together, though what Cancer truly wanted was for that final element to come within range of the team's FM net so they could exchange words without Duchess—or anyone else, for that matter—being any the wiser.

And by the time he finished his cigarette, he got his chance.

David transmitted, "*Radio check.*"

Cancer quickly mashed his transmit button and replied, "I've got you loud and clear. How was life as a drag queen?"

A pause.

"*I don't have to answer that.*"

Neither did Reilly, though the big medic wasted no time in offering his two cents.

"*Suicide really nailed it. Me and Rain Man didn't know whether to welcome him back or try and fuck him.*"

"*Or both*," Hass offered a moment later, "*not necessarily in that order*."

Cancer grinned.

"ETA?"

"*A few minutes*," David replied.

"Good. We're losing light fast and I want to stay ahead of the timeline as much as we can. How are you holding up?"

"*After hearing Doc spit the worst pickup lines in recorded history, I'm ready to shoot some people. It's a shame we won't be able to*."

"Tragic," Cancer agreed. "I'll have everyone ready to go here, let's do a quick powwow once you get in and then hit the road for the desert."

"*You got it*."

By the time Cancer climbed down from the trailer and set foot in the dusty courtyard, Worthy and Ian were already donning their plate carriers. Cancer followed suit, having just enough time to strap everything down and sling his weapon before receiving a transmission that David had the compound in sight.

He remained where he was, lowering his night vision and testing it before flipping it up again as Worthy and Ian moved to the rusty iron gate and heaved its twin doors open on creaking hinges.

The first cargo truck rolled into view then, pulling inside the compound as Cancer suddenly remembered that he had yet to report the event.

"Raptor Nine One," he transmitted over his command frequency, "the rest of our team is arriving now. Will update once we're moving."

By then the second truck had entered, following its predecessor down a row of car hulks before stopping beside the trailer.

Duchess replied, "*Good copy, Cancer*."

He heard footfalls behind him, which was all the notice he had before David wrapped him in a bear hug and said, "I missed you, fucker."

Cancer freed himself from the embrace and gave a disappointed shake of his head.

"I was hoping you'd still be dressed as a woman."

"I was going to surprise you," David replied, "but in the end, I had to change. Reilly was getting too turned on."

"Well, congratulations: you're ground force commander again, effective immediately. Have fun talking to Duchess."

David laughed.

"GFC for picking up a bunch of Tier One shooters who get to have fun while we sit around the desert? Not sure how I'll handle all that responsibility, but thanks. And talking to Duchess is an art and a science—you can't always lie to her, but if you stick to the truth we'd have been shut down a long time ago."

Worthy appeared, slapping David on the shoulder with the words, "Glad you made it. Sorry about what happened at the Palace Hotel."

"You and me both," David replied, then turned to greet Ian—but that next exchange was lost to Cancer as Reilly stepped in close and whispered in his ear.

"Dude. Between us, I got a picture of David in drag."

Cancer grabbed his collar and pulled the medic even closer, whispering back, "Not a fucking word about this. I don't want him finding out until we've got an eight-by-ten framed on the team room wall."

Reilly grinned maliciously. "Aye aye, Captain."

Releasing the medic, he saw that his team, Hass included, had formed a loose circle between him and David.

Cancer said, "You got a pep talk for us, boss?"

The team leader began, "All right, here's the score: no one's thrilled about working this hard only to be left behind on the final hit. It is what it is. All we can do is get the SEALs where they need to go and hope they speak favorably of us in their dozens of imminent memoirs and movie deals. But if they come out of this with Olivia secured, we can all chalk this up as a win. No matter what happens, I'm going home with my chin up, and if I can say that a couple hours after cross-dressing for the first and hopefully last time, it goes for all of us."

When he went silent, looking as if he'd become lost in his own thoughts that may or may not have involved the deaths of two counterparts less than 24 hours prior, Cancer elected to keep forward momentum by asking, "That it?"

"Yeah." David nodded. "That, and it's good to be back. Let's get loaded up and head out."

35

"*Raptor Nine One, Suicide Actual.*"

Duchess lifted her hand mic and replied, "Go ahead."

"*We're about five minutes out from the parachute landing zone, request update.*"

She took a moment to consult the time displays on her computer screen. "Rotary wing flight is on time, touchdown at planned staging area in seven minutes plus or minus thirty seconds. Assault force is airborne over the Mediterranean; they're still planning to drop in approximately ninety minutes, at half past midnight."

"*Righteous,*" David said, eschewing any attempt at professionalism over their satellite radio link. "*We'll let you know once we arrive. Suicide Actual, out.*"

Duchess set the mic down and remained sitting rigidly upright, warily glancing across the room.

The OPCEN was staffed at full capacity but almost eerily quiet. She could make out the low radio chatter of the helicopter pilots from a speaker box on Sutherland's desk, and a few exchanges from the J3 Operations desk as the staff there communicated with the military elements. But for the most part, everyone present had entered their inner sanctum of contemplation, likely their last chance at the calm before the storm.

It was funny how this worked—there was at first an insurmountable number of possibilities, factors, and considerations, all of which were gradually whittled to the requirements for a functional plan. That plan was then assembled in detail, reviewed ad nauseum, eventually approved with or without modifications, and then...then, she thought, the wait. An unbearable length of time, regardless of the duration where there was nothing she or anyone under her leadership could do to affect the outcome, when all the moving pieces had been sent into action and all they could do now was watch, and wait.

Whatever the mission, it never went exactly as envisioned; this was the universal law. At best, their well-laid plans served as a viable framework for adjustments when the inevitable minutiae of real-world considerations tried to offset all the collective brainpower of her operations center, a cumulative effect that seemed like the universe was trying to disrupt their efforts wherever, whenever, and however it could.

And that was where she was now—the pregnant pause, the darkest night that came just before dawn or, in this case, when things started falling apart worse than they already had. As much as she tried to assure herself this was a matter of her own perception and not reality, Duchess was unable to shake the feeling that she was about to experience an unalterable reversal of everything she thought she knew about the situation in Libya.

It was that notion that caused her to startle at David's next transmission.

"*Raptor Nine One, Suicide Actual.*" She held her breath as he continued, "*We are in position, clearing the parachute drop zone for unexploded ordnance and ground obstacles at this time.*"

A breath of relief. Had it been five minutes since their last transmission, she wondered, or was her perception of time merely stretching as it usually did during critical events?

Without bothering to check the clock, she replied, "Copy all, continue mission as planned and be prepared to reinforce the helicopter staging area in the event of a ground attack."

"*We should be so lucky.*"

That little bastard was pissed he wasn't on the main assault, and as much as the thought irritated her, she had to admit that people of his ilk were the type she was comforted by rather than concerned with having in close proximity to a possible enemy response.

No sooner had the thought occurred to her, with the mic still in her grasp, than Jamieson gave his next time hack.

"Night Stalker formation is sixty seconds out."

She relayed the update to David, noting with pleasure the odd circumstance of serendipity; all the moving pieces and potential pitfalls, with the travel time for vehicles over uncertain desert terrain least among them, and her Project Longwing team was arriving into position just over a minute ahead of the helicopters.

Under the original timeline, David's team would have roughly an hour to set up the landing zone while the Night Stalkers refueled their fleet, all before the SEAL Team Six operators parachuted in to utilize the fully prepared ground and rotary wing support from both elements.

But with only two of those three moving pieces launching on time, and the Night Stalkers losing one of two MH-6 Little Birds, the entire mission now fell at the mercy of an hour-and-a-half dead zone as the C-17 completed the flight from Italy to a designated exit point over the Libyan desert.

As this thought occurred to her, Lucios turned in his seat and spoke.

"Ma'am, Triton has detected significant activity at NAI 2. Multiple PTT exchanges and a cellular activation."

The push-to-talk exchanges were a promising indicator: everyone in Libya had phones, but the presence of handheld radios was far more often reserved for exchanges that were meant to usurp an easily monitored cell network.

"NAI 2?" she asked.

"The Italian fortress."

"Content?"

Lucios paused to read the reports now streaming onto his computer screen. "Push-to-talk intercepts are guard position chatter. Sounds like they're replacing shifts."

"Other indicators of hostage presence?"

"Stand by."

Jamieson announced, "Thirty seconds to touchdown."

Duchess didn't bother passing that fact along to David, far too engrossed in watching the back of Lucios's head until he spoke again.

"We've got it, ma'am. One location requested water for the 'nonbeliever,' said it was running late and the boss wasn't going to be happy if she died on their watch."

"'She,'" Duchess asked, "gender-specific?"

"Yes, ma'am. Definitely 'she.'"

Duchess drew a breath. "Brian, vector all ISR assets to that location at the highest feasible altitude and maximum possible offset—I don't want any audio compromise. If they can't see what they need to under those parameters, any exceptions will be cleared through me on a case-by-case basis."

Sutherland called back, "Done, I'll swing them high and wide. We can adjust from there."

"J2," she continued, "put the best visual of that objective on the main screen. Audio transcripts to secondary screens as they occur. Any indications that Khalil is co-located?"

"Not yet," Lucios replied.

"J3, inform the assault force: current assessment is Olivia held at the Italian fortress, eighty percent fidelity and trending to ninety. High-value target may or may not be there with his personal security detail, will advise once we have more."

Then she grabbed her hand mic.

"Suicide Actual," Duchess transmitted without being certain why—it wasn't as if David's team needed to know this information in real-time, after all, so long as the assaulters were aware. "Olivia is at the Italian fort. More to follow."

David responded almost immediately. "*NAI 2, understood. We'll pump Ramzi for any details he hasn't thought to mention.*"

Then Jamieson said, "Night Stalkers are wheels down, all systems operational, starting their refuel procedures now."

With the mic still in hand, she transmitted, "Suicide Actual, birds are on the ground, no issues."

"*Copy*," David replied. "*Still clearing the landing zone, we'll be standing by to receive the shooters.*"

There was a palpable sense of relief in the OPCEN, with conversations resuming as no crisis emerged with the final emplacement of both support elements at their respective staging areas.

By then Duchess saw the target being streamed from the Triton's orbiting vantage point—the OPCEN's central screen was alight with the black-and-white projection of four crumbling walls and minarets in various states of disrepair, the partially wooded central courtyard containing an assortment of what appeared to be Bedouin tents. No people were visible, and prior to the Triton's confirmation of wireless communications, she hadn't known whether to take that as an indication of enemy presence or abandonment.

Suddenly her intelligence officer shouted over the conversations in the OPCEN, silencing them with his first word.

"SIGINT hit," Lucios said, analyzing his computer screen while holding a headset to his left ear. "Voice intercept for that cell activation."

Finally, Duchess thought, *finally* some good news.

But the feeling of elation vanished as the transcript appeared on a screen at the front of the OPCEN, streaming in one line at a time as the recording was translated from Arabic to English.

[call begins]

UNKNOWN 1: *Pay attention: the forecast has changed.*

UNKNOWN 2: *How?*

UNKNOWN 1: *The imam is on the way. At midnight he arrives to dispatch the nonbeliever. Then, we summon the ghibli.*

UNKNOWN 2: *I will depart now with my men. Praise be to God.*

UNKNOWN 1: *Praise be to God.*

[end call]

Duchess knew beyond a shadow of a doubt what the call indicated. Khalil was well aware that the US response was closing in and was adjusting his timeline accordingly.

As for the ghibli, it had to mean an attack, but against what target?

She lifted her hand mic, hesitating as a new block of text appeared on the screen.

Analyst comments: *"Imam" is likely a reference to KN. Assess hostage (OG) is located at or near call origin at the fort, while KN is en route from an offsite location to conduct execution. In this context, "ghibli" could indicate a terrorist attack. Call recipient possibly in charge of a supporting effort related to one or both events.*

Keying her mic, Duchess transmitted to David.

"Khalil is on his way to the fortress now, he arrives at midnight." Summoning a breath, she continued, "And then he's going to kill her."

36

Upon hearing Duchess's transmission, I was hit with a wave of nausea.

My team had heard the helicopters coming in, though just barely at this distance. Absent any previous radio transmission to confirm, I could have just as easily attributed the whisper of rotor blades to the desert wind.

Now I sat atop the hood of my cargo truck, pulling security and maintaining communications as Ian sat in the back, grilling Ramzi for further details about the objective. I leapt to my feet atop the hood, turning to look past the row of neatly parked vehicles to see the rest of my team scattered in a loose row fifty meters away, using their infrared lasers to sweep the ground for IEDs, landmines, and unexploded bombs to clear it for the upcoming HALO jump.

I keyed my team radio and spoke quickly.

"*Net call, we're going in. Leave keys in the vehicles, grab any equipment that would be useful for a hostage rescue, and load up on my truck. We're hauling ass to the helicopter staging area, I'll get us approval on the way. Target is the Italian fort, they're executing Olivia at midnight if we don't get there first. Infil will be through the tunnel outlet.*"

I had every expectation that I'd immediately have to clarify that I wasn't joking, but the reaction I saw told me that wouldn't be necessary. The infrared floodlights extinguished immediately, and the distant figures turned in unison and began charging toward our vehicles.

Cancer breathlessly transmitted, "*Doc, you're driving. Racegun, route planning with Angel—*"

That was as much as I heard before Duchess's voice came over the opposite earpiece.

"*Suicide Actual, do you copy?*"

"Copy all," I confirmed, scrambling off the hood and moving for the back of the truck. "And at midnight the SEALs will still be flying to the exit point—they're not going to make it. But I know who can."

I was in the process of clambering into the cargo area to find Ian and Ramzi hunched side by side, their faces lit by the glow of a tablet displaying satellite imagery, when Duchess replied.

"*Convince me you have even a remote chance against such a large target.*"

Finding my assault pack, I threw it over my shoulders and took a seat on the floor as I answered her.

"If Olivia's execution is imminent, then sending in five expendable assholes is a justified risk to take."

Hass shouted at me, "Six."

I looked over to see him climbing into the back with me.

"Correction," I transmitted. "Six expendable assholes."

Hass was followed in short order by Cancer and Worthy, both toting kit bags from their respective vehicles—they'd packed nearly everything from the safehouse on the off chance that the SEALs damaged or lost any equipment during their jump. If a retention strap broke and a demo bag or set of bolt cutters went plummeting to the earth, we damn sure wanted to have extras on hand for them; never in a million years, however, had we expected to need any of it ourselves.

Duchess asked, "*Plan of action?*"

Feeling the truck's engine rumble to life, I braced myself for departure and replied, "It's simple. We've still got one MH-6 in the fight—"

My last word caught in my throat as Reilly floored the accelerator and nearly sent me sprawling.

"One MH-6," I repeated, "that can carry six shooters and is the quietest bird out there. So my team rides that to one of the preplanned HLZs, then moves on foot to the tunnel outlet in the cliff. We take care of any security, follow the tunnel to the fort, and make entry at the sublevel. Then it's a matter of penetrating as silently as we can and locating Olivia."

Looking across the back of my truck, I saw Worthy kneeling next to Ian and Ramzi, conducting an animated exchange over the tablet. They were determining the best helicopter landing zone, I knew—the Night Stalkers had already plotted them all the way across the Green Mountains, identifying every clear patch of ground where the rotors of their various birds could find clearance. They were supervised by Hass, who was transmitting to the Night Stalkers over the air frequency, while Cancer handed out various pieces of equipment from the spare bags we'd packed.

Duchess said, "*My J2 assesses that Khalil will be moving dismounted from some mountain bunker. Given the tree cover surrounding the fortress, we won't get a clear view of him, and even if we did, a UAV strike would result in Olivia's immediate execution. And under the best of circumstances, you'd be reaching the fort when Khalil is, or damn close to it.*"

"Perfect. Ask any bodyguard—the biggest vulnerabilities in security are during VIP arrival and departure. We can slip right in the back door while they're worried about greeting their leader. Then we slice and dice however we can."

Worthy shouted at me the moment I ended my transmission.

"Two seven bravo."

Keying my radio before Duchess could reply, I relayed, "We want HLZ two seven bravo, I say again two seven bravo."

"*Understood,*" Duchess said with crisp authority. "*I'm authorizing your launch. Let me be very clear that this is a preemptive measure—Khalil's arrival might be delayed long enough for the SEALs to take down the target. If we get an intel update to that effect during your flight in, I'm going to recall the Little Bird to the staging area. If it occurs once you're inserted, then I want your team to serve as a blocking force at the tunnel outlet.*"

"Agreed on both counts." Then, for the second time that night, I added, "We should be so lucky."

"*Luck hasn't been on our side tonight,*" Duchess pointed out.

"No shit," I readily agreed, trying to anticipate the tactical considerations of the upcoming mission in the precious little time we had before executing it. Then I continued, "We don't have the manpower to hold that objective. So if we manage to get Olivia, our first course of action is getting her back down the tunnel and onto a helicopter. If we can't manage that, we'll run her into the hills on escape and evasion until the SEALs are able to secure a pickup."

"Concur. One more thing—the intercepted communication referenced a ghibli, or sandstorm, to coincide with the hostage execution. We believe it's a terrorist attack of some kind. It's safe to say that it won't originate from the Green Mountains, but if you obtain any pertinent intelligence, then relay it asap. Do you need anything else from me?"

"Two things. First, somebody at the refuel point will have to babysit Ramzi. And second, Little Birds are quiet but we could really use a noise diversion. Maybe the remaining Night Stalker birds could fly another route to draw attention away from us?"

She replied, "*We're way ahead of you. And we're going to do better than helicopters.*"

I wasn't sure what she meant by that, and I didn't particularly care; we didn't have the luxury of time to overthink this, and whatever Duchess worked on the back end was what we were going to get no matter what I said.

Instead I replied, "Stand by for me to brief my guys."

Then I keyed my team radio and said, "All right, boys, we're headed for the tunnel entrance. Sounds like there's some kind of attack in the works, they referred to it as a sandstorm, a ghibli, so be on the lookout for intel. Here's your planning guidance: there's nothing to lose. We don't make it to the objective before Khalil, she dies. Racegun, I want you moving hard and fast on point. Favor speed over stealth until we get close to the tunnel entrance, then flip those priorities until we're compromised. We'll figure out everything else as we go, so trust your instincts and play it by ear."

"*So basically,*" Reilly transmitted back, "*fast and loose.*"

Worthy added, "*At this point, I've forgotten how to do things any other way.*"

Hass spoke next, his voice ringing with more amusement than despair. "*And to think I expected tonight to be boring. Fuck me.*"

Cancer was more to the point, executing his duties as second-in-command by clarifying the minutiae that I hadn't even considered up to this point.

"*Load order uses the same task org as the UAV hit*," he began. "*Split Team One, left bench. Split Team Two, right bench. Once we hit the ground, order of movement is Racegun, Suicide, Rain Man, Angel, Doc, and myself*."

Hass objected, "*I should ride next to the GFC for in-air updates*."

"*Fine. You're on right bench next to Suicide. Angel, flip to the left*."

"*Got it*," Ian confirmed.

Cancer continued, "*I want myself and Racegun seated up front to pop heads as they appear. Doc and Suicide in the middle. Angel and Rain Man, you're in the back*."

"Time hack?" I asked.

Reilly replied, "*Thirty seconds out from the birds*."

With that settled, I transmitted to Duchess.

"All right, we're almost to the FARP. Are the Night Stalkers tracking?"

She answered, "*They're ready. Your MH-6 is on the west end of the staging area, callsign Beast Three Six*."

I shouted toward the cab, "West side, west side, Little Bird."

"On it," Reilly called back, swerving the truck left.

Cancer appeared next to me, then leaned in and said, "You know what aircraft that is, right?"

"What do you mean?" I asked, having forgotten he still had a radio tuned to the command net from his previous duties as ground force commander. Then, before he could respond, I realized the significance of his question. "Oh, shit. It is, isn't it—same pilot, you think?"

He shrugged. "We're about to find out."

I transmitted to my team, "Going off comms for a sec."

We'd long since programmed all applicable radio channels, with the Night Stalker joint frequency chief among them. I flipped my tactical radio over to it now and transmitted, "Beast Three Six, Beast Three Six, this is Suicide, GFC."

By then Reilly was slamming on the brakes, and Cancer was gone—first out the back by the time the rest of us were bailing out of the truck.

I leapt to the ground amid a cloud of dust from the truck's sudden stop, then darted around the side and into a wave of fuel and exhaust fumes to get my bearings as a female voice responded, "*Moreno, Pilot in Command.*"

Reilly had driven us into a ring formed by Night Stalker aircraft, Blackhawks and Chinooks arrayed in a defensive perimeter of sorts to provide fields of fire for crew chiefs operating the miniguns. But the only bird I was concerned with lay straight ahead—a small, egg-shaped fuselage with a modest tail boom and triangular braces over the seating benches to allow for the use of fast ropes.

I heard myself laughing at the pilot's response even as we ran toward her helicopter in a file. This couldn't be happening.

She continued, "*I'm tracking HLZ two seven bravo, fastest possible drop-off, immediate departure once your team is 'boots on the ground.' Confirm.*"

"Confirm," I replied, seeing Cancer take up a position beneath the rotors to establish a head count; more of a formality than anything else with only six shooters, but those habits never died. I felt him slap me on the shoulder as I passed, then rounded the helicopter's bulbous glass windscreen to reach my center position on the right bench as I transmitted, "Remember us?"

"*Say again.*"

The loading process was a thing of beauty as everyone moved to their assigned positions as a result of Cancer's hasty planning. I'd barely taken a seat before Worthy and Hass boarded on either side.

I saw that Worthy mounted his seat cowboy-style, swinging one leg to either side of the bench and hooking his ankles together to maintain more stability for a forward-facing direction of fire. Little Bird pilots hated that, as it resulted in more wind being blasted through the open space beside their cockpit, but they understood the purpose, and I imagined Cancer was doing the same on the opposite side of the helicopter.

Then I transmitted back, "Josephine, you're about to haul the same guys who pulled you off Jolo Island. Just thought you should know."

I momentarily wondered if her presence here tonight was an intentional move by the Night Stalkers. Their aircraft rotated readiness cycles for immediate deployment under the Joint Special Operations Command—was this blind luck, or had they made an immediate switch once they knew Khalil was operating in Libya? Neither would have surprised me.

And to her credit, Josephine's response wasn't racked with sobs or emotional in the least. She transmitted, "*Copy. If you put down Khalil, give him an extra bullet for me. Or ten. Beast Three Six light on the skids.*"

Any clarification I needed on what those last four words meant was resolved when the Little Bird broke the bonds of gravity a moment later, lifting upward and then dipping forward on a charging ascent toward the Green Mountains.

~

Ian watched the ground fall away beneath him, the helicopter gaining speed as it slipped between an idling Blackhawk and Chinook before proceeding into the open desert at an altitude of twenty feet.

"*All right,*" David transmitted, "*I'm back up on comms. Fun fact: Josephine is flying this bird. Let's have some good news for her by the end of this.*"

Ian had to marvel at the fortuity of that fact—he was the only one on his team who hadn't met Josephine Morena during the rescue operation, having been stationed offshore to run the various signal intercepts required for that particular mission. His teammates, however, had spoken very highly of the Night Stalker pilot's grit in fighting alongside them on their way off the island.

And when it came to flying, her strategy seemed to be to fly as low as possible, as fast as possible. The wind whipped across Ian's face as David continued, "*Rain Man, talk us through the air piece.*"

Hass replied, "*Flight time is seventeen minutes, final approach will be on a heading of three zero five. The HLZ is a postage stamp of a clearing that barely has rotor clearance for a single MH-6, which limits our pickup options to this bird only. Once we're on the ground, she's going to return to the FARP, refuel, and drop off her copilot to open up seating capacity for seven in the event we get the hostage out. That means someone will have to ride shotgun on the way back.*"

As usual, Cancer had a plan for that option.

"*If we get Olivia out,*" he said, "*she goes on the left bench between me and Doc. Angel, you'll sit in the cockpit, and for the love of God, don't touch anything.*"

"Copy," Ian said, watching the desert landscape transition from a flat sweep of sand to an increasingly wrinkled series of dried-out streambeds.

Josephine adjusted the helicopter's pitch ever so slightly as the terrain gradually sloped upward.

Then David transmitted, "*Racegun, give us the route.*"

Worthy began, "*We'll depart the landing zone headed north-northeast. It's going to be an uphill slog for about three hundred meters before we hit a ridge, then follow it another four hundred meters to the tunnel entrance. Twenty to thirty minutes.*"

Ian checked his watch, felt himself shaking his head—even if the pointman's most optimistic estimate was correct, they'd still only have nine minutes to make it all the way through the tunnel, into the fortress, and locate Olivia before Khalil's arrival. That was assuming, of course, that he arrived exactly at midnight and no earlier, which was far from a sure thing.

David asked, "*Security at the tunnel entrance?*"

Worthy's response was spoken with casual aplomb. "*We'll be coming through pretty thick vegetation that leads right up to the cliff. My vote is we go from file to rank formation about twenty meters out, then creep forward on-line until we get eyes on.*"

"*Fine,*" David said, then, "*Angel, take it away.*"

Ian was about to answer him when the Little Bird tilted upward at an almost vertical trajectory, then rolled right until all he could see was the night sky. He braced in his seat as the helicopter rotated again to reveal the ground below, no longer a desolate landscape but a forested ravine. Josephine was now flying between tightly knotted hilltops, using the terrain to mask her approach as they threaded their way up the mountainous plateau.

Swallowing hard, Ian transmitted, "According to Ramzi, the tunnel entrance is between two limestone slabs at the base of the cliff. There's too much vegetation to confirm that from satellite imagery, but he gave us the exact grid from his GPS; what we don't know is how it will be secured. His last trip there was over four years ago, and at that time there was an iron gate secured by chain and padlock and manned by two individuals. The tunnel stretches two hundred and fifty meters through a limestone ridge to the westside fortress sublevel—another iron gate manned by guards, but that's as far as Ramzi ever went..."

His words trailed off as he detected a new sound, this one audible even over the rotors and wind: a low, throaty howl rising in volume behind the helicopter. Looking left past the tail boom, he identified a twinkling glint of flame streaking across the sky behind them. At first he thought it was a rocket, then realized what he was actually looking at as he keyed his mic and transmitted.

"Fighter jet, six o'clock, heading east."

Hass responded, "*It's one of ours—Navy F/A-18, audio diversion to cover our infil. Two more on the way.*"

It took Ian a few moments to identify the second, this one trailing the first by perhaps a half mile with its afterburners lit. A smart ploy, he thought; no tight formation but an extremely loose spread, which was beneficial not only in providing an echoing swath of noise but in presenting the appearance of a group of Libyan MiGs on a night sortie.

David went on, "*What about when we're inside the fortress?*"

"Based on what the geospatial and imagery analysts can make out," Ian said, "along with historical records of Italian colonial construction, there is likely only one sublevel with depots for ammunition and supply storage. That means big rooms, a lot of empty space that we can visually clear at a glance. At the main level we're looking at a two-story square with minarets at the corners. Original construction of the first floor should have the barracks, field hospital, chow hall, with few to no windows looking out. Still big rooms, but with full exposure to the courtyard and all the Bedouin tents there, so we'll have to be extremely careful. Second floor was constructed for fighting positions, which means maximum outward visibility, and since none of our surveillance has shown people external to the building, I think that's where we'll find the majority of enemy forces arrayed for 360-degree observation of air or ground assault."

He felt the MH-6 bank left on its sweep up the high ground leading to a ridge, then rock sharply to the opposite direction before descending. It was as if Josephine was trying to give them the most nausea-inducing roller-coaster ride possible; the reality, however, was far more grim. The only semblance of protection from ground fire to both the pilots and the main rotor assembly was the helicopter's underside, and keeping that de facto shield oriented toward the most likely enemy positions as the terrain unfolded was a matter of survival.

The same could be said for flying low and fast, thus minimizing the ability of a ground observer to identify, much less take aim at, a passing aircraft.

Despite the irrefutable necessity of these sharp and oftentimes violent maneuvers, Ian had ample opportunity to second-guess the pilot's judgment when she rolled the Little Bird left at an almost ninety-degree angle, leaving nothing but thirty feet of empty air between him and the ravine below.

David asked, "*Next up: where are they holding Olivia?*"

"It would be speculation on my part, but if I had to guess—"

"*You do,*" Cancer cut him off. "*You stared at that imagery until your eyes bled, so pretend you're Khalil and figure out where you'd put her.*"

Gripping the bench with one hand as the helicopter banked right, Ian provided the only answer he could.

"Northwest minaret. It's the most intact of the four, and equidistant from the tunnel and main-level entrance, which gives them the most reaction time to execute her if they detect a raid."

"*Perfect,*" David said. "*We clear counterclockwise from the sublevel, take the first staircase we can find to the first floor. Get to the northwest minaret however we can and go up it.*"

Then Hass transmitted, "*Hate to interrupt, but we're one minute out.*"

"*Last thing,*" David insisted. "*Khalil is wearing the dead pilot's dog tags. If we get the chance to kill him, I want those tags recovered for the widow.*"

Cancer replied, "*Copy. Anyone sees movement from here on out, shoot first and ask questions later.*"

No idle observation, this—Ian knew as well as anyone that they were approaching the most vulnerable period of their flight, when every advantage of the MH-6's speed and maneuverability evaporated amid the need to decelerate and descend to a stopping point that was fast approaching.

"*Thirty seconds,*" Hass said.

Ian could make out that stopping point now, an absurdly small, oblong field dwarfed by the treetops surrounding it. Academically, he knew the 160th planners could plot down to mere inches the rotor clearance available for landing and takeoff based on analyzing current UAV feeds, but instinctively, he had no idea how the hell Josephine was going to drop her Little Bird into an area that he'd be hesitant to fast rope into.

Nonetheless she continued her approach, maintaining altitude while bleeding off speed—they were going to overfly the landing area, Ian thought—and then it was as if the bottom fell out.

The MH-6 dropped in a perilously sharp descent, losing equal parts speed and altitude as the ground rose up to meet them. Ian instinctively straightened his legs, giving clearance to the skids a second before they vanished in the whipping grass and, with a soft thud of impact, the Little Bird was idling on the landing zone.

Ian leapt off with his weapon at the high ready, sprinting forward to the treeline at an oblique angle as Reilly and Cancer spread out to his right. They didn't have to go far, and within seconds he came to a crouched shooting position beside a tree trunk as he scanned the undergrowth for targets.

But all he saw was a forested slope dropping away before him, bearing a degree of vegetation he never thought he'd see in Libya. He searched for unnatural movement amid the mottled green backdrop of his night vision, the bushes and saplings shifting with rotorwash as Josephine applied throttle.

Amid the increasing noise of the MH-6 ascending skyward, Ian strained to hear David's transmission in his earpiece.

"*Little Bird away—Racegun, lead us out.*"

37

David transmitted, "*Well, Angel, your job as our intel guy is secure. I just realized why Khalil went to all the trouble with the campfires and incense.*"

Worthy cracked a smile despite his present exertion.

He didn't have the mental bandwidth to consider the point before this, but now that David had mentioned it, the reason was clear enough.

Aside from the thin, fresh mountain air, his nostrils were filled with the earthy scents of oak, juniper, pine needles, and tree sap, to say nothing of the fact that the humidity was markedly higher than it had been at sea level.

He was leading his team through a sprawling forest, and with the shallow, muddy streams and pine trees, it felt more like a North Carolina training exercise than anything he'd previously encountered in Libya. There was an odd sense of familiarity here, adding to the almost surreal feeling that he was going to awake at any moment from a dream. Less than an hour ago they'd resigned themselves to a supporting role and were clearing a landing zone for the esteemed gentlemen of SEAL Team Six; now, they were throwing themselves ass over teakettle toward an objective they wouldn't have been allowed anywhere near under anything but crisis circumstances.

Which, regrettably, described the present situation all too well.

The only real hindrance to their progress thus far had not been the forest but the elevation; they'd started more or less fully rested, setting off before the sounds of either Josephine's rotor blades or the trio of Navy fighter jets flying with full afterburner had subsided. But a few hundred meters of steep uphill at the fastest possible pace had burned out his quads and hamstrings long before they'd reached the ridge, which meant that everyone else was sucking for air just as much as he was.

Now that they were on relatively high ground, it should have been an easy walk save the deadline looming over them and, more importantly, over Olivia Gossweiler. Conducting a hostage rescue was about the last thing his team was organized, trained, or equipped to do, but right now they were the only show in town, and between letting that poor woman die or taking a Hail Mary shot at a rescue, he felt immeasurably grateful that the Agency and his government had done the right thing in approving their insertion. No matter what was about to happen, he could take solace in the fact that he and his team were doing everything they could to stop the execution of an innocent civilian.

Worthy descended a short slope that ended in boulders interlaced with deadfall from the surrounding forest. Far too dense, he thought, for them to pass in any meaningfully short period of time. He chose a bypass to the left while on the move, deeming the right side option, loose rock fragments that would broadcast the sound of their movement, far too risky this close to their destination.

Once he was five meters into this new direction of movement, Worthy looked back to ensure his team had seen him and followed suit. David was second in the formation, and the next two men in the file were identifiable at a glance by virtue of their equipment appendages: Hass with his twin long whip radio antennas, and behind him, Ian with bolt cutter handles protruding on either side of his head. Good enough, he thought as he continued.

Worthy conducted two azimuth checks and consulted his GPS before slowing his pace, then proceeded for another full minute before a final glance at his wrist-mounted Magellan told him the tunnel entrance was 24 meters to his front.

Without taking his gaze off the terrain ahead, Worthy transmitted in a whisper, "We're about twenty meters out, let's get on-line—"

He released his transmit switch as a dark shape emerged from behind a tree trunk in his direct line of sight—undoubtedly a human head, though the surrounding vegetation was far too dense for Worthy to make out whether this person was taking aim or not. It didn't matter either way, he considered as he raised his HK416 from the high ready to a firing position and activated his infrared laser. Muscle memory and endless repetitions across a hundred or more live fire ranges took hold then, and he was at a full stop observing with clinical detachment a bright green dot blazing on the exposed head's scalp, the difference between his laser's zero and the point of bullet impact at that range automatically taken into account and compensated for in the time it took him to register the sight.

Worthy fired twice and noted the head jerk backward before disappearing in the undergrowth, and his weapon was back on safe as he charged forward with a calculated blend of speed and stealth. He didn't know who he'd just shot more or less between the eyes; his concern at present was whether anyone else had seen or heard.

He tried to place his footfalls on solid ground in the interests of keeping quiet, fearing he'd just compromised his entire team and getting confirmation as a man ahead called out, "Jaheim?"

Worthy was in dangerous territory now, least of all because his teammates weren't in position to back him up. He felt reasonably certain he'd scored at least one fatal headshot but hadn't confirmed it, and was rapidly approaching whoever had peeked out with absolutely zero effort to assure his personal safety.

Suddenly the forest gave way to open ground beneath the treetops, a danger area that Worthy stopped well before reaching to see a pair of limestone slabs leaning against each other at the base of a vast cliff. To either side of the slabs was an armed man wearing night vision devices, one puffing a cigarette and the other walking directly toward him.

Worthy took aim at the advancing enemy without hesitation, shooting three subsonic rounds and transitioning to the other man as the final bullet struck. Then he fired again, seeing the glowing cigarette ember spinning skyward in a counterclockwise arc before both bodies dropped in place and Worthy advanced forward while sweeping for further targets.

He found none, though his halt near the edge of the treeline brought with it a sense of great concern and despair.

The sloping cliff face ahead was dotted with smaller trees and bushes growing out of rock ledges, though he saw no shortage of cave entrances amid the limestone—no telling if they were occupied, though a cursory scan of his options revealed that it didn't matter much either way. They were getting inside that tunnel, period. Whether or not they were compromised in the process was up to the enemy, but it wouldn't affect the team's calculus in proceeding at all costs.

He heard footsteps approaching from his rear shortly before they clattered to a halt and David whispered within audible range.

"There are worse ways to go."

Worthy looked over his shoulder to see what his team leader meant, seeing only his teammates as they took up firing positions.

At his first downward glance, however, Worthy received his explanation.

The corpse just behind him was missing a significant portion of its brain matter, with bullet entry wounds in the upper lip and right eye beneath a shattered monocle of his night vision. But whoever he was, the dead man was splayed out alongside a tree trunk whose base was unnaturally dark given the surroundings. He had an AK-103 slung over his back and, far more pertinent to David's proclamation, grasped his fully exposed manhood. Worthy assessed at a glance that the slain fighter had departed his guard position to take a piss behind the tree that had just become the site of his death and, secure in this knowledge, resumed his focus on the mission at hand.

David transmitted, "*Security down, linear danger area ahead—breachers up.*"

~

I remained in place as a combined element of Reilly, Ian, and Cancer scrambled toward the slabs of limestone between two enemy corpses.

As I prepared to transmit over my command radio, I had severely mixed emotions about entering the tunnel.

On one hand, things were progressing as smoothly as could be expected. But that could turn on a dime once we went underground, and I'd have no communications with Duchess—normally an enviable position for me, but not when she was my only link to receive updates in a rapidly unfolding crisis. If Khalil was delayed long enough for the SEALs to mount a rescue, we'd be endangering Olivia even further by proceeding. Part of me wanted that to be the case, for us to be ordered to serve as an isolation element here, because her odds of survival would go up by a factor of ten.

Keying my command radio, I spoke quietly.

"Raptor Nine One, we had enemy contact but remain uncompromised. Three EKIA at the tunnel entrance we're preparing to enter. I'm about to lose comms, and I don't think that will improve once we make it into the fort. Last call for guidance."

"*Understood*," Duchess replied over my earpiece, "*no change to status. Assault force is still over half an hour from jumping, additional radio chatter indicates Khalil is approximately ten minutes out. Still zero movement of personnel on the roof or in the courtyard, so any enemy forces are internal at this time. You are clear to proceed and accomplish whatever you can. Good luck.*"

"Copy all, we're going in, will report when able. Suicide Actual, out."

I'd no sooner finished the transmission than Cancer came over the team frequency.

"*At the gate—be advised, padlock is on the inside.*"

Not good, I thought.

That particular detail didn't make a difference as far as the bolt cutters went—they'd chop through a chain just as readily as a lock shackle—but it indicated that the guard shift here would only be allowed back in the tunnel when their replacements arrived, which spelled the unfortunate fact that anyone who heard my team's approach would accurately assume us to be hostile.

Cancer continued a moment later, "*Breach is clear.*"

"Moving," I replied, and with that, the remainder of the team ended our security effort—Worthy was the first to advance, with myself and Hass following behind him. The pointman approached the slabs and then vanished between them; it wasn't until I got closer that the triangular patch of blackness lit with the ambient glow of an infrared floodlight and I saw a square cutout in the stone, the entrance the size of two standard doorways combined. Ramzi hadn't been lying about bringing mules through here, I thought as I passed the open gate with bars threaded by a cut section of chain.

Then I was inside, and understood why the breaching team had risked activating their infrared floods, particularly now that we'd confirmed the enemy could see about as well in the dark as we could—there wasn't so much as a candle within the tunnel to allow our night vision to function. The square porthole ran almost perfectly straight until a slight curve blocked the view fifty feet ahead, the dank air pungent with the scent of wet stone.

"*Racegun*," Cancer transmitted from his position at the far left edge, "*take the right side*."

Worthy swept past me to position himself opposite Cancer, and the rest of us fell into position without prompting; with the best two shooters in the lead against either wall, Reilly and I moved to the center to exploit the remaining field of fire straight down the middle. Glancing over my shoulder, I saw Ian and Hass picking up staggered slots on the walls behind us to pull rear security until their services were otherwise required. With the six of us making an X-shaped formation, I transmitted, "Let's go."

And with that, Cancer and Worthy began their forward sweep, and the rest of our team followed them toward the fortress.

~

Reilly let David set the pace for their two-man contribution to the center of the team formation, adjusting his walking speed based on the better judgment of his team leader, who was a foot to his left.

Their every movement was constrained by the dual pointmen ahead—Cancer and Worthy were using their infrared floodlights sparingly, the ghostly green discs centered around the bright pinpoint of their aiming lasers as they appeared, sweeping the floor ahead to identify any noise-producing obstacles and tripping hazards, and then everything went dark for long swatches of time before the process repeated.

The effect was that of a nightmarishly slow-motion strobe that lapsed to a claustrophobic lack of visual input, though Reilly understood their intent well enough: David had explicitly stated that speed would take priority until they made it to the tunnel entrance, and now that they had, stealth was the predominant consideration until the now-imminent moment of compromise by enemy forces. And if so much as a single observer was positioned at the final stretch of tunnel with a cheap set of night vision, keeping their infrared signature to an absolute minimum could be the difference between a successful entry to the fort sublevel and having a rocket shoved up their collective ass.

Besides, he thought, if they moved any faster than this, the noise would give them away; even at the current walking pace, the echo of every footfall, however soft, reverberated in the tunnel like a slamming door.

They continued their methodical march forward until Cancer and Worthy's floodlights suddenly extinguished in near unison. Reilly was momentarily confused by the simple fact that he could *still see them*—his night vision was dark and grainy, but so much as five steps back it would have been a uniformly flat shade of green absent the assistance of an infrared source.

That meant ambient light ahead, though it wasn't until he proceeded around the next curve that he could make it out.

By then Cancer and Worthy had slowed to an almost imperceptible creep, their weapons raised toward a light perhaps twenty meters away. On second glance Reilly determined that it was a perfect square, the tunnel's outlet within the sublevel of the fort, though the edges of that outlet weren't uniformly straight: two silhouettes were clearly visible amid the glow, both seated from the looks of it.

Reilly took aim, his left thumb poised against the pressure switch for his infrared laser.

It seemed almost impossible that the pair of guards couldn't hear the team coming by now, though it wasn't until he detected a man's laugh that he understood why. They were conversing with each other, and that lack of discipline enabled Cancer and Worthy to continue closing the distance as seconds ticked by with excruciating slowness. Soon only fifteen meters remained, then ten—Reilly could now make out the barred gate between them and their ultimate targets, and shortly after that he could see the shapes of rifles in the men's laps while fragments of their conversation drifted down the tunnel. If his team got much closer, they'd be able to stick their barrels through the bars before opening fire.

This was almost too good to be true, he thought, and like every event of good fortune in combat, that meant it was bound to end at any moment.

Which of the dual pointmen ultimately compromised the team's presence, Reilly had no idea, but he clearly heard the skittering of a loose rock against the limestone floor. The dialogue between the guards halted mid-sentence, and at that exact moment both the barred gate and the men beyond were crisply illuminated by a pair of infrared floodlights as Cancer and Worthy opened fire simultaneously. Reilly heard the clangs of metal on metal and the spark of bullets ricocheting off the gate as he and David took aim and opened fire.

The volley of suppressed gunfire lasted only three seconds from start to finish. Reilly stopped shooting the instant Cancer and Worthy extinguished their floodlights, an action that was immediately followed by both men sprinting forward. He and David followed suit, the team leader transmitting as he moved.

"*Angel, get those fucking bolt cutters up here.*"

When the two pointmen skidded to a halt without shooting, he was certain both guards were dead—the only question remaining was whether anyone outside of the six Americans in the tunnel had heard the subsonic rounds cracking off metal or the guards hitting the ground.

But as he came to a stop and rotated his rifle rearward on its sling, he heard only Hass and Ian's footsteps behind him, his teammates' breathing, and an odd rustling and tapping of boot soles against a hard surface that was explained when he achieved an up-close view of the two dead men before him.

The guard on the left was stock-still, frozen as a statue with a half-dozen or more bloody exit wounds perforating his exposed backside, his night vision skewed sideways on his head. While equally dead, however, his partner was far from motionless—his body was convulsing in postmortem response, the sight both reassuring and tragic.

With Cancer and Worthy positioned against the tunnel walls and aiming in the opposite direction down the corridor, Reilly and David had precious little opportunity to provide security. They did the best they could, however, maneuvering behind the twin pointmen as Ian appeared with his bolt cutters in a two-handed grip. Extending the handles to their maximum reach, he aligned the cutting edges of the cutter jaw over both sides of a single link before compressing his grips. There was a sharp *click* followed by the high-pitched clatter of the link fragments hitting the ground, and Ian tucked the bolt cutters under one arm and threaded the entire length of the chain to the tunnel side before stepping back.

Reilly and David filled the void, pushing their respective gate doors outward as far as they could go—not very far, as it turned out, with each hitting a dead guard in remarkably short order. Then the medic shouldered his way through the gap, moving left to position himself along the far wall to take aim as his team leader did the same on the opposite side.

His view was down a stone hallway extending past a gas lantern on the floor, ending at an L-shaped intersection ten meters beyond; a moment later he saw Cancer appear on the opposite side of the hall and heard him whisper a message a fraction of a second before his earpiece crackled with the transmission, "*Angel and Rain Man, search those bodies and drag them into the tunnel.*"

It was all Reilly could do not to laugh at the absurdity of the latter part of that order: a medically significant amount of blood would have saturated the wall and floor by now, while both chairs remained upright as if nothing had happened. Still, nothing good would come of a pair of downed fighters visible at a glance from anyone who peered down the hall after they left.

He heard the scrape of the bodies being moved as the four shooters took turns reloading in sequence during the tactical pause.

Hass transmitted, "*Got a push-to-talk radio off one of them, I'll monitor it for traffic.*"

Then Reilly heard the soft clank of the gates being returned to their original position before Ian followed that up with, "*We're good.*"

David spoke next, his voice exuding a calm confidence as he issued his next directive.

"*Cancer, you're closest to the northwest minaret—lead us out.*"

The sniper whisked forward along the far wall, and Reilly fell into place behind him as the number-two man in the newly-forming stack.

~

Cancer approached the corner to his front and briefly considered whether to conduct a high-low maneuver or flow straight around it. He decided on the latter in the interests of time, dipping his barrel when he was a few steps out so he wouldn't provide any advance notice to anyone watching around the edge. Then he pivoted right and took aim, flowing forward as Reilly swept left to keep pace along the far wall.

No one in sight, which was far from a surprise—if there was, they'd have been deaf not to hear the two guards getting gunned down less than a minute prior, subsonic ammunition or otherwise.

He faced a long hallway carved out of the stone and reinforced with limestone blocks, with vaulted doorways on the right-hand side. None were lit, though a gas lantern at the far corner told him this corridor didn't go untraveled for long. His next decision point was how to negotiate the first wide entrance that was fast approaching, and rather than enter and clear it he ceded forward security to Reilly and panned his own rifle sideways to shine his infrared floodlight inside as he passed.

An enormous room was on the other side, empty save for a few scattered crates. Reaching the opposite side of the doorway, he reoriented his aim forward to repeat the process. The result was the same, so he ran the play a third time—just as Ian had predicted, each room on the sublevel appeared to be a large depot for storage and little else.

This was close-quarters maneuvering at its worst, but as the lead man, Cancer was the limiting factor in the team's progress. If he committed to entering and clearing each room in sequence they'd be down here all night, which wouldn't do them much good if Olivia got her fucking head sawed off in the next few minutes.

Cancer resumed his forward movement, only then seeing that the next doorway wasn't to his right, but appeared to be the sole opening on the left wall. It was only big enough for a single man to pass, which was his first indication that he'd found the spot they were looking for. His second came when he glimpsed stairs at the bottom edge of the doorway, at which point he knew they'd reached the only route leading up the northwest minaret. Cancer felt a rush of exaltation at the sight; six minutes ago they'd been making entry into the tunnel, and now they were about to take the assault vertical.

He flashed his left hand in a fist to halt the formation, then crossed to the left side of the hall to maintain his position as the number one man on their way up. It was a greedy move, sure, but then again he was the most experienced team member, and if anyone was prepared to deal with whatever second-by-second decisions would be required as they moved up the stairs, it was him.

Then he continued moving toward the doorway, hearing his team's footfalls resume behind him. Only as he dipped his barrel in preparation to spin into the staircase entrance did he realize that at least one set of footfalls wasn't behind him, but to his front.

A man emerged from the stairs attired largely the same as the two guards at the tunnel gate: dual tube night vision, Soviet-style chest rack with magazine and grenade pouches. Though by the Heckler & Koch G36 in his hand, Cancer instinctively knew this wasn't a foot soldier but a sergeant of some kind, probably trooping the lines to ensure his people were awake and conducting their duties as ordered.

And that rank had at least some bearing on the man's reflexes as well. Cancer scarcely had time to realize that they were far too close for either to fully raise, much less employ, their full-length rifles before the enemy fighter, clearly having come to the same conclusion, tackled him to the ground.

Now this cocksucker was literally on top of him, their night vision devices pressed together, and while one of his teammates would soon pull the fighter off him one way or another, Cancer would be damned if he was going to sit around waiting for help.

Instead he abandoned the attempt to maintain control over his rifle, but not before giving a forceful upward shove. Then he released his right hand from the pistol grip, jerked his knife free of its sheath, and tilted the blade upward in a backhanded motion while trying to keep the enemy fighter away with his left palm.

The force of the man's body descending on top of him pushed the knife handle downward with incredible force; it struck Cancer's front just above his mag pouches and in turn caused the armored front plate to compress against his chest. The effect was like a gut punch, suctioning the air out of his lungs as he gasped for breath.

Cancer was pleased to note that his opponent had fared far worse in the transaction; the man was struggling to breathe as well, though primarily as a result of the blade that was embedded up to the hilt just below his sternum. And *that*, Cancer thought, was why a well-balanced, maneuverable knife was worth its weight in gold, even when you were expecting a gunfight.

He had no further time to revel in his victory, however, when the pressure on his chest suddenly vanished. Cancer maintained an iron grip on his knife handle, the blade coming free as one of his teammates hoisted the enemy fighter upward until he was awkwardly straddling Cancer, then drove the point of an identical Winkler blade into the base of his throat.

A hot spray of blood pelted Cancer's lips and cheek, causing him to flinch before the wheezing, dying fighter was flung sideways. Wiping his mouth with the palm of his tactical glove, Cancer took the biggest breath he could and saw to his surprise that it wasn't Reilly who intervened—the medic had bypassed the hand-to-hand fight to take point and establish security down the hall, and Worthy stood at the base of the steps and aimed his weapon upward.

Instead it was David who knelt to wipe both sides of his blade clean on the enemy's shirt. Then he sheathed the knife and extended his hand.

Cancer gratefully accepted the offering, still struggling to catch his breath as David hoisted him upward.

"God*damn*," Cancer whispered, "this is a great knife."

He was in the process of replacing his recently-blooded blade at the appropriate location on his kit and resuming a two-handed grip on his HK417 when David, now forming up behind Worthy to pull security in their direction of movement, transmitted his latest command guidance.

"Anyone who hasn't stabbed someone with their Winkler by the end of this mission is buying beer for those who have."

A moment before they resumed their clearance effort, Hass asked for clarification.

"*What if my Winkler's not team issue?*"

"Doesn't count," Cancer replied, heaving a final breath and falling in behind his team leader. "You're playing by Longwing rules now, rookie."

Then he saw David reach forward to give Worthy's shoulder a squeeze, and the pointman took his first steps up the stairwell at the northwest minaret.

~

Ian followed his team up the tight confines of the spiral staircase, moving as the second to last man in the formation—Hass was just to his front, and Reilly, having provided hallway security until his team was safely on the stairs, brought up the rear.

Worthy transmitted from the front of their formation, "*Looks like this goes all the way to the top—how high do you want us to take it?*"

David said, "*Angel, is she on the first or second floor?*"

Ian had a pre-loaded response ready for just that inquiry, and it had consumed no small percentage of his thoughts since entering the fortress. Given the likelihood of a heliborne assault, any self-respecting terrorist would shy away from keeping his only bargaining chip near any potential rooftop insertion sites.

But his team wasn't in some standard urban objective; this was a hilltop fortress with panoramic views, and he stood by his assessment that the second floor had observers watching for any approaching aircraft. The enemy was far more likely to be surprised by a ground assault making it through the main gate after having appeared out of the forest, and that planning factor would compel them to keep Olivia as far from the ground as they could to maximize their lead time in the event a hasty execution was required.

"Second," he replied at once, forgoing any attempt to verbalize his justification.

David took him at face value, transmitting immediately.

"All the way up. Enter and clear the first room you see to get us out of the hallways and establish a foothold."

The ascent gave Ian ample time to question his judgment call. With the certainty of lookout positions on the second floor, he'd already proclaimed it to be the enemy stronghold. If Olivia wasn't there, he'd just sent his team into a lion's den that they would promptly have to fight their way out of, if they could at all; the only guarantee up there was that they would encounter bad guys, and probably a lot of them.

Worthy transmitted, *"Door right, first-floor entrance. Bypassing."*

The subtext to that notification was "every man for himself." There would be no security to cover the team as they leapfrogged past a stationary shooter posted at the door; instead, each man would have to scan the threshold for any enemy while they moved. It was the world's worst game of duck, duck, goose—except here, if one man encountered an adversary, it would mean a decisive engagement with no backup until the nearest teammate arrived.

Ian proceeded upward, trying to ascertain through his night vision exactly where the door was until he saw Hass make a split-second pivot that ended when he turned forward and continued his trot up the tightly spaced steps.

Then it was Ian's turn, and he held his breath as he rotated and lifted his rifle to sweep the open doorway beside a short landing.

The view beyond was a short expanse of floor ending at a far wall marked by a cutout that revealed a glimpse of the courtyard at the fort's center. Ian saw thick trees through the window, and beyond them the bright trace of the nearest Bedouin tent roof. Then he was past the doorway, resuming his jog up the stairs.

A moment later Reilly transmitted, "*Last man clear*," which should have been a relief-inducing announcement that they'd made it past the first floor without getting bogged down in a gunfight that wouldn't end well for the team or, more regrettably, Olivia Gossweiler.

But Reilly had barely finished his transmission when Worthy gave the inevitable follow-up.

"Door right, second floor."

There was a very tangible surge of speed as the formation compressed upward, everyone increasing their pace save Worthy, who had probably slowed his remaining footfalls to allow everyone else an opportunity to catch up. Because he was about to set foot onto some seriously uncharted territory—there would be no radio calls after he reached the top floor, at least not until everyone was consolidated in the first room—everything past this point would be a moment-by-moment reaction to the situation that was about to unfold. By the time Ian located the doorway in question, Cancer was vanishing through it followed in short order by Hass.

Ian set foot on the landing and crossed the threshold onto the dusty stone floor of a hallway amid the low drone of an unseen generator. His team was headed right and he followed suit, glancing in the opposite direction down an unlit hall before looking back at the corner to his front. A glow of light extended beyond it, visible for only a moment before Ian followed Hass through an open doorway.

He raised his rifle to join the clearance effort, but his teammates had already reached their respective points of domination and were reorienting toward the door. He stepped aside to make room for Reilly, who entered and audibly whispered the same thing Ian was thinking.

"Holy fuck."

The room reeked of human waste, its source a toilet bucket in the corner. Combined with the rumpled blankets on the floor and shackles bolted to the wall, Ian knew without a doubt he'd seen this room before.

This was the site of Khalil's video demanding that David present himself for hostage negotiations, where Olivia had appeared beaten, bound, and gagged, with the word *kafir* written across her chest in blood. He couldn't prove that fact as bedsheets had been strung up over the walls in that video, and while they were now absent he could see why Khalil had used them—the Agency would have otherwise had a field day analyzing the rough limestone surfaces of the walls, and probably been able to determine within a very small margin of error that it was of early twentieth century Italian colonial construction.

Ian stepped toward David and whispered, "They already removed her for the execution. We need to go left once we get into the hall, there was a light around the corner—"

That was as far as he got before David keyed his mic and quietly said, "Ninety seconds to midnight. Stack up and take a left out the door."

No other words were spoken; as the last man in, Reilly was already pulling security at the room's sole exit, and Cancer fell into position behind him, followed by Worthy and David. Ian scarcely had time to reposition himself before the stack flowed outside, moving quickly and almost silently toward the source of light around the hall corner.

~

Reilly cut left into the hallway, raising his rifle toward the corner ahead as he moved.

Becoming the number one man was more or less a roll of the dice in the ever-shifting formations of room clearing, and unless Ian or Hass ended up in that slot—the former through his lack of tactical experience, and the latter due to the simple fact that the team hadn't worked with him long enough to trust him with the responsibility—it would have been counter-productive to pause and adjust their order of movement.

That wasn't to say that the remaining teammates were necessarily equal in their capabilities, as no one would argue that Worthy was the fastest shot among them by a wide margin and would have cleaned house as a gunslinger in the Wild West. But Reilly, David, and Cancer were more or less on a level playing field when it came to holding their own for the fleeting seconds it would take for the other shooters to back them up. Besides, he thought, the notion of an innocent female hostage had imbued his normally easygoing demeanor with an edge of anger and urgent momentum that made him enthusiastic about the prospect of leading his team forward.

The buzz of a generator somewhere around the corner masked his team's movement, and he had precious little time to analyze the light spreading across the floor to his front. It was relatively bright and discernible even without night vision, but that meant two things: one, it wasn't a typical gas lantern like they'd seen on the sublevel, and two, whatever he was about to find was going to be unprecedented.

Reilly dipped his barrel before the corner, then pivoted right and raised it again.

Seven meters away was a closed door lit from within, the doorframe clearly outlined on the left side of the hall. To either side of it was a rigidly standing man holding an assault rifle at port arms, not undisciplined fighters but an honor guard of sorts that he couldn't make sense of and, fortunately, didn't have to.

Both men swung their night vision toward the sound of his team, alert but unalarmed; there must have been roving patrols inside the building, Reilly thought with detachment as he activated his infrared laser and made the exceedingly minor adjustment required to align it with the center of the right man's torso.

Reilly fired twice, transitioning left too late to kill the remaining guard, but that man was already on the receiving end of a completely separate grouping of suppressed gunfire, this one fired by Cancer, who'd fanned out to his left.

Both bodies were still falling when Reilly took off at a near-sprint, intending to remain the number one man before Cancer could somehow overtake him for the privilege as he had outside the sublevel stairs. The medic's reasoning went beyond personal pride; despite the presence of a power cord snaking beneath the closed door as a conduit to the generator that he could hear but not see, the odds were very high that someone inside the clearly occupied lit room would have discerned the dull thwacks of subsonic rounds striking the wall if not the far less subtle collapse of the men posted outside. That spelled overwhelming odds that his team was about to have more targets coming into view at any moment.

His assumption was justified in the seconds it took to close the distance by half as the door opened to reveal not bright but *blinding* light from within. Reilly's night vision was almost entirely washed out in one fell swoop, any ability to visually discern his surroundings made possible only by a human silhouette stepping into the doorway and partially blocking the blaze.

By then Reilly had no reservations about gunning down an unarmed person on the objective. He didn't bother trying to discern whether or not the figure held a weapon, only confirming it was a man before slowing to a jog to engage from a few meters out.

The lack of hesitation paid off: a fraction of a second before he pulled the trigger, the man halted at the sight of the bodies in the hall and began to shout in Arabic, his cry turning into a pained grunt as the first of three subsonic rounds lanced into his side. He dropped to his knees in the doorway, and Reilly had time only to shoot him again or use his left hand to flip up his night vision before entering the room. He sided with the latter as he converged with the blazing glow.

Then Reilly delivered a swift kick to the man's chest to knock him backward, vaulting the body to enter the room and move to the nearest corner.

And while he made it inside, he almost immediately abandoned the notion of clearing the room at all.

The first thing he saw to his front were two tripods. One supported an enormous professional-grade movie camera, while the other one behind it at a 45-degree offset held an elevated light angled downward.

That single light didn't account for the room's brightness, so great that there was a very tangible increase in heat as he entered. Reilly had grown up in southern California and seen his fair share of movie shoots in progress; he knew, therefore, that the light before him was only one of three forming a triangular illumination around a central target. Rather than move to his corner, he twisted his footing to follow the orientation of the camera lens before launching himself in a catapulting leap toward the object of focus for the room's lighting—in this case, the kneeling, gagged, crying, and exceptionally surprised-looking Olivia Gossweiler.

He registered figures in the room around him even as he leapt, saw the flash of barrels whipping toward the same target he was now flying at.

A captured service member would know goddamn well to hit the deck the second one or more fully kitted commandos cleared the doorway, but Olivia Gossweiler had no concept of the degree of devastation and death about to be visited upon everyone in this room, armed or not, except for her—if he could save her in time. Rather than go prostrate, she remained kneeling, her eyes locked on him as he leaped in what felt like slow motion.

In a perfect world, professional counterterrorism operatives would clear the room, doing it so quickly and precisely that only the hostage would be left alive. But, simply put, his team didn't train for this shit aside from the occasional Stateside exercise to push them far outside their operational specialty of dispatching the deserving. Even if that weren't the case, he had no idea if his teammates had actually kept pace down the hall, as under the circumstances he had been moving unusually fast for a man of his size.

Instead his only thought was that he had body armor over his chest and back and she didn't, and that one or more of the men he'd sighted in his peripheral vision were there for no other purpose than to serve as no-notice executioners for just such an eventuality.

He collided with Olivia as if executing a football tackling drill, flattening her body and covering her to serve as a human shield.

His last action before the gunfire began was to flex his limbs on either side of her and press his face to her cheek in a smothering motion that would have surely suffocated her in short order. Then he heard the sound of one rifle opening up, followed by two more in unison—all of it suppressed, thank God, with more entering the fray until the chuffing expenditure of subsonic rounds was so great he could no longer venture a guess at how many of his teammates were now gunning down Olivia's captors.

Reilly's nostrils were filled with the scents of Olivia's body odor and urine, his first indication that she'd either voided her bladder prior to his arrival or was doing so now. She was screaming through the gag as the floor reverberated with the thuds of falling bodies, the entire soundscape underscored by the tinny rattle of brass shell casings striking and bouncing off the flat surfaces. Everything sounded like it was going as well as could be hoped, though Reilly didn't so much as lift his head until he heard the gunfire subside and David speak a single word before the last pieces of brass had settled.

"Clear."

Reilly lifted himself off Olivia's prone figure, rising to all fours and glancing about the room, with one singular thought—namely, that he couldn't let Olivia see this shit—momentarily taking precedence over his duties as a medic.

"You're safe," he said, pulling the gag out of her mouth. "I'll help you up. Don't look, okay?"

It was a halfhearted effort to spare her the trauma of the sight that he was only now beginning to comprehend himself.

To say his team had slaughtered the men here would have been an understatement. With zero margin for error and tremendous consequences for so much as a single enemy getting a shot off, each man had probably expended half a magazine each in riddling their targets with kill shots, then follow-up shots, and then, once they'd fallen, follow-up *head* shots. Now the walls looked like Jackson Pollock had worked them over with a few buckets of blood, the floors more so with the addition of brain matter pouring from three bodies inside the room plus a fourth in the doorway, the one Reilly had to leap over upon entering and who, at present, was receiving an additional three rounds unceremoniously fired from none other than Ian before he took aim into the hallway, joined by Hass on the opposite side of the threshold. The remaining team members formed up on them in dual stacks, collapsing their security positions and reloading in pairs.

Reilly helped a badly shaken Olivia to her feet, noting that despite his admonition she did indeed look—not at her saviors but at the fallen enemy fighters and film crew he hadn't wanted her to see. And, to his surprise, she released a high-pitched, nervous titter of laughter.

"Can you walk?" he asked.

"Yes." She nodded, only then meeting his eyes with the question, "Who are you?"

Reilly had no idea what to say; he couldn't well mention that a highly compartmentalized targeted killing program had been and remained the only thing standing between her and certain death, and to explain that the men who'd just entered the room were simply fellow Americans seemed far too obvious.

So he sided with the only response that would be understood by a civilian with zero knowledge of their country's extensive military, paramilitary, or intelligence architecture, with popular culture serving as their only conception that any of the prior existed at all.

"We're Navy SEALs," he said boldly, his tone an octave higher than he'd meant to speak. "We're here to get you out."

Cancer released an audible groan.

"Racegun," David said quietly, opting for callsign in the presence of a civilian, "take us back to the stairs. Doc, you keep her in the middle—"

His order was punctuated by the muffled crackle of a transmission, not over Reilly's earpiece but in the room, and Hass quickly recovered his captured handheld radio and brought it to his ear to listen.

Looking to David in alarm, he translated, "Khalil just arrived at the main gate."

Then, after a moment of intense concentration as the Arabic words continued, he followed up that announcement with the addition of four words.

"He's coming here now."

David cut his eyes to Worthy, who'd already replaced Ian at the room's threshold and had his rifle pointed out the door and into the hallway beyond.

"Go," David said, and Worthy slipped through the doorway without so much as a moment of hesitation, moving back to the stairway.

~

Cancer took his place at the rear of the formation by design—as the first man in, or at least the first one to actually clear his corners instead of diving atop a hostage and leaving everyone else to do the killing, he'd moved deepest inside the room and was, by virtue of time required to rejoin the stack, the last one back out.

But even if that hadn't been the case, he thought as he flipped his night vision over his eyes just before the doorway, he would have gone well out of his way to place himself at the tail end. A rock-solid shooter was just as important at the back as the front, now more than ever: they had no idea who or what lay in the untested corridors up here, and with Reilly escorting Olivia at the formation's center, Cancer was unwilling to outsource their rear security to anyone else. His time of vying to be the lead man in the stack had come to an end the moment they secured a living hostage.

He swung his barrel down the far end of the hallway, confirming it to be empty before joining his teammates jogging back toward the stairwell. Worthy was setting a good pace, leading everyone quickly but smoothly forward while maintaining decent noise discipline, when David transmitted over the sound of a generator to their rear.

"Rain Man, you getting anything over the air frequency?"

"Negative."

That question held a very clear subtext, and it didn't bode well for the team.

The walls in this place were probably four-fucking-feet thick, which made satellite communications with Duchess impossible short of reaching an open window—ill-advised, under the circumstances.

That left the possibility of relaying a message via the aerial platforms overhead, and the fact that Hass couldn't reach them either presented a far greater problem. Whatever those UAV operators were seeing in real time was a mystery and would remain so, along with any relevant late-breaking radio intercepts aside from any messages passed over the handheld radio from a dead foot soldier. All that swoopy technology and vast military resources counted for nothing as far as his team was concerned; they were completely on their own.

He performed a quick check rearward to confirm a roving patrol wasn't entering the hall behind them, and was in the process of looking forward when he almost slammed into Hass. The formation had come to a complete stop, a disparity that was quickly explained by Worthy's whispered transmission.

"Go back—sounds like ten people headed up the stairs."

Cancer turned and bolted back down the hall, now fully gripped by fear. Worthy had been right to call for a reversal: an enemy force of that size would decimate them in a close-quarters shootout, particularly when Reilly was as good as removed from the fight trying to keep a hostage under control. Then again, the men coming up the stairs wouldn't need to wipe them out at all. A single unsuppressed gunshot would send every bad guy in the fort headed their way, and it was a literal miracle that hadn't occurred already.

He barreled past the dead guards and the room with the film studio, considering that if he didn't find a solution in horrifyingly short order, the most they would have accomplished would be to slightly relocate Olivia's place of death and add their own bodies to Khalil's propaganda machine. They couldn't hide for thirty seconds, much less until the SEALs finally showed up; survival meant finding another way back to the tunnel, no small feat considering they were on the second level, negotiating an unknown floor plan of a century-old building with questionable remaining infrastructure.

Cancer moved as fast as he could, past a room containing the humming generator, feverishly searching for stairs and not finding them until he approached the far corner—there, sure enough, was an open doorway with an identical set of stairs spiraling downward. The northeast minaret, he surmised, and about as far as they could get from the tunnel entrance they desperately needed to reach in order to escape.

He took to the stairs without bothering to look back, focusing his efforts on descending as far as he could to make way for the five men and one woman behind him. Because when the enemy fighters rounded the hallway corner behind him, they'd have a clear line of sight all the way to the far stairs, and if his team wasn't fully inside and on their way down by the time that occurred, they'd be taking their first casualties in remarkably short order.

So Cancer took the stairs two at a time, moving downward at the limit of his ability not to fall and only confirming with the briefest of glances that no one was posted at the first-floor landing below. He was immeasurably comforted when Worthy transmitted, "*Last man clear*."

Thank Christ, Cancer thought, though the reprieve lasted for exactly two seconds.

That was as long as it took for a new sound to reach him above the pounding footfalls echoing in the spiral staircase—shouts in Arabic from the second floor, proof positive that the slain guards and missing hostage had been discovered, and all but sealing the team's fate if Cancer couldn't find a pathway out in record time.

Then he saw that the first-floor landing wasn't a landing at all; it was a solid floor with a doorway representing the only outlet.

"No sublevel access," he transmitted, though his inner thoughts could be more accurately conveyed in three words: *shit*, *shit*, and *shit*.

Unable to slow down, he had fleeting seconds with which to calculate which way to go once out the door. A left turn would take him along the east side of the fortress, toward the main gate, while heading right would present a far more direct path toward the northwest minaret and, perhaps more importantly, the only staircase that they definitely *knew* provided sublevel access.

He cleared the bottom stair and exited the doorway into a long, dark hall that appeared to be completely unoccupied, the interior wall punctuated by vaulted window cutouts letting in ambient starlight from the courtyard. Turning right, he took two steps toward the nearest corner before stopping dead in his tracks—the white glow of multiple flashlights approached from the perpendicular hall, heralding the sounds of running footsteps and men shouting to one another.

Plan B, he thought, turning back to race in the opposite direction just as Hass and Ian spilled out onto the first floor.

Cancer ran southward past open cutouts exposing his team to the trees and tents in the central courtyard beyond, and didn't bother to look—they were seconds from a full compromise no matter what they did, and he was the only one in a position to lead his team to a route that would take them out of here. If they got spotted by someone in the courtyard, then so be it; they were out of options anyway.

He rapidly closed with the corner ahead, painfully aware that they were on the east side of the fortress and needed to get to the west. Rounding the next hall would put them on the southern boundary and headed in the proper direction, though there was a vast swath of interior space with an indeterminate number of enemy fighters to clear before their next chance of a descent into the sublevel. Not a good option, but the best they were going to manage.

But in an almost eerie sense of déjà vu, he encountered the exact same obstacle that had prevented his last attempt at westward progress in this hellhole: the approaching glow of flashlights, shouted commands, thundering footsteps.

Skidding to a halt, he transmitted, "They're coming from the south side, too."

Worthy added, "*And down the stairs behind us.*"

Well that settled it, Cancer thought; however many men were around the corner, it was probably fewer than the combined elements on the north side and stairwell.

David seemed to share his assessment, transmitting back, "*Bust the south side.*"

Cancer needed no encouragement for that; he'd already pulled one arm out of his sling, transitioned his HK417 to the opposite shoulder, and rotated around the corner to take aim while keeping as much of his body as he could behind cover. A teammate would be appearing at his side any moment now, and by the time that happened he intended to rack up as many kills as possible.

As it turned out, accumulating a healthy kill count wasn't going to be a problem, and for all the wrong reasons.

He began firing immediately, not bothering to take aim—for one, he couldn't see his infrared laser against the glare of flashlights coming down the hall, and for another, any bullet he put down the hall was going to hit someone, even if it bounced off the floor or ceiling.

The wave of enemy fighters was lined up wall to wall, shoulder to shoulder, and probably five deep to form a human shield to prevent anyone from passing. Cancer began blasting rounds as fast as he could, discharging a third of his magazine before yelling, "No way," as he ducked behind the wall amid a hailstorm of incoming fire chipping away at the corner.

Through the first salvo of enemy gunfire he heard David transmit in an unsettlingly restrained voice, "*Fuck the hallways—we're assaulting through the courtyard.*"

~

Ian hoisted himself through the open window cutout a moment after Hass vanished through it, sliding past a thick slab of the fortress wall before making a blind leap into the bushes of the courtyard beyond.

A glance to either side revealed his teammates hitting the ground in a staggered row, Cancer to his left and the remaining four plus Olivia strung out to his right. And as he scrambled to a position beside Hass to take his place for the hasty assault, he heard the Combat Controller shout, "I think we just found the ghibli."

David transmitted before he finished the sentence, his final one before the team began bounding through the trees and vegetation that gave way to the first in a row of Bedouin tents in the clearing ahead.

"*I want effects by the time we reach the west side.*"

Ian darted ahead, stepping high to avoid tripping amid the tangle of plants springing up between tree trunks, sweeping for enemy fighters ahead as he caught his first glimpse of what lay below the nearest tent. Hass moved directly beside him, speaking quickly.

"Reaper Two One this is Rain Man Eight Seven, requesting a Hellfire, looking for time on target, three mikes, with immediate reattack at the center of the courtyard."

At first glance, Ian had difficulty comprehending the object beneath the tent ahead—a ballistic missile, to be sure, one meter in diameter and close to twelve meters in length, tapering to a conical warhead. He momentarily assumed it was a Scud, one of several lined up in a staggered row, but such missiles belonged atop eight-wheeled transport vehicles while these were fitted to stripped-down components consisting of the erector-launcher units only.

He was reaching the end of the treeline, rounds cracking through the leaves and popping into tree trunks as fighters within the fortress to either side fired from the windows, before he accounted for the disparity—the only way to get missiles of this size into a mountain fortress was by moving the disassembled components overland or using a helicopter to airlift them in, and neither was conducive to transporting a seventeen-ton truck per missile. That omission had the added benefit—at least from Khalil's perspective—of packing far more of the weapons beneath the tent roofs than he otherwise could. Ian counted the tail ends of the missiles before him, determining that there were ten lined up in the same northwesterly orientation, spaced just far enough apart for the backblast of each launch to leave the nearest missiles unscathed.

He distinguished a long string of Arabic text on the fuselage of the one directly in front of him—and he only needed to read the first four words to know both what the rest of it said and that drones weren't the only technology Khalil had imported from Yemen.

God is the Greatest, Death to America, Death to Israel, Cursed be the Jews, Victory to Islam.

The Houthi slogan meant that he was looking at a row of Burkan-2s.

Ian took a final glance at the missiles' northwesterly orientation before transmitting, "Burkan-2 missiles, aiming for a target in Italy. Maybe Sigonella." With thousands of US military personnel and billions of dollars' worth of aircraft and equipment, the base would make for a target that was as spectacular as it was strategic. Then he went on, "They can fire these in minutes, if they have to. We can't waste any time."

David transmitted back, "*Thanks for the news flash, fuckface. We can't disable all this shit. Your job is to keep Rain Man alive until we've got munitions coming up off the rails.*"

Ian understood the logic of that simple command; on an objective with a newly-liberated hostage and enemies closing in, Hass's ability to call in air support as only he could was the difference between life or death for everyone involved. Anyone here would willingly give their life to save a fellow teammate, but Hass's death right now may well result in everyone else being killed.

He swung left around Hass as they ran, placing himself between the Combat Controller and the nearest source of fire at the south wall before taking aim at a fighter scrambling through a window. A laser appeared before he could illuminate his own, and the man fell dead.

Cancer shouted behind him, "I've got the walls—clear between the missiles."

Ian sprinted ahead of Hass, rounding the first munition and taking aim down its length as his teammates ran on the far side, with Olivia's white shirt almost glowing in his night vision. This was bad, very bad—ideally they could clear forward with more or less even spacing, maintaining clear fields of fire.

But the long missiles blocking the way forced them to split in two elements, pushing them closer to the walls and the enemy fighters they contained. Before they could rectify this with a deliberate linkup, they first needed to distance themselves from the east side, where the majority of fighters were firing at them. Doing so required them to press the initiative with speed and extreme violence, outpacing the enemy's ability to comprehend or react and doing so without shooting one another while clearing the gaps between missiles.

He was proceeding toward the tail of the second missile when Hass transmitted his follow-up from the Reaper's sensor operators.

"Time on target is three minutes."

David immediately replied, "*We don't make it across by then, we're dead anyway. Approved.*"

Ian heard Hass's next words transmitted over the air frequency as he relayed the order in an off-the-cuff delivery.

"Roger, 9-Line to follow. One through three n/a, lines four and six from your sensor, ten-by Burkan missiles—"

Rounding the second missile, Ian raised his barrel to see a man crouching halfway down the fuselage. He opened fire with three subsonic shots and saw him fall dead a split second before his body was lit by infrared lasers originating from the nose cone as the first shooters from the opposite element arrived into view.

The dead man was unarmed; who he was or what he was doing here remained a mystery, but it was clear enough that given the team's suppressors and the speed with which the assault was proceeding, he hadn't realized the American team was inside the courtyard.

Ian turned and moved toward the third missile, hearing a fragment of Hass's continued transmissions behind him.

"—danger close, GFC initials Delta Romeo—"

He slipped past the third missile and took aim, this time remaining as close as he could to the tail in case the north element of his team had to engage before he did. His infrared laser immediately crossed with another coming from the opposite direction. The odds of a friendly fire incident were catastrophically high.

Aborting his clearance, Ian ran past the tail of the fourth missile, pivoting around it and directly into the path of an incoming laser—if it belonged to an enemy fighter, he was dead—but mercifully, he saw an identically kitted team member at the far end.

Only then did Ian realize that the volume of unsuppressed enemy gunfire had subsided considerably since they'd cleared the first set of missiles. In moving toward the largely undefended center of the fortress courtyard, they were forcing the opposition to turn their barrels toward not only their counterparts in the opposite halls of the first floor but also toward God only knew how many millions of dollars' worth of equipment. They must've been fearful of either damaging the missiles, killing each other in the crossfire, or both; and without any apparent attempt to isolate them from reaching the west wall, Ian presumed they took this for a virtual suicide attack to sabotage the munitions rather than prioritize the hostage's survival.

Hass continued, "Stand by three minutes and zero seconds, ready, ready, HACK."

Then, over the team frequency, he transmitted, "Three minutes."

The words distracted Ian from the next message coming over his earpiece, and he was already rounding the tail of the fifth missile when he registered David's transmission too late to change course.

"*South element, move north and link up with us—*"

By then Ian was committed, already edging around the next tail to peer beyond with the hope that he was about to face another unoccupied gap. He could easily trot between the parallel fuselages, leading Hass and Cancer to a seamless linkup with the rest of their team to remove the looming fear of them shooting each other in a clearance effort.

Instead he saw that the fifth and sixth missiles were separated much more than the previous gaps—an entire Bedouin tent with the side flaps rolled up separated the two. Beneath it, a row of foam mats and sleeping bags represented the living quarters of a half dozen men clustered in the center, either unarmed or clutching weapons that they appeared wildly unqualified to use.

His only conscious thought was to remain close to the nearest missile as he would a wall during room clearing, and he opened fire on the move.

That measure paid off in full two seconds later, after he'd fired the remainder of his magazine at the group and was conducting a reload. Two more infrared lasers appeared as Hass and Cancer engaged the men from his left flank, by which time Ian knew who they were shooting based on the outdoor sleeping quarters as well as their inability to defend themselves.

These were the weapons engineers and firing crews, those most assured of their safety at the epicenter of a heavily guarded fortress. They'd probably been living there for days in preparation for a no-notice launch order from Khalil, standing by to conduct the attack in what would appear to be an abandoned fortress when viewed from anything but a ground-level vantage point within its walls.

Now they were falling dead amid the sustained volleys of three attackers, Ian included as he completed his reload and resumed firing.

It should have been a resounding victory for Ian, now leading Hass and Cancer north to consolidate with the remainder of their team for a unified effort to reach the west side of the courtyard before the first Hellfire impacted. But as the three-man element conducted a volley of follow-up fire on the downed opponents along with staggered reloads on the move, he noticed a row of what appeared to be rounded rectangular cubes lined up just beyond the living space.

The sight of them immediately resolved the many contradictions they'd encountered since entering Libya: Khalil's funding and resources, the extent to which he remained two steps ahead at every turn regardless of the incredible military and intelligence efforts to stop him. He was also reminded of his team's snatch operation in Montenegro, and the haunting words of their captive as they spirited him toward the Albanian border.

...the cargo was packaged in 25-liter jerricans...

Ian was looking at those cans now, and a quick tally assured him there were 250, maybe 275—and then, suddenly, the enemy's hesitation to open fire in the direction of the missiles was explained.

He looked from the cans to the conical warheads he was fast approaching, wondering exactly how they were set up. The best-case scenario was a burster charge that detonated on impact, spreading the VX over perhaps fifty meters, maybe more if the prevailing winds allowed.

But if the missiles were equipped with less primitive equipment, such as a fuse based on radar proximity or altitude, then an airburst would turn the VX payload into an aerosol whose range was increased tenfold, which, if detonated over a population center, had the ability to make the Cairo attack look like a barfight by comparison.

Ian keyed his radio and said, "Khalil is Weisz's man in Libya—these missiles are equipped with the remaining VX. I'm looking at the jerricans now."

Hass transmitted back at once, "*Do we need to call off the strike? The Reapers only have thermobaric rounds.*"

A valid question, to say the least—Ian hadn't been privy to official studies concerning the effects of such warheads impacting the tightly spaced missiles with a VX payload. Instead he did a quick mental rundown of what he knew of the nerve agent, thinking aloud while transmitting as he closed the distance to his teammates, who he could now see posted up ahead as they delivered fire to targets on the north wall.

"The first Hellfire will detonate some of the rocket engines and their fuel, and secondary explosions should take care of the rest. VX isn't volatile; you can't even boil it into a gas. I'd expect any distribution to be limited to the courtyard, with any droplets being incinerated well before they make it to the far side. As long as we make it over the west wall before the blast, and don't touch any of the shrapnel, we should be fine."

"*Should* be?" David asked.

This time Ian was so close to the warheads that he heard his team leader's response over his earpiece as well as audibly, and he came to a stop before him to reply without bothering to transmit, "The alternative is getting gunned down before we reach the stairs."

"Fuck me," Hass muttered aloud, though his voice returned to a clinical detachment as he relayed the development over the air frequency. "Be advised, missiles have VX warheads—"

David transmitted, "Racegun, move out. Me and Cancer on right flank, Rain Man take the left, Angel you're on trail security."

There was no guidance for Reilly, nor did there need to be—while Worthy took off into the trees along the courtyard's northern perimeter, the remaining four men surrounded the medic as well as the woman he guided forward with an iron grip on her arm.

The lopsided formation was intended to safeguard Olivia from the greatest risk at present, in this case shooters entering the courtyard from the north wall. But only slightly behind that in terms of imminent danger were those who'd pursued the team from behind, trying to get close enough for a kill without endangering the missiles; for all they knew of VX, he thought, they probably feared a single wayward bullet puncturing a warhead would fill the entire courtyard with gaseous nerve agent.

Ian took up a position behind a tree trunk, turning rearward to take aim while his team was still untangling their formation. Finding targets to their six o'clock wasn't an issue. The real problem was engaging them with accuracy, and Ian resorted to firing a controlled pair of subsonic rounds at each of perhaps the half-dozen flashes of movement he saw flitting through the undergrowth. All he had to do was slow them down enough to safeguard his team re-entering the fortress at the northwest corner; any enemy fighters remaining in the courtyard when the Hellfire struck and ignited a chain reaction of rocket engines exploding would either be killed immediately, or wish they had.

With close to half his magazine expended, Ian turned to follow his team.

To his horror, he saw that they were already gone.

He charged forward through the strip of woods, feverishly trying to catch sight of them as Hass transmitted, "Sixty seconds."

With his team using suppressors, Ian's only clue as to their location was the volume of enemy gunfire to his right, and through breaks in the foliage he could make out not only the fort's north wall but the bodies of slain combatants who'd tried to leap through windows only to be gunned down by Worthy, David, and Cancer in short order. The corpses were soon obscured by a pale, wafting cloud—his teammates had wisely employed smoke grenades to disrupt the enemy's lines of sight, reminding Ian that he should do the same with the one and only canister he'd packed in his kit.

Finally he caught sight of Olivia's shirt, distinguished in his night vision long before his teammates' camouflage fatigues and plate carriers. He sped up as much as he could, leaping over a fallen branch and gradually closing the distance until he made out Hass to his left, Reilly to his front with the hostage, and Cancer to their right, the latter barely visible through the trees as he engaged windows on the north wall.

Now well over halfway across the courtyard, his team should be able to outpace the strike by a short but sufficient margin; the question remained, however, whether Ian would catch up in time.

He closed the distance beyond what would have been acceptable tactical spacing, trying to buy some lead time for his next rearward engagement as he selected a tree and rotated around it, resuming his rearward aim.

This time he was dismayed to see that the enemy fighters proceeding through the brush behind him were even closer than last time. He directed three bullets for each shadowy figure he could identify, his HK416 going empty as he ducked behind the trunk for an emergency reload, then shifted around the opposite side to repeat the process. Confirmed hits were in short supply amid the limited visibility, though he heard a few pained yelps and saw some of the shadows drop with a speed that told him he'd been at least partially successful.

He turned and ran forward to catch up with the team once more, this time dipping a hand into the cylindrical pouch on his plate carrier that contained his lone smoke grenade before yanking the pin and tossing it behind him.

Then he continued forward, a glance to his left showed that he was approaching the end of the row of missiles. The assessment was confirmed with David's next transmission.

"Racegun, you and I are first through the windows—strongpoint the hall in either direction. Everyone else, cover Doc until he gets Olivia inside."

Ian had his first breathless realization that they might actually survive this thing—they could hold their own far better now than they could while divided on either end of a row of twelve-meter-long missiles. From the current pace and the ever-dwindling volume of enemy fire to his right, he and his teammates were finally gaining some semblance of an upper hand, however fleeting.

"Thirty seconds," Hass transmitted.

Ian now knew that one of the Reaper UAVs was lasing the center of the compound to guide the munitions of the second, its sensor operator waiting to fire until the exact instant it had the target in sight on a wheeling arc overhead.

Worthy was next over the net, speaking two words—*"Breaking cover"*—that were the first and only indication he'd have that the end of the planted area was approaching. Ian charged ahead, first making out the breaks in the treeline ahead and then catching glimpses of his teammates scrambling through the window cutouts in the fortress wall.

But he wasn't prepared for Hass's next transmission over the team frequency, coming as he was still meters away from any semblance of protection.

"Rounds away."

Well this was going to be a doozie, Ian thought—he was still mid-sprint on his way to the wall, and while he didn't know the exact flight time of the first Hellfire, he was certain it wouldn't be long. Nor could he gauge how long remained until impact from any discernible urgency in Hass's voice; a man like that, who'd spent his entire professional career communicating with pilots and UAV operators in life-or-death situations, simply didn't know how to sound panicked over the radio. He could have been seconds from death, and his tone over comms would still have all the excitement of an operating room surgeon requesting a scalpel during a routine procedure.

Ian abandoned his final piece of cover and darted across the remaining distance, identifying a window ahead he planned to scramble through before the impact.

But then he saw Hass running to his left and perhaps two paces behind him; if Ian was at risk of dying in the upcoming explosions, then Hass was even more so. The intelligence operative sprinted into position behind him in the interests of providing an assist over the wall and inside the building.

Whether Hass registered Ian's course adjustment was impossible to tell—he reached the wall and leapt atop the bottom edge of a vaulted window cutout, and Ian scrambled beneath him to shove the Combat Controller up and over.

The effort was successful, though as Ian leapt atop the cutout, he heard Hass say, "Splash out."

Ian jumped and gained purchase on the ledge, scraping his boots against the wall in an effort to pull himself to the fortress interior. He'd be too late, he thought, until he felt Hass grab the back of his armored plate and heave him upward with incredible force as he shouted, "Incoming, incoming!"

Then Ian was inside, falling to the floor as the Combat Controller dropped to the prone beside him.

The Hellfire missile rocked the courtyard, initiating secondary explosions in a high-pitched series of blasts that sucked the air out of Ian's lungs. A shockwave of incinerated dirt and plant matter whipped overhead, his first attempt to breathe met with the stench of explosives and rocket propellant.

He suddenly remembered the possibility that he could be inhaling VX droplets along with the hot air now entering his mouth. If that was the case, they were all seconds away from experiencing a headache, difficulty breathing, or outright paralysis before the connection between their muscular and nervous systems was completely severed and everyone died of asphyxiation.

Hass seemed to have no such reservations, saying over the air frequency, "Request BDA," before the echo of the blasts had subsided.

The pair of Reapers would have to change slots now, with the one that had just fired assuming the duties of lasing the target as the second rotated into position in the high-altitude choreography that was unmanned aerial warfare. Ian struggled to a kneeling position and tried to gain his bearings in the smoky hall as Hass continued, "Roger, approved for immediate reattack."

Ian saw his teammates moving out to his right and was eager to follow them before the next round of missiles exploded. He caught sight of David at the corner ahead, rapidly closing with the stairwell of the northwest minaret.

~

Only when I had the minaret stairwell in sight did I realize we weren't the first to arrive—through the smoke of the courtyard blasts I saw a man vanishing inside. It was possible that the enemy fighter was trying to lock it down to prevent our passage, though far more likely that he was trying to reach the tunnel in order to escape, the same as we were.

I picked up my pace to deal with the latter possibility; if I was wrong, I was about to pay dearly for the miscalculation.

But as I reached the doorway and took the briefest moment to clear the space with my rifle, I saw that I'd been correct: a small file of men, four or five in total, was hustling down the spiral staircase with the aid of a flashlight and rapidly approaching the sublevel outlet. My visibility of them was limited by the tight confines, and if they reached the bottom, they'd be the single greatest threat to our exfil. I wouldn't be able to reliably engage one, much less all of them, with my personal weapon.

Which was fine, I thought as I dropped my HK416 on its sling and reached for a pouch on my kit, because I didn't need to.

The advantages of an elevated position were of immeasurable importance in combat—whoever controlled the high ground usually won the fight through superior visibility and fields of fire. In this case all I needed was the benefit of gravity, and I pulled the pin on a fragmentation grenade and tossed it down the center of the staircase with all the effort of a kid letting a half-eaten apple fall to the ground. It only took me a moment to repeat the process, sending a second grenade freefalling by the time the first was impacting at the sublevel.

I felt a hand squeeze my shoulder.

It was a teammate cueing me to move, and at the worst possible time. They thought I was halting my advance until I had a second man to clear, when nothing could have been further from the truth. I shuffled backward to force them away, and was resuming the grip on my rifle as I said, "Frags out."

But neither of us heard the statement; the first detonation's blast was channeled upward by the vertical stairwell, so loud that the decibel cutoffs of my earpieces couldn't contain the effect. A shockwave of scorching heat and sand blasted upward like a mushroom cloud, whipping my face to the side as my teammate guided me backward with a hand on the drag handle of my plate carrier. I'd barely staggered free from the doorway when the second grenade exploded, though this time I was better prepared for the effects as a dust cloud billowed out of the doorway.

I heard Cancer say behind me, "We're up."

Taking a breath and holding it, I proceeded through the doorway onto the stairwell landing. As sand particles stung at my eyes and I entered a near-total brownout of dirt and smoke, I considered I may well have done significant structural damage to the very stairs we needed to descend.

At that point I was committed, however, and it wasn't like our odds would get any better by retreating into the fort. Sure, a good deal of enemy fighters had probably just been vaporized by the Hellfires and secondary explosions in the courtyard, and while I hoped that any survivors were retreating into the mountains, it was entirely possible we'd face a mass exodus seeking the tunnel if not mounting a counterattack from our rear.

Gingerly testing the ground with my boot as I advanced, I found the edge of the first stair, placing my shoulder to the wall for stability and working my way off the landing and downward across the steps, probing the ground with my boot soles. The entire fort shook with a deep concussion, followed in short order by a second—the Reapers were launching their second strike, and now that my entire team had lost communications once more, Duchess would be in control of what the aircraft did from here on out. And if I were her, with the recent knowledge that the entirety of the missing VX was located in that courtyard, I'd have something a whole lot bigger than a Hellfire missile launch inbound at the soonest possible opportunity.

I'd moved perhaps halfway down when my foot collided with something on the stairs beneath me—a human body, no doubt—and I lowered my suppressor to it before firing two rounds. No movement, not so much as a flinch, which meant I was wasting ammo, but I'd be damned if I was going to follow that up with a broken femur on our way out. Crouching down, I used my left hand to grab a bloody fistful of fabric before sliding the mass sideways.

It didn't take much, maybe eight inches of hoisting, before enough of the body cleared the edge of the stairs to shift the center of gravity and take the entire corpse with it, falling down the center of the spiral staircase with such sudden momentum that I was almost pulled down with it. A moment later I heard the satisfying crunch of a body striking the hard limestone floor.

With that accomplished, I continued my descent, proceeding down three more stairs as my teammates followed me. All at once, I could see again—I'd just cleared the rising cloud of sand and smoke, and my newly-acquired visibility revealed that the stairs served as a perfect funnel to channelize the retreating force into my grenade blasts. Two bodies were strewn across the stairs below, with an additional one on the landing and a fourth, surely the one I'd dumped off the side, lying in a contorted position at the center. All were clearly dead or close enough to it to not represent a threat, but with a hostage in tow I wasn't taking any chances.

Activating my laser, I gave each body an additional two rounds to center mass, then conducted a tactical reload as I continued downward, stepping over two of the corpses before hitting the final landing and angling outward to establish security in the hallway beyond.

There was a black scorch mark on the ground, radiating oblong sooty marks in a star-shaped pattern—one of my grenades had bounced just out of the stairwell—and a single body had been thrown clear of the blast in the otherwise empty hallway.

I lowered my barrel and was about to deliver another double tap to the motionless figure when a sudden tug of instinct caused me to hold my fire, and it was only a second later that I realized why.

There was something eminently familiar about the prostrate man. He wore traditional Muslim attire, a long-sleeved white gown with decorative stitching, an elaborate ceremonial belt bearing a sheathed dagger beside a clipped satellite phone on one side and a sword on the other. I must have been looking at Khalil, I suddenly realized, and the slimy little bag of shit had clearly outrun his bodyguards on his way out of the fortress. That made me want to shoot him all the more, but I resisted the impulse. As soon as I felt the first teammate arrive behind me and give my shoulder a squeeze, I said, "Cover me," without further explanation.

Then I exited the stairwell and knelt beside the man as Cancer and Worthy advanced to either side, pulling security down the hall.

Rolling the body over, I confirmed that indeed, this *was* Khalil, half his face covered in fine sand powder marred by the trickling blood from a gash on his forehead. The satellite phone on his belt had just gone from a potentially useful piece of intelligence to an utterly invaluable one, particularly now that we knew he was unquestionably connected to Erik Weisz.

I ripped off one of my tactical gloves and pressed two fingertips into his neck. He was alive, all right, his pulse strong and consistent despite the shrapnel wounds.

Cancer spoke as I hastily pulled my glove back on.

"Boss, if you want to do the honors, you better make it fast."

I glanced behind me, seeing Reilly and Olivia exit the stairwell, followed in short order by Hass and then Ian pulling trail security.

Then I glanced back down at Khalil, and in a moment of total and instantaneous certainty, knew what I had to do.

38

Duchess sat at her OPCEN workstation, body rigid, eyes focused somewhere above her computer screen. There was a muted hush among her staff; at this point, everyone knew better than to try and speak to her, and that was unlikely to change until there was another pertinent update.

She never thought she'd see the day, but David had been so dismissively lax in his reporting that she was beginning to miss having Cancer as ground force commander.

It wasn't a matter of transmissions being blocked by the thick fortress walls, which was entirely understandable. She hadn't expected to hear much from the time his ground team entered the tunnel until they exited—then again, she also hadn't been expecting a fucking assault across the open courtyard, during which time US Air Force Master Sergeant Jalal Hassan had delivered an abbreviated close air support 9-Line briefing that could have been used as a textbook case study at the JTAC schoolhouse, and done so while bounding across enemy-held ground and probably shooting people between transmissions.

The Combat Controller had maintained steady communications for almost four minutes, delivering almost everything she knew about the situation the team had encountered. And maybe, she considered, that was why

David had decided not to bother keeping her in the loop, tactical priorities aside.

Because in that time, she'd received exactly two transmissions over the command net, consisting of a grand total of fifteen words. A moment after the grainy images of heat signatures had piled out of the windows at the courtyard's east wall, he'd sent the spectacularly concise message, "*We've got her, trying to get out*," followed by the equally underwhelming intel dump of "*Rest of the VX is here, cruise missiles*" shortly before the eruption of a smoke grenade indicated they'd made it over halfway across.

And that was it, she thought incredulously; by the time the Hellfires struck, she'd resigned herself to being completely dependent on Hassan's messages over the air frequency for any semblance of information, and even those had consisted only of a request for the battle damage assessment of the initial strike, followed by clearance for a reattack. Both doctrinally correct for a Combat Controller but in no way fulfilling the requirements of the ground force commander who'd remained notably silent in the interim.

The results of the two Hellfire strikes thus far had been better than anyone could have hoped, however: the first two missile impacts had ignited a chain reaction of rocket engines amid the Burkan-2s and surely killed a significant number of enemy in the courtyard as a result, rendering the second round of Hellfires largely redundant. Although at this point she wasn't taking any chances.

Everything else was a black box to Duchess, who'd been fielding nonstop requests for information from everyone up to and including Senator Gossweiler and the Director. The only response she could give was that UAV footage seemed to indicate at least five of seven individuals had re-entered the fortress at the courtyard's western wall, with the fate of the final two impossible to determine given the thermal flash of the initial airstrike. They could have made it or been fatally wounded by shrapnel; everything else remained unknown. Had the rest of the team made it to a stairwell, or been killed by an enemy counterattack within the building? Had they so much as reached the tunnel before being wiped out? No one could say.

And that was before she considered the only explanation as to how the remaining VX was in Khalil's possession: the entire hostage situation was anything but an opportunistic snatch-and-grab. For over two years, Erik Weisz had been corralling otherwise disparate terrorist groups, criminal syndicates, and corrupt governments toward some larger and more sinister goal. He must have ordered Olivia's kidnapping to get to Senator Gossweiler as a power move, a retaliation of sorts after having his progress slowed by Project Longwing. Weisz's goal was unquestionably to send a message, executing the senator's daughter in tandem with launching a VX attack against Italy—and taken in that context, Khalil Noureddin was little more than a proxy if not a pawn.

When David finally transmitted, Duchess reached for her satellite hand mic with a trembling hand.

"*Raptor Nine One, Suicide Actual.*"

"I've got you," she said, almost breathlessly. "Status?"

"*We just exited the tunnel, will reach the landing zone in approximately twenty minutes. Olivia is secure.*"

"You got her out?"

"*I'm looking at her now. She's safe. A bit banged up, but she'll live.*"

David's voice was strained, racked by exertion. Which made sense, she supposed, given what he'd just been through—but still, he was normally calm on the radio no matter the circumstances. At the moment it sounded like he was keying his mic while deadlifting.

She brushed the thought aside and asked, "And your team?"

"*Everyone's alive. Some minor injuries, nothing we can't patch up at the staging area.*"

"Any status on Khalil?"

It was almost a foolishly presumptuous question, one that she almost hesitated to ask. Given everything that had just transpired at the fort, it was simply unbelievable that those six men were able to reach Olivia, much less make it out with her alive. The odds were low that they'd even seen Khalil whether alive or dead, and with all enemy radio and cell traffic ending the moment the first airstrike hit, she'd resigned herself to even more uncertainty surrounding the terrorist leader who'd gone dark for over two years between major operations.

But she wasn't prepared for David's response to her inquiry—which was, simply put, nothing at all.

Duchess waited, not wanting to pressure any member of a team who'd just accomplished the impossible, much less the ground force commander.

When he didn't respond after a full ten seconds, however, her patience turned to anger.

"Suicide Actual," she said, then repeated more forcefully, "any status on Khalil?"

39

Duchess's inquiry forced me into do-or-die time on fully committing to a course of action that I was already hellbent on executing—all that remained were the final arrangements.

Worthy led us along the forested ridge leading away from the cliff, where we were making good progress on our way back to the helicopter landing zone. With three hundred meters of easy downhill fast approaching, things were about to get even better; at least, for everyone but me.

I was toting Khalil's unconscious body in a fireman's carry, an awkward arrangement at best given that his wrists and ankles were flex cuffed together. We'd already removed his ceremonial belt with its attendant blades, and most importantly the satellite phone that I planned to exploit fully once everyone was safely back at the refueling point.

My reserves of adrenaline were fading now, giving way to a bedrock of anger and stubborn pride that prevented me from handing off Khalil to anyone else. I had a grudge with him that went all the way back to Jolo Island, and if anyone was going to make sure he got where he was going, it would be me.

I accelerated my pace to a shuffling jog to catch up with Reilly. The medic was still escorting our hostage, who lacked the benefit of night vision.

It was only then I noticed Olivia had a camouflage poncho tied around her waist—Reilly was never without one for casualty transport in situations where carrying a rescue stretcher was out of the question. She must have soiled herself, I thought, and the medic had sought to provide whatever measure of dignity he could under the circumstances.

"Hey, Olivia," I asked, "are you gangster?"

Without looking back, she replied, "I don't know what that means."

"We're going to need you to 'unsee' some things. Is that a problem?"

Her next response caught me off guard, preceded by a long and weary sigh.

"You get me the hell out of here," she began, "and I'll keep any secrets you want."

Nodding in approval, I said, "Yeah. You're gangster."

Duchess transmitted again, sounding firm now. "*Suicide Actual, any status on Khalil?*"

I fell back to my previous formation spacing, grunting as I resituated Khalil over my shoulders—he wasn't a tremendously large man, but deadweight was deadweight—and keyed my team radio.

"Rain Man, I need you to get any overhead surveillance away from the landing zone before we get there. Push them way the fuck out, I don't care how you do it—"

Cancer intervened, "*Rain Man, 'metal rabbit' the HLZ.*"

"*Got it,*" Hass replied.

And while I had no idea what that meant—I'd missed out on a lot of things during my solo stay in Libya, it seemed—I replied to Duchess at last.

"Raptor Nine One, comms are going in and out, say again?"

She repeated, "*Khalil. I have to ask.*"

Following Reilly and Olivia left around a massive evergreen, I saw the terrain ahead sloping downward; this was the home stretch.

Then I replied, "We engaged him and his bodyguards when they were trying to reach the tunnel. He's dead."

"*You're certain?*" Duchess asked.

"I am. Chalk it up. And we grabbed his satphone, so expect a full data dump as soon as we get back to the FARP. Now if you'll excuse me, I've got to focus on the terrain."

"Good copy, birds are on the way and we'll handle the rest on the air frequency. Nice work out there."

Oh Duchess, I thought, if you only knew.

Then I felt a sudden rush of fear at Duchess's mention of birds, plural. Our landing zone could fit a single MH-6 and barely even that, and my plan now hinged upon exploiting that seemingly minor detail. But I received my explanation by way of multiple approaching helicopters with a decidedly un-Little Bird-like sound profile, and Hass came over the net.

"Be advised, two-by MH-60 DAP gunships coming on station to secure the HLZ."

Tremendous, I thought. Olivia was willing to play ball, sparing me the need to convince her that our enemy prisoner had bled out from wounds sustained in the grenade blast; on top of that we were mere minutes away from pickup, and Duchess seemed to have been sufficiently deceived for the time being.

And at that moment, just as the wave of exaltation hit me and I allowed myself to crack a smile, Khalil awoke.

I knew this because the deadweight transitioned to muscle rigidity, then resistance, as he tested the flex cuffs and then wrestled against me. The last thing I needed while trying to negotiate a downhill slope was for him to throw off my balance, and I spoke my first words to him since our last meeting together.

"Stop moving, motherfucker, or I'll knock your ass out. Again."

His body went still then, his polished voice ringing in my left ear as I scanned the ground ahead to determine my best footing.

"You must know by now," Khalil said, without a trace of panic, "that I will never talk."

"Yeah, I figured you'd say that."

"My faith is such that—"

"You can stop right there," I cut him off, "and save us both the speech about your religious convictions. You're not making it to a waterboard table, I assure you."

"Is that supposed to make me fearful?"

Stopping in place to hoist him higher atop my shoulders, I continued moving and said, "I don't really give a shit what it *makes* you, it's a fact.

There's a shortage of good places to land a helicopter around here. Where we're headed, there's room for one bird and it's only got seats for seven. I know you don't have night vision, so take my word for it: we're moving with eight, including the woman you were about to kill. Go ahead and take a wild guess who's not making it out."

There was a long pause before he replied, "If this is true...then why have you not killed me already?"

"You'll see. And believe me, it's going to be one hell of a surprise. Keep your mouth shut or sing like a bird, it's not going to make any difference. As much as I've enjoyed our little chats, Khalil, I'm all done fucking around with you."

There was steel in my voice, and I meant every word; the value of Khalil as a live detainee was considerable, but I wasn't about to risk the lives of my team or our supporting pilots any more than I already had by leaving men behind while the Little Bird made two trips to a potentially compromised landing zone. We'd been exceedingly lucky to make it this far in a last-minute bid to do what we could for Olivia, and regardless of what Khalil did or did not know, my risk tolerance beyond this point had simply dropped to zero. There was still a chance of an enemy counterattack trying to pursue us through the mountains, or the bird getting shot down with or without us in it; there was simply no fucking way I was going to muddy those waters further by trying to get Khalil out alive.

Besides, I thought, I had something in mind that was far more important than any intelligence he could offer.

Khalil's response was a tad rushed, I noted, the first indications of fear creeping into his voice.

"I know many things."

"Really?" I asked, now getting angrier than I already was. "Because I thought you weren't going to talk, and while we're on the subject, I already know you're sponsored by Erik Weisz. There's nothing you can tell me that your satphone can't. If I have one question for you, it's how in the fuck you got off Jolo Island when a few hundred shooters combed every inch of it looking for you."

"Your question indicates your ignorance. He did not simply sponsor me, Suicide. I was his creation."

His last word was interrupted by Worthy's voice over the team frequency.

"*We're a hundred meters out.*"

Cancer must have heard me talking to Khalil, because he began issuing commands at once.

"*Suicide, I'll take it from here. West side security: Racegun, Angel—*"

I pulled my earpieces free and let them hang on the cables, then replied to Khalil with the only conclusion I could draw from his last statement.

"So the shootdown in the Philippines wasn't your plan, it was his. He was grooming you for international terrorist fame and had an escape plan in place, years ahead of actually acquiring the VX."

Khalil said nothing, and I took his silence as confirmation that I was right—and the revelation was horrifying in its implications.

The entire existence of my team, after all, was to address a capability deficit in America's strategy against terrorism. Namely, that despite an abundance of elite military and intelligence units, everyone had their hands full in trying to find and terminate the top leadership. No one was addressing the rising talent, the ambitious lieutenants in various terror organizations with the vision and leadership capacity to mobilize the fanatics and disenfranchised youth in the years to come. It didn't take more than a brief study of Bin Laden's rise to understand that he was a clear threat that could have been eliminated with ease at numerous junctures given sufficiently generous political authorities that simply hadn't existed before 9/11. By the time someone like him garnered America's attention, they were well-protected enough to evade detection for months or years.

Project Longwing was created to identify and deal with people like that *before* they became famous with one or more catastrophic terror attacks, not after. And if Khalil was telling the truth, Erik Weisz was doing the exact same thing—except by removing those rising leaders from the battlefield, he was giving them the tools and strategy to dominate it.

Finally I asked, "What's his endgame?"

Khalil replied with casual dismissiveness, "From my perspective, it hardly matters. If you were handed everything you ever wanted, on a silver platter as it were, would you question the motives?"

"If that silver platter involved the slaughter of a few thousand of my own people," I said, "yeah, I probably would. Nice act pretending to be furious about Cairo, by the way—you had me fooled."

"I knew nothing of Cairo until it happened. And your country has 'slaughtered,' as you put it, nearly one million people worldwide in its response to a single attack by an Egyptian, a Lebanese, two Emiratis, and fifteen Saudis. All in the name of a greater good, all while the fire of resistance grows stronger, not weaker, as a result. We may debate ideologies, Suicide, but on the topic of morality, you have no right to judge me."

His reference to the 9/11 hijackers almost went unnoticed by me—I saw the team formation ahead split apart, with Worthy cutting right as Ian went the other way, and Reilly leading Olivia toward the small clearing ahead.

Stopping in place, I saw Hass and Cancer slip past me to either side, the former to a security position and the latter to ensure everyone was placed to his liking for what was about to occur. The pair of DAP gunships were flying in a wide orbit around the landing zone, the sound of their rotors distant as they searched for targets and, apparently, found none.

I clarified to Khalil, "I didn't come here to judge you. I came to beat you—there's a big difference—and now that you're gone, Weisz is next. So unless you can tell me where to find him, there's nothing left to say."

"I cannot tell you *where* to find him," Khalil responded icily, "I can only tell you that you *will* not—"

I tossed him off my shoulders before he finished the sentence, hearing him hit the ground with a grunt as I flexed my back and stretched—after a kilometer or so of hauling him, I was finally unencumbered.

Loosening my sling, I took my HK416 in one hand and keyed my mic with the other.

"Cancer, please secure the captive."

Then I turned to look at Khalil on the ground behind me. He was still on his side and making no effort to rise, just staring up at me in total defeat; without night vision, he probably saw me as little more than a black silhouette against the trees.

I re-inserted my earpieces and heard Hass transmit, "*Thirty seconds out.*"

Keying my mic, I asked, "Any eyes on the HLZ?"

"*Just us. We're clear until I order the UAVs otherwise.*"

Transitioning to my command frequency, I said, "Raptor Nine One, we're at the HLZ and standing by for pickup."

Duchess said, *"Good copy, the MH-6 is twenty seconds from touchdown."*

Then Cancer appeared, pushing his weapon back on its sling and hoisting Khalil to his knees.

"Go ahead, boss. I got him."

Turning to approach the clearing, I arrived at the edge of the trees in time to hear a thin buzz approaching from the south, the unmistakable sound of Little Bird rotors piercing the ambient noise of the gunships.

"Net call," I transmitted to the team, "hold fast once the helo touches down. Doc, you can get Olivia situated on the left bench. Everyone else stays on local security—this will only take a minute, maybe two."

Then I caught my first sight of the MH-6 as it roared over the treetops and descended, the egg-shaped fuselage revealing a single pilot at the controls as the skids made landfall.

I didn't have to run far to reach the open hatch at the side of the cockpit —this field was scarcely large enough to fit the tiny bird's rotors with enough clearance for landing and takeoff. Running the blade of my hand across my throat, I shouted, "Shut it down and get out."

Josephine's hands remained on the collective and cyclic as she turned her four-tubed night vision device toward me and yelled back, "What?"

"Get out," I repeated. "We brought you a present."

I pointed to the treeline, where a flex-cuffed Khalil Noureddin knelt like a gift-wrapped Christmas present from God himself, with Cancer standing over him.

By the time I looked back to Josephine, she was already spooling down the engines and unbuckling her harness. I stepped back to allow her to climb out, and when she did it was with an M4 carbine in hand.

"Use mine," I said. "For the suppressor."

The real reason was that no one was accounting for our ammunition on a bullet-by-bullet basis, and I had no idea whether that held true for an aviator. Even if it didn't, a formal investigation could change all that in a heartbeat. At this point, as with many others in my relatively short Agency career, I was concerned only with plausible deniability.

Whether or not Josephine sensed that remained unclear, but she set her M4 back in the cockpit and accepted my HK416, advancing toward Khalil with a determination that made Cancer quickly step out of the way. I would've too, in his position—she hadn't so much as confirmed that no UAVs were watching us right now, either assuming we'd taken that precaution or otherwise too consumed with rage. I was barely keeping up with her, and it was only when she'd made it five paces out that I cried, "Wait!"

Then I raced past her and reached into Khalil's shirt collar, finding the black cord around his neck before pulling it over his head. I turned to Josephine, now standing a few feet behind me, and handed the cord over with the words, "Almost forgot. Andrew Musante's dog tags."

She took the offering, holding the tags for a moment before pocketing them in her flight suit. I stepped out of the way for her to face the man who'd shot her out of the sky in the Philippines.

Josephine took another step forward and spoke to Khalil.

"I'm the pilot who escaped from Jolo Island. And this," she continued, raising the HK416, "is for the pilot who didn't."

She shot him twice in the heart; he flinched with the bullet impacts and fell forward to the earth, dead before he hit the ground. And then, to her eternal credit, Josephine lowered the barrel and fired a third round, then a fourth, and then the remainder of the magazine, increasing the speed of each trigger pull until the weapon was empty.

I heard her inhale sharply, and for a moment I thought she was going to cry, but the breath ended in a sigh of relief. She handed my weapon back and spoke quietly.

"I feel much better now. Thanks."

"Don't mention it," I replied, ejecting the empty magazine. It was a ridiculously understated memento, but with Musante's dog tags going to his widow, the only viable alternatives consisted of Khalil's sword and dagger, both which were far too reminiscent of her former lead pilot's death and the latter of which had been stained with blood when he last displayed it to me. By contrast, the magazine that held bullets now lodged in Khalil's body seemed a far more fitting tribute to counterpoint the grief and guilt she surely still felt, and I offered it with the final words, "Something to remember this by."

She accepted the gift and departed immediately, striding back to her helicopter and climbing inside the cockpit as I keyed my team radio.

"Exfil, exfil, exfil."

The security perimeter collapsed toward the bird with surprising speed. Reilly already had Olivia snaplinked in on the center of the left side, I could see through the open cabin, and by the time I reached my seat, Worthy was straddling the front edge of the right bench with Hass taking a seat at the back end. I took my position between them amid the sound of the rotor blades spinning up, giving a rearward glance to see Ian scrambling into the remaining cockpit seat beside Josephine.

"*We're up,*" Cancer transmitted.

I flipped my team radio to the air frequency before saying, "Beast Three Six, we're ready when you are."

"*Roger,*" Josephine replied.

The engines continued to spool amid additional radio chatter until I changed back to the team net and said, "Hell of a job back there, guys. Hell of a job."

My gaze fixated on Khalil's body, now barely visible in the treeline directly to my front. Good riddance, I thought; there was one less terrorist leader out there and the world would be better off for it. Most importantly, Olivia was free, at least provided we made it back to the staging area without incident. Then my thoughts turned to the bricklike object in my drop pouch: Khalil's satellite phone, powered on when I recovered it from him and remaining so now.

I forgot about it in short order as the MH-6 ascended almost vertically, whipping in a flat clockwise turn to face south before accelerating in a dive to hug the terrain as we flew south out of the Green Mountains.

~

From his seat on the rear of the left bench, with Olivia safely clipped in to his right, Reilly looked ahead to see theirs wasn't the only aircraft on its way out—the two DAP gunships had formed up in an echelon right formation to clear the route ahead, flying considerably higher in anticipation of a diving "gun run" should anyone decide to open fire.

Altitude wasn't on Josephine's agenda, though, as she continued her nap-of-the-earth flight with all the same precision she had on infil.

Reilly leaned toward Olivia and shouted over the rotor blades, "Are you okay? It's only a short flight—"

"Fine," she called back. "I like rollercoasters."

"Then you're in for one hell of a ride."

This verbal exchange didn't quite represent the first time they'd spoken all night, but it was damn close to it. In the race to escape, he'd had time to ask her if she was injured, and then he'd said little more than rushed instructions while guiding her around obstacles for the remainder of the mission. Reilly hadn't even had a chance to tie his poncho around her waist until they'd left the tunnel, and while she seemed to be doing as well as could be expected, he was all too keenly aware that her worldview of saving baby whales had just come within a sword swing of ending forever.

Reilly reached for the flexible hose leading to his water bladder and asked, "You want any more water?"

"Not right now. Thank you—"

Her last word was high-pitched as the MH-6 suddenly banked in the opposite direction, and then she emitted an uproarious shout that was equal parts laughter and exhilaration, like she was a schoolgirl at the world's greatest carnival. It was hard to tell where the shock ended and any real sense of enjoyment began, but given the several lifetimes' worth of trauma this woman had accrued over the past seven days, Reilly was glad to see her achieving some release however she could.

The bird leveled out and Olivia, suddenly self-conscious about her outcry, said, "Sorry."

"You probably can't see them," Reilly answered her, "but there's a couple gunships up ahead that'll deal with anyone who has a problem with you yelling. Knock yourself out. Here, I'll join you."

Reilly released a victory whoop and was soon joined by Olivia as the Little Bird angled to tilt them both downward, then pulled a hard left turn to skirt a ridgeline.

As Josephine flipped the bird to its opposite side, Worthy transmitted, "*Sounds like Olivia's doing okay. So who gets the case of beer for this one?*"

"*Josephine does,*" Cancer replied, "*plus me and Suicide. And you fuckers are buying—everyone who didn't put the business end of their Winkler into an enemy combatant tonight.*"

Hass said, "*Wouldn't have counted even if I did. Longwing blades only, right?*"

"*Yeah, that's right. But you've earned your keep and I'm a man of my word. When we get back I'm giving Daniel Winkler a call to order knife number six.*"

"*That's what I wanted to hear,*" Hass replied, exultant.

Cancer concluded, "*If anyone else used their blade, speak now or forever hold your peace.*"

"No," Reilly transmitted back, sounding louder and angrier than he intended. "Shit."

Olivia called out, "What's wrong?"

"Sorry, nothing. Just some trash talking among the guys, that's all."

"Oh. Where are the rest of them?"

"The rest of who?"

"Your guys," she clarified in a low shout.

Reilly was initially confused, then recalled that devoid of night vision, Olivia had no idea whether there had been a half-dozen shooters or a hundred coming to rescue her. Most of what she'd been able to see once they pulled her out of the death chamber-slash-film studio was a whole lot of darkness filled with gunshots and explosions, and even if she was able to view the desperate flight of their small team, Hollywood may well have conditioned her to think the situation was totally normal.

He thought about lying in the interests of not adding insult to injury; after all, they were all lucky to be alive, but no one more so than Olivia herself. How much worse would her nightmares be if she truly understood how narrow the margin of her rescue was?

But then he realized she was about to land at a desert staging area to see a few dozen fully equipped SEALs sitting around for seemingly no good reason at all, and finally admitted, "It's just us."

She asked the obvious question then.

"Why didn't you send more people?"

Reilly was careful to omit any mention of the word "execution" before replying, "There was a big assault force coming to rescue you, but they hadn't arrived yet and Khalil made his move ahead of schedule. My team wasn't supposed to go into the fortress at all, but we were the only ones forward-staged to make it in time."

"So you guys are like...what, SEAL recon?"

He shrugged amid another soaring turn along a canyon. "We prefer to think of ourselves as six expendable assholes."

"And you came for me anyway."

"Well, yeah. What choice did we have?"

Then he heard Hass transmit, "*F/A-18 inbound with a 2,000-pound JDAM.*"

"*Seriously?*" Ian replied.

Hass continued, "*WMD, brother. They're not fucking around.*"

Reilly called out to Olivia, "Hey, you want to see the fortress blow up?"

"What fortress?" she asked.

"The place they were holding you at."

"In that case, yeah. Yes. I mean fuck yes, I want to see it blow up."

"Take a look behind us."

He leaned back as far as he could to maximize her view, then looked past the Little Bird's tail and wondered if he'd gotten her hopes up for nothing. Josephine was yanking and banking, whipping the tiny airframe around like it owed her money as Hass transmitted, "*Round away.*"

Reilly said, "The bomb's falling now, so you should see it any—"

There was a flash of light behind them, the spark of flame visible for a split second before the Little Bird performed an arcing turn away from it, barreling downward along a narrow ravine that ended amid a crisscrossing series of ancient streambeds in the desert.

The sound of the explosion finally arrived, echoing across the hills like the world's loudest gunshot, a crashing boom that made the bench shudder beneath them.

Olivia said, "No more fortress?"

Reilly gave an approving nod. "No more fortress."

The aircraft leveled out then and Reilly looked down to see that Josephine was flying a conservative fifty feet off the ground, just enough that she could autorotate the bird to a hard landing in the event of a mechanical issue. Now that they were over open and increasingly flat desert free of any discernible surface-to-air threat, Reilly felt like someone pulled the plug on his energy levels. First was the final evaporation of any residual adrenaline, and second the realization that he was fast approaching the end of his brief encounter with the freed hostage. The SEAL Team Six medics were going to take control of Olivia the moment the skids hit the ground, and when that happened, his team would be relegated to that of an obscure supporting effort whose biggest job in Libya would boil down to getting the hell out as soon as possible.

Whether by intuiting his thoughts or merely by spontaneous admission now that the hardcore aerial maneuvers had ended, Olivia leaned toward him and shouted, "Jesus Christ, I'm glad you guys came."

"I'm glad we made it in time," he replied, "and that you're safe. Once we land, you're going to be checked out by medics. They're good, the very best, so don't try and play tough—answer them honestly, okay?"

"Sure."

After taking a breath and holding it for a moment, Reilly exhaled and continued, "But they probably won't make you see a psychiatrist until you're back in the States, or close to it. Until then, just keep in mind that you made it. I don't know what you had to do in order to survive, but whatever it was, you succeeded. Remember that."

"I feel fine—I'm free, after all. I don't need a shrink."

"Look, I don't mean to profile you as an aid worker, but—"

"But what?"

Reilly tried to choose his words carefully. "I'm guessing you're super optimistic, own more than one pair of BIRKENSTOCK sandals, and consider granola a major food group."

"So what if I do?"

"Even people who kill bad guys for a living come home with issues. You've been through a lot, Olivia. With trauma, you usually don't get hit with the hangover until later. Don't ask how I know." Then, intentionally repeating her wording, he continued, "And when you do see a shrink, I want you to be completely honest with them, too."

Olivia scoffed.

"Why would I want to talk about it with someone who wasn't there?"

Reilly had the bemused thought that the woman had been a hostage for all of a week and she'd already voiced the same question that every combat veteran in history had asked themselves at one time or another. It was the same question that he himself had before finally seeking help from someone outside his own brothers in arms.

He explained, "Because while people like us were racking up traumatic experiences, people like them were helping out the ones who came before us. Remember that, all right? Promise me."

"Sure, I promise."

"And don't forget, we passed Khalil's body just before reaching the tunnel. Especially if your dad asks. You remember that, right?"

"I was in shock," she said, "the whole thing was a blur. But for the record—"

"Yeah?"

"You could have at least let me shoot him, too."

Then it was over—Reilly felt the Little Bird descend suddenly, and looked ahead to see the formation of grounded Night Stalker birds at the refueling site. The aircraft were interspersed with all four cargo trucks, indicating the SEALs had successfully parachuted in and driven themselves to the FARP; so where the hell were they?

As Josephine flared to land, he got his answer: fully kitted operators came streaming off an MH-47 ramp and debarking the transport Blackhawks. They must have arrived in the past ten minutes, and yet they'd immediately loaded up in preparation to secure a crash site if the Little Bird got shot down or suffered a mechanical issue on its way back.

The skids alighted softly, and Reilly unclipped Olivia's tether before escorting her beneath the rotor blades as his team dismounted. He saw a group of three SEALs jogging toward them—medics, he could tell by the aid bags—trailed by an officer and his attendant radio operator.

Olivia turned toward him before they arrived, asking after a brief pause, "What's your name?"

"Reilly. My name's Reilly."

She extended a hand. "Nice to meet you. And please thank the other five expendable assholes for me, would you?"

He laughed as he shook her outstretched hand, a polite and absurdly formal sendoff that ended when the SEAL medics surrounded her and led her toward their treatment area.

Then he turned to locate his teammates, and moved toward them to begin the long journey home.

~

"Hurry up, fucker," I said to Cancer, waving impatiently. "I've got to call Duchess."

Cancer produced his lighter and mumbled around the unlit cigarette between his lips, "Anything worth having is worth waiting for."

Then he lit the smoke, drawing a half-inhale to ensure it was lit before handing it to me.

I gratefully accepted the cigarette, then heard an increase in the volume of rotors a short distance away. Josephine's Little Bird suddenly rose ten feet from the ground, then pivoted a quarter-turn clockwise before ferrying toward the fuel point to top off before her return flight to the ship.

The sudden absence of the MH-6 revealed Olivia being shuttled away by a trio of SEALs equipped with aid bags. Reilly was shuffling toward us unaccompanied, along with another pair of Navy operators moving with a decidedly urgent gait.

Judging by the long-range antennas extending from the radio pack of the second one as he followed the first like a shadow, it didn't take a savant to know that the SEAL Team Six ground force commander wanted an audience with us.

After sucking down my first drag of the cigarette, I said to Cancer, "Deal with him. I've got to see what Duchess wants to do about this satphone before everyone's wheels-up."

"I'm sorry," Cancer replied sardonically in the closest thing I'd likely ever hear to him issuing an apology, "but all I heard was 'I don't want to end up in a SEAL memoir.'"

"That too. Have fun."

I strode away before he could object further, signaling the incoming operators with a feverish wave followed by pointing adamantly at Cancer and shaking my hand for emphasis.

He called after me, "I hope that cigarette gives you cancer, you little shit."

Transitioning my pointer hand to an extended middle finger for his benefit, I continued walking as I transmitted.

"Raptor Nine One, Suicide Actual. Be advised, Angel is getting his data kit from the truck but I've got Khalil's satphone if you want to get started."

"*Good copy*," Duchess replied. "*First question—was the device switched on when you found it?*"

"Check," I replied, coming to a stop and pulling the phone from my drop pouch as I extended the telescoping antenna.

"*Then it's critical you leave it that way until it reaches our analysts. Let the battery die if you must, but don't turn it off.*"

I knew she wasn't going to tell me what technical nuances of the Agency's exploitation equipment resulted in that particular directive, and even if she was, I wouldn't have cared in the least. The tech geeks had spoken, and I was in no mood to request clarification.

"Sure," I said. "Whatever."

Raising my night vision, I activated the red-lens headlamp hanging around my neck and turned the phone over in my palm as she continued, "*Next: we need to know the make and model. There should be a marking somewhere on the case—*"

"Iridium," I cut her off, already scrutinizing the fine print, "9575A Bearcat."

She paused before replying, "*Go figure. That model is for US government sales only.*"

Taking another drag, I laughed and responded, "When you care enough to send the very best. Want the serial number?"

"*Not yet. First we need to enter service mode to reset the passcode without blocking the SIM card. This is a factory process with seventeen steps. Are you ready to begin?*"

"No need," I said, staring at the illuminated screen on the device. "There isn't a passcode. I'm in."

"*You're serious?*"

"It's unlocked, with a good signal. Khalil was nothing if not overconfident. What's next?"

"*Okay*," Duchess replied, the severity of her tone assuring me we were in exceedingly serious territory. "*Priority number one is the call history. To access that—*"

"Hang on," I said, uncertain if my heavily noise-damaged sense of hearing was playing a trick on me as I discerned a high-pitched series of chirping noises.

But then I saw that no, the sound was not only occurring in reality but emitting from the device in my hand. The already-illuminated screen had seamlessly changed displays, and while the signal strength, battery level, time, and date remained, the word *IRIDIUM* had been replaced with *INCOMING CALL, RAYIYS.*

"Duchess," I transmitted, "I'm going to need you to stand by."

She sounded almost panicked at the intrusion.

"*What's happening?*"

Rayiys was Arabic for chief or boss, and I quickly replied, "If I'm right about this, and I'd like to think that I am, it seems Erik Weisz is calling."

I plucked out my earpieces before she could object or my team's ongoing radio traffic could distract, then answered the call and brought the phone to my ear. Angling the antenna skyward from its new orientation, I took another pull off Cancer's cigarette and blew a plume of smoke toward the stars.

"Hello."

There was a slight chuckle on the other end of the line before a distinctly Italian-accented voice replied.

"Funny. You don't sound like Khalil."

I smiled—whatever his real name, Weisz had a sense of humor.

"He's indisposed at the moment. May I take a message?"

"You could," Weisz replied, "but I imagine he will remain quite occupied with his 72 virgins for some time. Perhaps I should deal with you directly instead."

Now I was smiling outright, the expression surely reflected in my tone as I issued my response.

"It would be my pleasure. How may I be of assistance, Mr. Weisz?"

He responded without hesitation, "What I want most from you would be best established face to face."

"Just tell me when and where."

"There is no need to trouble yourself with the details."

"No?" I asked, drawing another lungful of smoke. "Then how do you propose we conduct our meeting?"

Now I could hear Weisz's smile through the veneer of his words. "It is quite simple. Keep trying to find me, and I will ensure it."

"Well that sounds—"

The words trailed off when I realized I was talking to myself. The line was dead.

I removed the phone from my ear and analyzed the display to confirm that, indeed, the call had ended. Now I was out here alone, standing beneath the desert starscape amid a perimeter of SEALs and Night Stalker Birds that would soon be gone, as if they'd never been here at all.

Then I heard footsteps thundering up behind me at a run.

Turning, I saw Ian come to a stop while shouldering a bag of his tech equipment over one shoulder. He scanned me from bottom to top—my night vision rotated skyward, radio earpieces abandoned in a deliberate attempt to unplug from both the tactical and strategic necessities of my job title and duty description, cigarette in hand and moving toward my ever-spreading grin.

"David," he gasped, "what the fuck just happened?"

THE BELGRADE CONSPIRACY:
SHADOW STRIKE #6

A lethal shipment of military hardware.

An international terrorist group on a mission of mass destruction.

One man stands to forever change the course of history...unless David Rivers can stop him.

David Rivers is an expert in the art of violence. Together with his team of CIA operatives, he's executed dozens of covert assassinations—but this mission might turn out to be his deadliest yet.

One man stands behind the transfer of high-level military hardware to an international terrorist syndicate. The CIA has uncovered his identity: Yuri Sidorov, a Russian arms dealer with state protection. With the arms deal only days away, David and the team are faced with an impossible challenge: to get close enough to take out their target, they must first win his trust.

David and the team infiltrate a black market arms network in Serbia, negotiating a web of secret police and mafia hitmen. Each wrong turn may prove fatal, but they're determined to succeed at any cost.

But Sidorov is still alive for a reason, and when the team uncovers dark forces at work in the Balkans and America, they realize that killing him is the least of their worries.

By the time they learn the truth, it's too late...and now they're the ones being hunted.

ABOUT THE AUTHOR

Jason Kasper is the USA Today bestselling author of the Spider Heist, American Mercenary, and Shadow Strike thriller series. Before his writing career he served in the US Army, beginning as a Ranger private and ending as a Green Beret captain. Jason is a West Point graduate and a veteran of the Afghanistan and Iraq wars, and was an avid ultramarathon runner, skydiver, and BASE jumper, all of which inspire his fiction.

Sign up for Jason Kasper's reader list at
severnriverbooks.com/authors/jason-kasper

jasonkasper@severnriverbooks.com